The Remains of an Altar

Phil Rickman

# THE REMAINS OF AN ALTAR

Quercus

First published in Great Britain in 2006 by

Quercus
21 Bloomsbury Square
London
WC1A 2QA

A CIP catalogue reference for this book is available
from the British Library
ISBN (HB) 1 905204 51 5
ISBN-13 978 1 905204 51 9
ISBN (TPB) 1 905204 52 3
ISBN-13 978 1 905204 52 6

10 9 8 7 6 5 4 3 2 1

PART ONE

'The Bible record is unmistakable in its references to the old straight track as having partly or wholly gone out of use: "the ancient high places are in possession of the enemy"; "my people have forgotten me, they stumble in their ways from the ancient paths."'

Alfred Watkins
*The Old Straight Track* (1925)

1

# On the Bald Hill

MORE THAN A DAY later, there was still wreckage around: a twisted door panel across the ditch and slivers of tyre like shed snakeskin in the grass.

It had rained last night, and the Rev. S. D. Spicer's cassock was hemmed with wet mud. What might have been a piece of someone's blood-stiffened sleeve was snagged in brambles coiling like rolls of barbed wire from the hedge. The countryside, violated, wasn't letting go. It felt to Merrily as if the air was still vibrating.

'Other vehicle was an ancient Land Rover Defender,' Spicer said. 'Must've been like driving into a cliff face.'

Ground mist was draped like muslin over the hedges and down the bank and the early sun lit the windows of a turreted house in the valley. Looking back along the road Merrily could see no obvious blind spots, no overhanging trees.

'Boy died in the ambulance.' Spicer nodded at the metallic red door panel, crumpled and creased like thrown-away chocolate paper. 'Took the fire brigade best part of an hour getting him out the car. Fortunately, he was unconscious the whole time.'

Merrily shook her head slowly, the way you did when there was nothing to be said. No act of violence as sudden and savage, massive and unstoppable, as a head-on car crash. She was thinking, inevitably, of Jane and Eirion out at night in Eirion's small car. One momentary lapse of attention, a snatched caress, and . . .

'He was in his mid-twenties. Lincoln Cookman, from north Worcester. The girl . . . no hurry to get her out. She'd had her window

3

wide open. No seat belt. Head almost taken off on impact. Sonia Maloney, from Droitwich.'

'Oh God.' Merrily took a step back. 'How old?'

''Bout nineteen.' Spicer's London accent was as flat as a rubber mat. 'All horribly brutal and unsightly, but mercifully quick. No suffering. Except, of course, for Preston Devereaux.'

'Sorry, Preston—?'

'Local farmer and chairman of the parish council. And, as it happened, the driver of the Land Rover. Returning late from a family wedding.'

'Oh, hell, really?'

'Could've been any of us, Mrs Watkins. Parish Council's been asking for speed cameras since last autumn. Not that that would've made a difference, state these kids must've been in. They come over from Worcester, places like that, at the weekends. Windows open, music blasting. Sixty-five, seventy, wrong side of the road. Poor guy's still reliving it. He'll need a bit of support – my job, I think.'

'And what, erm . . . what's mine, exactly, Mr Spicer?'

It was a reasonable question, but he didn't answer. Parish priests would often have difficulty explaining why they'd resorted to Deliverance. Spicer had been been terse and cagey on the phone yesterday. *Can you come early? Before eight a.m.? In civvies. Best not make a carnival out of it.*

OK, just gone 7.50 on a Monday morning, and here she was in discreet civvies: jeans and a sweatshirt. And here's the Rector, all kitted out: cassock, collar, pectoral cross. Merrily felt wrong-footed. Why would he want that? She'd never met him before, didn't even know his first name. Never been to this village before, out on the eastern rim of the diocese where it rose into the ramparts of Worcestershire.

'Well, the point is,' Spicer said, 'this is the worst but it's not exactly the first.'

'You mean it's an accident black spot?'

Sometimes, when a stretch of road acquired a reputation for accidents, someone would suggest that a bad pattern had been established, and you'd be asked to bless it. One of those increasingly commonplace roadside rituals, support for all the road-kill wreaths laid out by bereaved relatives – how *did* all that start? Anyway, it was a job for the local guy, unless there were complications.

'How many actual accidents have there been, Mr Spicer?'

He didn't respond. He was standing quite still; shortish and thickset, with sparse greying hair shaved tight to his head and small, blank eyes that seemed to be *on* his face rather than embedded there. Like a teddy bear's eyes, Merrily thought. *Poor man*, Sophie had said last night on the phone. *She took the children, of course.*

It was as though some part of Spicer had withdrawn, the way a computer relaxed into its screensaver. Not many people could do this in the presence of a stranger – especially clergy who, unless they were in a church, tended to treat silence like a vacuum into which doubt and unbelief might enter if it wasn't filled with chatter, however inane.

OK, whatever. Merrily let the silence hang and looked up at the tiered ramparts of the sculpted fortress-hill called Herefordshire Beacon, also known as British Camp. This was the most prominent landmark in the Malverns. Where the Celts were said to have held out against the Romans. The misty sun was hovering over it like a white-cowled lamp.

The name *Malvern* came from the Welsh *moel bryn*, meaning bald hill, and bald it still was, up on the tops of this startling volcanic ridge, while the foothills and the Alpine-looking valleys were lush with orchards and the gardens of summer villas: well-preserved remains of Elgar's England.

'Three ... four now,' Spicer said. 'Maybe even five, including this one. That's inside a couple of months. One was a lorry, took a chunk out of the church wall.'

'And on a stretch of road as open as this, I suppose that's ...'

'Drivers reckoned they swerved to avoid a ghost,' Spicer said.

His tone hadn't altered and his eyes remained limpid. A wood pigeon's hollow call was funnelled out of the valley.

'That took a while to come out, didn't it?' Merrily said.

'Come back to the house.' He turned away. 'We'll talk about it there.'

2

# Uncle Alfie

AFTER VERY LITTLE SLEEP, Jane awoke all sweating and confused. On one level she was lit up with excitement, on another fired by the wrongness of things: injustice, greed, sacrilege.

Bastards.

The thinness of the light showed that it was still early, but the Mondrian walls were already aglow: ancient timber-framed squares, once wattle and daub, then plastered and whitewashed and finally overpainted, by Jane herself, in defiant reds and blues and oranges.

It was more than two years since she'd coloured the squares – just a kid, then, disoriented by the move to this antiquated village with a mother who used to be normal and had suddenly turned into a bloody priest.

Just a kid, determined to make her mark: *Jane's here now. Jane takes no shit. This is Jane's apartment. This is the way Jane does things, OK?*

In a seventeenth-century vicarage, it wouldn't have been at all OK with the Listed-Buildings Police, but it had seemed unlikely that they'd ever come beating on the door with a warrant to investigate the attic. Looking back, Mum had been seriously good about it, letting Jane establish a personal suite up here and splatter the walls with coloured paint they couldn't really afford . . . and never once suggesting that it might look just a bit crap.

But that was over two years ago and now Jane was, Christ, *seventeen*. And this once-important gesture, these once-deeply-symbolic walls, were looking entirely, irredeemably naff. Not even much like a Mondrian – in the middle of an A-level art course, she could say that with some certainly.

More like a sodding nursery school.

Decision: the Mondrian walls would have to go. You were in no position to fight senseless public vandalism if you couldn't identify your own small crimes.

That sorted, Jane sat up in bed and looked out of the window at the *real* issue. Full of the breathless excitement of new discovery and a low-burning rage which, she'd have to admit, was also a serious turn-on.

Below her, beyond the front hedge, lay Ledwardine, this black and white, oak-framed village, embellished with old gold by the early sun. Defended against neon and advertising hoardings by the same guys who would've freaked if they'd ever been exposed to the Mondrian walls . . . while totally missing the Big Picture.

The focus of which was just beyond the village: a green, wooded pyramid rising out of a flimsy loincloth of mist.

Cole Hill. She'd always assumed that it had simply been named after somebody called Cole who'd tried to farm it a few centuries ago. Now . . . *Cole Hill* . . . it sang with glamour.

Jane sank back into the pillows, last night's images coalescing around her: the slipping sun and the line across the meadow. Drifting down from the hill, with the blackening steeple of Ledwardine Church marking the way like the gnomon on the sundial of the village. Amazing, inspirational.

*But, like, for how long?*

Tumbling out of bed, she dislodged from the table the paperback *Old Straight Track* she'd been reading until about two a.m. – photo on the back of benign-looking bearded old guy, glasses on his nose. Alfred Watkins of Hereford: county councillor, magistrate, businessman, antiquarian, photographer, inventor, all-round solid citizen. And visionary.

Jane Watkins picked up the book.

*You and me, Uncle.*

This book . . . well, it had been around the vicarage as long as Jane had, and she'd thought she must have read it ages ago. Only realizing a week or so back that all she'd done was leaf through it, looking at Watkins's pioneering photos, assuming his ideas were long outdated, his findings revised by more enlightened thinking. Now, because of this A-level project, she'd finally read it cover to cover. Twice. Feeling the heat of a blazing inspiration. And it was all *so close.* Mum was probably right when she said there was no family link, and yet it was as if this long-dead guy with the same name was communicating with Jane along one of his own mysterious straight lines.

Saying, *help me.*

Jane turned her back on the clashing imperatives of the Mondrian walls, stumbled to the bathroom, and ran the shower.

She needed back-up on this one.

Two years ago, telling Mum would have been a total no-no, the issue too left-field and the gulf between them too wide. Two years ago, the sight of Mum kneeling to pray would have Jane shrivelling up inside with embarrassment and resentment. But now she was older and Mum was also more balanced, a lot less rigid.

Except for the rumble of the old Aga and the rhythmic sandpaper sound of Ethel washing her paws on the rug in front of it, the kitchen was silent.

Jane found a note on the table. It said:

J. YOU'VE PROBABLY FORGOTTEN ALL ABOUT THIS ... BUT HAD TO LEAVE EARLY THIS MORNING TO MEET PARANOID RECTOR IN THE MALVERNS. THICK-SLICED LOAF IN BREAD BIN, EGGS IN BASKET. DON'T FORGET TO LEAVE DRIED FOOD OUT FOR ETHEL. SORRY ABOUT THIS, FLOWER. SEE YOU AFTER SCHOOL. LOVE, M.

*Flower.* Like she was seven.

But, yeah, she *had* forgotten. In fact, there'd been so much on her mind when she'd come in last night from Cole Hill that she'd hardly listened to anything Mum had said, before pleading fatigue and bounding up to the apartment to research, research, research well into the early hours, until she'd finally fallen asleep.

Jane left the note on the table, went to find the dried cat-food for

Ethel and grab a handful of biscuits from the tin. No time for eggs and toast.

What about school?

*What about not going?*

She didn't remember ever bunking off before. But some things were too important for delays, and anyway school was winding down now towards the long summer break.

Trying to open the biscuit tin, she found she was still gripping *The Old Straight Track*, having brought it down with her like a talisman. On the front was a misty photograph of a perfect Bronze Age burial mound swelling behind a fan of winter trees.

Yesterday evening, at sunset, she'd seen – and she must have been around there a dozen times in the past without spotting it – what must surely be the remains of a burial mound, or tumulus, or tump, on the edge of the orchard behind Church Street. The magical things you could so easily miss, bypass, ignore . . . or destroy.

Jane felt this swelling sense of responsibility towards a man who had already been dead for well over half a century when she was born.

*You and me, Uncle Alfie.*

3

# For the Views

MUST HAVE BEEN IN one of Jane's pagan books that Merrily had read how, in primitive communities, the local shaman was often a social outcast, both feared and derided. Being a female exorcist in the Church of England gave you some idea of what this must have been like.

'*Deliverance Consultant.*' The Reverend Spicer was shaking his head wearily. 'What exactly does that ... you know ... ?'

She'd watched him moving around, pulling down tea caddy, mugs, milk and sugar from strong, beechwood units. He knew where everything was. After what Sophie had told her in the office, she'd been half-expecting some kind of desperate chaos in the rectory kitchen – unwashed dishes, layers of congealed fat on the stove – but it was clean and functional, if not exactly cosy.

He spilled a single blob of milk, frowned and ran a dishcloth over it.

'I know what "exorcist" used to mean. Deliverance is a bit more ... And *consultant*?'

'That just means I don't get involved personally unless I'm invited to. On the basis that these ... slightly iffy things are usually best handled by the guy on the ground. Which would be you, Mr Spicer.'

'Call me Syd.' He opened a cutlery drawer, extracted two spoons. 'You ever *done* an exorcism?'

'Minor exorcism, mainly – Requiem Eucharist for the unquiet dead, variations on that. Never had to stop a small child abusing herself with a crucifix, never been sprayed with green bile. Although, naturally, I live in hope.'

You got this all the time. A recent survey had shown that more people in Britain believed in ghosts than in God. Whereas parish priests still tended to believe in some kind of God but often had a problem with ghosts. Even more of a problem with exorcism, last refuge of anachronistic misfits in the desperately modern C of E.

Spicer didn't smile. Behind him, on the Rayburn, the kettle hissed.

'So what qualifies for a minor exorcism?'

'Usually, an unhappy atmosphere that doesn't respond to concentrated prayer. Would you like me to lend you a book? That'd take care of the consultant bit.'

'I think I need the personal service.' He sat down opposite her. 'I'm just ... not sure, frankly, about where you ...'

Merrily sighed. That other familiar barbed hurdle.

'My spiritual director is a bloke called Huw Owen. Runs deliverance training courses in the Brecon Beacons?'

'Yeah, I know the area.'

His small, passive eyes said, *too well.* Curious.

'At the end of the course he gave me the regulation warning. Told me ordained women were becoming the prime target for every psychotic grinder of the satanic mills who ever sacrificed a chicken. Therefore a woman exorcist might as well paint a big bull's-eye between her ... on her chest.'

'Maybe you saw it as a bit of a challenge.' Spicer, decently, didn't look at Merrily's chest. 'A chance to carry women's ministry into a dark and forbidden area.'

'Well, no, the point I'm making ... I'm not a militant feminist, I'm not a post-feminist, I'm not pioneer material and I'm not—'

'Honestly.' He held up his hands. 'I don't have a problem with women priests. Nor even women deliverance consultants. In principle.'

'So the problem is?'

The kettle came whistling to the boil.

'Problem is,' he said, 'taking it seriously, as you're bound to do – being comparatively new to the job and with the side issue of the women's ministry still having something to prove – it occurs to me you might not be up for what could be a PR exercise.'

'You've lost me.'

'I mean if I, as Rector of Wychehill, were to ask you, as official

11

diocesan exorcist, to perform a public ceremony of, shall we say, spiritual cleansing, whatever you wanna call it, simply to make the community feel happier – take some pressure off?'

'Off whom?' Merrily reached down to her shoulder bag: cigarettes.

'Off me, for a start.' Spicer poured boiling water into a deep brown teapot. 'See, these people who say they had an accident because they swerved to avoid a spectral figure on the Queen's Highway ... I'm having difficulty with it. They're decent people, but ...'

'That's OK.' Merrily brought out the Silk Cut and the dented Zippo. 'Really.'

To a stranger, the road was the least ghostly aspect of Upper Wychehill. It glided down the valley in a long, slow slope, with the wooded hills hunched behind it like a giant's shoulders. As many of its dwellings were invisible, it had been hard to make out where the village began and where it ended.

The reason why many of the homes were invisible was that they were on different levels, with rows of houses above and below the road. The ones above were set back into the hill and the ones falling away below it, all you could see of them as you drove past were hedges, walls and gates. They seemed to be mainly bungalows with colonial verandas or flagged patios with sundials and statuary, barbecues and big views across Herefordshire.

The few grey buildings at road level were weighted by the church, this immense neo-Gothic barn, probably late-Victorian, screened by two substantial oak trees either side of the entrance. Further down, built of the same stone, with a dramatic view of the Beacon, was the rectory. A big family house with a home-made swing in the front garden. From what Merrily understood from Sophie, the Spicer kids had been long past the swing stage. But it still looked starkly symbolic of loss, with its peeling frame and one side of the wooden seat fallen off its chain.

When they were inside, she'd asked Spicer, without thinking, if he had help in the house.

'What? A cleaner? A housekeeper?' He'd laughed. 'Do you?'

Point taken. No private income.

'I get occasional offers,' he'd said. 'We've got several nice ladies in Upper Wychehill. The Ladies of Wychehill? That sound like a book? Listen. First rule for the solo priest. Don't give anybody room for gossip. My wife left just over three months ago. Since then, I've done all my own cleaning, cooking, gardening, painting, the lot, plus keeping three parishes on the go. Which makes for a long day.'

He'd looked at her, his soft-toy's eyes unmoving.

'But a mercifully short night.'

Outside the bay window, the still-shadowed long back lawn was tidily mown and trimmed but had no flowers. It ended where a bank of fir trees lifted the land into the hills.

'I can give you a list of people to talk to, so you can make up your own mind.' Syd Spicer crossed to the Rayburn. 'You want some toast? Or I can do full English. I'm fairly capable.'

'I can see that. Tea'll be fine, thanks.'

He brought two white mugs to the table, and then sugar and milk.

'Point is, Mrs Watkins, country areas—'

'Merrily, do you think?'

'Yeah, OK. Country areas, Merrily, are superstitious, just like they've always been – you know this. Where are you based, North Hereford-shire?'

'Ledwardine. 'Bout an hour from here.'

He nodded. 'Only nowadays the superstition comes from a different direction. The locals might be less credulous than their grandparents were, but your city-bred incomers always include the kind of people who're living in the sticks because they *want* to get back to a primitive belief system. They're the ones who organize the wassailing and stuff at Christmas, dangle charms off their porches.'

'Everything except go to church,' Merrily said. 'But if you have an accident black spot, they'll be the first to suggest the area might be haunted?'

Spicer shook his head sadly.

'I've got three parishes and the others are a healthy mix of locals and new blood. In Upper Wychehill, a real local person is somebody who's been here twenty-five years. It didn't really exist until the 1920s, when the church was built – gesture of apology by the owner of one of the quarry firms mutilating the Malverns.'

'He must have been *very* sorry.'

'Yeah, big, innit? Especially in the middle of a few farms and not much else, as it was then. The bloke saw it as a concert hall as well, however – strictly religious, of course. Same time, he had this house built for the minister, and a sum of money donated to the Church, to pay him – long exhausted, of course but, by then, more housing had gone up and it was a legit parish.'

'So, what you're saying, it's not—'

'Not a *real* village, no. Just a mess of mixed-up dwellings either side of a road with no pavement. So people never walk about and they rarely meet each other. Some are weekend cottages. Bloke died in one last year, wasn't found for three weeks. That's the way it is. No village shop, no cosy pub. Just a church that was always too big and people who move here for the views.'

Spicer had taken a folded piece of notepaper out of his cassock. He opened it out and placed it on the table in front of Merrily.

*Dear Rector,*

*I am sorry to bother you, and I never thought I would write a letter like this, but I am worried sick about my daughter who as you know is a district nurse and has to go out at all hours in her car. I am terrified that something will happen to her on that road. These stories are hard to credit, but something is wrong here. I do not get to church as often as I would like since I have become disabled but I beg of you to take whatever measures are necessary to deal with this problem. I do not care who or what it is, it must be got rid of by whatever means are open to you.*

*I feel foolish writing a letter like this but Helen is all I have left in this world.*

*Yours sincerely,*

*D. H. Walford.*

'Poor old Donald. His wife died three years ago. Daughter got divorced and moved in with him. He's an entirely rational man, retired primary school head. But this . . . this is how it escalates.'

'What was the first reported accident?'

'Lorry. Came across the road, into the church wall, like I said. Still waiting for the insurance to get sorted.'

'Did you talk to the driver?'

'I was out at the time, but the guy told Mrs Aird, who does the flowers in the church. She was in there when it happened. He said he'd seen this white orb coming towards him down the middle of the road.'

'So this was at night?'

'Early morning. Police suggested the bloke had been driving too long. We tidied up the wall, thought no more about it.'

'Until . . .'

'Week or so later, Tim Loste, the choirmaster, hit a telegraph pole. Not injured, fortunately. And then there was a woman, lives up the hill, flattened her sports car on a tourist's Winnebago.'

'And they both saw this light?'

'They both . . . saw a figure behind the light.'

He turned to the window. The summer sun had finally penetrated his flowerless garden, but it still looked as if it was clinging to winter. Syd Spicer too, Merrily thought, as he turned to face her.

'And there might be another one, which is . . . a bit weird. Joyce Aird can tell you. They won't talk to me about it. Joyce was waiting for me after the worship yesterday. We'd had some prayers for the victims of the night before, and Joyce said . . . She gave me a piece of paper with your phone number on it, which she'd obtained from the Diocese. Said it was time to seek help to remove the evil from our midst.'

'So, essentially, you had me forced on you,' Merrily said.

'Me, I've been telling them, let's get the council in . . . surveyors . . . examine the road camber. Let's not get *carried away*. Famous last words.'

'What about the Land Rover driver, the chairman of the parish council. Did *he* see—?'

'I haven't even asked him, Merrily.'

She sighed. 'Would you mind if I had a cigarette?'

15

Spicer put his head on one side.

'You disapprove?'

He shrugged. 'I have one occasionally. When I want to. You go ahead, if you need one.'

'Doesn't matter.' Merrily dropped the Silk Cut back into her shoulder bag. 'You said there was something a bit weird.'

'Oh, well, that . . . Joyce wouldn't talk about it. Not to me. Said it was best discussed with a woman. I suppose I'm getting a bit . . .'

'I can imagine.' She lowered her bag to the floor. 'How do you want me to go about this?'

'Well, that's up to you, Merrily. But the way some of them are reacting, I'm not sure that a simple blessing of the road would be quite enough. I suppose I'd like you to talk to them.'

'Well, obviously I'd have to—'

'No, I mean all of them.'

'All of them?'

'Everybody,' Syd Spicer said.

4

# A Very Public Ghost

'ALL OF THEM?' SOPHIE said in the Cathedral gatehouse office. 'Are you sure you know what you're doing? At a public meeting?'

Merrily sighed.

'It's a very public ghost.'

'Merrily . . .' Sophie looked pained. 'Has there ever *been* such a thing as a public ghost?'

Merrily thought about this, elbows on the desk, chin cupped in her palms. She'd been thinking about it for many of the fifty gridlocked minutes she'd spent watching guys in cranes playing pass-the-girder on the site of another new superstore that Hereford didn't need.

'No,' she said. 'In the real sense, I suppose not.'

'There you are, then,' Sophie said. 'Let the Rector have his public meeting and then you go along afterwards – quietly – and do what you think is necessary.'

Sophie Hill, crisp white blouse and pearls. Very posh, discreet as a ballot box. The Bishop's lay secretary who, essentially, didn't work for people or organizations. Who worked for The Cathedral.

Except on Mondays, when Sophie worked more or less full-time for Deliverance. For most parish priests, Monday was a well-defended day off; for Merrily, only a day off from the parish. Monday was when she and Sophie met in the gatehouse office at the Cathedral to deal with the mail and the Deliverance database, and to monitor outstanding cases.

'I need to remind you that the Crown Prosecution Service have warned that you may still be called to give evidence in the Underhowle case when it finally comes to trial. And *on* that issue – aftercare. The

17

new minister there would welcome some discreet advice on, as he puts it, disinfecting the former Baptist chapel.'

'In which case, I might need to go over. Could we stall him until next week? If he could just keep it locked, meantime . . . keep people out.'

'Next week also, you've agreed to talk to that rather persistent Women's Institute in the Golden Valley . . . unfair to postpone again. *Don't* look like that – you agreed.'

'OK.'

Problem here was that WIs always wanted lurid anecdotes, and this was a small county population-wise: one of the audience would always be able to fit names into whichever sensitive issue you were discussing. The policy was to avoid WIs, but occasionally one squeezed through the net. And, sure, there was a pile of parish stuff accumulating on the diary, including a christening tomorrow, and two weddings looming. Big months for weddings, June and July. So . . .

'What you're telling me, Sophie, is that I really don't need Wychehill.'

Sophie said nothing.

'What if I walk away now, and it happens again?'

'Oh, for heaven's sake, Merrily, what if it happens again *after* you've been involved?'

Which it sometimes did, hence the need for aftercare.

'There are still two people dead, and while linking that to something paranormal is deep water, I'd feel safer going along. Even if it means opening the whole thing up at a public meeting. I mean, I can understand Spicer's problem. He's got a worried community which he says isn't really a community at all. Houses are widely separated, people don't know one another. He wants to make sure that everybody at least has a chance to find out what the score is.'

'Merrily, deliverance is about discretion – how many times have you said that? You don't like addressing WIs about past cases, but you're perfectly happy to—'

'I'm not *happy*—'

'—To discuss an ongoing problem with a roomful of people, probably including the media.'

'I don't think the press would cover anything that local, do you? Hope not.'

'You don't *think*,' Sophie said. 'That's hardly satisfactory, is it? I'd be inclined to get the Rector to absolutely guarantee it. What's the format going to be?'

'I listen to the evidence and then outline the options.'

'Oh, I see. You present them with a series of options, and then they *vote* on it?'

'No, I listen to what they have to say and then I make a recommendation based on my . . . experience.'

Sophie gave Merrily a resigned look and opened the desk diary. 'When is it? And where?'

'Wednesday evening at the church. They haven't got a village hall in Wychehill, I think it was converted. This gets tagged on to the end of the bi-monthly parish meeting, which is open to the public— Look, I'm not going to go in cold, Sophie. I'm going to check it all out thoroughly.'

'In which case you really don't have much time.'

'Which is why, unless you can think of anything more pressing, I think I'd better go back there now.'

Merrily walked over to the window. There was something *else* . . .

'Oh yeah . . . Sophie, have there been any inquiries to the Diocese from Wychehill – anybody asking for my number?'

'No. I'd have been told. I'm very strict about that. And they don't give out your number, they give this number in the first instance. Why?'

'Nothing, really.'

Merrily looked out of the window over the Cathedral green and sunny Broad Street with its library and museum, its extensive hotel, its classical-pillared Roman Catholic church, its shops and cafés . . . and at least two well attested ghost stories that *she* could think of.

From behind Merrily heard the faint clinking of the chain on

19

Sophie's glasses as she shook her head in sorrow – with just a hint, Merrily thought, of foreboding.

# 5

# Between the Lines

ON TOP OF THE HILL there was a clearing and the remains of what might have been a cairn of stones.

Lol had never been all the way up before, but Jane had said there was something of serious, *serious* importance here, and not just to her or even to the whole community of Ledwardine. This was possibly a *national treasure*.

She'd dragged him out to the edge of the village and then across the main road and over the fields to the first stile, which had a public footpath sign next to it. But if there ever had been a footpath it was long overgrown, and it had been a steep and slippery climb to the top of Cole Hill.

'You can't see much now,' Jane said, among the gorse clumps on the summit, 'but there was a Celtic settlement here once. So obviously that makes it Ledwardine's *holy* hill, right?'

'If you say so.'

Lol had felt slightly uncomfortable about walking through the woods with his girlfriend's daughter, her navel exposed below the sawn-off summer top.

No, actually, it wasn't so much this as her attitude: intense, no frivolity, Jane carrying a sense of purpose like storm clouds around her, intimations of war.

Now she was telling him about the name. How, in *The Old Straight Track*, Alfred Watkins had identified three other Cole hills, or similar, in Herefordshire. One definition of the word, apparently, was juggler ... or wizard.

'"Cole-prophet" – that's another ancient term,' Jane said. 'So Cole

Hill – serious, serious magical associations, Lol. I hadn't realized that. And if *I* hadn't realized it . . .'

Jane stood in the sunlight. Her hair was pulled back and her eyes seemed to be full of tiny sparks.

'We live in an enchanted landscape, Laurence. And most of us just don't see any of it any more. How dispiriting is that?'

Below them, the village was wrapped in greenery, and the mist made smoke rings around the church steeple. The view was dizzyingly seductive: you felt that if you fell into it, it would just absorb you and by the time you reached the ground you'd have evaporated.

Lol shook his head. His day had already been tilted. Monday mornings, he needed to establish a work pattern for the week: sit at the desk by the window, write songs. His livelihood. What he did. What he was *supposed* to do. So why had he been almost grateful to see Jane crossing the street from the vicarage, wearing her skimpy orange top and her sense of purpose?

Jane said she had the day off school to work on a project connected with A-level art, a portfolio she was compiling on landscape mysteries. Something in connection with this that she needed to discuss, and Merrily had gone off early to meet some angsty priest, so, like, if Lol could spare just *one hour* . . .

All around Cole Hill the paths were overgrown; there were broken stiles and barbed-wire fences. It had taken most of an hour just to get here.

Jane shouldered her canvas bag.

'Nobody comes up here now, and that's wrong. We all need to go to the high places. It says that in the Bible, so even Mum—'

'Had *you* been to this . . . particular high place before, Jane?'

She frowned. 'I'm here now, that's what matters. It's where the ancient energy is drawn down, to feed the village spiritually, to feed its soul. You know?'

'Alfred Watkins actually said that, did he? About feeding energy into Ledwardine?'

'Not exactly, but he *would* have said it if he hadn't been a magistrate and stuff, with civic duties and all that crap. You have to *read between the lines*, Lol.'

'Right.'

Lol would have to agree that reading Alfred Watkins entirely altered your awareness of the humps and bumps of the countryside – the way Watkins's own had been altered when he'd stood on top of a hill not far from here and noticed, in a flaring of wild revelation, how ancient sites, from prehistoric stones and mounds to medieval churches, seemed to have been arranged in straight lines. But Watkins had seen them as the earliest British trackways; most of the rest was New Age conjecture.

'So what do we do now, Jane?'

'Watch the church. Keep watching the steeple.'

The steeple must have been half a mile away, at least, but from up here you felt you could prick your hand on the tip of the weathercock. Beyond it, to the west, you could see distant Hay Bluff over the mist, a dent in the sky at the end of the Black Mountains.

Jane put on her sunglasses.

'And then we walk towards it.'

Lol followed her, keeping a few feet behind, sure now that something else was bothering her. Some problem between her and Eirion? They'd been together a long time. Maybe too long, for teenagers.

'We came up the easy way,' Jane said over her shoulder. 'But we have to follow a different route down, to more or less keep to the line. The path zigzags a bit, but if we keep the steeple in view . . .'

'Eirion OK, Jane?'

'Fine.' Her voice was a little too light. 'Off to uni in September.'

'Where?'

'Depends on his A-level results. Oxford, if he does well. Bristol or Cardiff if he fluffs. Or, if he *really* fluffs, one of these joints that used to be an FE college until, like, last week?'

'I see.'

'I mean, it's ridiculous how like *everybody* has to go *somewhere*. You need a degree to be a hospital porter now. You probably need a degree in, like, hygiene studies to clean lavatories. It's—'

Jane slid on a small scree of pebbles and grabbed a sapling to keep from falling.

'—All complete and total bullshit. Just a Stalinist government scam to destroy the individual, get everybody into a slot. Result is you've got people walking round with a string of letters after their name, and they're like, you know, Homer Simpson?'

'So, you, er . . .' Lol thought he was beginning to get the picture. 'If Eirion does well, you won't see as much of each other, will you?'

A grey squirrel scurried up a fir tree ahead of them.

'I just don't see why,' Jane said. 'I mean *why?* Why do you have to waste precious years being lectured to by all these hopeless losers so you can wind up with some totally meaningless qualification that everybody else has got. Why can't you just *do stuff?* Original stuff. I mean . . . *you* did.'

'You got something original in mind?'

They climbed over a rotting stile on the edge of a decaying copse at the foot of Cole Hill. Jane waited for Lol. She was squeezing her hands together.

'I want to find out things for myself – like, not formalized curriculum shit that just qualifies you to be like every other—'

She spun away. She might have been in tears. She moved rapidly through the trees and out to where another stile had been strung with barbed wire. When Lol reached her she was bent over the wire, breathing hard. The canvas bag was at her feet.

She had both hands around a pair of wire-cutters.

'Jane?'

'It's supposed to be a public footpath. Nobody has any right to—'

Two ends of barbed wire sprang apart and Jane stepped back.

'Jane, where did you get the wire-cutters?'

'Gomer.' Jane clambered over the stile. 'You coming?'

All his foreboding becoming justified, Lol climbed over the stile and stumbled after Jane through tall grass, holding his hands up above the nettles. They came to a five-barred gate set into an overgrown hedge, strands of orange binder twine hanging loose from it.

'I pulled that off last night.' Jane opened the gate. 'Now. Look at *that.*'

'What?'

'*Just look!*'

Lol closed the gate behind him and stood and looked. He saw a gently sloping meadow full of Hereford cows, red-brown and cream, classic. You didn't see enough Herefords in Herefordshire these days, but that clearly wasn't what Jane had meant.

'Oh,' Lol said. 'I see.'

Like the shadow of a tall pole, a path cut directly across the meadow. A visible path that could have been contructed or simply made by sheep crossing the field from gate to gate – dead straight from the gate they'd just come through to another one at a slight angle in the hedge at the bottom of the field. Both gates and the path were directly aligned with the smokey, sepia steeple of Ledwardine church.

Lol walked towards the centre of the field, keeping to the path, and turned to see that the path was perfectly aligned, in the opposite direction, with the top of Cole Hill.

Some of Watkins's lines demanded imagination, but this one spoke for itself.

Jane stood on the line, as if she was standing before an altar. Although the sun was high and warm, Lol saw her shiver. She wrapped her bare arms around herself.

'Before you reach the village, there's a mound just inside the orchard – behind Church Street? It's not marked on the map, but it must be an ancient burial site, if only by its position in the landscape. Absolutely on the line. Like, it's not very high now, but a lot of them aren't any more; they've been ploughed in over the centuries. And then, on the other side of the mound, you're dead on course, across the market place, for the church.'

'You've convinced me,' Lol said. 'It's a nice one.'

'And . . . *and,* Lol, if you continue the line, *through* the church – I've only done this on the map, but it works, it totally works – within a mile, on the other side, you've got an ancient crossroads and a genuine prehistoric standing stone which is not very big but is actually marked on the map.'

'Well, congratulations,' Lol said. 'You've found a new ley line.'

'*Ley*,' Jane snapped. 'Alfred Watkins called them leys. Ley *lines* – that's just a term that's been adopted in almost a disparaging way by so-called experts who say they don't exist. And, OK, some of them you can draw the line by circling the sites on the map, but when you go there you can't really see it. But this . . .'

'Textbook,' Lol said. 'I suppose.'

'I mean, *I* can't claim any credit – except maybe for rediscovering it. This side of the hill's been more or less hidden away for years, probably since the orchards went into decline. And, oh yeah, you know what this field's called? *Coleman's Meadow.* Geddit? The field where the track was laid out by the *Cole*-man, the shaman, the wizard . . . ? And you can feel it, can't you?' Jane stamped a foot. 'Come *on*, Lol. You're an artist, a poet. Do *not* tell me you cannot feel it.'

'Well . . .'

'You stand on the track and you're, like, totally connected with the landscape. And with the *ancestors* who lived here and marked out the sacred paths. Thousands of years ago when people were more in contact with the elements? So like whether or not you believe the leys channelled some form of mystical life-force through the land, or they were spirit paths where you could walk with the dead, or whatever . . . I don't *care*. I don't need to understand the science. I just need to know that I can stand here and feel I'm, you know, part of something . . . bigger. *Belong*.'

'It's probably the most any of us can ever hope for,' Lol said. 'To belong somewhere.'

They stood quietly for a few seconds. You could hear neither the sounds of the village nor the traffic on the main road, only birdsong and the grass wrenched from the meadow in the jaws of the Herefords.

The sun was already high. Caught in its glare, Jane, in her yellow crop-top, looked young and uncertain.

'I need some information off you, Lol.'

'For this ... project?'

'Sort of. I need to know who decides what happens around here. Like with the council and stuff. I mean, I think I know the basics. Just want to be sure before I make a move.'

'A move?'

*Oh, hell.*

Jane looked at her feet.

'Jane ...'

'What?'

'This day off school, to work on the project ...'

'Look,' Jane said, 'it's nearly the end of term, the exams are over, nobody really *cares*. And this is a major crisis. And anyway it's *connected* with the project, which is about how artists have dealt with earth mysteries, the secret harmonies in the landscape.'

'You're not making this very clear, Jane.'

'All right.' Jane unfolded her arms and pointed. 'You want it made clear, go and read it what it says on that sign.'

A small placard was affixed to the gate on the opposite side of the field. Lol wandered over. On the other side of the five-barred gate the path broadened out, and he saw that he was in the orchard at the back of his own cottage, which fronted on to Church Street. When he looked back, Jane's ley was no longer obvious, which presumably was why she'd brought him down from the hill.

Lol adjusted his glasses and read what it said on the sign, which was headed HEREFORDSHIRE COUNCIL PLANNING DEPARTMENT.

What it said, basically, was that an application had been submitted to turn Coleman's Meadow into an estate of twenty-four high-quality detached executive homes. It invited observations from the public.

Oh.

Lol turned, at a click of the latch on the gate, to find that Jane had followed him.

'Only they'll need to kill me first,' Jane said.

# 6

# The Sunset Chair

JOYCE AIRD'S DRIVE SLOPED steeply down from the road in a tunnel of dark trees. It was like entering a badger set, until you emerged into a vastness of light.

'Oh dear,' Mrs Aird said. 'Your sins always find you out, don't they? Yes, bring that chair out, dear, we can sit together in the window. Bring your tea.'

The sun-lounge overlooked the valley, across the long village of Colwall and on and on over Herefordshire, all the way to the Black Mountains and Wales.

'How *did* you know?'

Mrs Aird had the kind of West Midlands accent which wore anxiety like old and trusted slippers. She was about seventy-five, soft-featured and with lightly blonded hair.

'Oh . . .' Merrily put down the cane chair with its thick, padded seat. 'It's just that if anyone's inquired about exorcism, the arrangement is that the office tells me or our secretary, Sophie. And nobody seems to have.'

'Well, no, I never rang the Diocese. That's just what I told Mr Spicer. He's a good man, Mr Spicer, at the bottom of him, give him his due, but he's a *man* isn't he? And he *has* had a lot of personal problems lately. I thought, he's just not going to *do* anything, is he? And I was telling a friend – we used to be neighbours when I lived in the Forest of Dean and we've kept in touch, and I was telling her on the phone about what had happened, and she immediately said I should get the Rector to ask for you. That's how I got the number. Her name's Ingrid Sollars.'

'Oh.' That was OK; nothing wrong with Ingrid Sollars. 'Yes, she was involved in . . . a problem we had. She's a nice woman.'

'A much stronger person than me, I'm afraid. I get very frightened about things I don't . . . well, none of us understands them, do we? We can't. We're not supposed to. But Ingrid gave me your number and she said you'd take it seriously, but it would be best to go through the Rector, for *political* reasons. But I get so frightened, now, you see.'

Mrs Aird had a single, lonely chair in the window. Called it her sunset chair. Never missed a sunset. You could just see Herefordshire Beacon, on the far left, but nothing of the road, although you could hear the traffic above you, like a sporadic draught in the attic.

'I used to think it was better this time of year with the holiday cottages starting to fill up and the village more like a *real* village. I've got to know some of the holiday people, and they're quite nice. Gave me their keys to go in and make sure their cottages were all right, switch the heating on in winter. Made me feel useful and I thought it made them feel more welcome so maybe they'd stay for a bit. But I've had to give the keys back. I don't like to go into a strange house alone any more. Well, would you?'

Merrily must have looked blank because Mrs Aird leaned forward, going into a whisper.

'There was a *poor man* – a bit solitary – who'd come in the summer for weeks at a time and we never knew whether he was there or not, and one day . . . someone noticed all the flies.'

Mrs Aird gripped the arms of her chair, shuddering.

Merrily apprehensively balanced her tea, in its willow-pattern china cup, on her knee.

'Doesn't the Rector go to see people?'

'Well, he *does.* Comes to see me about once a week, but then I'm a regular churchgoer. But some people don't like it – see it as an intrusion, as if he's going to evangelize. But of course Mr Spicer's not like that, is he? And he's got these other parishes to look after. And he's on his own, too, now. Not been easy for him, with his wife . . . and his daughter. And everything that's happened.'

Mrs Aird sat with her arms folded, looking expectant.

'You were there when … the lorry driver …'

'It was like an *explosion*, Mrs Watkins. I have a key to the church and I'd gone in early to put the flowers out because there was a funeral that day – Mrs Hatch, a mercy – and *bang*. I went rushing out, and the cab of the lorry was almost flattened on the driver's side. He had to come out of the other door. I brought him in here and I gave him a cup of tea while we were waiting for the police and the breakdown people. He had his hands to his eyes, just thinking about it, and he said – I'll always remember – he said, *It was like a little sun.*'

'But it wasn't a sunny day?'

'It was later, but it was very dull then. Only about half past seven. When the police came, they breathalysed him straight away, and he was completely clear. They said he couldn't have seen a light, but he *insisted* that was why he'd swerved, and he was a nice man – not young. One of the policemen said to me afterwards, *Oh, I expect he fell asleep at the wheel and dreamed it.* I said, *That's not fair, you don't know …*'

An orb, Merrily was thinking without much enthusiasm. Very fashionable with cable-TV ghosthunters, orbs. Bit of glare got recorded by the camera and it was an *orb*, a semi-formed manifestation. What Huw Owen called a spirit-egg, though you were never quite sure when Huw was being disparaging.

'Did the driver think there was anything … strange about the light?'

'Well, it was certainly strange, but I didn't think there'd have been anything *ghostly*. Not then. But then there was Mr Loste … and the others.'

'Mrs Cobham.'

'She's a bit …' Mrs Aird put her nose in the air '… if you ask me. And not over-friendly. Mr Loste … well, some people think *he's* a bit … what's the word …?' Mrs Aird waved her cardiganed arms about in a random sort of way. 'Maniac … manic. Obsessed with his music and his choirs … and, give him his due, he's marvellous. He's done wonders. But some people think he's not reliable in other ways. And his friendship with the American woman who goes to the wells. *Bit* peculiar. But . . . he saw what he saw, and he'll tell you as much, give him his due.'

'I'm hoping to see him later. I'll probably need to go back and see the Rector first.'

'He's not in,' Mrs Aird said. 'His car's gone.'

How did she know that from down here? Had she got a periscope?

'He's got three parishes, you know. And all his problems.'

Merrily drank some tea.

*Oh, well.*

'I'm . . . afraid I don't really know anything about that. Don't really like to ask him these things.' Peering over her cup. 'Sounds like I'm prying.'

Mrs Aird looked up at the ceiling and made a sad, wounded noise.

'It was his daughter wrecked everything. Emily. Got a son as well, but he's too young to cause trouble. Emily would be . . . what, eighteen? Mrs Spicer, Fiona, she was from Reading, somewhere like that, near London. She didn't really like the country, and when Mr Spicer left the Army— You know what he was, don't you?'

'Erm . . . no.'

'S . . . A . . . S.'

Mrs Aird mouthing it silently, like a breach of the Official Secrets Act.

'Really?'

No wonder Syd Spicer was familiar with the Brecon Beacons.

'Been out about eight years,' Mrs Aird said. 'But there's something that doesn't leave them, if you ask me.'

'Mmm.'

Probably right. And they often didn't leave the area. After many years based in Hereford, learning to become the most efficient killers in or out of uniform, they formed connections with the people and the land. Married local girls. Surprisingly – or maybe not – Spicer wouldn't have been the first of them to become a priest.

'Imagine the stress she must've been through,' Mrs Aird said. 'Never sure where in the world he was at any time, but knowing it was always going to be somewhere terribly dangerous.'

Merrily nodded. The SAS had probably the worst matrimonial record outside Hollywood. Breakfast with the wife, late supper in a cave in Afghanistan. Then retirement, still hyper, and they couldn't settle down. The wives had to be very special to survive all that. Long periods alone, counting the Regiment graves in St Martin's church-yard.

'Sometimes . . .' Mrs Aird leaned forward again '. . . Fiona came to talk to me on her own. She said he'd always promised her that when he came out of the Army they'd go back down south – bright lights and no sheep, she used to say. But then I suppose he found his faith. I don't know *where* a man like that finds it.'

'Oh . . . sometimes it's just lying there, in your path, like an old coat, and before you know what you're doing you've picked it up, tried it on and it seems to fit.'

'That's nice,' Mrs Aird said. 'I suppose.'

'How did Mrs Spicer react to that?'

'Oh, she stuck by him.'

Merrily smiled. Like Spicer had come out as a transsexual.

'At least she knew where he was. He was a curate in Hereford, at first, and she didn't mind that, thinking they'd move south as soon as he won his spurs, so to speak. They'd bought themselves a little house near his in-laws down in Reading, and they'd spend holidays there. But then he was offered Wychehill and the surrounding parishes – a *bit* closer to London, but it turned out to be the worst of both worlds. And the girl, Emily, she hated every minute she had to spend here. Off with her friends to nightclubs, every chance she got. And that, of course, led to boys and . . . the other thing. You know?'

'No . . . what?'

'That's what . . .' Mrs Aird leaned further forward as if the place was bugged. 'That's what broke up their marriage. The stress of dealing with the girl.' She paused. 'Drugs.'

'Syd's daughter?'

'It's everywhere, my dear. Young people can't seem to face normal life any more, can they? Mr Spicer's daughter . . . even Mr Devereaux's elder son, when he gave up his job with the hunt. Went clean off the rails when it was banned, and they say *he* went on drugs. Luckily, he came round. But Mr Spicer's daughter ended up in *rehab*.'

'Oh.'

'So you can imagine what it was like for them when the Royal Oak changed hands.'

'Sorry?'

'And that's very much part of it, if you ask me. The evil.'

'Evil . . . ?'

'Ingrid said you weren't the kind to dismiss it like so many of the modern clergy do.'

Mrs Aird looked out of her wall-to-wall picture window across the valley with its pastures and orchards.

'Expect I'll have to go, soon. You wouldn't believe how often the houses change hands up here. It's like Mr Walford says – he's disabled but a very intelligent man, we do crosswords together – and he often says, *This is what I always wanted, a place up here, and then when you get it you suddenly wake up one day and realize you're too old for it.* This is not a place to be old, Mrs Watkins, though I'll miss my sunsets.'

Merrily looked around the room, everything modern and convenient and sparkling in the sunshine.

'The Royal Oak,' she said. 'Is that a pub?'

'*Pub?*' Mrs Aird said. 'It's the gateway to hell. I don't even want to talk about *that*, if you don't mind. I've had all the locks changed and I shut myself away at weekends, go to bed with my mobile phone in case they cut the wires. And unfortunately it's not something *you* can do anything about.'

'Is there anything I *can* do for you while I'm here?'

'No, I'm quite self-sufficient really. I've been a widow nearly twenty years, and I can cope with most things.'

'Everybody needs help,' Merrily said.

Mrs Aird looked down into her lap for a moment; when she looked up she seemed, in some way, younger, her expression more focused.

'If you don't mind me saying so, Mrs Watkins, you seem a nice girl. But you don't look very much like my idea of a ... you know.'

'Yes, I'm sorry.' Merrily looked down at her sweatshirt. 'The Rector asked me to ... I don't think he wanted to draw attention to me being here.'

'No, I'm sorry. I shouldn't have said that. Ingrid says you know what you're doing. It's just that I don't have many friends in Wychehill, and this girl ... that's what worries me most.'

*And there might be another one,* Syd Spicer had said, *which is ... a bit weird. Joyce Aird can tell you. They won't talk to me about it.*

'She's a single mother, Mrs Watkins. She's on her own in that house. And she's had the worst of it. She's ... this is why something needs to be done.'

'I'm a single mother, too. I have a daughter of seventeen.'

'*You* can't be old enough for ...' Mrs Aird's eyes lost their focus. 'Oh, you lose touch at my age. Everybody under fifty looks like a child.'

'What's her name?'

'Hannah.'

'She lives in Wychehill?'

'Thinks she's possessed,' Mrs Aird said. 'It's not good, is it?'

# The Dead of Ledwardine

LOL LET JANE INTO his terraced cottage in Church Street. In the living room, the sunlight jetted through the window-hung crystals – Jane's house-warming present – making quivering rainbow balls on the walls and the face of the Boswell guitar. Making the guitar seem to vibrate with possibilities which would vanish like the rainbow balls as soon as he picked it up.

'Well, go on.' Jane planting herself next to the writing desk. 'Ring them.'

'I don't know the—'

'I have it here. Copied it from the notice.'

Jane consulted her right wrist, read out the row of numbers biroed on it. She was left-handed. Sinistral. Therefore dangerously unpredictable. How was he supposed to handle this? Encourage her to go ahead with what seemed like a valid protest? Or, bearing in mind Merrily's situation in the village, do what he could to talk her out of it?

'And the code, of course, is 01432,' Jane said.

Lol rang the council's planning department, Jane drumming her fingers on the desk the whole time. What he eventually learned, from a guy called Charles, was in no way likely to wind her down.

'He says it's up for discussion next week.'

'They'll make a *decision* then?'

'The impression I got is that there've been no objections. The site being fairly secluded, inside the development line as laid down in the local plan, and not visible from the village centre. Perfect housing site.'

'But it's on a ... Why didn't you tell him it's on a crucial—?'

'Jane—'

'Yeah, yeah, the council doesn't believe they exist. Anywhere else with, like, a really major figure like Alfred Watkins, there'd be a statue in High Town, and all the key leys, like Capuchin Way, would be marked by brass plaques. But this bunch of crass, self-serving tossers—'

'Jane, the government's demanding new housing all over the country. And there *is* a case for Ledwardine needing . . . starter homes?'

'And like, *luxury executive dwellings* fit into that category?'

Lol sighed. They'd called in at the Eight Till Late to quiz Big Jim Prosser on the ownership of Coleman's Meadow. Jim had identified a farmer called G. J. Murray, who lived at Lyonshall, about seven miles away. This Murray had inherited Coleman's Meadow from his aunt and had been touting it to development companies ever since.

Which was the way of it. People wrote to the *Hereford Times*, moaning about all the locally born young people being driven out of the county because they couldn't get onto the housing ladder, but when they had a chance to develop some field for housing, it was usually *luxury executive dwellings*. Where the safe money was.

'And, like, even with starter homes, most of them just go to people from outside,' Jane said. 'All the guys in my class who were born around here, they just can't wait to get the hell out . . . rent an inner-city apartment near some cool shops. Or emigrate. We're a nomadic race.'

'Unfortunately, the council can't operate on that basis.'

Didn't you just hate playing the responsible adult? Especially when she was right. They really needed more executive homes, another two dozen SUVs clogging the village?

'Anyway, it's not going to happen, is it, Laurence? We're going to get it stopped.'

'We?' Lol said. '*We?*'

'Either you're for me or against me.'

'Jane, I am one hundred per cent *for* you. It's just that we're not talking about protecting an ancient monument, are we?'

'Of *course* we are . . . sort of.'

Jane sat down and drew a diagram on Lol's lyric-pad.

◆ Cole Hill . . . ◆ Coleman's Meadow track . . . ◆ tumulus . . .

◆ market place . . . ◆ Ledwardine Church . . . ◆ ancient crossroads . . . ◆ standing stone.

'. . . Six, seven points if you include the market place. It's beyond dispute. If I had a big enough map, I could probably trace it all the way to the Neolithic settlements in the Black Mountains. It's a *living* ancient monument.'

'Still be there in essence, though, won't it, even if they build on it?'

'It won't be *visible*. This is a genuine, existing old straight track, probably an ancient ritual route, right? By the time *they*'ve finished, the way the land slopes, you probably won't even be able to see Cole Hill from the church any more for all these identical luxury homes with their naff conservatories. It's a crime against the ancient spirit. It'll *sour the energy!*'

'Energy,' Lol said. 'That's not something you can easily see, is it?'

'It's something our remote ancestors were, like, instinctively aware of.'

Jane went into lecturer mode, telling him things he already kind of knew: how the old stones had been erected on blind springs and the leys had energized and sustained the land and the people who lived on the land. How the oldest churches had also been built on ancient pagan sites because even in medieval times the people still *remembered*. And, of course, the leys were also lines of contact with . . . the ancestors.

'The dead. Burial mounds. Circular churchyards growing up on the sites of Neolithic stone circles. The spirits of the dead were believed to walk the alignments so, in the old days, a coffin would have to be carried to the church along a particular track to prepare the spirit for the afterlife. It was a crucial thing. We should get Mum to reinstate it.'

'It's a theory,' Lol said, nervous.

'Ties in with folklore the world over, Lol. What it means is that the path through the church to the holy hill is the village's link with its ancestors . . . its origins. You obliterate the path, you sever the link, and Ledwardine loses its . . . its soul!'

Jane sprang up, as though the ancient energy was surging underneath the cottage floor.

'Who do I complain to? Who do I lobby?'

'The MP? Downing Street?' Where it would go into the shredder marked *fruitcakes.* 'Maybe best to start with the local councillor.'

'Gavin Ashe?'

'Gavin Ashe resigned, Jane. New guy is Lyndon Pierce. Lives at the end of Virgingate Lane.'

'Which party?'

'Non-party. He's an independent.'

'Well, that's good, isn't it? That means he doesn't have to follow any party line on housing, right? It's a start.'

Lol said nothing. 'Independent' also meant you were free to jump into anybody's pocket.

'Well,' he said, 'I suppose you could approach him on a preserva-tion-of-heritage basis. If you show him the picture in *The Old Straight Track.*'

'Erm ... yeah,' Jane said. 'I *could* ...'

'Because I'd guess that area hasn't changed at all since Watkins was around in the 1920s?'

'No. Probably not.' She looked uncertain, suddenly. 'Right. So that's Lyndon ... ?'

'Pierce. He's a chartered accountant. Jane ...' Lol didn't really want to ask this. 'Coleman's Meadow *is* shown in the book, isn't it?'

'Look, Lol, you couldn't ...' Jane frowned. 'Obviously Watkins couldn't include every ley in the county.'

'You mean, no picture?'

'Well, no, but that doesn't—'

'The most perfect, visible ley and he didn't take a picture of it?'

'Maybe he just didn't *use* it.' Jane was backing awkwardly towards the door. 'Maybe it didn't come out, *I* don't know. Don't look at me in that sorrowful, pitying—'

'So, basically, this is not an Alfred Watkins ley, this is ... a *Jane* Watkins ley.'

Lol thought he saw a glitter of tears. This was about more than just a ley line and the soul of the village. It was also about being nearly eighteen and the realization that you were entering a world where changes were seldom for the better.

'Jane, did ... did Watkins even mention this line, or even Ledwardine?'

'No.' Jane looked down at her feet. 'It's the one thing I can't understand.'

'Oh.'

'It's the real thing, though, Lol.' She looked up, defiant again. 'I mean *you* thought it was. You weren't just—?'

'Well, I suppose it doesn't *necessarily* mean he didn't find it.'

'Now you're humouring me. Don't do that.'

'No, really. He might have discovered it too late to get it into the book.'

'You think?'

'It's possible. And I mean, I'm no kind of expert, but it does seem like a perfect ley.'

Jane looked him in the eyes. 'So you think I'm doing the right thing.'

A weighty moment. For a second or two, Lol felt the presence in the room of the cottage's last owner, Lucy Devenish, Jane's friend and mentor. His, too. Dead for over two years now. But sometimes when he came in at night he could still believe he'd seen, in the fractured instant of snapping on the lights, the folds of Lucy's trade-mark poncho hanging over the newel post at the bottom of the stairs.

'I suppose that depends very much on what you're planning to do,' he said carefully.


When Jane had gone, Lol could still feel her agitation in the air, bobbing and flickering around like the rays from the crystals.

He picked up the Boswell guitar. Prof Levin had studio time available in the second half of September, which left less than three months to develop this horribly difficult second-album-after-the-comeback. The one which had to be appreciably better than the first or your career was in meltdown.

Again.

Lol sat down on the sofa with the Boswell and tried again with 'Cloisters', a mainly instrumental number which, no matter how he moved it around, and despite the experiments with Nick Drake tuning, continued to sound ordinary. As in flat. As in lifeless. More or less like every other song he'd half-finished in the past several weeks – a period in which, otherwise, he'd felt contented, balanced ... normal. It was surely too much of a cliché that you had to be emotionally raw, broken, ragged, wretched or lovelorn to write a worthwhile song.

Maybe it just needed a string arrangement.

He lay back on the sofa with his arms around the guitar, an image coming to him of the dead of Ledwardine in some half-formed procession from the steeple to the holy hill, bisected by a stream of unheeding SUVs.

# 8

# Dead to the World

CARACTACUS.

It was carved into a stone slab by a gate in a hedge enclosing a house and an empty carport. A flat, blank house built of the same squarish stones as the church. It was about a minute's walk down the hill from the Rectory but very much on its own.

Merrily had a sudden sense of isolation, vulnerability. She shook herself.

Caractacus, as most schoolkids learned, was the ancient British hero defeated by the Romans and taken back to Rome, where he was treated with some respect. The final conflict was supposed to have taken place on Herefordshire Beacon, but that was only a legend, discredited, apparently, by historians.

If Caractacus had retired here at least he'd have been spared a view of the Beacon. The house was tucked so tightly into the hill that all you could see behind it was a steep field vanishing rapidly into the forestry.

To get to the front door, Merrily had to push away a sapling taller than she was. Disbelieving, she inspected a leaf.

An *oak*? Within a couple of years it'd be pushing the glass in. In thirty years it would probably have the house down. Tim Loste must surely be planning to transplant it somewhere – but where? His front garden was the size of a smallish bathroom and there clearly wasn't much space behind the house, either.

On the wall beside the front door was a bell pull. Merrily could hear the jingling inside the house. No other sounds. She waited at least two minutes before edging around the oak and walking back to the road, pulling her mobile from her shoulder bag.

'Couldn't check out a couple of things for me, could you, Sophie?'

'Tell me.'

'The Royal Oak. It's a pub not far from Wychehill which seems to have undergone some kind of transformation, making it . . . unpopular. Might be something on the Net.'

'I may even have *heard* something about this. I'll look into it. Anything else?'

'Syd Spicer. Is it true he's ex-Regiment?'

'I don't know. The Bishop would be able to tell us for certain, but he's taken his grandson to a county cricket match in Worcester. That's rather interesting, Merrily, isn't it? I'll find out what I can about Mr Spicer's history which, given the traditions of the SAS, is likely to be very little. What are you doing now?'

'Trying to understand what's happening here.' Merrily looked up the hill towards the church, concealed by dark deciduous trees. 'Spicer's right about this place. You wouldn't know you were in it.'

She'd left the twenty-year-old Volvo in the parking bay in front the church. She walked up past it, seeing nobody, following the grey-brown churchyard wall into a short, steep cutting which accessed a lane running parallel to the main road but on a higher level, like a sloping gallery.

*Time to seek help to remove the evil from our midst,* Joyce Aird had apparently said to Syd Spicer.

Midst of what?

All the same, she brought her small pectoral cross out of her bag and slipped it on, letting it drop down under the T-shirt. You could never be too careful.


Hannah's cottage was low and pebble-dashed and painted a buttermilk colour. Rustic porch and a clematis, and a mountain bike propped up under a front window.

It was just gone one p.m. and the sun was hot and high. Hannah was wearing shorts and a stripy sleeveless top revealing a butterfly tattoo on one shoulder.

She didn't have sunken eyes or a deathly pallor.

'I feel dead stupid now.' She was maybe a year or two younger than Merrily: pale hair in a ponytail, no make-up, a diamond nose-stud. 'I'm glad you're not . . . you know . . .' Pointing at her neck.

'Too hot for all that.' Merrily had shed the sweatshirt, was down to her green Gomer Parry Plant Hire T-shirt. 'I used to have a black one with a dog collar on it in white but I couldn't find it this morning.'

'It's OK, I know you're the real thing. Joyce Aird rang.'

'Mmm. Thought she might.'

'Nothing wrong with Joyce,' Hannah said. 'Better than local radio, normally, so it's killing her keeping quiet about this.'

Hannah wasn't local either. Northern accent. East Lancashire, maybe.

'This is nice.' Merrily looked around. 'You live here on your own?'

'With my son. He's nine. This is my parents' holiday cottage, had it years and years. They said we could come down here, me and Robin, after my husband left us. Last year, that was, and I'm still feeling a bit, you know, impermanent. You coming in?'

The cottage was tiny, no more than three or four small rooms, Merrily guessed. The living room was furnished like a caravan – bed-settee with drawers underneath, a table that went flat to the wall, a Calor-gas stove in the fireplace. Hannah guided her to a compact easy chair with a yellow cushion and put herself on the edge of the bed-settee. The single window was wide open to a honeysuckle scent.

'Luckily, you caught me on the right day. I've a part-time job at the tourist office in Ledbury. Three days a week. Keeps us going. Do you want tea or coffee or a cold drink?'

'Could we maybe talk first?'

'Yeh, 'course. I'm afraid I've not been to church since Robin was christened. Bad that, isn't it? I might go if it was a bit smaller. But it's horrible, our church. I mean, isn't it? You don't feel anything particularly holy in there, that's for sure.'

'It seems very . . . pleasant in here, though.'

'Well, it's very *small*. Had to put a lot of furniture in storage. But it . . . Oh, I see what you mean. No, there's nothing wrong *here*. We used to come year after year and for weekends when I was a kid. I love it. It's gorgeous round here, i'n't it? No, there's nothing like *that* here.'

'Well, that's good.'

'I did feel really *free* again, biking to work down the hill to Ledbury. Bit hard going coming back, but it keeps you fit.'

'Lot of long hills. Don't think I could do it.'

'Your leg muscles ache like anything at first, but it's worth it. Listen, I'm sorry, I've never been in this sort of ... I was going to look for your website on the computer at work, but there was always somebody there. I don't want you to feel I'm wasting your time, that's all. I don't even know if there's a charge.'

'Er ... no.'

'Bit nervous now,' Hannah said.

'Actually,' Merrily said. 'I've never had a case of possession. Shameful thing for a so-called exorcist to say, but there we are. So ... what's it like?'

'What's it *like*?' Hannah grinned. 'You having me on? I don't know what to say. I'm not a person that gets scared. I'd love a dog, mind, but I'd have to leave him in when I went to work and that wouldn't be fair.'

'Got the same problem, Hannah. Sorry, I don't even know your last name.'

'Bradley. That's my married name. It's a bit better than what I was called before – Catterall – so I thought at least the bugger can leave me that. Look – this is just between us, right?'

'Don't worry.'

'I think about it all the time, but it's still hard finding the words,' Hannah said.


'It was next to me. *That* close. I'm not kidding.'

Spacing it out with her hands, looking at Merrily for signs of disbelief. Merry just nodded. Hannah wet her lips with her tongue.

'Mouth's gone all dry now. Can I get a ... ?'

Hannah brought a can of Diet Pepsi for each of them and sat herself down again, rolling the cold can between her hands.

'It's a long hill, and I'm not that brave yet that I can just let go. I'd be sod-all use in the Tour de France, I tell you.' She shook her head. 'I don't know why I'm laughing, I was—'

'Which side was it on?'

'Towards the middle of the road. That side. I keep as close as I can to the verge 'cos some of these drivers are bloody maniacs.'

'And it was . . . this was definitely another bike.'

'What it's like . . . it's like when two of you are going along side by side and you turn your head to say something and . . . nothing! Soon as you turn your head . . . gone. First couple of times I was thinking it was me, how you do.'

'This is the daytime?'

'Morning . . . afternoon. I don't take the bike out at night, I'm not stupid.'

'What happens when you don't turn your head?'

'That's what I was coming to. If you don't look, you can can see it. If you keep your eyes on the road ahead and you don't— Sounds daft, I know. In fact, that's wrong. You can't *see* it, that's not what I meant. You're just fully *aware* of it. It absolutely completely exists. Two of you biking along side by side. And you can feel the wind coming at you along the hedge, but on the other side you're shielded from it by . . . by this other cyclist. Really. Honest to God.'

'And how do *you* feel when that's happening?'

'At first . . . just weird. Uncomfortable. So I'd keep turning and looking, just to get rid of it. And then . . . Oh God . . . I was so busy looking to the side I nearly went into the back of a tractor and trailer that'd just pulled in to the side. Another second I'd've been *splat*. Great big metal trailer. Go into that on a bike it's broken bones at least, Mrs Watkins.'

'Merrily.'

'That's nice. Merr-ily. Have you got to be psychic for your job?'

'Not essential. Sometimes it can be counter-productive. What happened after the trailer incident?'

'We've come to the bit I don't like.'

'I don't think I'd like any of it.'

'What happened . . . I thought about what'd become of Robin if I was in an orthopaedic bed for six months, so I decided that if I ever again got the feeling there was somebody cycling next to me I'd have to stop looking to one side.'

'Did you . . . ever think what it might be?'

Hannah shook her head.

'I didn't think too hard. You'd go daft, wouldn't you? What I was really afraid of, to be quite honest, was that it might be a brain tumour or something. When you've got a child, these things . . .'

'I know.'

'So it was almost a relief when it . . .'

'What was the bit you didn't like?'

'Well, like I say, if you keep on and you don't look, it just becomes more and more real. And close. I didn't like that. It was a day like this, maybe not quite so hot, but I could smell his sweat. And yet it was cold. Very cold, suddenly.'

'It was a man, then.'

'Oh yeh. I could smell his sweat. There's something about a man's sweat, i'n't there? And his *tobacco*. Tobacco breath. Not like cigarettes – I used to smoke till I had Robin – this was real strong tobacco breath. And after a while – I'm just concentrating on pedalling as fast I can, see, just gripping the handlebars and gritting my teeth, no way was I going to stop – I was feeling his thoughts. Just look at my arms, Merrily, I've got goose bumps thinking about it. Feeling his thoughts! Not – don't get me wrong – not what he was *thinking*, exactly. It was more the *colour* of his thoughts. The texture. The *feeling* of his thoughts. I'm not putting this very well, am I?'

'You're putting it brilliantly well, actually. You must've been very scared by now.'

'I was afterwards. When I got to work the first time they thought I must be ill. My colleague at the information centre, she wanted to send me home in a taxi, but I needed to work. Talk to people. Get over it. I did go home by taxi that night, mind. Had to go back next day on the bus to pick up the bike.'

'Anything happen then?'

'No. It never does when you're afraid it might.'

'When you say you weren't scared till afterwards ...'

'Because you're too much like ... too much like a *part of it* to be scared. That's what I meant by possessed. He was there. He was breathing all over me. I was wearing shorts – this was a week or so ago, this was another time. I was wearing shorts like these, only a bit tighter and he – I swear to God, I felt his hand on my thigh, and I was angry, instinctively, you know? Gerroff! And he bloody chuckled. He *chuckled.*'

'You *heard* him chuckle?'

'I *felt* him chuckle. And that's worse. You feel him chuckling inside your head. That's what I meant by being possessed.'

'How long did it last, usually?'

'Probably no more than a few seconds, but a lot can happen in a few seconds when it's something that's never happened before.'

'And how many times?'

'Three. No, four. Until I realized what was happening and just ... got off.'

'When you got off the bike, it was all right?'

'I realized then that it only happened when I was on the bike. As if I was actually generating it by pedalling.'

'And there was nothing wrong with you physically. Unlike the others, though, you never actually saw anything.'

'Never.'

'When did it last happen?'

'Earlier this week.'

'Same man?'

'Oh, yeh.'

'*What* happened?'

'Bugger-all, 'cos I jumped off quick this time and wheeled the bike along till I got on the main road.'

'Just to get this right, this is the hill where you come out of this lane, at the church and then go past the Rectory ... down past there.'

'That's right.'

'Could you just tell me . . . when you were feeling his thoughts, what were they like?'

'Dark, usually,' Hannah said. 'Angry.'

'Angry with you?'

'No. He doesn't know me. I'm sure he doesn't. He just gets into my space. It's like he just needs somebody's space to get into, and it doesn't matter who you are.'

'So who was he angry at?'

'Something bigger than me. Everything. God? I couldn't say.'

'And the time something touched your leg . . .'

'You're thinking it might've been a leaf or something, aren't you? That's what I thought. And I'm not going to insist it wasn't. I just know what it felt like. Are you married, Merrily? You are allowed to, aren't you?'

'Yes, you are. And I used to be.'

'Join the club. All I'm trying to say . . . when you're in bed with a bloke, right? And you wake up and he's still asleep . . . but his hand's sliding up your nightie? Like that. Shall we have a cup of tea? Tea's better on a hot day, sometimes.'

Merrily smiled. 'Love one.'

Hannah stood up and opened the sliding door into a kitchen that must once have been part of the same room.

'Blokes, eh?' She looked over her shoulder at Merrily. 'Hand up your nightie and dead to the world.'

# 9

# Mutated

WALKING OUT OF HANNAH'S gate into the warmth of the afternoon, Merrily felt mixed emotions circling her like bees: primarily, a certain wild excitement that was close to the edge of fear. You realized how much time you spent coasting the safe surf between the hard sandbank of scepticism and the unfathomable deep blue abyss.

She stepped down through the cutting, with the church on her left and the sun in her eyes and the phone chiming in her bag. Aware of the layers of Wychehill. The layers of experience.

'The Royal Oak,' Sophie said, as she reached the Volvo. 'Some things you might want to know.'

'Go on.'

'I have some information from the Internet which I can send to you at home, if you aren't coming back to Hereford. However, I ran into Inspector Bliss and took the liberty of mentioning it. He said he'd be most interested to talk to you.'

'About the Royal Oak?'

'Discreetly,' Sophie said.

It was probably worth going back. Merrily had a christening in Ledwardine tomorrow afternoon; if she dealt with parish business in the morning she could probably come back here on Wednesday and talk to Tim Loste and Preston Devereaux before the public meeting.

Feeling tired now. Up before six a.m. and two trips to Wychehill, and she hadn't eaten yet.

Still . . . She smoked half a cigarette, then turned the car around and drove down past Ledbury . . . Trumpet . . . Stoke Edith. Midsummer in a couple of days, the first hard little apples like green nuts on the twisty trees and the hops on the wires. A potent landscape of cider and beer.

She felt light-headed. It was humbling and slightly shocking when, amongst all the self-delusion and the wishful thinking and the mind games, you encountered someone as guilelessly direct as Hannah Bradley.

Sophie said, 'My attempts to log on to the Royal Oak's actual website were frustrated by the inadequacy of our software. Apparently, the Diocese has failed to provide us with something called *Flash Seven*.'

'Anything to save a few quid.'

'From what I've been reading about the Royal Oak elsewhere, I'm quite grateful we *don't* have it. There you are. You may understand some of this.'

Merrily went round the desk to peer at the screen over Sophie's shoulder.

*HIP-HOP . . . RAGGA . . . GARAGE . . . HOUSE . . .*
*DRUM'N'BASS . . . BHANGRA . . .*
*. . . IN THE MALVERNS?*
*Believe it!!! A big old country pub – used to*
*be all darts matches and Rotary Club –*
*has MUTATED . . .*

'My first experience of nightclub websites, I confess.' Sophie said.

'You surprise me.'

'To save you some time, this establishment is just across the boundary into Worcestershire – and out of the diocese. Another good reason not get involved.'

Sophie scrolled up to uncover a picture of a bejewelled black man called DJ Xex. Instantly dismissing him with a contemptuous flick of the mouse.

'It appears that the Royal Oak is now owned by a Mr Khan – apparently quite a well-known entrepreneur in the West Midlands?'

Sophie glanced at Merrily, who shook her head. Never heard of him.

'Quite a number of local press reports about local people calling on the appropriate authority to have Mr Khan's licence withdrawn. I've printed them out for you.'

'But you didn't print the picture of DJ Xex for the noticeboard?'

'This would be less amusing to you, Merrily,' Sophie said, 'if you had to live with it.'

Possibly true. All the innocent fun of inner-city clubland in the romantic Malverns: punters swarming in every weekend from the teenage wastelands, cars screaming through the village at one a.m., windows open, *boom, boom, boom*. Kids stopping to throw up in front gardens, relieve themselves in the churchyard. Have sex on graves . . . allegedly. And now a fatal road accident of the kind that people always insisted had been waiting to happen.

'Sounds as if the victims of Saturday's crash had spent the evening at the Royal Oak.' Merrily gathered up the on-line news stories Sophie had printed. 'Colliding with the chairman of the parish council, returning from a wedding.'

Sophie winced.

The stories were mainly from the *Malvern Gazette*: petitions to Hereford and Worcester councils, letters to MPs. Counter-allegations of NIMBYism and racism by the leader of a youth project who thought the restyled Royal Oak was the best thing to happen in the Malverns this century.

'What did Frannie Bliss say?'

'We didn't have much time to talk. He asked how you were, and I explained that you were looking into an alleged occurrence at the eastern end of the diocese and then simply asked if he knew anything about the Royal Oak.'

'Or, as it's now apparently called . . .'

'*Don't.*'

Merrily smiled at Sophie.

'Inn Ya Face? That's quite good, really.'

'In Elgar's hills.' Sophie's lower body trembled slightly as if the ground beneath her feet had shifted. 'One day, Merrily, I think we may be pushed just slightly too far.'

'I wonder . . .' Merrily tapped her lower lip with a pen '. . . if that's why Syd Spicer's a little sceptical. I wonder if he thinks that the ghost of a traditional cyclist – an image symbolic of gentler times – is someone's idea for stirring the pot.'

Sophie raised an eyebrow.

'It happens. Just occasionally. But then Syd doesn't seem to know about Hannah Bradley.'

'You found that convincing?'

'It's about as convincing as it gets.'

'The girl thinks she's been sexually assaulted by . . . ?'

'I wouldn't put it that strongly, and neither does she. Quite a healthy attitude towards it, really. That's one of the things that makes it so credible.'

'What will you do?'

'Collate all the reports. Try and find out if anybody's ever been killed on that road on a bike. If I can tie it down to an individual, the obvious answer would be a straightforward Requiem Eucharist in the church, with as many of the witnesses as we could get. Plus the Rector, of course.'

'Ah, yes.' Sophie picked up a notepad. 'The Rector.'

'You checked him out.'

'Ordained eight years ago.' Sophie raised her glasses on their chain to read her shorthand notes. 'Installed as Rector of Wychehill, with two other neighbouring parishes in autumn 2003. Renowned, apparently, for his strenuous youth-work – previously, he ran a shop in Eign Street specializing in Outward Bound-type pursuits. Mountaineering, geology. And before that, his career, as you say was with the Army. The file doesn't mention which regiment, but then, if he served in Hereford, it hardly needs to.'

'No.'

Merrily was thinking of Spicer's distinctly unemotional response to the carnage at Wychehill, the minimalism of his kitchen, his total self-reliance. *I'm very capable.*

'My experience of the Special Air Service, Merrily, is that they tend to dispense information on a need-to-know basis.'

'If at all,' Merrily said.

Remembering a story someone had told her about a Hereford dentist with a serving-SAS patient who'd dropped in for a heavy-duty root-canal filling and – by way of an exercise – had declined the anaesthetic.

Might have been apocryphal, probably not.

# 10

# Firewall

MENTIONING THE ROYAL OAK to Frannie Bliss . . . this had been like opening the door of the CID room and rolling a grenade through the gap.

They were in the café in the Cathedral cloisters, with a Gothic-framed view of the Bishop's garden. Bliss was doing his eager-fox smile, raspberry jam from his doughnut oozing between his fingers.

'Clever little bastard, though, Merrily. His old feller's some kind of professor of Islamic Studies in Wolverhampton. Also, a consultant to the Home Office.'

He evidently thought she knew more than she actually did.

'The lad's been doing his bit, too, advising the council on community relations in Worcester. Oh, and he also runs an ethnic art gallery in Malvern, where the Prince of Wales once attended a reception.'

'Yes,' Merrily said, 'I'm sure the Prince of Wales would have enjoyed that, but—'

'In fact, so snugly has Raji fitted himself into the system that the little shit was actually one of the speakers at a symposium last year on new directions in community policing. Having earlier – this may surprise you, or not – had lunch with my esteemed ruler.'

'Annie Howe? Why would that surprise me? Frannie, just give me the building blocks . . . How does this guy come to be the owner of a country pub in the Malverns?'

'Oh, and *then*, following the symposium – attended by civic leaders and other useless suits – I get meself formally introduced to young Mr Khan. Merrily, he *patronized* me.'

'Oh dear.'

"'From *Liverpool*, then, sergeant.'" Bliss putting on this poncy public school accent and a twisted smirk. "'That's quite a cultural quantum leap, isn't it?'"

'He called you sergeant?'

Bliss leaned back. His red hair was receding slightly, and something throbbed in his temple.

'Full name Rajab Ali Khan. Twenty-seven years old, and already the owner of – as well as the nice gallery – nightclubs in Worcester and Kidderminster. And now, yeh, the Royal Oak Inn, as was, in the heart of the glorious Malverns. I think he even had grant-aid. He's good at that.'

He put down the remaining half of his jammy doughnut. On the side plate, it looked like debris from a post-mortem.

'And at this point I've *gorra* say, Merrily, that I believe Raji to be a main player in the supply of a substantial percentage of Class A drugs entering the Border counties.'

Merrily stirred her coffee. 'You know that?'

'No, I said I *believe* it.'

'I believe in God, Frannie, but—'

'And I also believe there's a firewall around him, for reasons I'm either not sufficiently elevated to have been told about or because . . .' Bliss picked up his doughnut. 'Ah, what's the point? The service is in flux again, and the best we can do is keep our noses down until it's over.'

Merrily said nothing. He meant the proposed merger of West Mercia Police with two other regions, creating a superforce supposedly more capable of tackling terrorism and major crime but probably in the process, also saving the Home Office milllions of pounds by raising the bar and reducing aggravated burglary to a misdemeanour.

He held up a hand, a raspberry globule like a stigmata in the centre of the palm. He was a Roman Catholic, fond of symbolism.

'A warning, Merrily. We're becoming hopelessly politicized. It's no longer about nailing villains to the wall.'

Merrily poured more coffee.

'Can I take it Mr Khan is a practising Muslim?'

'Practising? Bastard's got it off to a fine art. See, these days, if there's a Muslim who speaks out publicly against terrorism, as Raji's been known to do – *I'm a Brit, don't I* sound *like a Brit?* – some clowns tend to be less concerned about what else he's into.'

'And you think drugs are passing through the Royal Oak in significant quantities? I mean, what are we talking about – crack, speed, heroin . . . ?'

'And acid,' Bliss said. 'Acid is back. Turn off your mind, relax and float off a sixth-floor balcony.'

'Is all this widely known?'

'What *is* widely known, but not widely highlighted, is that there are suddenly more drugs – *by far* – on the streets of these old market towns than we can hope to control. Coke and cannabis – recreational stuff for the middle classes – and cheap nasties for the kids. I expect Jane—'

'I'd know.'

'What they all say, Merrily. Moorfield . . . a famously liberal headteacher.'

'School director.'

'Eh?'

'What he prefers to be called.'

'God help us.' Bliss took an angry bite out of his doughnut. 'I mean, look at Pershore. You imagine anything like that happening in Pershore?'

'Remind me.'

'Lad called Chris Smith found shot through the head in his van in a car park near the river. Signs of torture. Mouth taped, cigarette burns. Other things I won't describe with food around. Local CID didn't know him – no form – but subsequently identified as quite a prominent local dealer, operating in the area for over a year.'

'Linked to this Raji Khan, you think?'

'We don't know. Less than half an hour from the Oak. If you were to twist my arm . . . *Aaah.*' Bliss made a frustrated hissing noise. 'Lot of us coming round to thinking it should all be decriminalized, everything you can smoke, swallow or inject. We're pouring billions down the pan, in man-hours and paperwork, and we're losing the battle. And we're bored with it and all the ancillary villainy by brain-dead street-trash supporting a thousand-a-week habit. Some point, we're gonna back away, wash our hands, say fuck it.'

Bliss put up both hands, pushing it all away.

'And I have told you *nothing*, Merrily. In fact, we haven't even had this little meeting in the lovely old cloisters that your lot pinched off my lot in fifteen-whenever-it-was.'

'Like that, huh?'

'You're a mate.' Bliss beamed bleakly. 'And I like to be there for me mates. And I hope you feel the same way.'

'So what you're saying . . . if I happen to come across anything in Wychehill that might be pertinent to the inquiries you're not allowed to make . . .'

'*Not actively encouraged* to make. Yes, that would be helpful. You priests, so intuitive. Even the Prods.' Bliss tucked the remains of his doughnut into his mouth. 'Just one thing – if you do happen to learn anything—'

'Call you at home.'

'Exactly. Or on the mobile, if urgent.' He fingered up a bead of jam left on his plate and licked it off. 'So . . . the good people of Wychehill are claiming that all the extra traffic and the nasty music has disturbed something a bit . . .'

Bliss waggled his fingers and made spooky *woo, woo* noises.

'Sometimes, Merrily, I don't know how you keep this up.'


It was very warm now, and the Cathedral green was smudged with people in T-shirts and summer frocks, some of them camped around the recently installed life-size bronze sculpture of a pensive Sir Edward Elgar gazing up at the tower.

A teenage girl sitting by the plinth was wearing cans and had an iPod in her lap. Walking back towards the gatehouse, Merrily thought it unlikely that the kid was listening to *The Enigma Variations*. If it had been Jane, not in a million years; to Jane, unless attitudes had changed, Elgar was just some pompous, imperialist old fart.

*I'm not keeping up any more, that's the trouble.*

Merrily stopped in dismay, looking back at the Cathedral tower, under major repair again – scaffolding around it like a thousand interlinked Zimmer frames. And she was not yet forty, but she'd reached the age when 'keeping up' required consistent effort. Jane never bothered about staying ahead of the game, because Jane knew she *was* the game.

Scary. Everything was scary. Like the thought of a centralized police service directed by nervous politics. Merrily went across to the Hereford tourist information centre and picked up what she could on the Malverns before climbing the stone steps to the Deliverance office, where Sophie was putting the phone down.

'Just came in to say that if there's nobody I need to see, I think it might be best to go back to Wychehill. Get this over. Is that all right?'

'Did Mr Bliss clarify things?'

'Mr Bliss muddled things further, as Mr Bliss so loves to do.'

'Merrily, three things . . . I resorted to the telephone, from which I learned that the Royal Oak used to be a favoured meeting place for rambling clubs because of its capacious carpark and access to several footpaths. The Ramblers' Association, needless to say, has lodged a complaint with the tourist authorities.'

'It's what they do. I don't think I'm going to worry too much about the Royal Oak.'

'I also checked with Worcester Deliverance. It appears that mysterious balls of light are not unknown in the Malverns. Usually connected with UFOs rather than anything psychic. Unexplained cyclists with lamps, however . . . that's a new one.'

'Oh, well. Thanks, Soph—'

'And, thirdly, the Reverend Spicer rang. The public meeting in Wychehill planned for Wednesday . . . I'm sorry about this, Merrily.'

'Called off? No, you wouldn't be sorry about that, would you?'

'Brought forward. To tomorrow evening.'

'*What?*

'For reasons of discretion, according to Mr Spicer. They want to be sure there are no press people there. Or, indeed, employees of the local authorities or the tourist associations, who've been known to attend such meetings. He says it's something that should be settled by local people ... and you, of course.'

'But I've got a christening in the afternoon!'

'The part of the meeting relevant to you won't start until eight-thirty.'

'No, I mean, I still have people in Wychehill to see.'

Sophie sighed. 'Sometimes I think you try too hard.'

'You either do the job or you don't. I'll just have to go back tonight.'

'Merrily...' Sophie rocked back. 'That's ridiculous. You've been there twice already, you've been up since dawn ... Have you even eaten?'

'Sort of.'

'Right,' Sophie stood up. '*I'll* take you.'

'No, it's—'

'If you fall asleep at the wheel on the way back...'

'I'll ask Lol, OK? Give me a chance to see Jane before we go – I'm starting to feel like a part-time parent.'

Maybe it was what Bliss had suggested, about Jane and drugs. She rang Lol, and there was no answer.

# 11

# Idyll Chipped

WHEN LOL CALLED BACK, Merrily was already in the car in the Bishop's Palace courtyard. She switched off the engine. Lol was asking if she knew about Jane's *project*.

Merrily sank back in her seat, twisting the rear-view mirror, smoothing out what could be a new line under her left eye.

*Jane* and *project*. Curious how sinister those words sounded together.

'She said she was going to explain it all to you this morning,' Lol said, 'if you hadn't had to dash off so early.'

'If I hadn't had to dash off so early, she'd have been at school, and she knows it.' Merrily closed her eyes. 'She's never *done* that before. I don't think.'

'The exams are over ...'

'I don't care, it's a school day.'

'Do you want to call in, if you get home earlyish?'

'Thing is, I'm only coming home to change. I've got a job out near Malvern. For which I think I need to look like a minister of God.'

'Oh. Well, she knows I'll tell you. She just uses me as a filter. It'll wait.'

'No, it won't,' Merrily said. 'I can tell it won't.' *Bloody* Jane. 'Lol, I was wondering if you could come with me. Sophie wanted to drive ... thinks I might fall asleep at the wheel. Actually, it's a situation that might benefit from a second opinion, and I'm not sure Sophie's would be the right one.'

'I'm just a humble songwriter. Sure. Whatever.'

'You undersell yourself. A humble songwriter who once did half a psychotherapy course. If you come over to the vicarage in, say, fifty-five minutes, I should be changed and ready to leave.'

Small silence. Through one of the Bishpal windows, she could see Gary, the Bishop's West Highland terrier, standing on the back of a sofa waiting for the boss to come back from the cricket.

'If I come round in, say, *forty*-five minutes,' Lol said, 'will you still be undressed?'

No time, of course, for *that*. Jane was home, anyway – quiet, obliging, and therefore suspicious. Sure, she'd get her own meal. *No problem, you two get off to . . . wherever.* Exhibiting no particular curiosity about what might be going down. Which meant that something was printed on her own agenda, in heavy type.

But worrying about Jane could eat up your life. And now, for the first time in many years, she was a problem shared . . . kind of. At least, Lol . . . well, at least they were officially an item at last, nothing clandestine any more.

On the road, Merrily driving the Volvo, he told her about Jane and Coleman's Meadow. The ley line and the luxury executive homes. Something about all this seemed to bother him but, for once, Merrily couldn't see a major problem.

'Kid's been involved in far worse things. I mean, *I* don't like the idea of an ancient trackway to the top of Cole Hill being obliterated to accommodate luxury executive homes. We've had two new estates in eighteen months.'

'Small starter homes would be OK?' Lol said.

'We need a few starter homes. I'm just not sure we need any more . . .'

'Sedate, comfortable middle-class people?'

'Let's back away from that one for the moment. Whatever we need, there have to be better places to put them. OK, so Jane gets up a petition to the council. Fair enough. She's seventeen. Next year she gets the vote.'

Lol polished the lenses of his brass-rimmed glasses on the bottom of his T-shirt.

'Far be it from me, as a failed psychotherapist, to try to tell you about your daughter, but, like . . . do you think maybe it goes deeper? Bored with A levels, not lit-up by the idea of university, because *everybody* does that.'

'You think she doesn't want to leave home?'

'Maybe she's afraid to. Afraid that she'll come back to find everything destroyed. Lost a lot, over the years. Her dad. Lucy . . .'

'Mmm.'

Jane's dad, her mother's unfaithful husband. Dead in a car crash, but Jane had still been little then. When the formidable Lucy Devenish, the kid's first real friend in Ledwardine had been knocked off her moped and killed on the outskirts of the village, that was worse, an idyll badly chipped. Jane, town-raised, had bonded with the countryside very quickly, thanks to Lucy and her rural folklore and her – OK – possible paganism.

And it was in Lucy's old shop, Ledwardine Lore, that Jane had been the first of them to encounter a damaged musician, trying to reassemble his life after a criminally unjust court conviction, a family breakdown, a bad time in a psychiatric hospital. So many daughters could barely tolerate their mothers' boyfriends, but Jane had virtually engineered this relationship. Lol putting down a deposit on Lucy's cottage in Church Street, just across from the vicarage . . . that was the final piece in Jane's mosaic.

And Lucy Devenish was still a presence for all three of them.

Lucy's primary *raison d'être* had been the defence of old Ledwardine against misguided incomers and the slashing scythe of crass development.

*Uh-oh.*

Merrily glanced at Lol, trying to look like a respectable companion for a vicar in a dark jacket over a dark T-shirt with no motif. Jane and Lol were, in their own way, also an item. Jane knew how to work him.

'So the imminent destruction of Coleman's Meadow and the ley line . . . you think she sees that as something that would've sent Lucy ballistic. What's she going to do, do you think?'

'She wanted to know who to complain to.'

'Councillor Pierce?'

'What else could I say? She'd only find out somewhere else.'

'Well. I instinctively don't like Lyndon Pierce *much*...'

'But at this moment you could almost feel sorry for him, right?'

'It's going to be an experience for him, certainly.'

Merrily drove into Ledbury, with its oak-framed market hall, its clock and its sunny old bricks. Last town before the Malvern Hills, the eastern ramparts of Herefordshire reflecting the Black Mountains of Wales in the west. Between these purple-shadowed walls, the county was a twilit, peripheral place.

Normally, she liked that. The out-of-timeness of it.

*Bloody Jane.*

The Malverns were so familiar, an eleven-mile ripple on the horizon, that it was easy to miss how strange they were. They were *sudden* hills, a surprise happening in an otherwise eventless landscape

Driving in from a different side tonight, Merrily watched the scenery acquiring scaled-down Alpine dimensions: sunlit, serrated ridge, inky valley. Eleven roller-coaster miles with a long history of recreation, ever since they'd been reserved as a hunting ground by the conquering Normans.

Never more famous, however, than in Victorian days when the healing waters of one-time holy wells had briefly been more sought-after than champagne and Great Malvern had become a fashionable resort.

The guidebook she'd bought in Hereford and checked out over tea explained how these hills had been given special protection, for one reason or another, throughout recorded history.

But it hadn't stopped the quarrying.

'Apparently, George Bernard Shaw remarked that so much stone was being taken away that the Malvern Hills were in danger of becoming the Malvern Flats.'

'But they've stopped it now?' Lol said.

'Not that long ago.' Merrily slowed, approaching a green-bearded cliff face. 'But at least quarrying's good for concealed car parks.'

A segment like a slice of layered cake had been cut out of the hillside, and someone had built a shambling stone house on raised ground at the apex. A house which, at some stage, had grown into a country pub. Lol inspected it with no discernible awe.

'This is the gateway to hell?'

Maybe there had once been a tiered garden in front; now it was this huge parking area with walls of natural rock, partly curtained with conifers. Merrily pulled onto its edge, under the discoloured swinging sign on a pole in the entrance: an archaic-looking painting of a squat tree and *Royal Oak* in faded Gothic lettering. Below, another sign, plain white, pointing at the pub.

*Inn Ya Face* >>>>

Nine or ten vehicles on the car park but no people around. She wound her window down. No sound other than birdsong. No visible litter. No smell of moral cesspit.

'If the gateway to hell was jammed with people burning, nobody would be tempted into sin,' Lol said.

'That a new song?'

'Not yet.'

'OK, let's go and talk to people about a ghost on a bike.'

The Volvo jangled on the long incline.

It was half a steepish mile further on, towards the top of the hill. Coming in from the south-west, you could see how the community had been constructed on the ravages of quarrying, houses and bungalows forming alongside new forestry, on their separate levels.

More than half hidden, it was like the shadow of a village.

But tonight it was sprinkled with gold dust.

Both their windows were down as they drove in, and, on the cusp of evening, the warm air around Wychehill was glistening with the moist and luminous soundtrack of medieval heaven.

# 12

# Nearness

A RIBBON OF ROAD under hunched, conifered shoulders. Like Spicer had said, no evidence of community or enclosure: no shop, no pub, no kids on bikes, no dog-walkers. Only on the top of Herefordshire Beacon, maybe two miles away, could you see figures moving, like flies on a cow-pat.

At just after seven p.m. Merrily pulled into a long bay in front of the church behind five other cars.

The church was set well back from the road but the distance was reduced by its size. At the end of an aisle-like path from the bay, its porch door was closed, its squat tower had no window slits. It stared sightlessly towards the road and couldn't see the lushness of the valley which opened up below it on the other side.

And yet this unpromising, sullen hulk – post-Victorian-Gothic, built of still-unmellowed stone blocks – was . . . exalted.

Merrily shut her car door as softly as she could.

'It's got to be a record . . . a CD.'

'I don't think so,' Lol said.

He stood in the church entrance by the black sign with gold lettering: St Dunstan's. Above it, a heavy lantern on a wrought-iron bracket, one of its glass panels shattered.

The voices, male and female, poured down like a slow fountain.

'It's . . . Gregorian chant?' Lol said.

'I don't know. I mean, that's . . .'

'Something like that, maybe. It's certainly Latin.'

'But that's . . . I know things aren't as hard and fast these days . . . but this is an Anglican church.'

Lol shrugged.

'You want to go in?'

'Better deal with what we came for.'

Merrily unfolded the order-of-service for a funeral, on which Syd Spicer had written the names and addresses, beginning with *Tim Loste, Caractacus Cottage. Down the road, past the Rectory.*

'He's got to be conducting it, hasn't he?'

'Hell of a choir for a village this size,' Lol said.

'A village where, according to the rector, people don't even talk to each other much. So, like, they just sing? Why didn't Spicer tell me Loste wouldn't be available tonight?'

'I don't suppose he knew you were coming. How far away are the others?'

'Chairman of the parish council has a farm about half a mile away. I was going to save him till last, as he apparently hasn't yet claimed to have seen anything. The other's a Mrs Cobham. Converted barn. Two minutes' walk, according to Spicer. Call that ten for the likes of us.'

'He *was* in the SAS?'

'Mmm.'

'Is it common for an ex-SAS man to go into the Church?'

'Church welcomes hard men. Good for the image. Bit of balance.'

They walked through the cutting, past Hannah Bradley's cottage. No sign of Hannah. Although there was nobody about, Merrily felt conspicuous and zipped up her thin black fleece over her dog collar. Now the road was curving away around a hill defined by ascending houses and bungalows, several of them hidden behind conifer walls.

'How about for him?' Lol said. 'Not a bit tame?'

'We have people in the C of E make the Taliban look like a tennis club.' Merrily stopped, looked up the hill. 'Do you think *that's* it?'

The barn-conversion was set back from the lane, its bay filled with plate-glass panels, mirrors of gold in the early-evening light. Expensive. The new gravel driveway had been given a curving route to make it seem longer, maples planted in careful stockades either side of it. A white Mercedes 4×4 sat at the top, outside the oak front door.

'This is the woman whose car apparently went out of control and hit a camper van.'

But, again, there was nobody in. Merrily felt that, even before Lol let the knocker fall twice against its steel plate, the clunks echoing inside the barn like footsteps in an empty ballroom. She stepped back.

'Not my night, obviously.'

'Maybe it's the wrong house.'

'So which other one couldn't we miss?'

Lol knocked again.

'Maybe they're in the choir.'

'A whole village of brilliant, classically trained singers?'

Merrily moved back towards the lane which, beyond the barn, became a dirt track.

'It's like someone we can't see is laughing at us.'

Maybe Syd Spicer. Maybe the Rector of Wychehill was laughing at them. Laughing silently, lying in some ditch, covered with branches, his face streaked with dark mud, like in the old days.

He should be here, as back-up. The protocol was that the local priest came with you, the first time, didn't just throw the addresses at you and leave you to get on with it.

Merrily went to the edge of the lane and looked down into a bucolic kaleidoscope: swirls of woodland and cider-apple orchards and maybe vineyards, around sheep fields which glowed like emerald and amber stained glass as the sun began its scenic dive into the Black Mountains forty miles away.

By the time they'd walked back towards the church, the chant had stopped.

'Maybe the whole community turns out to listen.' Lol walked into the entrance, along the gravel path bordered with yew trees, turning to look back at Merrily. 'You're *allowed.*'

'I don't know that I am, to be quite—'

'Pardon me?'

A blur of movement. Merrily turned slowly. A woman had appeared out of the trees by the entrance. She wore a pale sleeveless dress so long that it completely covered her feet, and it seemed somehow as if she'd risen from the ground.

'You're looking for someone?'

'Well, we—'

'Is there a concert on?'

Lol had wandered back. The woman smiled at him.

'Choir practice, is all.'

She had a loose, wide mouth and big, deep-sunk eyes that seemed swirlingly aglow.

'You're in the choir?'

'I don't sing, although I have an interest. I was taking some air during the break. I live in a cottage back there. Wyche Cottage? Like the Wyche in Wychehill, which means salt, only, the real-estate guy in Ledbury, when he told me the name on the phone, I thought it was *witch*, and I'm like . . . *woooh*.'

She shook her tumble of brown curls.

'Disappointing, really,' Lol said.

'How so?'

'That it just means salt.'

'Yeah. I guess. I changed it, anyway. Starlight Cottage now. Look—'

She came forward, stumbling over the dusty hem of her dress, coming up very close to Lol and peering at him. Contact lenses, Merrily thought.

'Pardon me,' the woman said to Lol, 'I don't want to appear . . . but I think I know who you are?'

He took a pace back. Occasionally he was recognized, usually by someone who'd bought a Hazey Jane album nearly twenty years ago and was mildly pleased that he hadn't killed himself like Nick Drake. He never relished it.

'OK . . .' The woman gazed hard at Lol. 'Listen, I may have this totally wrong, but see, I'm not so stupid. I was expecting an old guy in a big hat with like a black bag, and it's no business of mine, really, but you should know that some people in this place are just a little crazy.'

'How so?' Lol said.

'Not so simple. Like, you're talking about something, you know, sacred?' She looked down and brushed a leaf from her dress. 'I'm sorry. This is not my place. But there's something here that must *never* be parted, you know what I'm saying? Like, you can walk out on the hills at twilight and you can sense his nearness. It's a strange and awesome thing.'

'Yes,' Lol said. 'I can imagine it would be.'

'So, like, you know, I mean no disrespect here, but the whole idea of exorcizing this ... wonderful, magical thing – from the Malvern Hills, of all places – that's gotta be a bone of contention, right?'

This was the third time they'd stood outside a front door getting no response, but Merrily had heard the radio playing inside the house and she kept her finger on the bell.

It was still more than a minute before the door opened and Spicer stood there, unsmiling, in jeans and a black clerical shirt.

'A word, Syd.'

He stared at her without expression, then looked at Lol. The sleeves of his shirt were rolled up, as if he'd been dealing with one of those household tasks he performed privately to prove he had no need of outside help.

'*Why* didn't you tell me?'

She'd pulled down the zip of her fleece to reveal the collar, show him she was kitted out this time.

Spicer said, 'Who's your friend?'

'I realize local loyalty is a good thing,' Merrily said, 'and crucial for a parish priest, I accept that. But there's also the question of loyalty between people who share a ... a calling? So you give me half a story, set me up to appear in front of the entire parish—'

'It won't *be* the entire parish. It won't even be *half* the parish. Who's your friend?' he asked again.

'This is Lol Robinson. He's standing in as witness, back-up, second opinion. All the roles normally filled by the particular parish priest who's requested assistance. *If* the parish priest can be bothered.'

'I'm sorry, Merrily, I just assumed you'd prefer to check things out on your own.'

'No, you didn't. You just didn't want, for some reason, to reveal the alleged identity of the alleged presence.'

'Look,' Spicer said. 'The people out there who wanted an exorcist called in, I thought it was down to them to explain exactly why. I just went through the motions. I told you I had reservations, but I didn't think it was right to spell them out to you before you'd had a chance to check out the situation for yourself.'

'Maybe you wanted me to come back this evening to hear the music, just to underline it a little?'

'I didn't know you'd be coming back *at all* before the meeting. That's why I set it up. For God's sake, Merrily—'

She turned away in frustration. The evening sun threw an unearthly light on Herefordshire Beacon so that it looked like a cake aflame on a hot-plate.

'I mean ... Elgar?' She swung back to face him. '*That* Elgar?'

13

# Another Sphere of Existence

OH SHIT, SURELY NOT this one? *Please* don't let it be this one.

The late sun was bleeding into a false horizon of cloud, an old tractor coughing and retching across a field somewhere.

Jane standing in Virgingate Lane, radiating dismay.

She'd looked up Councillor Pierce in the phone book. The address was given as *Avalon*, which had been kind of promising: anyone who'd named his house after the legendary land of apples in the west, where King Arthur had been laid to rest, must have *some* kind of a soul.

Yeah, well . . .

There obviously *had* been apple trees here, in the days when Ledwardine was almost entirely surrounded by productive orchards. In fact, you could see a few of their sad stumps in the shaven piece of former field through which a tarmac drive cut like a motorway intersection, all the way to the triple garage.

Half a dozen cars were parked along the drive, which was actually wider than Virgingate Lane itself, where all the cottages were old and bent and comfortably sunk into the verges.

The extensive dwelling at the top of the tarmac drive was built of naked, glistening bricks, the colour of a Barbie's bum. It had a conservatory, a sun-lounge, three fake gaslamps.

Jane could hear music and faint laughter from the house.

*Great.*

The plan had been to maybe encounter Councillor Pierce in his garden, casually ask him about the Coleman's Meadow project and then perhaps educate him a little on the subject of leys and natural

71

harmonies. He couldn't turn her away, could he? He was a politician. She'd be able to vote for him next time. Or not.

It was clear from all the cars, however, that Councillor Pierce was hosting a dinner party or something. *Bollocks.*

Stupid idea, anyway. Jane felt deeply self-conscious now, standing there in her white hoodie like some shameless stalker. Unlikely that she'd gone unobserved from inside.

As if in confirmation of this, security spotlamps came blasting on below the broad pink patio which surrounded the house like a display plinth. Jane saw the hulk of a plundered cider-press with a slate plaque attached to the stone wheel. The plaque said – inevitably – AVALON.

Maybe it was irony. Sod it, anyway. She turned away from the horror. Maybe she'd just write a letter of protest to the planning department, with a copy to the *Hereford Times* who wouldn't print it. Sod them all.

'Excuse me!' A man behind her. 'Excuse me ... you looking for anyone in particular?'

Jane turned. Two guys in middle-aged leisureware – polo shirts, chinos, golfing shoes kind of kit – were strolling down the drive towards the nearest car, a gold Lexus. One of the guys beeped open the car doors and balanced a beer can on the roof.

Jane was starting to shake her head, walk away, when one of the pinkening clouds over Avalon reminded her, somehow, of the bird-of-prey profile of Lucy Devenish. She sighed.

'You're not ... Councillor Pierce?'

The guy with the car keys grinned, opening one of the rear doors.

'How far would it get me if I said I was?'

'Excuse my friend, he's an oaf,' the second guy said. 'Did you want to see Lyndon?'

'Erm ... Well, you know, not if he's like, you know, busy.'

Both of them laughed. The guy with the keys pulled a black leather briefcase from the Lexus.

'You think Lyndon will be too busy to see this lovely young thing, Jeff?'

'Lyndon is a man always mindful of his civic duties,' the other guy said. 'Follow us, if you like.'

'No, really,' Jane said, 'it's not urgent or anything. I can—'

'No, no, you can at least come and have a drink. You'll be quite safe. My colleague's in Social Services.'

They laughed. The cloud formation that had looked for a moment like Lucy Devenish had broken up.

It wasn't exactly a pool party or a barbecue. That is, there *was* a pool *and* a barbecue behind the house, but neither was in use. However, one of those extraterrestrial-looking patio heaters was working, and seven people – four men, three women – were spread over a couple of hardwood tables, with drinks. Papers on the table seemed to be architect's plans.

'So what would *you* expect of a new community centre, Jane?' Lyndon Pierce said.

He handed her a glass of white wine. He didn't seem to recognize her, which was probably a good thing. He'd asked her name, and she'd just said Jane and left it at that.

*New community centre?*

'So, like, what's wrong with the *old* community centre?'

'That's *precisely* what's wrong with it.' Lyndon grinned. 'It's old.'

Lyndon was quite a lot less old than she'd imagined. Maybe thirty. Gelled black hair and a plump mouth. Tracksuit bottoms and a Hawaiian shirt open over a red T-shirt. Not too gross yet, but he probably would be in a couple of years.

'Chance of a National Lottery grant, you see, Jane,' one of the chino guys said. 'We'll be holding a public meeting to let the people of Ledwardine have their say. We're drawing up a list of options for them.'

'What if the people of Ledwardine don't *want* a new community centre?' Jane said.

Lyndon Pierce looked at her like he didn't understand the question. Beyond the swimming pool, the view was across a couple of darkening fields towards Ledwardine square. Lights were coming on in the Black

Swan, the church steeple fading back into the evening sky like another sphere of existence.

'I'm sorry,' Lyndon said. 'Cross purposes, I think. We were just all having an informal chat about the new community centre, look, but you wanted to talk about ... ?'

'Coleman's Meadow,' Jane said.

'Oh. Right. Actually, Jeff's in Planning, he might be able to to help you on that one.'

Jeff said doubtfully, 'Well, I'm afraid they'll probably be fairly pricey, if you're ...'

Jane could tell he was trying to work out if she was old enough to be getting married or setting up home with someone. It was almost flattering. She took a sip of wine, thinking hard. She'd just stumbled, unprepared, into what seemed to be an out-of-hours gathering of top council people. When would she get another chance like this? Probably never.

OK.

'I think you've ... got this wrong ...' Trying to keep her voice steady. '*I* wouldn't live in Coleman's Meadow, if the alternative was, like, a cardboard box in Jim Prosser's shop doorway.'

Eyebrows went up. A thin woman of about Mum's age gave Jane a hard look.

'Because, like, Coleman's Meadow is a very important ancient site which should be protected,' Jane said. 'I'd have thought somebody might've noticed that.'

Nobody was smiling much now.

'I'm sorry, Jane,' Jeff said. 'This particular development would be what we would call acceptable infill. We're very pleased that site's become available. So I don't think any of us quite understands what you're getting at there.'

'Right.' Jane swallowed more wine. 'I can draw you a proper plan if you want but, basically, Coleman's Meadow is the key point on an ancient alignment from the top of Cole Hill, through a burial mound and Ledwardine Church and then on to, like, a couple of other sites. Coleman's Meadow is really important because the field gates are perfectly sited on the alignment and because the old straight track actually exists there ... like, you can see it, and ...'

She was going to say *feel it.* Decided to leave that aspect alone at this stage.

Lyndon Pierce blinked. Jeff and another guy looked at each other.

'So ... so, what I'm saying, if you have new houses – totally *unnecessary* new houses – built on Coleman's Meadow it would completely obliterate the most perfect, like one of the clearest examples of ... of a ...'

'Ley line?'

An older guy, wearing a cream sports jacket, half-glasses and a half smile.

'*Ley,*' Jane said.

The older guy nodded. 'I wondered if that was what you were talking about.' He looked relieved.

'So ...' Lyndon Pierce lowered the wine bottle to the flags at his feet, '... you know what she's on about, Cliff?'

'I'm sure you must've heard of ley lines, Lyndon.'

'I've *heard* of them, yeah—'

'Periodically, someone revives the idea that prehistoric stones and burial sites were arranged, for some mystical purpose, in straight lines, along which old churches were also built. If you ask the County Archaeologist, he'll tell you it's a lot of nonsense. But, like many ideas discredited by the archaeological establishment, it's become a cult belief among ... well, usually old hippies or New Age cranks.'

'So it's like, flying saucers and that sort of stuff?' Lyndon Pierce asked.

'Exactly,' the older guy said.

'So nothing to ...?'

'No, no.' The older guy shook his head, smiling faintly. 'Not at all.'

Jane thought of Alfred Watkins, reserved, bearded, magisterial, a pillar of the Hereford community but with an open, questing mind. Everything she'd been taught suggested that society in the early part of the twentieth century had been nowhere near as liberal and adventurous as today's.

*Yeah?* Well, no wonder there was no statue of Alfred Watkins in Hightown, with bastards like this running the county.

'How can you . . .' She couldn't get her breath for a moment. 'How can you *talk* like that? How can you, like, just rubbish something that throws a whole new light on the countryside . . . that makes it all light up? Especially in *Herefordshire*, where Alfred Watkins was, like, the first person in the world to . . . to . . .'

'Ah . . . Watkins, yes.' Cliff smiled at her, cool with this now. 'Charming old chap, by all accounts. Typically English eccentric, very entertaining, totally misguided.'

'That's a typical Establishment viewpoint!'

'Oh dear,' Cliff said. 'I'm terribly sorry, but I rather suppose that's what we are.'

'So, thank you for coming, Jane,' Lyndon Pierce said. 'But I'm afraid a fantasy conjured up by some old, dead eccentric guy is really not going to cut much ice today. I was elected, as I'm sure your parents will tell you, on an expansionist ticket. Nowadays, rural communities grow or die, and I want to see Ledwardine getting more shops, restaurants, leisure facilities . . . and *far* more housing. We could have a thriving little town here.'

'But it's not a t—'

Jane stared at Pierce, who seemed to be bloating before her eyes into something obscene.

'Jane . . .'

It was the woman who'd given her the hard look. Short curly hair, dark suit. Possibly seen her somewhere before, but not here.

'Jane, is this just a personal issue for you?' the woman said.

'Well, I'm also doing a project for school. On the interpretation of landscape mysteries?'

'*Ah.* How old are you?'

'Seventeen.'

Somebody started to laugh.

'And which school do you go to?' the woman asked.

'Moorfield High?'

'Robert Morrell,' the woman murmured to Cliff. 'Jane, does Mr Morrell know you're here?'

'Look ... sorry ... what's it got to do with him?'

'Quite a lot, I should have thought, as he's the head of Moorfield High.'

'Well, he doesn't live here, does he?' Jane felt herself going red. 'Like, I *care* about this place. *I* don't want to see it ruined. I don't want to see the ancient pattern all smashed for the sake of a bunch of crap, bourgeois piles of pink brick like ... like *this*. I mean, sod your new community centre, you should be having a public meeting about the annihilation of Coleman's Meadow, don't you think?'

'I really *don't* think we should be arguing about a plan that's not yet come before the council,' the woman said. 'Certainly not with a schoolgirl.'

'But if nobody says anything, it'll just get quietly pushed through, won't it, by people who don't give a—'

'I should be very careful what you say, if I were you,' the woman said coldly.

'Particularly to the vice-chair of the Education Committee,' Cliff said.

A rock landed in Jane's gut. This was, of course, the woman who'd been sitting next to Morrell on stage at the prizegiving ceremony.

Jane looked down at her wineglass; it was empty.

'Well, I can see I'm not going to get anywhere with *you* guys. I think I need to get home to ...'

She backed away to the nearest corner of the house called Avalon and then looked at each of them in turn.

'... Work out how best to shaft you,' Jane said.

And turned and ran through the summer-scented dusk, past the crooked, sunken, black and white cottages of Virgingate Lane.

# 14

# A Dim and Bleary Light

SPICER LED MERRILY AND Lol into his spartan kitchen, offered them seats at his table but no tea. The sun had dropped into a bank of cloud, and the conifers at the end of the garden were turning black.

Spicer switched off the radio.

'I suppose it's like people seeing Shakespeare's ghost in Stratford-on-Avon.'

He joined them at the table but didn't put a light on.

'Or Wordsworth in Grasmere,' Merrily said. 'Brontës in Howarth. Yes, I do get the picture.'

Recalling once looking up a number under E in the Hereford phone book and noticing *Elgar Carpets and Interiors, Elgar Coaches,* the *Elgar Coffee Shop, Elgar Fine Art* . . . like that for about half a page.

In all these establishments, you'd be shelling out twenty-pound notes with an engraved portrait on the back of a man with neat grey hair, a generous moustache, faraway eyes.

'See, in comparison,' Spicer said, 'Wordsworth and Shakespeare are remote figures. Elgar's been dead barely seventy years. It's like he still lives around here, with everything he's come to represent. Go to the Elgar museum at Broadheath, they say you can see his betting slips.'

He had his back to the window bay, blocking more light from the room, which had three doors, all shut. One thing was sure: you'd never see Syd Spicer's betting slips. Merrily wondered if visitors were confined to the stripped-down kitchen so they wouldn't clock his books or his CD collection or pictures of his kids.

'I should've realized. The soundtrack of the Malverns. The obvious spirit of the place.'

'Maybe more obvious than you know,' Spicer said. 'Joseph Longworth, the quarry boss who built the church, as well as being a born-again Christian or however they put it in those days, was an Elgar fanatic. The church was built that size to accommodate an orchestra and choir able to perform the great man's works. Elgar's said to have attended the dedication.'

'It's all coming out, isn't it?'

'If Longworth could've called it St Edward's he would have.'

'But Elgar was a Catholic, wasn't he?'

'Yeah, he *was*,' Spicer said, 'and he wrote extensively for the Catholic Mass, as you ... presumably heard. But, of course, his music was played in Anglican cathedrals, and cathedral sound was what Longworth was paying for.'

'Sounds like he was getting it.'

'Not for long. They held a few concerts here, but Longworth died and then Elgar died. And nothing much happened until Tim Loste arrived. Who thinks Elgar's God. So this is becoming Elgar city again after many years. I'm sorry, maybe I *should*'ve told you.'

'And should I have heard of Tim Loste in a wider context?'

'Nah. Used to be a music teacher at Malvern College, now he's a private tutor. Got an amateur choir drawn from miles around. At least, it started amateur; they're making a bit of money now. From my point of view, the parish gets its cut, and if most of the music's heavily Catholic, well...'

'Fills the church.'

'Yeah. Situation now is, we've a whole bunch of people in Wychehill and down the valley who've moved here *solely* because this is Elgar country. Listen to some of them, you start picking up this maudlin kind of patriotism. "Land of Hope and Glory." Don't you hate that song?'

'Apparently, Elgar hated it, too,' Lol said. 'But then, he didn't write the words.'

Merrily glanced at him. She didn't know he knew any more about Elgar than she did, which, frankly, was not much.

'Let's deal with the bottom line, Syd. Who's saying the supposed presence is Elgar?'

'Out loud, nobody. It's one of those situations where an idea develops. Can I tell you why I'm not happy about it?'

'Please.'

'Well, let me tell you about Tim. Good conductor, great teacher, they say . . . but would like to be a great composer and isn't. Some part of him is deeply frustrated. He's prone to depression. So this particular night he goes off the road, hits a telegraph pole. Nobody else involved, no injury, no need for police. Which was just as well, because Tim was pissed.'

'Oh.'

'Happened just across from the church. I heard the crash. I go over, help him out of the wreckage – this is about half-nine at night, month or so ago, getting dark. Bring him back here, administer the black coffee. He's shaking all over. I was going down to Ledbury, he says, to buy a light bulb for my desk lamp. Trying to write, bulb blew. *Going down to Ledbury for a light bulb* – that tells you the state he was in. I'd've given him a bloody *bulb*, for God's sake.'

'Is he often . . . ?'

'Drunk and incapable? Now and then. Couple of us had to go down the Oak one night, get him away from the bouncers. He'd broken a window. I didn't tell you about the Oak, did I?'

'I know about it.'

'Naturally, Tim really hates the Royal Oak. A disruptive force sent to destroy his life's work. Lost it completely one night when the wind changed and all this rap music . . . it kind of rises up and bounces off the hill. Anyway, that's by the by: this crash was on a week night, and the Oak was quiet. Tim reckoned he'd just pulled out of his drive when he saw what he described as *a dim and bleary light*. When it got closer, he could see it was a bicycle lamp. He said.'

'But he was drunk.'

'Very. Anyway, the light's some distance away at first. And then he said it was like he must've blacked out for about half a second – which doesn't surprise me – and the next thing the cyclist is coming straight at him. He says he can make out what seems to be a high-buttoned jacket and a hat. And a big, dark slice across the face.'

'Moustache.'

'That's the inference. And the eyes are white, according to Tim, like the eyes in a photo negative. Tim swerves, goes into the pole.'

Spicer fell silent. In the fading light, he was very still, hadn't moved since sitting down, didn't seem to need to rearrange himself like most people, to find a comfortable position.

'But how did he know it was Elgar?' Lol said.

'Mr Robinson, he's got pictures of Elgar all over his walls, Elgar music seeping through the brickwork. Tim sees Elgar every-bloody-where. He's ... I like the guy, most people like him, but nobody's gonna deny he's well off his trolley. Planted an oak tree in his front garden. Have you *seen* the size of his front garden?'

'And what did you do?' Merrily said.

'Sat him where you're sitting now, told him to stay there. Rang a mate, runs a bodywork garage the other side of Colwall. Got him to bring his truck and get Tim's car away before the police got word. If he'd lost his licence I think he'd have gone into a depression he might not have come out of easily. I said, Go home, get some sleep, Tim, and don't even think of telling anybody what you just told me. *As if.*'

Spicer snorted.

'He did tell people?' Merrily said.

'He told Winnie Sparke. That was enough. The American lady? Winnie is Tim's ... protector. Nurtures his sensitive talents, knows about his problems. Find out about you very quickly, Americans, because they just ask. *You have an alcohol problem, Tim? I have herbs for that.*'

'So it was Winnie Sparke who spread it around?'

'Couldn't've timed it better. There's a retired geezer, Leonard Holliday. Been here about two years. Leonard's chairman and secretary of WRAG – the Wychehill Residents' Action Group. Committed to getting rid of Inn Ya Face and restoring the Royal Oak to the gentle hostelry where Elgar himself ... it's said that Elgar used to drop in for a pint of cider when he was staying at his summer cottage over at

Birchwood. So, anyway, there was a meeting of Holliday's action group to appoint a deputation to lobby the council. Somebody says what a pity we don't have a celebrity living here, like some of the villages have. Holliday says, pity we don't have someone like *Sir Edward* here any more. And Winnie says, You're sure we don't . . . ?'

'Oh dear.'

Merrily closed her eyes, suddenly quite deflated.

It all made sense. A gift for a protest group, the idea of England's greatest serious composer rising up from the grave against Raji Khan and his filthy jungle music.

'When was this, Syd?'

'The meeting was about ten days ago. Winnie Sparke says it just slipped out, but it couldn't've worked better if she'd timed it. Sir Edward Elgar riding into battle on Mr Phoebus?'

'Who?'

'Elgar called his bike Mr Phoebus. Name of a Roman sun god.'

'What happened then?'

'I think, to be honest, Holliday was dithering a bit. On the one hand, it would get in all the papers, attract massive publicity to their cause. On the other – apologies, Merrily, but who *really* believes ghost stories? It could easily be the wrong kind of publicity. But then there was another accident.'

'Mrs Cobham?'

'Stella. Stella and Paul. Famous for their very loud rows. Stella's little BMW roaring down the middle of the road after some fracas, practically spitting flames. Cyclist coming down the middle of the road. Stella swerves. Family of German tourists in a mobile home looking for their campsite. Bam.'

'Anybody hurt?'

'Bit of whiplash for Stella. And shock. Says she'd never believed in anything like that, until . . . I don't think you'll get any change out of her. Doesn't like talking about it any more. Doesn't want to get a reputation as . . . you, know . . . a bit of a Winnie Sparke. Actually, Winnie's much more intelligent.'

'You don't have many illusions about your flock, do you, Syd?'

'I'm supposed to? I thought it was our job to lead them to God. Merrily, there *is* no flock. This is not a village, it's a bunch of disconnected houses jammed into rock crevices.'

'So what about you?' Merrily said. 'What would you like to happen?'

'I'd like people to be sensible. I'd like Donald Walford to stop worrying about his daughter, Joyce Aird to get her Polo out of the garage again instead of having all her groceries delivered. Sounds insane, doesn't it?'

'Not in an isolated community. I suppose a lot now depends on whether the driver of the Land Rover is claiming to have seen anything immediately prior to a crash that makes the other three look trivial.'

'Yeah.' Spicer nodded slowly. 'It does, doesn't it?'

'*Has* he said anything yet?'

'Not to me. Not yet. But he's chairman of the parish council. Which means he'll be chairing tomorrow's meeting. You got the message about that?'

'It's why I came back tonight. Do you think I should go and see Mr Devereaux now?'

'Whatever he's decided, you won't change his mind.'

'I don't want to change his mind.'

'Merrily.' Spicer stood up. 'With respect, if you've spoken to Joyce, I think you've done enough. She's the one wants an exorcism of some kind. What we've done, by getting you in, is brought it all to a head. Wychehill's split three ways: the ones who don't believe any of it, the ones who want whatever it is exorcised because they're afraid of what will happen next and ... the Elgar fans.'

Merrily thought about the American woman, Winnie Sparke. *There's something there that must* never *be parted, you know what I'm saying? Like, you can walk out on the hills at twilight and you can sense his nearness. It's a strange and awesome thing.*

Sensing his nearness.

Like Hannah Bradley who, quite reasonably, didn't want it put around that she'd been been touched up, from the other side of the grave, by England's most distinguished composer.

Consider the implications of this situation. Try not to panic.

# 15

# Only Me

'WHY DON'T I EVER listen?' Merrily was driving too fast down the hill towards Ledbury, as if the Malverns were ramming the Volvo from behind. 'Jesus, she might be a touch loopy, this Winnie Sparke, but she cut to the essence of it: *am* I going to be the mad priest who stands at the roadside and publicly prays for the soul of a musical genius, a national icon, a man with his face on twenty-pound notes, to be at peace and stop causing fatal bloody road accidents? Am I going to be the person who – for heaven's *sake* – exorcizes Elgar?'

'Just ... slow down. Please?'

Lol thought she looked tiny and vulnerable, at the wheel of a car that was too big for her and grated out its age on every bend. She'd refused to let him drive. He held on to the sides of his seat.

'There'll be a way out. Spicer doesn't want that.'

'No, Laurence,' Merrily said, 'What he doesn't *want* is to have to do it *himself*.'

And she was probably right. One thing you learned, being close to a vicar, was that other vicars could be scheming bastards.

'Whatever happens, he's going to want to keep it discreet. They're very publicity-shy, the ex-SAS. And *that's* likely to be the main reason he's switched the meeting from Wednesday night to tomorrow. He doesn't want TV crews from America.'

A single light up ahead was dim and bleary. Merrily braked.

'If it gets out,' Lol said.

'You don't really think ... ?'

'Big figure, Elgar, worldwide.'

They passed the vintage motor-scooter. It was on the correct side of the road. Merrily drove slowly in silence for a while. A lorry overtook the Volvo. Lol caught her glance.

'We've never discussed this, Lol, but I got the feeling in there that you knew rather more about Elgar than I did.'

'Depends how much you know.'

'Well . . . bugger-all, really. That's what makes this so much worse.'

Jane stumbled, panting, into the cobbled market square with its hanging aroma of apple-wood smoke from the fire the Black Swan kept lit for the tourists on all but the warmest summer nights.

She looked around. Nobody about. No lights in the vicarage. No lights in Lol's cottage, which used to be Lucy's. Maybe he and Mum had locked the dog collar in the glove compartment and stopped to *do it* on the back seat in a lay-by.

Jane grinned. God, what was she turning *into*?

Whatever, at least those guys from the council hadn't found out her full name. All she had to do was keep clear of Lyndon Pierce for a while and she could ride this out.

Which of course would be the coward's way out.

It was about 10.15 p.m., the deep red veins of evening yielding to the cooling blue of early night. Jane moved between the lumpen 4x4s of the Black Swan's clientele and slipped under the eaves of the oak-pillared market hall.

Thinking about the winter after Lucy died, when she'd seriously embraced some kind of goddess-worship, lying about her age to join this women's esoteric group, The Pod, in Hereford. Wondering now why she'd more or less abandoned paganism which, on nights like this, seemed a kind of healthy spiritual response to nature and the environment.

A better relationship developing between her and Mum probably had something to do with it. Mum becoming more liberal as she became more secure in her own job. And then there was Eirion. Meeting Eirion, falling in . . . love, probably.

Which was looking like a dead end.

Jane moved out of the shadow of the market hall and across the cobbled square, walking towards the church until the top of Cole Hill came into view, smoky and seductive in the dusk. The hill of the shamans.

Eirion. She badly wanted to see him, but it was pointless. Within three months he'd be at university. Emma Rees at school – not a particular mate, but you had to feel sorry for her – had been *engaged* to some bloke, and he'd gone to college in Gloucester (*that* close) and within about a month it was *Dear Emma* ... a bloody text message!

Jane didn't do texting any more. Texting was for kids and adults with emotional dyslexia.

She took out her mobile, switched it on and watched it lighting up. Brought up the Abergavenny number from the phone book. This would be a small test, right?

Jane drew in a long, ragged breath and pressed the little green-phone sign, listening to it ringing. Decided *no* and was about to hit the little red-phone button when ...

'Jane Watkins.' Eirion said in her ear. 'I know the name from *somewhere*. Hang on ... Yes! Didn't we used to go out together at one time?'

Eirion's phone had, of course, flashed up the caller's number. So good to hear his stupid Welsh voice. Actually, not good at all.

'Listen,' she said, 'I'm sorry I haven't rung. It's been ... it's like ...'

'Thought I was being phased out, I did.' Eirion exaggerating the accent. 'In view of my imminent departure to some distant seat of learning. Strange how we become paranoid, isn't it?'

'That's ridiculous.'

'Would've slashed my wrists in the bath,' Eirion said, 'except I've only got an electric razor.'

'You could always have plugged it in, dropped it in the bath and electrocuted yourself. Lateral thinking, Irene.' Jane smiling, in spite of it all. 'Look, what would it cost to set up a website?'

'Shit,' Eirion said. 'Any thoughts of you still wanting me for my body ...'

'It was *never* about your body, fatso.'

'Thank you.'

'Anyway, how soon could you organize it?' Jane said.

Feeling that sense of *what have I got to lose?* urgency. Thinking of the council pygmies trashing the reputation of the great Alfred Watkins: *lot of nonsense ... New Age cranks...*

*Jane* Watkins standing on the market square in ancient Ledwardine feeling the lines of energy, the ancestral spirit, glowing and pulsing all around her, rippling through her in the numinous dusk.

'It was when Simon St John was laying down the cello parts for *Alien,*' Lol said, 'and I said I'd like something pastoral but moody. So Simon starts playing this lovely, sorrowful tune. And there it was. Hills ... *real* hills. Texture. Dull day. Low cloud. And some diffuse, underlying emotion. Elgar's *Cello Concerto.*'

'Wow,' Merrily said.

No particular reason for Lol *not* to know about Elgar. His own dead muse, Nick Drake, had, after all, been inspired by the likes of Delius and Ravel.

But Elgar had always seemed so *Establishment.* Hadn't he been made Master of the King's Music? Hadn't he composed all these marches and patriotic anthems? Hadn't he written *Pomp and Circumstance,* whose very title ...

'Misunderstood,' Lol said. 'Most of his life people were getting him wrong. Even his appearance ... Looked like an army officer. Or a country squire. Misleading.'

'You mean you *like* Elgar?'

'Son of a piano tuner with a shop in Worcester. Self-taught. Lived for nine years in Hereford where he employed his daughter's white rabbit as a consultant because his wife wouldn't let him have a dog. Kept trying to invent things. Had a home laboratory. Seems to have blown it up, once. What's not to like?'

Merrily drove a little faster. You slept with someone – albeit rarely for a whole night – and you thought you knew everything about him.

'And even when he was famous,' Lol said, 'he was often mentally, emotionally and spiritually ... totally messed up.'

She glanced at him, sitting there with his hands on his knees, watching the dark, burnished landscape. How much common ground was there in the creative landscapes of classical composers and guys who cobbled together, albeit sometimes brilliantly, four-minute songs on their guitars?

'He smoke?'

Thinking about Hannah and the strong tobacco.

'Lifelong,' Lol said.

'What about women? Did he ... like women?'

'A lot. His wife was nine years older and a lot higher up the social scale than him. Her dad was a general or something. She helped him and encouraged him. It seems to have been a good marriage.'

'But?'

Some people suggest he had affairs with younger women. It's more likely to have been just ... crushes.'

'Where'd you learn all this?'

'Couple of biographies.'

'It's just ... you've just never mentioned him. You've never once mentioned Elgar.'

'Well, you don't, do you?' Lol said. 'He's just too ... too *there*. Part of the tourist trail. Every few miles, another sign saying *Elgar Route*. Nobody notices any more. He's official. He's a thousand people waving Union Jacks at the last night of the Proms. Which is why it's so interesting how ambivalent he was about all that.'

Lol looked out of the side window towards a round hop kiln spiking the sunset like the tower of a Disneyland castle.

'In fact, he was a romantic, a dreamer. And the landscape was everything. *This* landscape. When he was dying, he—'

He broke off, pretending to correct a twist in his seat belt, Merrily slipping him a glance.

'Lol?'

'Sorry?'

'When he was dying *what*?'

'Bit of whimsy, that's all. Maybe not a good time.'

Merrily sighed.

'OK,' Lol said. 'He's lying there. He knows this is it. Coming up to the big moment he famously orchestrated in *The Dream of Gerontius*.'

'That's the one about the guy who's dying and what happens afterwards? I'm sorry, I ought to know. I feel so . . .'

'Heavenly choirs, conversations with angels, stodgy theology, heavy-duty dark night of the soul.'

'Right.'

'Anyway, inches from death, Elgar – I suspect – is trying hard not to think about the implications of all that. And *Gerontius* goes on for ever, while the *Cello Concerto* comes in at less than half an hour.'

'Your kind of music.'

'Look, I'm *sorry* I didn't tell you I was checking out Elgar—'

'No, you've every right— Just . . . carry on.'

'So there's a friend at the bedside. And Elgar beckons him over and feebly whistles the main theme from the *Cello Concerto*.'

Lol began to whistle softly, this rolling tune that rose and fell and rose and then fell steeply . . . and the road swooped down among long fields and hop yards under a sheet-metal sky warmed by bars of electric crimson.

'This isn't going to be a joke, is it?' Merrily said.

'No, but it has a punchline. Elgar says to the guy, "If ever you're walking on the Malvern Hills and hear that, don't be frightened . . . it's only me."'

'That's it?'

'That's it.'

'Only me, huh?'

'For what it's worth,' Lol said, 'he didn't mention the bike.'

# 16

# Animation

Just when you very much needed to talk to your daughter...

MUM. EIRION'S COMING THROUGH EARLY. WILL PICK ME UP. WE NEEDED TO TALK. E. WILL GIVE ME LIFT TO SCHOOL. SEE U TONITE. LOVE, J.

Seven-thirty, Merrily had come stumbling downstairs in her towelling robe and the note was on the kitchen table, suspiciously close to where she'd left her own message yesterday for Jane.

Eirion and Jane needed to talk? *We need to talk. Do you want to talk about this?* What an ominous cliché *talk* had become, thanks to TV soaps. It meant cracks, it meant falling apart.

Not that Merrily hadn't been conscious of a reduced intensity in the Jane/Eirion department. Not so long ago, one of them would phone every night, maybe in the morning, too – on the landline from home, Jane having gone off mobiles because they fried your brain and texting was for little kids.

That was something else: of late, Jane had become kind of Luddite about certain aspects of modern life. A year before leaving school, feeling threatened by change and destruction – was Lol right about that?

And the biggest change was the one affecting her relationship with Eirion – a year ahead of her and about to become a student. Big gap between a university student and a schoolkid. The gap between a child and an adult.

Nearly a year ago, Eirion had been sitting at this very kitchen table, on a summer morning like this, humbly confessing to Merrily that he and her daughter had had sex the night before. Both of them virgins. It had been almost touching.

Merrily put the kettle on, made some toast. Hard not to like Eirion, but liking your daughter's boyfriend was a sure sign, everybody said, that it wouldn't last. In an ideal world, Jane would have met Eirion in a few years' time, when she'd been around a little. But society wasn't programmed to construct happy endings. Relationships were assembled like furniture kits, and everybody knew how long *they* lasted.

The sun was swelling in the weepy mist over Cole Hill, evaporating the dew on the meadow. The mystical ley recharging. But Jane was stepping off it, moving safely out of shot.

'Oh, come *on*, Jane!'

Eirion lowering the digital camera. A Nikon, naturally. He'd shot the view from the top of Cole Hill and the low mound on the way to the church, the hummock that Jane was convinced was an unexcavated Bronze Age round barrow. And then they'd walked another half-mile and crossed a couple of fields to find the prehistoric standing stone, half-hidden by a hedge and only three feet high but that was as good as you got in this part of the county. Fair play, he'd taken pictures of them all and he hadn't moaned. Until now.

'*No.*' Jane flung an arm across her face. 'For the last time, this is not about me, it's about—'

'Yeah, yeah, the balance and harmony of the village and the perpetuation of the legacy of the greatest man ever to come out of Hereford. But I have to tell you, Jane – speaking as a person only a few short years away from a glittering career in the media – that a shot of you, with your firm young breasts straining that flimsy summer-weight school blouse, will be worth at least a thousand extra hits.'

'You disgust me, Lewis.'

Jane stepped behind a beech tree beside the bottom gate. A mature beech tree, full of fresh, light green life. One of several that would soon be slaughtered in the course of an efficient chainsaw massacre to accommodate twenty-four luxury executive homes.

Eirion tramped towards the tree, along the ley. Stocky, dependable Irene, his Cathedral-school jacket undone, the strap of his camera bag sliding down his arm.

'Jane, listen, I'm serious. A view means nothing, basically. Just a field with a church steeple in the background? It needs a figure to suggest the line of sight. I'm not kidding. We have to persuade the various earth-mysteries organizations to run this on their sites.'

Eirion had reasoned that, if it was speed she was after, a website was probably not the answer at this stage. What they needed – a whole lot cheaper – was an initial explanatory document which could be emailed to interested parties and influential on-line journals.

Made sense. On that basis, if he shot the pictures this morning, he could have it laid out by late tonight, email her a copy for approval and by this time tomorrow they'd be up and running: the full horror of Coleman's Meadow disclosed to the world before the weekend. Scores of people – possibly hundreds of people – lodging complaints with Hereford Council. Hundreds of *New Age cranks and old hippies* telling them exactly where they could put their *acceptable infill.*

Eirion stood watching her, keeping his distance.

'What?' Jane said

'You clenched your fists. You looked positively homicidal. What have I said now?'

'Irene, it's not—'

Jane shook herself. Oh hell. To fit in this shoot, he must've been up at five, driving over from Abergavenny about ninety minutes earlier than usual. Face it: how many other guys would do that for you? She felt totally messed up again, her emotions all over the place, hormones in flood. For a moment she felt she just wanted to take him into a corner of the still-dewy meadow and . . .

. . . What would it be like making love on a ley? What kind of extra buzz would *that* produce?

What it would produce would be a golden memory.

'Jane, are you all right? I mean you're not ill . . . ?'

'Sure. I mean, I'm fine.'

Jane clasped her hands together, driving back the tears. It was no use, she had a battle to fight, against slimy Lyndon Pierce and the chino guys and lofty, patronizing Cliff and the thin woman from Education. The mindless, philistine Establishment.

She sniffed and stepped out from behind the tree and walked back on to the ley, her head lowered.

'How do you want me to stand?'

'You're perfect the way you are.' Eirion smiled his glowingly honest, unstaged Eirion smile. 'Just don't look at me.'


Sophie displaying emotion was a rare phenomenon. When it happened it tended to be minimal: slender smiles, never a belly laugh. Disapproval, rather than . . .

'Merrily, that is quite *disgusting*. It dishonours him.'

Sophie was looking out of the gatehouse window, towards the Cathedral green. There might even have been tears in her eyes.

'It dishonours all of us.'

It was like you'd vandalized a grave. Spray-painted the headstone, trampled the flowers.

'He lived in this city for nine years, at the height of his fame. Even after he'd left, he'd come back for the Three Choirs Festival, when it was held here . . . as it is *this year*.'

Sophie swung round, her soft white hair close to disarrangement. 'Do you *really* want to besmirch that, Merrily?'

'Me?'

'I'm sorry, but this is giving credibility to something very sordid.'

She meant the road accidents. Merrily hadn't even mentioned Hannah Bradley. Just as well, really.

'Involving the Church in a campaign which might be laudable in itself but is extremely questionable in its execution is . . . I realize it's not your fault, but you *can* stop it going any further.'

'I didn't expect you to be quite so . . . protective?'

'I'm a former Cathedral chorister, I'm proud of my county's link with Elgar. His homes at Birchwood and then here in the city. His many connections and friendships at the Cathedral—'

'I know.'

Embarrassed by her ignorance, Merrily had picked up a slim guide to Elgar's Herefordshire, skimming through it before Sophie came in. It was a start.

'So what are you going to do about it?' Sophie said. 'May one ask?'

'Well, with your help, as an Elgar enthusiast and a Cathedral chorister for ... how many years ... ?'

'Fourteen.'

'... I want to look at it sensibly. Because whatever your misgivings about the idea of Elgar's ghost, my instinct is that there is *something*.'

Sophie scowled.

'Please? I've a christening this afternoon, and then I'm supposed to go to this parish meeting. Or not.'

Sophie went to sit at her own desk, waved a limp hand.

'Go on ...'

'I need to know enough to be able to discount crap, but I have to be prepared for the possibility of it *not* being crap. Which would leave two options: an imprint or what Huw Owen would describe as an *insomniac*.'

'A restless spirit.'

'In this case, an *angry* spirit, disturbed – much as you are – over the invasion of the Malverns by the hoodies and bling element. Which is a potentially sensitive issue because of ... well ...'

'Racism. Always the weapon used against us. As if appalling behaviour and criminal acts should be protected for so-called cultural reasons.'

'Lol reckons that, with Elgar, it wasn't so much political patriotism as a pure love of the countryside – the landscape itself. That in fact he even developed a bit of a distaste for "Land of Hope and Glory"? That true?'

'I suppose he had misgivings about the jingoism in the words. He *was* a lifelong Conservative, however, Merrily, never forget that.'

'Although, unless I'm wrong –' Merrily remembering something else from *Elgar – A Hereford Guide* '– a good friend of lifelong socialist George Bernard Shaw?'

'No, you're not wrong,' Sophie said, maybe through her teeth. 'What point are you making?'

'Just trying to form an opinion on whether, in theory, the raging essence of Edward Elgar might be summoned, like King Arthur from his cave, by a blast of trip-hop over his sacred hills. If something's happening, then something must have set it off.'

'You don't believe that for one minute.'

'Open mind, Sophie. It's what this job's about.'

'And what's the alternative?'

'The alternative, if we're accepting the possibility of a paranormal element, is an imprint. Spicer says Elgar used to bike through Wychehill, maybe stopping for a pint of cider at the Royal Oak.'

'Possibly when he was exploring the location of his cantata *Caractacus*, in the 1890s. Its main setting is Herefordshire Beacon.'

'It's about the last stand of the Celts against the Romans?'

'A legend now discredited. The final defeat of Caractacus was probably not, as once suggested, on the Beacon. Which wouldn't have bothered Elgar too much. He simply loved the drama of it and . . . was fascinated, I'm afraid, by Druid ritual. Blood-sacrifices and prophecies in the oak groves.'

'I should listen to it.'

'Yes, you should, but you'll find it essentially a patriotic work dedicated to Queen Victoria. Ending with what I expect *you* would call an imperialist rant – the British might have been defeated this time but would rise again, with an empire greater than Rome's.'

'I expect it was . . . of its time. And presumably – again – he didn't write the words?'

'Elgar told his publisher that he'd suggested the librettist should *dabble* in patriotism, but didn't expect the man to "get naked and wallow in it."'

Merrily smiled.

'Actually,' Sophie said, 'thinking about this, his cycling phase might have begun later, although it certainly started at Birchwood. Possibly while he was completing his masterpiece, *The Dream of Gerontius*.'

'That's not set in the Malverns, though, is it?'

'Merrily, your ignorance of great music astonishes me. It's set in the *afterlife*.'

'Erm ... OK. But we can assume Elgar was familiar with Wychehill? Travelling that road – on his bike or on foot – drawing from the landscape and also projecting his imagination *into* it. Fitting the criteria for an imprint – a recurring image in a particular location. A recording on an atmospheric loop.'

Sophie's face was expressionless. Merrily wondered sometimes if she believed any of this. Even for someone as unwaveringly High Church as Sophie, Christianity could still be a discipline rather than a journey of discovery.

'He undoubtedly did draw from the landscape and always saw his music through nature. Even as a boy, sitting by the river, he said he wanted to write down what the reeds were saying. Much later he was to say that the air was full of music and you just took as much as you required.'

Interesting. Merrily made a note.

'His principal biographer, Jerrold Northrop-Moore, an American, says the *Cello Concerto* projected to *him* – in America – an image of a landscape he'd never seen, and when he finally came over to Worcestershire it all seemed strangely familiar. He also suggests that Elgar's pattern of composition reflects the physical rhythm of the Malvern Hills.'

'And Lol said that when he was dying ...'

'Either he was being gently humorous in his final hours or he truly believed his spirit belonged in the hills. Does *that* fit your criteria for an imprint?'

'Maybe more than that,' Merrily said. 'But let's settle for an imprint for the moment.'

'And is that necessarily *bad*? An animation that simply replays itself?'

The phone rang and then stopped as Sophie reached out a hand. She sat back and rearranged her glasses on their chain.

'Linking Elgar with road-death, however, is abusive to the point of indecency.'

'People are *worried*.'

'And to allay their fears, you call upon God to banish the spirit of a genius?'

The phone rang again, and Sophie hooked it up. 'Gatehouse.' She covered the mouthpiece. 'Might it not be appropriate to bring this whole issue to the attention of the Bishop?'

'Not yet. Let's see what happens tonight.'


So where did you go with this?

Perhaps you started by strolling across the Cathedral green to confront the compact, tidy gent in bronze, leaning . . .

. . . On his bike. Of course he was.

Mr Phoebus, if this *was* Mr Phoebus, didn't have a lamp. But then his wheels didn't have any spokes either.

It was, Merrily thought, essentially a modest, unobtrusive piece. Life-size, dapper: Elgar the bloke. She sat on the grass in the sunshine with an egg mayonnaise sandwich, contemplating him from a distance while finishing off *Elgar – A Hereford Guide*.

Finally, she wandered across.

*Could you . . . ?* Keeping a respectful distance. *Could you possibly help me, Sir Edward?*

Look, this wasn't stupid. Sometimes . . . call it intuition, call it divine inspiration, call it . . .

But Elgar had higher things on his mind. Overdressed for the weather, he was gazing at the Cathedral tower with its unsightly scaffolding. The Cathedral where he'd spent so many hours – even, in later years, recording some of his music there.

*Look, I accept that I don't know enough about your work. I'm sorry. I hope to deal with that.*

No reaction.

No impressions. No guidance. Elgar was miles away, and music was Merrily's blind spot. In church, anyway. All the trite Victorian hymns she'd been trying to edge out of services for the past two years.

Everything the sculpture had to say to her was written on its plinth. A quote which someone – maybe even a committee – had thought essential to an understanding of the man and his work.

But it was interesting.

'This is what I get every day. The trees are singing my music – or am I singing theirs?'

Merrily walked around Elgar, looking over his shoulder, following his gaze.

'You're asking *me*?'

17

# Isolated

IN THE SCULLERY, THE answering machine was bleeping petulantly when Merrily got in. Bride's mother requesting a *second* rehearsal for one of next week's weddings – how much time did these people think you had? Then a reminder that she was expected to chair the Ledwardine Summer Fair planning meeting next Monday, and finally a hollow pause, a throat-clearing and this mild but slightly pompous southern Scottish accent.

'*Mrs Watkins, my name is Leonard Holliday, and this concerns your visit to Wychehill. Pointless calling me back, I shall be all over the place. I simply wanted to say, as the chairman of the Wychehill Residents' Action Group, that I've inspected your Hereford Deliverance website, and frankly I think your presence at the parish meeting would not be helpful.*'

Sounded as if he was reading a prepared statement.

'*I'm afraid there's been quite an hysterical reaction to some regrettable incidents. Some people are seeking to sensationalize a serious issue, in a way which would only make our campaign look fatuous. Therefore, on behalf of my committee – and we've made our feelings clear, also, to the Rector – I'd like to request that you do not attend this meeting. I'm sure you can see the sense of this. Thank you.*'

Merrily sat down at the desk, watching the machine reset itself. Some insect rammed the window and bounced away.

*Right.*

She called Syd Spicer. If there'd been some change of heart in Wychehill, he ought to have told her about it before now.

No answer. Not even an answering machine. What kind of rectory didn't have an answering machine? With less than an hour to spare

100

before she'd need to leave for the christening, she rang Directory Enquiries and obtained numbers for Preston Devereaux and Joyce Aird.

Devereaux first.

'No, this is Louis.' A deep drawl, but a young man's drawl. 'He's out, I'm afraid. Who's that with the rather sexy voice?'

'Thank you. My name's Merrily Watkins, I'm calling about—'

'The *exorcist*. Cool.'

'You're Mr Devereaux's son, I take it.'

'I'm going to be fascinated to see what you *do*.'

'You may be disappointed.'

'I really don't think so, Mrs Watkins. My little brother found your picture on the Net. I think he's taken it to his bedroom.'

Merrily sighed. 'When will your dad be in?'

'Not for hours. He has meetings all day. But he'll be back for yours, you can count on that.'

'I'll look forward to it.'

Good to know there was still respect for the Church. She hung up and dialled Joyce Aird's number.

Engaged.

Merrily was close to being late for the christening when Frannie Bliss phoned. 'As I hadn't heard from you, Merrily, I assumed you'd stumbled upon something in Wychehill which your conscience was telling you it was inadvisable to share with the Filth.'

'For once, I don't actually think I know anything useful – not to you, anyway.'

'Witnesses never know *what* they know until it's squeezed out of them by a master interrogator.'

'How long would it take to fetch one? I'm a bit pushed right now.'

'I hope God finds you less offensive, Merrily. All right, I'll tell *you* something. Our experts, examining the remains of the Mazda car belonging to the late Mr Lincoln Cookman, killed in Wychehill in the early hours of Saturday, had occasion to remove the spare tyre. And found a neat little package containing forty assorted rocks. And, no, he wasn't a geologist.'

'Oh dear.'

'Quite.'

'You're assuming he'd just picked up the package at the Royal Oak.'

'If you only knew how hard I'd tried to come up with a better explanation.'

'And are the police planning to do anything about this? Raid the Oak?'

'I think that would be an embarrassingly fruitless exercise, don't you? Something like this, you only get one chance, and I'm waiting for firm intelligence. I gather there's a meeting on in Wychehill, at which the problem of the Royal Oak is likely to be raised.'

'Yes, it's – tomorrow. Isn't it?'

'It's tonight, Merrily.'

'How did you find out?'

'I'm a detective. We *were* planning to look in, on an unofficial basis, but I'm told that would now be rather obvious.'

'Look, I've got to leave for a christening in a couple of minutes and then I was hoping to have a serious discussion with my only child when she gets in from school. What are you looking for?'

'Well, certainly something more than general rowdyism and weeing over walls. Like if illegal drugs were coming into Wychehill itself? Must be a few likely teenagers there. If we were to receive a serious complaint from a parent or two . . . Something I can dangle in front of Howe. I'm looking for a lever, Merrily.'

'I'm a vicar, Frannie.'

'And a mate,' Bliss said. 'I hope.'


After the christening of *Laurel Catherine Mathilda* and a brief appearance at the christening tea in the village hall, Merrily walked up to the market square under an overcast, purpling sky, and decided to wait for the school bus.

She looked up towards Cole Hill, but you couldn't see it from here, although you could from the church. Wished she had time to investigate this ley line for herself. Leys ... well, they were something she still wasn't sure about. They could never be proved actually to exist, but they had ... a kind of poetic truth. They lit up the countryside.

And if Jane had found a way of lighting up the countryside without drugs ...

Best not to get too heavy about her taking a day off school. As long as she didn't make a habit of it.

Merrily looked down into Church Street, at Lol's house. Wished she could light up the countryside for him. Under the shadow of middle age, he was understandably uncertain about his future. Set for stardom at eighteen and then robbed by bitter circumstance of what should have been the glory years. Too old, now, to be the new Nick Drake. His comeback album was selling *reasonably* well, he'd done gigs supporting Moira Cairns and the two old Hazey Jane albums had been remastered. But it still wasn't quite a career.

Now he was writing material for the second solo album. It wasn't going well. Although he didn't say much, she could feel his fear sometimes.

She turned, as the school bus drew up on the edge of the square and some kids got off.

And Jane didn't.

Merrily's heart froze. Stupid. This didn't automatically mean she'd skipped school again. Sometimes Eirion picked her up. However ...

She went straight home and called Jane's phone from her own mobile. Jane's was switched off. She left a message: call *now*. Put the mobile on the sermon pad and then sat down and rang Joyce Aird in Wychehill.

'I've caused a lot of trouble, haven't I?'

Merrily was cautious. 'In what way, Mrs Aird?'

'I had a visit ...' Her voice sounded unsteady. 'I was told this could bring us the wrong sort of attention and I've done the community a great disservice. I've lived here more than *twenty years*, Mrs Watkins ...'

'Asking for me to come and look into . . . ? *That's* the disservice?'

'I only did what I thought was best.'

'This is Mr Holliday, is it?'

'It's what we've become, I'm afraid. It's all about how it *looks*. Doesn't matter what the truth is any more.'

'Matters to me.'

'You don't live here, Mrs Watkins. It's not a nice place to live any more. Nobody's friendly.'

'Is that *since* these ghost stories—?'

'I feel I'm becoming a prisoner in my own home. Locked doors and drawn curtains and . . . and the lights on all night. That's what it's come to. I can't be in the dark. And I love my bungalow. I love the view . . . I *did* love it. Now it feels so isolated. I was going to give it till next year, but I've been thinking I'd better put the house on the market in the summer.'

'Do you have anywhere to go?'

'Back to Solihull, I expect. I should've moved back when my husband died. It's never the same on your own, though I do love my sunsets.'

'I'm really sorry, Joyce, but I don't think you should jump to—'

'Anyway, don't you worry. If they don't want you, there's nothing you can do about it, is there?'

'I'm sorry . . . I'm a bit confused here. I've had a message on the answering machine from Mr Holliday, who obviously doesn't want me . . . but I'm not sure it's his decision to make.'

'He said the Rector was going to tell you.'

'*Tell* me?'

'Not to come to the meeting. That they don't want you.'

'I see,' Merrily said. 'Would this . . . have anything to do with the late Sir Edward Elgar?'

'We haven't to use that name, Mrs Watkins. That's what I've been told.'

# 18

# What Remains of Reason

INSIDE, THE HUGE PARISH church of St Dunstan was as plain and functional as Syd Spicer's kitchen. Its Gothic windows were puritanical plain glass, diamond-leaded, and the light on this overcast Midsummer's Eve was cruelly neutral, showing Merrily how dispiriting it must be for Spicer on Sunday mornings, his meagre congregation scattered two to a pew and less than a quarter of the pews filled. Like a village cricket match at Lords.

But, as Wychehill didn't have a community hall, the church accommodated the parish meetings, so maybe its ambience would confer stability, calm, wisdom, dignity.

Or not.

'They found drugs in that car, you know.' Leonard Holliday – she'd recognized the voice at once – was on his feet across the aisle: crimped gunmetal hair, neat beard. '*Did* you know?'

Holliday must have police contacts. Maybe Masonic?

'No, I didn't know,' Preston Devereaux said wearily. 'I have a business to run. I don't have much time for gossip.'

'Ecstasy tablets, Chairman. They say one can buy them like sweeties at the Royal Oak.'

OK, maybe his contacts weren't *that* good.

'And you know why the district council, as the licensing authority, will not act against that place?' Holliday jabbing a forefinger at nobody in particular. 'You know why they won't shut it down – and I can disclose this with some authority, having worked in local government for forty years, and damned glad to be out of it ...'

'Mr Holliday—'

'The reason they *will not act*, Chairman, is that, as with so many tourist areas, the level of government grant-aid is now, to a large extent, dependent on the council and the tourism bodies being able to prove that they are attracting a sufficient number of *black and Asian visitors*. This is a *fact*. And these . . . music nights at the Oak are seen as especially attractive to that particular—'

'*All right.*' Preston Devereaux banging his gavel. 'As most of you seem to be members of the Wychehill Residents' Action Group, I don't think we need to complicate matters by going further into this issue tonight.'

He was at a table set up at the foot of the chancel steps, the chair next to him empty. The chancel was large and unscreened, its choir stalls in a semicircular formation, like a concert hall. More like a concerthall, in fact, than a place of worship, and as stark as a Welsh chapel.

It was just after nine p.m., the atmosphere thickening. Merrily wore a dark skirt and one of Jane's hoodies, zipped up to cover the dog collar. She'd slipped into a shadowy and empty back pew, just after eight-thirty. Thirty or forty people sitting in front of her, including . . . was that Joyce Aird? The normal parish meeting seemed to have started at seven; three people had left in the past half-hour.

Syd Spicer didn't seem to be here. She wasn't sure what this meant, but it probably wasn't a good sign. Preston Devereaux leaned back, looking through half-lidded eyes out into the uncrowded nave.

'I think we need to keep cool heads as we come to the final item . . . although, to be quite honest, I don't *want* to come to it at all. In fact, I feel embarrassed to be chairing a discussion of this nature, having no wish to watch this community casting off what remains of its reason.'

Devereaux was lean and weathered and keen-eyed, with longish hair the colours of Malvern stone, sideburns ridged like treebark. His accent was local, educated, grounded. He wore a brown leather jacket over a shirt and tie.

'However, because I find myself tragically implicated in this situation, I feel obliged to give it a public hearing. Essentially, we have a road-safety issue caused, I believe, by an increase in traffic through the village, due to increased tourism and . . . other developments.'

Somebody laughed. It had a bitter edge.

'However,' the chairman said, 'there *has* been quite a sharp increase in the number of road accidents lately, which has given rise to rumours which I shall describe conservatively as outlandish. Who's going to start us off on this? Helen—'

A woman stood up in one of the front pews.

'Helen Truscott. I use this road probably more than any of you, and I don't believe in ghosts.'

Someone clapped. Helen Truscott turned to face the assembly. Mid-fifties, brisk, attractive. You'd trust her judgement.

'I'm a district nurse by profession, and I'm also the carer for my disabled dad. And he worries when I'm out, particularly at night, and I'd like to clear this matter up, so that he can *stop* worrying.'

This would be the daughter of D. H. Walford who had written to the Rector.

'Thank you, Helen. We take your point. Anybody else? Mrs Aird?'

'Well . . .' Joyce Aird stood up, alone in a pew halfway down the nave. 'I think when there are a number of accidents, one after the other, we're all bound to feel a little nervous, and we can't help wondering if there's something going on that we don't understand. Especially those of us who live alone and perhaps have too much time to think. I'm a churchgoer, so I . . . when I get upset I turn to God. But I suppose I'm in the minority these days, so I . . . I'll . . .'

She sat down. Merrily noticed that the two vases of fresh lilies she must have put out on the chairman's table were on the flagged floor beside it.

'Thank you, Mrs Aird,' Devereaux said. 'As we're all churchgoers tonight, I'm sure God will be sympathetic. But I think this issue lies rather with the creations of man. The problem here's always been that, because of the positioning of the dwellings in Wychehill, mostly out of sight of the road, motorists do not realize there's a community here – scattered though it may be – of more than two hundred people. And so they tend to speed. Mr Holliday—'

Holliday was back on his feet, making it clear that the Wychehill Residents' Action Group, now extending to at least four other communities in the area, would be dissociating itself from any course of action designed to legitimize superstition.

'And indeed, Chairman, the very idea of suggesting that the ghost of Sir Ed—'

*Clack.* The end of his sentence was chipped off by the gavel.

'*The cyclist*, sir, if you please. There'll be no ridiculous conjecture in my meeting.'

'The idea that the story of *the cyclist* –' Holliday smirked '– would generate wider publicity for our campaign now seems . . .' He coughed. 'It seems clear to me that this would succeed only in leaving us open to ridicule.'

'But you thought about it, didn't you, Leonard?' Devereaux said.

'It did occur to me, yes, I'm rather ashamed to say, and I've now rejected it.'

'Very wise of you, sir.' Devereaux smiled. 'Now, I think we have a proposal . . .'

A man stood up.

'I'd like to propose that, in the wake of the weekend's fatality, we renew our call to the County Council and the police for the installation of speed cameras.'

'Right, proposal by Mr Sedgefield, of The Wellhouse.'

'Seconded,' another guy said without getting up. 'Perhaps they'll capture this bloody ghost on film – then we'd all be able to see it.'

Laughter. Preston Devereaux gavelled for silence, letting his smile fade.

'I don't really see there's much more we can do than that. But before I close the meeting, regarding the very regrettable incident involving myself at the weekend, several people have asked me two questions which, with the meeting's permission, I'd like to answer publicly tonight. Question one: no, I'm glad to say I was *not* hurt, for which I have to thank the famously robust physique of the British Land Rover. I very much wish, mind, that I'd been in my ordinary car – might've been able to get out of the way in time and the whole thing might've been less serious. But fate decided otherwise. Therefore, I'd like to propose that the whole community join me in expressing our condolences to the families of the two young people. Because, whatever some us may think about the Royal Oak . . .'

Subdued murmurs were lifted by the church's crisp acoustics into a substantial expression of assent.

'Good,' Preston Devereaux said. 'Now . . . question two. Simple answer: no, of course I bloody didn't!'

Laughter. Devereaux half-rose.

'Thank you, ladies and gentlemen. Now, unless anyone has something to add, I'd like to formally close this meet— I'm sorry, was that a hand at the back?'

'Yes, if I could just . . .'

She'd probably regret this later, Merrily thought, but you could only stand so much of this kind of crap.

She stood up, pulling down her zip.

The admonishing angel in her head looked a lot like Sophie.

'Oh, wow, look over there . . .'

Jane was standing on the massive, half-collapsed capstone, this huge jutting wedge. She was gazing to the south-west, the evening light thickly around her like the pith of some vast luminous orange, and she felt that if she jumped off now she'd go on flying, in a dead straight line to the crooked mountain on the horizon.

Arthur's Stone was the most impressive prehistoric monument in Herefordshire. It crouched like a dinosaur skeleton on Merbach Hill, above the Golden Valley which melted like grilled cheese into Wales. Arthur's Stone was not one stone but many . . . the remains of a dolmen or cromlech, a Bronze Age burial chamber which had once been covered with earth.

Alfred Watkins had found several leys passing through here, connecting it with country churches and unexcavated burial mounds and the remains of a medieval castle on an ancient hilltop site at Snodhill.

And if you stood where Jane was standing, on top of the monument, you could see, in misty profile . . .

'It's the Skirrid, isn't it?' Eirion said.

Like he could fail to recognize the holy mountain of Gwent, which he could see every day from his bedroom window just like Jane could see Cole Hill. The volcanic mountain cleft in two, according to legend, at the moment when Christ died on the cross.

Lying in Eirion's bed in the heat of the afternoon Jane had found herself visualizing the elemental force that split the mountain just as . . .

Oh God, was that some kind of sacrilege?

The day replayed itself in her memory: one of those wild, hazy days when you weren't aware of how magical it had been until it was nearly over.

She'd persuaded Eirion not to go to school – school hardly mattered at his stage of the game, A levels over, future in the lap of the gods. They'd gone back to his dad's place at Abergavenny and compiled the Coleman's Meadow document on his computer, with the photos and quotes from *The Old Straight Track*. Eirion had rewritten Jane's rant, draining off some of the vitriol and, she had to admit, it now seemed more rational and convincing. And then, with his dad and his stepmother safely away at the same conference in North Wales, they'd gone to bed.

Afterwards, she'd tried to ring Mum at the vicarage to imply subtly, without actually lying, that Eirion was picking her up from school. But Mum wasn't there, and the mobile was switched off most of the time. And then she'd remembered that Mum was going to be at a meeting over on the other side of the county for most of the evening, which left her and Eirion whole hours to go in search of the old straight track.

Eirion, in his post-coital *whatever* mood, had been cool about it, so they'd started off by looking for Alfred Watkins himself. *First and foremost a Herefordshire man*, it had said in his obituary in the *Hereford Times* in 1935, *as native to the county as the hop and the apple.*

Jane had found that in the Watkins biography by Ron Shoesmith, which had taken them in search of Vineyard Croft, the house near the

River Wye, on the edge of the city, where Alfred had lived for about thirty years with his wife, Marion. But they couldn't find it; they found a Vineyard Road, but it seemed all suburbs around there now. It was much easier to locate the house the Watkinses had moved to, just off the Cathedral green. It actually had a plaque on it, identifying its importance – probably the nearest thing to a monument to Alfred in the entire county.

'There ought to be an official Watkins memorial ley,' Eirion had said. 'Where you can stand and have the whole line pointed out for you.'

'So that even councillors could see what it was about?'

'They'd only be able to follow it if it was marked out in new branches of Asda and B & Q.'

We really understand each other, don't we? Jane thought. And in a few weeks he'll be gone.

She felt very close to tears and climbed down from the stone before she was tempted to throw herself into the horizon.


In the normal way of things, you were consulted by worried individuals whose world-view had been jogged out of focus – frightened people mugged by skewed circumstance. Since yours was the only hand reaching out they switched off their scepticism and clasped it.

Always individuals. Never a community, a society, a committee. In any random group, scepticism ruled.

'I'm confused, Mr Chairman,' Merrily said.

'Can't have that.' Preston Devereaux peered into the growing gloom. 'I pride myself on clarity. May we have your name, madam?'

'I'm, erm, Merrily Watkins.'

'Are you indeed?'

'I'm a consultant to the Diocese of Hereford on matters ... paranormal. And ...' she saw Joyce Aird had turned, looking both grateful and worried '... the Rector asked me to come tonight.'

'He must've forgotten to mention it to me,' Devereaux said. 'And as that particular item has now been dealt with—'

'It hasn't *really* been dealt with, though, has it? It's just been pushed under the table.'

Lot of heads turning, some muttering. No going back now.

'Mrs Watson—'

'Watkins. And I'm not a big conspiracy theorist, but I've encountered enough cover-ups in the past couple of years to recognize—'

'Madam!' The gavel came down with a crack that must have dented the table. 'Let no one accuse me of *that*.'

'I'm not accusing—'

'I think you'd better forsake the shelter of your back pew and attempt to justify it, Reverend.'

Preston Devereaux pulled out the chair next to his, calling out to the back of the church.

'Can we have some decent light on the proceedings?'

# 19

# Unload It

MERRILY STOOD UP IN the brittle, glassy light. She felt weak with fury.

Moved into the aisle, reaching into her bag to switch off her mobile. Would have felt better about this if Jane had called. In the end she'd gone round to Lol's, asked if he'd mind staying behind and trying to find her. OK, she was seventeen, for heaven's sake, nearly an adult. And yet . . .

*Oh God, get me through this.*

She stepped behind the table next to the chairman, looking out at twenty or thirty people, widely spaced, Winnie Sparke standing out in a crocheted white woollen shawl.

Lights came on, as if to dispense with the possibility of anything beyond normal occurring here. They were theatre-type spotlights, directed at the chancel, presumably for use during the choral concerts. The lights put the congregation into shadow and hurt your eyes when you looked up.

Merrily looked down.

'The main qualification for this job is, I've discovered, a high embarrassment threshold.'

Nobody even smiled.

'I was told – by the Rector, who doesn't seem to be here tonight – that at least four people had had experience of an inexplicable light, sometimes accompanied by a figure, in the road outside. Each sighting preceding an accident of some kind.'

She paused. Were they out there now? Tim Loste, Stella Cobham? Or had they been persuaded, by whoever had gagged Joyce Aird, to stay away? She thought about all the hours she'd spent, dragging Lol out to Wychehill, fruitlessly knocking on doors, needlessly infuriating the uniquely invaluable Sophie.

'The message spelled out tonight by Mr Holliday is that it's all superstitious rubbish. And he was thoughtful enough to put all that on my answering machine earlier today, when he phoned to advise me not to bother coming.'

A few murmurs at last. She could see Holliday, stiff-faced, in a left-hand pew, second row.

'Now what I'm gathering from what's been said is that Mr Holliday had earlier considered that the alleged phenomenon might have been useful as a publicity gimmick . . . to focus attention on his campaign against what's happening at the Royal Oak. Get the protest into the national papers. Maybe on TV.'

Merrily paused again, looking over to where she'd last seen Holliday, giving him a warm smile – the pompous, duplicitous git.

'You can see the TV reports now, can't you? Long shot of the hills at sunset, overlaid with some suitably serene pastoral music written by . . . *the cyclist.*'

Preston Devereaux's chair creaked.

'Mrs Watkins, I think—'

'And then it goes dark,' Merrily said. 'And we see the Royal Oak throbbing with purple strobe lights and a blast of drum-'n'-bass all over the forecourt. And then Mr Holliday steps into shot with a grim face and a petition to the council.'

'*Mrs Watkins.*'

'All right . . . I'm sorry.' Putting up her hands, turning to Preston Devereaux. 'Mr Chairman, I take it that you were tacitly informing us a few minutes ago that in the moments before that horrific crash you did not see a strange light or a strange cyclist. But where are the people who insist that they did? Is Mr Loste here tonight, for instance? Because I'd've thought if this meeting was to make a decision it ought to hear all the evidence. *Mr Loste?*'

She peered into the lights. Silence.

'Well . . . thanks, Mr Chairman. That's all I wanted to say, really. Just didn't want anyone to think that, having been invited, I'd failed to show up. Thank you.'

Merrily shouldered her bag amid a rush of whispers. Preston Devereaux said nothing. She slid around the table and walked away, out of the spotlight pool, down into the shadows of the left-hand aisle, aware of hushed discussions opening up on both sides, like a small motor coming to life, and then the scuffling sound of someone standing up.

'Wait . . .' A tall woman, black top, spiky red hair, standing sideways in the pew space.

Merrily stopped and leaned against a pew-end.

'I saw it,' the woman said. 'This fully formed man on a bike – high up on his bike, this great, black . . .' she stared around the church '. . . *pulpit* of a bike. Right there in front of me. And I wasn't drunk, whatever people are saying. I hadn't been drinking. When they gave me a breath test, it was totally negative. But I'm telling you I saw him. He was there. Absolutely and totally . . . bloody *there.*'

'You're . . .' Merrily felt a small worm of excitement uncurling in her spine. 'You're Mrs Cobham, right?'

'Correct. I swerved and he vanished and I went into this bloody camper van about half a second later.'

'How did you feel at that moment?'

'Feel? Mixture of . . . shock and . . . just sheer, primitive terror. I thought I was actually going to die. Die of shock, you know? All I remember after that was being out of the car and just standing at the side of the road, shivering. They wouldn't come near me, the people in the camper, they wouldn't leave their vehicle, I must've looked—'

'Was there any . . . change in the atmosphere when you saw the cyclist? The temperature?'

Merrily saw that the focus of the room had altered, people drifting to the ends of pews on either side, two semicircles forming and Preston Devereaux on his own by the chancel, sitting upright, his long sideburns like the chinstrap of a helmet. Stella Cobham gripped the pew in front of her.

'I felt cold. Whether that was just the shock . . . Couldn't seem to keep a limb still until daylight. Couldn't sleep. Couldn't think of anything else. Kept seeing him again and again in my head. I can see him now.'

'Mrs Watkins . . .' Preston Devereaux was on his feet. 'This is neither the time nor the place . . .'

Merrily just kept on talking to Stella Cobham, a damped-down silence around them, the windows in the nave filled with a dull purple half-light that didn't go anywhere.

'Could *he* see *you*, do you think?'

'I don't think he could see anything. His eyes were . . . somewhere in the distance. It was the eyes I remember most. It was the eyes that . . . there's a photo of him on the back of one of these books we bought – it's called *Elgar, Child of Dreams* – and it's one of those double exposures with his face superimposed on the hills, and his eyes are looking away, into some sort of infinity? You know? And there are these pinpoints of light in his eyes. Where's . . . where's Tim Loste?'

'Gone,' a man said. 'Or he didn't come.'

'Well, can somebody get him back? Because he'll be able to tell you—'

'Leave him alone.' Helen Truscott had appeared in the aisle next to Merrily. 'He's not well.'

'Oh God, the fount of all medical bloody knowledge. I'm trying to give him a chance to *unload* it.'

'And you think he'll be happy to have his beloved Elgar exorcized? There, I've said the forbidden name, too. You don't understand about Tim, do you?'

'I understand what I *saw*, Mrs Truscott . . .'

'You don't understand what state that man's in. You leave him alone.'

'Look, *I* was told people would say I was sick or mental or drunk, like Loste, and I . . . I've forgotten your name.'

'Merrily.'

'Well, Merry, whatever they're saying.' She swung her head angrily from side to side like a gun turret. 'I'm telling you there *is* something wrong here. *The cyclist* . . . Jesus.'

In the swollen silence, Merrily looked around and saw ... individuals. All these people together but essentially still pews apart. Maybe they knew one another by sight, by name, by reputation, but they were no more than a cluster of islands with separate climates, separate cultures.

Isolation. Midsummer Eve, and a chill in the air in a too-big church.

'Excuse me.' Preston Devereaux was brushing past. 'I suspect this meeting is now over. Would the last lunatic out of the building please turn off the lights?'

'Yeah, you go, Mr Devereaux!' Stella Cobham snarling at his back. 'You piss off. You keep nice and quiet about whatever you saw. You play it down. You weren't for playing everything down when the fox-hunting thing was on, were you?'

Devereaux stopped. 'That's over. It's over and we lost. You *move on*.'

Which was what he did. He walked out. At the same time, Merrily saw Leonard Holliday and three or four other people moving down the second aisle towards the main door ... and more faces were swimming towards her.

'If this—' She took a breath, inspiration coming. 'If this is really an issue, I'd just like to point out that the possibility of me or anyone attempting to exorcize Sir Edward Elgar ... that is very much not an option. And even if there *was* a connection with Elgar—'

'You can take it from me,' Helen Truscott said, 'that the connection was entirely in one unbalanced mind.' She glanced over her shoulder. 'And the devious heads of a few opportunists, who I hope have now seen the error of their ways.'

'What I was going to say, Mrs Truscott, is, if there really is evidence of some pervading negative spiritual presence here, then a small roadside blessing is probably neither sufficient nor appropriate. I was going to say that another way of dealing with it would be to hold a full Requiem Eucharist, here in the church ... perhaps extending out to the roadside?'

'What's that?' Stella Cobham said.

'A requiem is basically a funeral service. It's not something we do lightly, but it's sometimes a way of drawing a line under something.'

117

'You want to hold a service for the cyclist?'

'As some of you are a bit unsure about that, I'd be more inclined to suggest a service for the two people who died here last weekend, Lincoln and . . . Sonia? But I wouldn't do it unless I was persuaded that there was a good reason, and I'd need to consult the relatives.'

The mobile began to chime in Merrily's shoulder bag. She didn't even remember switching it back on. She saw Joyce Aird staring at her, mouth half-open.

'You want to hold a full requiem – a communion service – for those *drug dealers?*'

'Think I need to take this call, if you don't mind.' Merrily backed off. 'Look, that's just a proposal, OK? If you want to have a bit of a discussion about this, I've got some cards in my bag with my phone number and my email if anyone wants to . . . talk about anything privately or tell me anything. Excuse me, I'll be back.'

She hurried to the door, pulling out the phone, slumping on a bench in the porch with her bag on her knees.

'Jane?'

'Where are you, Merrily?'

Bliss.

'I'm at Wychehill Church. Why? What's happened?'

'You don't know?' Bliss said.

She went cold, thinking as always, *Jane.*

'Stop messing about, Frannie.'

She could hear the sounds of a car engine, the intermission of Bliss thinking.

'Don't go away,' he said. 'Might pick you up on the way, if that's all right with you.'

'The way to where?'

'We've gorran incident.'

'What's that mean?'

'Look, if you want to stick around I'll pick you up on me way. Be about half an hour. Yeh, do that, would you? Stick around.'

The line was cut. Bloody cop-speak. Why did they never spell it out? What was she supposed to do now? She stood in the church doorway, the sky outside the colour of the flash around a blackened eye. It must be nearly half past ten.

Behind her, the church door swung to and someone coughed lightly. There was a whiff of jasmine on the air.

'You're cute,' Winnie Sparke said. 'I thought the exorcist was the guy with you, and you didn't put me right.'

Her face was white and blurred, her hair curling into the shadows in the porch.

'What's *wrong* with this place?' Merrily said.

'You noticed that, huh?'

'Sorry, I think I was talking to myself.'

'Well, I'll tell you, anyway. Too much quarrying, way back, is what's wrong. Way back for us, that is, but like yesterday in the memory of rocks millions of years old. The hills are still hurting.'

'You think?'

'This is not a place to settle, believe me. Bad place to be, when the rocks are in pain, and you can take it from me, lady, these rocks hurt like hell.'

# 20

# Accidents happens

HE WAS WINDING THE NEW lime-green line into his brush-cutter head without even looking at it – finishing up with the two ends of line exactly the same length and pointing in different directions, the way the manufacturers and God had intended.

Incredible. Jane had tried this once, with just an ordinary garden strimmer, and about fifteen metres of the stuff had come spinning off the reel like one of those joke snakes out of a tin.

Gomer Parry had probably left school at about fourteen, and he could reload a brush cutter in three minutes, sink a septic tank, devise a stormproof field-drainage system . . .

. . . And he also knew where the bodies were buried in Ledwardine. Knew better than anybody since Lucy Devenish.

'Bent?' Jane said. 'You're serious?'

'Not as I could prove it.' Gomer snipped off the nylon line with his penknife. 'But I'd prob'ly give you money on it.'

He clicked the rubberized top back on to the head and, whereas Jane would've been beating it against the church wall and still one corner would be hanging off, it just . . . stayed in place.

She became aware that she was squeezing her hands together, impatient. Which was really childish. And this was not a childish matter. It had to be got right . . . might just turn out to be the most important thing she would ever do.

With Mum still not back when Eirion had dropped her off at home, Jane had walked down to Gomer's bungalow, ostensibly to return the wire-cutters she'd borrowed but really to sound him out about Lyndon Pierce. Gomer hadn't been at home but then, coming back across the square, in the gloom of a now-sunless sunset, she'd heard the whine of the brush cutter in the churchyard.

Gomer propped the cutter against the lych-gate while he took out his ciggy tin and opened it up and inspected the contents through the specks of shredded grass on the thick lenses of his glasses.

'Gotter be a bit careful, Janey. Walls got years. Even church walls.'

Jane looked around the churchyard and out through the lych-gate to the village square. Nobody in sight except James Bull-Davies getting into his clapped-out Land Rover.

'Please, Gomer . . .'

Gomer made her wait until he'd rolled his ciggy. He was wearing his green overalls and his Doc Martens and a new work cap that looked pretty much like the old one and probably the one before that.

'Ole churchyard's gonner need doin' twice a week soon.'

'*Gomer!*'

Gomer did his gash of a grin, the little ciggy clamped between his teeth.

'En't no rocket science, Janey. Councillors . . . all this on the election leaflets about directin' their skills for the good o' the community . . . load of ole wallop, and they knows it and they knows *you* knows it.'

Gomer sniffed the air.

'Well, all right, mabbe 'bout thirty per cent of 'em is straight-*ish*. Or, at least, when they first gets elected. Don't last, see, that's the trouble. All them good intentions goes down the toilet soon as they gets a chance of a slap o' free tarmac for their path, or their ole ma needs plannin' permission for a big extension to the house what her's gonner leave 'em when her snuffs it. So all I'm sayin' is, if you *has* to have dealings with your local councillor, best way's to start off assumin' he's bent. Saves time.'

'But, like, Lyndon Pierce, *specifically* . . . ?'

'Lyndon Pierce, he en't the sort of feller gets hisself elected juss so's he can call hisself *Councillor* Pierce.'

'Well, yeah, I realize councillors are always taking bribes from builders and people like that, so the chances are Pierce is getting a bung to make sure the Coleman's Meadow scheme—'

'Janey—'

Gomer started coughing, snatching his ciggy out of his mouth.

'I'm only saying that to *you*, Gomer. I'm not going to shout it all over the village, am I?'

'You don't even *whisper* it, girl, less you got the proof.'

Gomer took off his glasses, blotted his watering eyes on his sleeve. Jane bit a thumbnail, dismayed. Reticence was not his style. Gomer did not do restraint.

She stood there, chewing her nail. Since Minnie died, Gomer had become almost family, which was cool, because he was good to have around – like a grandad, only better. Well past normal retirement age now, but he'd never given up work. Kept his plant-hire business going with the help of Danny Thomas, dug graves for Mum with his mini-JCB, free of charge, treated the churchyard like his own garden.

And the great thing about Gomer was that he was ... *untamed.* Untamed by age. In a way that made you think there might actually be something quite interesting about being old, if you knew the secret.

He went over to one of the ancient caved-in tombs, where there was a big gap in the side and it was obvious that the body was long gone. He sat down on it and smoked for a while, Jane watching him and the tomb fading into the dusk.

'When I first went into Coleman's Meadow,' she said, 'I felt ... I felt the last person to go there and actually *see* it for what it was ... was Lucy Devenish.'

Gomer's ciggy was like an ember in the shadows.

Jane said, 'I could almost see *her.*'

Could almost see her now, in fact: the batwing swirl of the poncho, the hooked nose of an old Red Indian, the sharp gleam of a glancing eye, like a falcon's.

'Lucy hovers over this village, like a guardian of the old ways,' Jane said. 'That's the way I see it.'

'All right.' Gomer stood up, brushing ash from his overalls. 'First knowed him when he was a mean-minded little kid.'

'Sorry?'

'Pierce. One day, middle of January, Lucy caught him shooting at the blue tits with his air-rifle, when they come down to the nut feeder Alf Hayden used to hang by the ole gate into the orchard.'

'Bastard. How old was he then?'

'Mabbe fourteen? I wasn't living yere then, but we was dealing with a drainage problem, side of the orchard, for Rod Powell, and I'm in the ole digger when I years Lucy's voice shoutin' at somebody to hand over that gun *now*, kind of thing. So I goes trundlin' over, in the digger, and there's Lyndon Pierce pointin' the bloody thing at Lucy.'

'He was threatening to shoot *Lucy*?'

Jane started to tingle. It was – *wow* – like she'd been guided to this.

'Kids is daft,' Gomer said. 'Don't think 'fore they acts. 'Course, when he sees the digger, he hides the gun behind his back, but I leaves the engine running, see, jumps down the other side, grabs it off him. As I recall, it wound up under one of the caterpillars of the JCB. Accidents happens, Janey.'

'I am so proud of you, Gomer.'

'Boy tells his dad I've stole the gun off him. Dad rings me, threatens me I'll get no more work in this village ever again.'

'How could he do that?'

''Cause he was on the *council*. Two councillors representin' Ledwardine in them days, see – Garrod Powell and Percy Pierce. Then they had a big reorganization, and it was reduced to one, and Percy lets Rod have it uncontested, like. Real noble of him. Har! Amazin' all the arrangements as went through after that, to the benefit of Percy. Had a dealership in farm machinery, see, and some interestin' contracts comes his way, through the council, as wouldn't have looked quite right if he'd still been *on* the council. Also – you know what agricultural occupancy's about, Janey?'

'That's where there's a house that nobody can live in unless they can prove they're making a living from the land?'

'More or less. Point bein', a dwellin' with an agricultural restriction, you can't ask much money for him. So there was this bit of a jerry-built 1960s bungalow, bottom of Virgingate Lane, feller name of Ronnie Carpenter owned it, with fifteen acres, and he needed the money and he couldn't find nobody wanted to buy this ole place on account of fifteen acres don't give you much of a livin' no more. So Ronnie tries to get the restriction lifted so's he could flog it to somebody with the money to replace it with a proper house. Ronnie keeps applyin', keeps gettin' turned down . . . and then suddenly it goes through. Good ole Rod Powell, eh? What nobody knows is Ronnie Carpenter's arranged to sell the bungalow and the land, provisional-like, to Percy Pierce for his son Lyndon, who'd just qualified as a chartered accountant.'

'You're saying they only got to build that piece of pseudo-Beverley Hills crap because of a dirty deal between Rod Powell and Percy Pierce?'

Gomer dropped his last millimetre of ciggy onto the tomb, crushed it out and reminded Jane how people had always quietly helped each other in the country. And Rod Powell was dead now and Percy Pierce had retired to Weston-super-Mare, and now his boy had his seat on the council.

Was Lyndon Pierce really going to abandon a family tradition of being bent?

'So is it possible Pierce is tied up with this guy Murray, who owns the meadow?' Jane asked.

Not that it would matter. No need for corruption when you had council planning guys who thought appalling desecration was *acceptable infill.*

'Not many folk he en't in bed with, truth be told,' Gomer said. 'Accountant by profession, specializin' in smoothin' things out between farmers and landowners and the ole taxman. Local accountant who's also on the council? Popular boy, Janey. Popular boy.'

'A boy who used to shoot blue tits off a nut dispenser?'

Jane looked up at the church steeple, a sepia silhouette against a clump of cloud like dirty washing. Was this the Herefordshire of Alfred Watkins, who led genteel parties of gentlemen in panama hats and ladies with sunshades to explore ancient alignments of stones and mounds and moats and steeples? Was this the Herefordshire of the mystical poet Thomas Traherne, who was clothed with the heavens and crowned with the stars?

She hugged herself, wishing she could be back in Eirion's bed – and then wondering if she ever would be again.

'Makes you sick,' she said.

'Ar, it do,' Gomer said. 'Evenin', Lol, boy, ow're you?'

Jane turned to see Lol, in one of his alien sweatshirts, leaning against the lych-gate and shaking his head.

'You know how I hate to interfere, Jane,' Lol said in his mild, tentative way, 'but is it possible you're avoiding your mum?'

'Lol, she's been *busy*. She's *out* all the time.'

'A situation you might just be . . . you know . . . exploiting?'

'Not true at all. What I'm doing is, I'm actually trying to protect her, OK? She has a position in this village, obviously, and, like, how often have I done anything . . . OK, anything *locally* . . . that could cause her embarrassment? OK, don't answer that, but listen . . . this is what *Lucy* would want.'

Jane looked at Lol and then at Gomer, hoping they would both understand this.

Not that it mattered. She could almost see Lucy Devenish rising above the lych-gate, the darkening sky woven into the shadowed folds of her poncho.

## 21

# Playing Purgatory

Winnie Sparke looked past Merrily, out through the porch door into the waxy evening. Her white shawl was hanging loose like a priest's stole.

'You really shook things up in there, lady.'

'Wasn't me. I think something was just waiting to blow. You can't just sit on something like this.'

Winnie Sparke walked out into the night, Merrily following her.

'I don't suppose *you* know where Mr Loste is?'

'He isn't here.'

'I'd gathered that. But I *would* like to talk to him.'

'Maybe I could fix that. It's possible. Leave it with me.'

'With you?'

'Tim is . . . kinda fragile. Like a lot of people with huge talent, he needs someone to hold him together. Oops, mind you don't—'

'Oh my God, what's—?'

It had risen up like a column of smoke in the dusk, its eye sockets black, its mouth hanging open and the wings half-extended behind its arms. Its shoulders were black against a slash of red in the sky like the bar of a burning cross. Hands reaching up, palms outwards as if they were awaiting nails.

'Kinda weird, huh?' Winnie Sparke said. 'They say kids from the Royal Oak come in here and make out on the graves. But, hey, not on this one.'

The angel was standing on a tomb the size of a double-oven Aga, the lettering on the side big enough to read even in the ebbing light.

JOSEPH LONGWORTH, 1859 – 1937.

'ALL HOLY ANGELS PRAY FOR HIM

CHOIRS OF THE RIGHTEOUS PRAY FOR HIM.'


'Guy who built the church,' Winnie Sparke said. 'Found God and Elgar, not necessarily in that order.'

'I'm trying to place the quote.'

'You're excused. It's Roman Catholic. Newman – *The Dream of Gerontius.*'

'I was listening to it on the way here.'

While she'd been trying to engage Elgar in conversation, an exasperated Sophie had gone out and bought her three CDs. Next to the spare and moody *Cello Concerto*, the fifty minutes of *Gerontius* that she'd heard seemed both complex and a little dreary, heavy on the deathbed angst.

'Scary stuff,' Winnie Sparke said. 'All those layers of celestial bureaucracy. OK, you know how after the soul comes round on the Other Side, he gets a pep talk from his guardian angel and then these demons start messing with him? Then he gets just one tantalizing glimpse of God?'

'I'm not sure I got that far.'

'OK, well, between the demons and God he gets handed over to this guy.' Winnie Sparke reached up and tapped the arm of the grotesque figure on the tomb. 'The Angel of the Agony.'

'I don't know anything about him.'

Merrily looked up into the wretched marble face, grateful, on the whole, that there was nothing like this in Ledwardine churchyard.

'His job is to plead with Jesus to spare the soul of Gerontius,' Winnie Sparke said. 'It's a judgement thing. But you know what I think? I'm like, the hell with this guy, I think we can deal with purgatory right here.'

'In Wychehill?'

'On Earth, I meant. But Wychehill ... yeah, sure. Wychehill's as good, or maybe as bad a place as any for throwing off your demons.

127

Maybe we can discuss this sometime.' She flicked her shawl over a shoulder. 'You're gonna come back, now you won through?'

Merrily shrugged.

She lit a cigarette under the church lantern, one of its glass panes spider-cracked as if by a thrown stone or an air gun pellet. If Bliss was picking her up, she didn't want to go back in there and get pulled into a discussion. Besides, if a requiem was going to be held, Syd Spicer would need to make the arrangements.

There was a mauve, last-light glaze on the road, a faintly rank smell. She kicked what appeared to be a shrivelled condom into the side of the wall. Obtained from a vending machine at Inn Ya Face?

'Smoker, eh?'

She jumped.

Preston Devereaux was leaning on the wall under one of the oak trees. He, too, had a cigarette.

'Congratulations, Mrs Watkins.'

'I'm sorry. I was just . . . a bit . . .'

'You were bloody furious. A woman scorned.'

'I'm sorry. You've had a pretty bad week, too.'

'Had better.'

'How are you feeling now?'

'Me?' Devereaux leaned back against the wall, scratched his jaw. 'Well, since you ask, last night I got drunk. Today, I sold the offending Land Rover for peanuts. Couldn't stand to see it any more. I'm OK. Something happens, you live with it, move on. You don't *pick at it*, like a townie.'

'How do you mean?'

'Sorry if I'm causing offence again. I assumed you were local, name like Watkins.'

'Local origins. I've moved around.'

'Well, me too. But we came back, didn't we? God help us.'

'I hoped I'd be able to talk to you before the meeting,' Merrily said. 'But I think you answered my questions back there, anyway.'

'You were really going to ask me that? If I'd seen the ghost of Sir Edward Elgar on his bike before the crash? Good God.'

Merrily shrugged. 'My job.'

'Well, if you get to know me better you'll know it's not in my nature to make excuses or throw the blame at anyone living or dead. I was tired. Had a long drive, wanted to get home. Perhaps, if I hadn't been so tired, I'd've reacted quicker and there'd be two fewer funerals in Worcester. Who knows?'

'If you'd been less tired, you might have been going faster and the result would have been the same. Only you'd probably have been seriously injured.'

'I really don't know.' Devereaux shook his head slowly. 'But what I won't do, Mrs Watkins, is associate myself with the clowns who say this road's haunted. So if that's your idea of a cover-up, I'm sorry.'

'Clowns?'

'I don't know what's happening to places like this. At one time, we *absorbed* things. We, the community. Communities closed ranks, healed themselves. Scabs formed that eventually dropped off. Kind of people you got here now, the townies, they just got to keep picking and picking at it.'

'What about the Royal Oak?'

'The *Royal Oak*?' He snorted. 'Problem at the moment, but it won't last. They never do, these places. We just got to sit it out. Make a fuss, you just give them more notoriety, and they love that. Look, I'm more sorry than I can say about what happened to those two kids. I was a wild boy, too, drove too fast, inhaled my share of blow. Not for me to take a moralistic stance. But, this all-encompassing fear of the Royal Oak ... *live with it*, is what I say. Nobody can seem to live with anything any more.'

'Well, yeah, everybody expects a perfect life. But it's been suggested that a lot of Class A drugs pass through the Royal Oak. I don't know if that's right, but that's what they say.'

Devereaux stared at her. 'Do they? Who?'

Merrily didn't know how to reply, never entirely happy about being Bliss's snout, even if it was a two-way street.

129

'Aye, well, they're probably right, Mrs Watkins. And that's not good. But it'll pass. Be surprised if that place hasn't changed hands again by this time next year. Raji Khan's a businessman. When it goes off the boil he'll get rid.'

'You know him?'

'Stayed with me when he was looking over the Oak. Stayed in one of my lovely holiday lets. Clever man, young Mr Khan. Knows how to surf the economic tides.'

'You mean Mr Holliday was right about tourism grants to bring ethnic groups into the sticks?'

'It's the way this government operates.' Devereaux took a long pull on his cigarette, holding it between forefinger and thumb. 'But you know what makes me, laugh, Merrily – you don't mind I call you that . . . ?'

'Not at all.'

'What makes me laugh, my dear, is the way middle-class white folks move here from the harmless, peaceful suburbs, saying how glad they are to get away from the big, bad city, with all the drugs and the crime. Truth is, that was an imagined situation fuelled by *Crimewatch* and the *Daily Mail.* They'd never *actually* seen any of it . . .'

He laughed, at length, the cigarette cupped in his hand.

'And now here's the so-called ghost of Edward Elgar – poor dysfunctional bugger *he* was – and half of them of them think he's a traffic hazard and half of them think he's on their side against Raji Khan. What can you do with people like that? *Hello*—'

A young man in a rugby shirt was edging round the church gate. He stood in front of Devereaux and did a theatrical salute.

'They'll be out in approximately five minutes, sir.'

'Good lad.' Devereaux turned to Merrily. 'My younger boy, Hugo. Took the precaution of stationing him in the vestry, out of sight. What's the verdict, son?'

Hugo shrugged. 'No problems, really. Well, that Stella got a bit hysterical, but they talked her down. I think they're going for what Mrs Watkins suggested.'

'Which is what? I'd left by then.'

'Well, I'm not really . . .'

Hugo was about nineteen, lean like his dad, gelled dark hair and an earring. He looked at Merrily.

'Mr Devereaux,' she said, 'are you saying you had a spy in the vestry all the time?'

'Dad's the worst kind of control freak,' Hugo said.

'Local intelligence is very important,' Devereaux said. 'You live in a village, Merrily, you know what it's like. They weren't going to say much with me there, were they? Too official.' He smiled. 'No, I exaggerate. Hugo was at the back already, doing the lights.'

He put out his cigarette in a fizzing of sparks against the church wall.

'Tell me what you're proposing,' he said.

'Well . . . it's a requiem service in the church. A holy communion for the dead. So that would be a service for the two people who . . . died in the accident.'

'Why them?'

'Because they're dead. It's a big thing, death, but funerals today are often cursory and don't bring . . . don't always bring down the curtain. Don't bring peace, or even the promise of peace, for the living.'

'And how would this service achieve that?'

'Mr Devereaux, we could sit down and I could give you the theology in depth and take up the rest of your night. Let's just say that it does.'

'You're very confident.'

'I'm not confident at all. That is, it's not *self*-confidence, it's . . .'

She raised her gaze to the darkening sky. Preston Devereaux laughed.

'Well . . . who am I to argue with that? All right, then, go ahead. It's your show now. This is just a straightforward service, I take it?'

'Inasmuch as any service is straightforward.'

'What I mean is, you wouldn't be conducting what the press could call an exorcism?'

'You're right, I wouldn't.'

'Because none of us wants silly publicity, and if you can deal with it for us in a discreet and dignified fashion we'd be most grateful to you. Discuss it with the Rector, I should. I think you'll find he agrees.'

'Really.'

'Nice to talk, Merrily. Goodnight to you.'

Preston Devereaux clapped a hand on his son's back and they walked away to a dark 4x4 parked in front of Merrily's Volvo. She watched them go, feeling faintly sick. A bat sailed in front of the church lamp like a blown leaf.

*Deal with it for us.* Coming out of the church she'd felt halfway in control again, now she was a puppet with strings so tangled you couldn't tell who was pulling them. Merrily heard the voices of the villagers emerging from the church and walked rapidly away along the roadside towards the vicarage.

A car pulled alongside.

'You all right, Merrily?'

Bliss's face at the car window. She'd actually forgotten all about Bliss and his incident. She pulled back in mid-stride.

'Is this going to improve my night, Frannie?'

'Quite honestly,' Bliss said. 'I'd say probably not.'

## 22

# Power of Place

MERRILY JERKED HER HEAD away. '*Oh* God . . .'

The DC, who was called Henry, pulled back his lamp.

'You could've waited over by the truck,' Bliss said. 'I did warn you.'

And maybe she *would* have hung back, but a call a few minutes ago from Lol to say that he'd found Jane had fortified her, made her feel obliged to go across to join Bliss and what lay, in its abattoir splatter, across the jutting shelf of stone.

Bliss had driven up to the car park opposite the Malvern Hills Hotel at the foot of the Beacon, where they'd got into Henry's police 4x4. A roundabout route along dirt tracks had taken them to the other side of the hill, Henry parking in some woodland before leading them by lamplight, like a shepherd, along an uphill mud footpath.

It had brought them to a wide-mouthed cave in a wall of rocks, like a black gable under a roof. Two uniformed policemen were in the opening, smoking cigarettes. *Incident room*, Bliss had said, and laughed.

Merrily swallowed. Being sick wouldn't help the forensics.

'Frannie?'

'Uh?'

'You think there's a chance he did this to himself?'

The Home Office pathologist, Dr McEwen, looked at Bliss, probably to check that it was OK to speak in front of the woman in the dog collar. Bliss nodded.

'I'd say the chances that your man did this to himself are fairly remote.' McEwen was a soft-voiced Irishman in a red and blue baseball cap. 'With a suicide – if we assume this is something the individual has never attempted before – he's usually unsure of the best place to go in, so you'll normally find two or three test cuts above and below the main wound. Now, if you see here . . .'

This time Merrily didn't look, turning away towards the few lights of somewhere in Worcestershire laid out like a broken necklace under the ochre-streaked charcoal sky.

'But there *is* more than one cut.' Bliss's fluorescent orange hiking jacket creaking as he bent down.

'Sure, but they're not what anybody would call *test cuts*,' McEwen said. 'This one here looks like knife-skid, but *this* one, arguably a secondary slash, is far too deep. See what it's done to the trachea and the muscle there? There's also a wound on the back of the head, which might . . . Look, give me a few minutes more, all right?'

'Are these wounds consistent with that knife?'

'Back of the head, though, that looks more like your blunt instrument. I haven't seen the knife – you got it there?'

'Bagged up,' Bliss said. 'Kitchen knife, eight-inch blade. Found in the grass not far from his right hand.'

'Assume he didn't do it to himself. And I'd guess you're looking for more than one person, Francis. Probably more than two. If it happened here, which is how it looks by the blood-spatter, then . . . a muscular young feller like this, he'd take some holding down, wouldn't he?'

'Maybe somebody else holding his head back by the hair over the top of the stone to expose his throat for the knife. Henry, what did you say about this stone?'

'Known locally as the Sacrificial Stone, boss. That's all I can tell you.'

'There you go, Merrily. Can't say fairer than that.' Bliss took her arm and led her away, back up towards the cave. 'And this is Midsummer's Eve, right? Talk me through this.'

'Through what?'

'Ritual sacrifice. Just to get me started.'

'*That's* why you wanted me to come up with you?'

'No doubt we'll find a proper expert tomorrow, if we need one. But as you're here ... fair to say your personal experience extends to aspects of pagan worship?'

Merrily glanced back at the stone, a steep wedge in the hillside, the dead man, with his black bib of gore, arching back over it like he'd been been using it for working out, about to perform some dynamic form of sit-up.

'Frannie...' She dug both hands hard into her jacket pockets, turned away to where the path wound around to the earthen ramparts of the Iron Age fort. 'It doesn't happen, does it?'

'What doesn't?'

'Ritual sacrifice.'

'Yes, it does,' Bliss said. 'You think of that poor kiddie found in the Thames a few years back.'

'Yes, but that wasn't—'

'*One of ours*? Tut, tut. This is multicultural Britain, Merrily. Suggesting that the only valid form of ritual sacrifice in this country should be conducted by white men in white robes with sickles is tantamount to—'

'Oh, I see. Because this guy's *black*—'

'A black man found with his throat cut at a famous Ancient British monument ... that's slightly *cross*-cultural, isn't it? I don't think it's anything like that, but we need to eliminate it. Tell me about Midsummer's Eve.'

'Most traditional forms of paganism would focus on the solstice sunrise. Which is still a few hours away. But it's stupid anyway ... modern pagans just don't do this kind of thing.'

'Never say that, girl. There's always some bastard who'll do anything. But I take your point.'

'Also ... I mean, how long's he been dead?'

'Few hours, max. Found by some kids. Teenagers.'

'So he was probably killed before dark. Still be a few walkers about. They're going to stage a sacrificial ritual with the constant risk of an audience?'

A burst of light made Merrily turn in time to catch the second contained flash from a crime-scene camera, bringing the horror luridly alive: the obscene hole in the victim's throat like parted lips with a protruding tongue. She thought of hostages in Iraq dying on video, heard the keening of the knife in the air, saw the blade shining red-golden in the sunset. A slash, a spurting, a choked-off scream. She shivered.

'You're doing well,' Bliss said. 'This is what I wanted to hear.'

'Huh?'

'Look, if you need a cig, go ahead, just don't drop the stub.'

'I'm OK.'

'You don't look it. I'm sorry, Merrily, I didn't think. I do tend to use people, me.'

'Really? I've never noticed that side of you.'

Bliss grinned. Headlights washed across the sloping trees below them. The turf under Merrily's feet felt as springy as an exercise mat. With the smoky hills snaking away before her, it was like standing on some kind of natural escalator. Power of place.

'It's an execution, isn't it?'

'Possibly,' Bliss said. 'Of sorts.'

'And you're thinking the victim's connected with the Royal Oak.'

'A good detective is open to all possibilities.'

'Only . . .' She hesitated. '. . . A guy in the parish meeting just now was insisting that the licensing authority had been tolerating what was happening at the Royal Oak because you got better tourism grants if you could show the government you were encouraging black and Asian visitors.'

'Must send the council a picture. This could be worth thousands.'

'So I was wondering . . .'

'A *racist* execution?'

'I don't know.'

'You know what I think, Merrily? I think if this lad had been found with the same injuries behind one of the garages on the Plascarreg Estate we wouldn't be asking ourselves any of these questions.'

'Power of place,' Merrily said.

It was another ninety minutes or so before they went back to the

British Camp car park. Bliss had offered to get Henry to take Merrily back to her car at Wychehill, but she'd hung on, watching the police tape going up, lights bobbing around the hillside.

Bliss had wandered off to consult with his team and Merrily had phoned Lol, asking him to get a message to Jane: don't wait up.

'Henry says people come up here for the Midsummer sunrise,' Bliss said as they climbed down from the 4×4. 'In which case they'll be disappointed tomorr—' He looked at his watch. 'Dear me, it *is* tomorrow. Anyway, I don't want any bugger on that hill until we've been over it in daylight.'

'How long are you staying?'

'I'll drive you to your car and then I'll come back for an hour or two. See if I can make enough progress to stake a claim.'

'On the case?'

'Soon as Howe gets in tomorrow, she'll be working out how to remove me from the investigation. Being so close to the Worcester border doesn't help.' Bliss unlocked his car. 'Don't want to be too tired to put up a decent resistance.'

He drove past the side of the Malvern Hills Hotel and into the road that led back to Wychehill.

'However,' he said, 'if I did want to keep going until sunrise, and probably the sunrise after *that*, the answer would be in the knapsack that one of the lads has found among the rocks. Up by the Giant's Cave, as it's known.'

'A knapsack ... full of ... ?'

'In very saleable quantities. We'll know for certain in the morning if it belonged to our friend.'

'He was a dealer?'

'Not for me to defame the dead without forensic evidence, but ... yeh.'

'He was *dealing on Herefordshire Beacon*?'

'Oh heavens! A purveyor of narcotic substances on a national monument. Merrily, imagine for a moment, if you're a Malvern professional person throwing a dinner party, how much more civilized it would be to stock up on the After Eights on a balmy summer evening with all-round views.'

'Luckily I'm a vicar who can't afford to throw dinner parties. Bloody hell, Frannie.'

'But what puzzles me is who would brutally unthroat a drug dealer ... and then not even nick his flamin' stash?' Bliss cruised down the hill past the darkened Royal Oak in its tree-lined quarry. 'I'm norra great believer in coincidence, Merrily.'

'Look ... what can I tell you? I've been to a public meeting where the community had to decide what it wanted me to do about the ghost of ... of a cyclist. If anything in that connects with an appallingly nasty murder of a drug dealer on the lower slopes of Herefordshire Beacon it isn't obvious to me. But then, it *is* late.'

'But you'll be coming back, I take it.'

'I suppose.'

'And I might not be. So keep me informed.'

'And you keep *me* informed.'

In the north-eastern sky, she could see amber strips. Probably a false dawn. Midsummer morning in Elgar's England.

'Not only did they not take his drugs,' Bliss said, 'they didn't even nick his mobile. Work *that* out.'

PART TWO

'Both in prehistory and in the medieval period, the Malverns were in effect a ritual landscape against which various religious rites were played out.'

Mark Bowden, with contributions by David Field and Helen Winton
The Malvern Hills:
*An Ancient Landscape* (2005)

## 23

# Freelancing

JANE, AT BREAKFAST, SAID, 'I *haven't* been trying to avoid you.'

'Did I say you had?'

'Lol said you had. Which means the same thing.'

'Actually,' Merrily said, 'I was feeling bad that I hadn't been, as they say, here for you. Maybe you could take me to see this Coleman's Meadow? When you get home from school.'

After some sweaty, befuddled dreams that she couldn't remember but knew were unpleasant, Merrily just wanted to do something *normal*. She sat and looked at Jane across the refectory table. Wished they could stay here like this all day.

Jane said, 'What's wrong?'

'Difficult night.' Merrily put an extra spoonful of sugar in her tea. 'After the meeting, Frannie Bliss took me to look at a murder scene.'

'Scousers really know how to show a woman a good time. Like ... *why*, exactly?'

'Because the dead man was found with his throat cut on something called the Sacrificial Stone at Herefordshire Beacon and Bliss wanted to eliminate the possibility of it being a ritual midsummer slaughter by pagans.'

'Wow. For a vicar, you really—'

Merrily watched her daughter, translating every facial twitch: Jane trying not to be impressed while remembering she had guilty secrets and couldn't afford to be *too* abrasive over ...

'Pagans doing ritual murder? That is so insulting.'

'As Bliss pointed out, there are pagans and pagans. Anyway, it was bloody horrible, and I didn't get back until nearly two a.m. So if you've been trying to avoid me, I've not been aware of it.'

'Who was the vic?'

Kid watched too many American crime shows on Channel Five.

'When I left, he was still unidentified. Jane ... do you know anything about a dance venue called Inn Ya Face?'

'Best thing about that place –' Jane spread a slab of honey, obscenely, on a crumpet '– is its name.'

'How do you know?'

'I've been, obviously.'

'*When*? You never mentioned that.'

'We didn't stop long. I mean, it's a good place to go because there's masses of parking space, supervised by these hard-looking guys so you don't get your car nicked, and it's free. We thought we might go again some time, if there was anybody particularly cool appearing, but we somehow never have.'

'You and Eirion?'

'Dr Samedi was supposed to be on – you remember Jeff, from Kidderminster?'

'Oddly, I was only thinking about Dr Samedi last night. He's still in business?'

'Yeah, but we got the wrong night. There was this really poxy band on, thought they were the new Chemical Brothers. Really bad. Not bad as in wicked, bad as in ... crap.'

'Talking of chemicals—'

'Whoever told you I'm doing drugs is—'

'I meant the Royal Oak. Inn Ya Face. Could you – if you wanted to – get much there?'

'Mum, how naive *are* you? You can get it *anywhere*. There are like ten-year-old dealers outside playgroups? I mean, all that meet-me-on-the-corner-when-the-lights-are-going-on stuff ... that's costume drama.'

'That's an exaggeration, right?'

'Not much of one. Prices have never been lower in Hereford. So I'm told. Look, Mum ... erm ...' Jane's eyes flickered. 'You heard from anyone? About ... me?'

'Like who?'

'I don't know ... Morrell?'

'The head?' Merrily drank some hot tea. What was this? 'Why Morrell, Jane? Does he know about your serial truancy?'

'Serial—? Mum, that is absolute sh—'

'How many times?'

Jane picked up a piece of crumpet, put it down again, stared at it and sighed.

'Two.'

'You're sure?'

'I swear. Look, if I'd asked for time off the premises to work on my project I'd've got it. I just didn't want to ...'

'Tell them exactly what the project involved.'

'Because ... All right, because I went round to Councillor Pierce's place to ask him about this housing plan, and there were all these county council guys there, and one was a woman from the education authority.'

'Why don't I like the sound of this?'

'I mean I wasn't, you know, rude to them or anything. Just tried to get my point over about Coleman's Meadow being, essentially, an important ancient monument, and they said that was all crap, and Alfred Watkins was a misguided old man. They called it "acceptable infill". And Lyndon Pierce said he wanted to build Ledwardine up into a thriving little town with like restaurants and massage parlours?'

'He said *that*?'

'Well, he said restaurants. And a new village hall – leisure centre – that's already going ahead, apparently.'

'That's rubbish. I'd have heard. Been consulted, even.'

'No, really. They're getting a Lottery grant.'

'Seems very unlikely to me. I was at a christening tea in the village hall yesterday. It's going to be redecorated next month.'

'It sounded like a seriously done deal to me,' Jane said.

'I'll check it out. What did you say to them?'

'Nothing. Not really. When this woman started banging on about Morrell, I just got out of there.' Jane stood up, brushing cat hairs from her skirt. 'You do look knackered, Mum.'

'I *am* knackered – let's not get sidetracked.'

Merrily inspected Jane in her school uniform, hoping it wasn't only familiarity that made her daughter look innocent rather than sultry and faintly menacing like some of the other girls you saw waiting for the school bus. Jane going, on her own, to see Pierce . . . that was kind of admirable, but whether Pierce would regard it as mature and socially aware was a different matter.

'You haven't done anything else I should know about, have you?' Call it intuition.

'He used to shoot blue tits off nut dispensers,' Jane said.

'What?'

'Lyndon Pierce. When he was a kid. Lucy Devenish tried to stop him and he pointed his airgun at her, and then Gomer—'

'Gomer told you this?'

'Gomer took the gun off him and flattened it under his JCB. I bet the bastard didn't put *that* in his election leaflets.'

'Jane—'

'Don't worry, I'm not going to try and blackmail him or anything.' Jane shouldered her airline bag. 'I'm probably not even going to say anything about his old man, Percy Pierce, doing a dirty deal with the disgusting Rod Powell to get this, like, agricultural restriction lifted.'

'What?'

'So he could build Lyndon's revolting Las Vegas-style villa. I'm not going to hang that on him . . . yet.'

'Good,' Merrily said. 'I'm delighted you're probably not going to attempt to blackmail the local councillor, because it is, as you know, a serious crime.'

'Building on Coleman's Meadow is also a crime,' Jane said. 'Well . . . better get off, I suppose.'

The phone starting ringing. Merrily rose.

'There *is* something I don't know, isn't there?'

'Well, obviously, there must be lots of things, Mum,' Jane said. 'But I can't imagine anything that would cause you a particular problem.'

'When did you ever?'

As soon as Merrily heard Spicer's voice in the phone, flat and neutral as underlay, it came to her how much she didn't want to go back there.

'You had a good night, then,' he said.

'I had a bloody awful night. But how would you know?'

The time for civility was long gone. It was clear that Wychehill – whatever Wychehill *was* – needed help, the element of nervous dysfunction quiveringly obvious. And, as Lol had said when she'd rung to tell him about last night, it was surely time that Spicer did something about it, rather than some outsider. Of course, that could just have been Lol not wanting her to go back either.

'I'm glad you went,' Spicer said.

'You were told to call me off, weren't you?'

'Yeah, but I couldn't reach you, could I?'

'Of course you could.'

'Sure.'

'Who told you to call me off?'

'Preston.'

'Why?'

'He's just a funny bloke. Proprietorial. His family goes back. I mean, *really* goes back – Norman times. I'm not saying he doesn't like outsiders, exactly – the guy's running upmarket holiday accommodation on his farm – but he likes to be in control. And people in Wychehill like him to be in control. They're all outsiders and they like to buy into the history. Even Holliday.'

'So Holliday was firing Devereaux's bullets?'

'Holliday would've run with Elgar's ghost, all the way to the *News of the World*, even if he doesn't believe a word of it. Maybe *because* he doesn't believe a word. I can understand Devereaux not wanting that – *I* wouldn't want it.'

'But you weren't there last night.'

'No point. It was a stitch-up. But like I say, I'm glad you went. It worked out. A requiem will be spot-on. Everybody happy.'

'Why do I feel *I've* been stitched up?'

'Trust me, it's the best thing. Devereaux respects you now. That counts.'

'What about Stella Cobham?'

'Oh, he isn't gonna forget that, is he? She came close to making a fool of him.'

'And what's your feeling now about ... what we're dealing with?'

'Don't matter what my feelings are. What are yours?'

'It's impressive. But if there's going to be a requiem, maybe you should do it.'

'*No.*'

Startled by the force of Spicer's response, Merrily said nothing.

'It's not my thing. All right? I can get you the names and addresses of the dead kids' parents. Been in touch with the priest handling the joint funeral in Cookman's parish. I can make the arrangements – all you have to do is show up.'

'This coming Sunday? Evening?'

'Why not? Thank you, Merrily.' A long expulsion of breath; he was smoking. 'I hear you were up on the hill last night.'

She was getting used to how long it took him to get around to crucial issues.

'All it was ... a CID man I know was in charge up there. He thought I might be able to help. He was wrong.'

'Why'd he think that, Merrily?'

'Because it looked as if there was a ritual element to it.'

'Nah,' Spicer said. 'It's urban business, innit?'

'How do you mean?'

'He was a bouncer. At the Oak.'

'I didn't know that. Syd ...'

'Yeah?'

'Are there still serious drugs coming out of there, in quantity?'

'That what your pal thinks?'

'Not my place. But I did hear something about Preston Devereaux's boy. Not Hugo, the other one.'

'Louis. He's about twenty-three now. What did you hear?'

'That he'd gone off the rails after the hunt ban.'

'Yeah, that's true. Youngest-ever master of the East Malvern hunt. Lived for it, totally. Ban came in, he had a breakdown, of sorts. Like his life had been cut off at the roots.'

'But his father ... moved on?'

'As he likes to say. Yeah, he sold the horses. All the other hunts, with the tacit approval of the gutless wankers in the Cabinet, are doing pretend drag hunts where foxes just accidentally get killed. Preston's too proud.'

'So when he says, *you move on...*'

'He means, you move on, disguising your rage and loathing. Don't give them the satisfaction.'

'And does that also explain his attitude to the Royal Oak?'

'You're doing very well, Merrily,' Spicer said. 'It usually takes outsiders years to acquire that level of local understanding.'

'I live in a village.'


'He's right,' Bliss said. 'Roman Wicklow. A hard-boy.'

He wouldn't talk on the phone, so it was back to that same table in the Cathedral cloisters. Outside, it was an all-too-typical midsummer morning: small, white sun crowded by sour clouds, not very warm.

'His form includes ABH, malicious wounding and possession of Class A. Bromsgrove's his old playground, so they'll be looking there.'

'They? Not you?'

'Mr One-night-stand, me.' No doughnut this time, Bliss was drinking black coffee. 'Left to meself, I'd be roasting Raji on a slow spit. But when you're off the case, you're off the case.'

'Annie Howe's taken over?'

'Since first light. Legitimately. It's a Worcester thing now, from all angles.'

'But you're still interested?'

'In an academic way.'

'I bet.'

'I managed to . . .' Bliss sipped his coffee, winced, added sugar. 'Before they broke the news, we had another word with two of the little scallies who found the remains. Thirteen-year-olds sharing a six-pack of Fosters, so a little mild pressure was permissible. Finally admitted this wasn't the first time they'd seen Roman up the Beacon.'

'Birdwatching?'

'Mr Khan was terribly shocked. Assuring me he'd have fired Roman at once if he'd so much as suspected. And, you know, strange thing, I think he *was* shocked. Mr Wicklow dealing on the Beacon? Handful of rocks and a few piffling grams?'

'You think he *really* didn't know?'

'That kind of trade would be far too trivial for Raji, not to mention *dangerously* close to home. Yeh, I believe him when he says he'd have had Wicklow's balls if he'd found out. Wicklow was freelancing. Probably made the arrangements in the pubs in Great Malvern, then met the clients in the fresh air, with those wonderful, far-reaching views of anybody approaching and a nice cave to shelter in.'

'Therefore Khan's not involved?'

'Oh, I never said that.' Bliss looked down into his coffee, lowered his voice. 'If he'd found out that one of his people was operating on the side and figured it was time an example was made of someone foolish enough to abuse his position . . . well, that just might explain why the goody bag was left at the scene.'

'*He* had Wicklow killed?'

Bliss smiled. 'Try and prove it.'

Merrily leaned back. A stray blade of wan sunlight tinted an edge of the Bishop's lawn. Another world.

'So ritual murder's definitely ruled out?'

'It was never really ruled in. Also, Doc McEwen's knocked down his own theory that it would've taken several people. Wound on the back of the head now suggests that Wicklow was clobbered first and then dragged to the stone before his throat was cut. Assuming an element of surprise, one person could have done that.'

'And it wouldn't have taken long, I suppose?'

148

'By comparison, no time at all.' Bliss looked at her, his eyes slitted. 'Still funny it should happen when you're around, though.'

'You're considering the possibility that *I* did it?'

'Can you think of a better way of little Francis becoming Annie Howe's favourite detective in the whole world? Instead of off the flaming case.'

Merrily hadn't yet been to the office, slightly worried about facing Sophie, whose reasoning, on the issue of Wychehill and Syd Spicer, had been, as it had turned out, flawless.

Sophie wasn't in, however – probably over at the Palace, dealing with the Bishop's mail. The computer was switched off, but four messages were on the answering machine, one of them non-routine and left less than four minutes ago.

'Mrs Watkins, this is Winchester Sparke.'

*Winchester?*

Sophie came in with a cardboard file under her arm, sat down opposite Merrily and began to unpack it, assembling a small pile of letters on the desk.

'I need to speak with you.' Winnie Sparke's voice was harsh and frayed. Please call me back. I— The cops have taken Tim. Came pounding on his door ... took him away.'

# 24

# Lord of Dread

MERRILY RANG BLISS on his mobile.

'Hold on a mo.' She heard the sound of feet on stairs and then an outside acoustic, city traffic. 'Yeh, I've just heard. It was a surprise to me, too. You know anything about this feller?'

'He's a composer. A music teacher. What's the basis for it?'

'I don't know, Merrily, it's not my case.'

'Can't you find out?'

'If I make a nuisance of meself. Hate to use a hackneyed old phrase, but what's in it for me? And I *don't* want a mention in your prayers; you're a Protestant.' He sniffed. 'All right, here's my inspired guess: an outrage crime.'

'Is an outrage crime what I'm thinking it is?'

'Way I'm looking at it is, we've got two local dealers taken out within a fortnight, both in rural areas. I told you about the guy in Pershore?'

'But didn't you say he was shot in his car? *Modus operandi* doesn't exactly tally, does it?'

'*Modus schmodus*, Pershore's still only half an hour's drive from Wychehill. But is Annie Howe looking at it from that perspective? Oh no, too small-time and messy. Annie wants an *outrage crime*. By which I mean where some normally law-abiding person or persons is pushed well beyond the limits of socially acceptable behaviour by the perceived collapse of everything he or she holds dear.'

'That's vigilantism, Frannie. That's *Death Wish 2*. I've never met Tim Loste and I don't know that much about him. But a musician and choirmaster, however troubled, doesn't really strike me as the most obvious serial killer of drug dealers.'

'Doesn't matter. Annie wants Loste because he's white and middle-class. I'll see what I can find out and get back to you.'

Merrily held the phone to her ear long after the click, watching Sophie sorting the Bishop's correspondence, recalling her reaction to the Royal Oak becoming Inn Ya Face.

*One day, I think, we may be pushed too far.*

'You were off sick on Monday,' Robert Morrell said.

*Sick* was a dirty word to Morrell. He worked out three nights a week in the school gym, did the London Marathon, and his skin was lightly tanned all year round. You had to be suspicious of a head teacher with a sunlamp.

Jane nodded. 'It was a migraine. I get them sometimes in summer.'

'And it persisted through yesterday.'

'Well, I *was* going to come in yesterday, and I went out to wait for the bus and it . . . it just came on again.'

'You been to the doctor, Jane?'

'Well, no . . . I know what it is. It's a migraine. I've had it before. It's like . . . it's horrible. First of all, you see these big black spots in front of your eyes, and then it . . .'

'Comes and goes, I imagine.'

'Yes, it does. That's what it does. Comes and . . . goes.'

'And this . . . conveniently capricious migraine was presumably in remission on Monday night when you paid a surprise visit to Councillor Pierce at his home.'

Oh God. Any vague hope that Jane had had that this was *not* why Morrell had sent for her hit the deck like a bag of flour. It was going to take a lot of sweeping up.

'I . . . erm, the migraine seemed to be easing off by the evening, so I went for a walk in the cool air to clear my head . . . and I just happened to be passing that way and . . . you know . . . got chatting to these people. Not knowing who they were, at first. Only, the thing is, I'm using aspects of local history for my art project, and I was thinking that now I was feeling better I could at least do some work on the, erm, project, and so ... I'm sorry, Rob, this probably sounds ...'

'Yes, it does, Jane.'

'I didn't ... I mean ...'

Jane's resolve collapsed. She really didn't like this new policy of Morrell's where, when you reached the sixth form, you were permitted to call him Rob. Like you were all mates. So that when you did something wrong, it was like you'd let down your mate. Which was totally ridiculous because there was no way Jane would ever get close to having a mate like Morrell, with his tracksuits, his sunlamp, his neatly shaven head, his minimalist office, his Tony Blair smile ...

He did it now, that ghastly smile, and then he leaned back in his executive chair and spoke with the kind of horrible lazy fluency that must have persuaded the thick bastards on the education authority that he was smooth enough to do this job.

'Jane, tell me ... which particular part of your project involves haranguing elected members and officers of the Herefordshire Council for performing their democratic duty in opening the way for the kind of much-needed rural housing that may enable you and your fellow students to remain in this area when you leave the education system, rather than becoming economic migrants?'

By the time Jane had worked this out, it was too late for any kind of smart response. Morrell's smile vanished, like that of the tiger deciding it was time to stop playing with his prey and get down to the meal.

'Perhaps I need to make it clear to you, Ms Watkins, that, as a sixth-former, you are an ambassador for this school in the greater community. Do you understand what I mean?'

Jane just nodded; couldn't even manage a respectable display of dumb insolence.

'All right. On this occasion, to save further embarrassment, and to protect our exemplary record on truancy, I informed Councillor Mrs Bird – the vice-chairman of Education and one of our governors, as I'd have thought you would remember – that on this occasion you'd been given time off to work on your project.'

'Thank you,' Jane said feebly.

'And I'll thank *you*—' Morrell's palm slammed down on his desktop '—not to drag the name of this school into disrepute in future, with your lies and your childish fantasies. Do you understand what I'm saying? Far from covering up for you, *next time* . . .'

Jane nodded.

'Good,' Morrell said lightly. 'Off you go.'

Bending his shaven head over some report, he highlighted a line of type with a yellow marker pen. In the doorway, ashamed of her craven attitude, Jane turned round.

'It's not *low-cost* housing, you know. It's luxury, executive—'

'Geddout, Jane,' Morrell murmured. 'You're beginning to bore me.'

Jane just like *fell* out into the corridor, knowing her face would be red and scrunched up. Feeling the heat of tears and weight of the Establishment. It was like . . . Stalinist: the Council, intent on crushing all opposition, putting the word out to the chief of police to warn her off.

She stumbled into the toilet to wash her face and then went into one of the cubicles and fumbled out her mobile to leave a message on Eirion's phone, see if he could pick her up after school. Needing someone to howl to.

Soon as she switched on, the voicemail signal buzzed, and she clapped both hands around the phone because Morrell was strict on the use of mobiles during class-time – confiscation had been known, for as long as a week, and in this case would be guaranteed, and then the secret police would have all her private contacts.

*You have one message. To access your messages, press one.*

Probably be Eirion, saying he was going to be tied up tonight. Jane pressed *one.*

'Hello, Ms Watkins.' This strange, cheerful man's voice. 'My name is Jerry Isles, and I work for the *Guardian* newspaper. I'd like to discuss your campaign on behalf of the, um, Ledwardine ley? Could you please call me back?'

Jane stood there, with her back to the cubicle door, staring into the toilet, the mobile feeling like a stick of dynamite with a fizzing fuse. When she and Eirion had done the document for the Net, she'd put her mobile in as the contact number, mainly because she didn't want anybody ringing the vicarage. Expecting maybe a couple of concerned ley-hunters who might be prepared to send letters of protest to the council.

The *Guardian*? Jeez.

'And what do *you* know about this man Loste?' Sophie asked.

'Nothing.' Merrily spread her hands. 'Hearsay. I've never met him. I've never even seen him.'

She'd just called Winnie Sparke. The call had lasted around half a minute, Sparke insisting that she didn't like to speak on the phone and could they meet this afternoon, somewhere other than Wychehill? Great Malvern would be appropriate. She knew a place they could be private.

'You're *going*?' Sophie said.

'What can I do?'

'This man has been taken in for questioning about a peculiarly savage and revolting murder and you propose to meet his girlfriend somewhere *private*.'

'I'm not sure she's his girlfriend.'

'Do you even know anything about *her*?'

'There are only twenty-four short hours in a day, Sophie.' Merrily slumped back in her chair, leaning it against the wall. 'And I'm already working most of them.'

'I'm sorry. I'll see what I can find out.'

'I'm sure you've a stack of letters to do for the Bishop—'

'Shush,' Sophie said, as the phone rang. 'Gatehouse. Yes, she is.' Sighing. 'One moment, Inspector.'

Merrily sat up, groping for the phone.

'Mr Loste, Merrily.' Bliss coming at her like a fast train hissing from a tunnel. 'If you wanna know, in absolute, pain-of-death confidence, why they've brought him in, listen up, because I don't have much time. You got shorthand?'

'Sophie's is better.'

'Then put me back to Sophie. And this really doesn't go any further than the two of you, understand, or I'll be in more shite than you could ever imagine.'

'Sure.'

'What I'm giving you is a text message received by Raji Khan last night, transmitted from Wicklow's mobile. Read and destroy, then call me back and tell me what you think.'

'Texted *by* Wicklow?'

'Texted, almost certainly, after Wicklow's death by Wicklow's killer or an accomplice and passed on to Howe by Khan in his capacity as an upright citizen. You'll find it fairly unbelievable. Gimme Sophie.'

Merrily handed over the phone and played nervously with her Zippo, watching Sophie reaching for a notepad and pen, beginning to write.

'Sign? Oh, *thine*. I'm sorry . . . continue.'

Arcane Pitman loops and whorls and dots. Everything suddenly moving unintelligibly fast.

'Yes . . . yes . . .' Sophie's eyebrows raised. 'My God, *yes* . . . so it is. No, I won't do that. Thank you, inspector.' She hung up, tore off the top page of her notebook and sat down to transcribe. 'I recognized it at once.'

'Recognized what?'

'Let me finish.'

Sophie reversed the shorthand notebook, pushed it across the desk to Merrily. She'd hand-printed the transcription. 'I was instructed not to put it into the computer.'

*Lord of dread and lord of power*
*This is thine, the fateful hour.*
*When beneath the sacred oak*
*Thrice the sacred charm is spoke,*
*Thrice the sacrificial knife*
*Reddens with a victim's life,*
*Thrice the mystic dance is led*
*Round the altar where they bled.*

'What is it? Merrily looked up. 'Black Sabbath?'

'It's ...' Sophie frowned '... Elgar, I'm afraid. His librettist, anyway. It's an extract from the cantata we discussed.'

'*The Dream of*—? It can't be.'

'*Gerontius* is an oratorio,' Sophie said with no sarcasm. 'Of a kind. The cantata is *Caractacus*.'

'Oh. The one set on...'

'Herefordshire Beacon. British Camp.'

'Bloody hell.'

'Literally. The passage relates to where Caractacus, facing his final confrontation with the Romans, is directed by various prophecies from what you might call Druids of the old school. The libretto ... particularly on paper, it lacks a certain subtlety of expression. Elgar wasn't famous then. It was written by a neighbour, a Mr Acworth. A retired civil servant, as I recall.'

'And this bollocks was texted to Khan?'

> ... *the sacrificial knife*
> *Reddens with a victim's life*

Merrily stood up and turned to the window: Broad Street traffic, T-shirts, summer frocks.

Inn Ya Face.

The phone went again and Sophie took it, her reading glasses dropping down on their chain. She wasn't on long.

'I'll tell her,' she said. 'If I see her. Thank you.' When she looked up at Merrily, her face was creasing with an unexpected, almost motherly concern. 'You can't react to everything.'

'Just tell me.'

'Detective Chief Inspector Howe's office. She would like to meet you in Wychehill later this afternoon.'

'Howe wants to see *me*?'

'The sergeant said she very much hopes it will be convenient.'

'Which means if I don't show there'll be a police car outside the vicarage at some ungodly hour.'

'I'm sorry, Merrily.'

What the hell was *this* about? Merrily sat down, laid her palms on the desk, took two long breaths and called Bliss back.

'No idea,' Bliss said. 'But whatever the bitch wants, you keep me well out of it. What do you reckon about the text?'

'If it wasn't so bad it'd be creepy. How many people would recognize the words of an Elgar cantata?'

'In the Malverns,' Sophie murmured, 'about four thousand.'

'Not a great many rival dealers,' Bliss said. 'That's for sure. We must be looking at one of the principal reasons for them picking up Mr Loste.'

'Maybe he's just advising them, as an exper— No. Sorry, I'm overtired. It was texted to Raji Khan personally?'

'To the Royal Oak landline.'

'Would that work?'

'You can text a landline and the message gets read out over the phone.'

'Loste has an oak,' Merrily said.

'Sorry?'

'I just thought. Loste has an oak planted in his front garden.'

'That's uncommon?'

'It is when your garden's barely big enough for a dwarf apple-tree. A lot of oaks here, that's all I was thinking. Sacrificial oak. Royal Oak . . .'

'And the oak was the sacred tree of the Druids. Even I know that. What does it tell us?'

'I don't know. Maybe Annie Howe does?'

'You know,' Bliss said, 'if it turns out Annie's pulled the right man within just a few hours . . . I'd really hate that.'

When Merrily got back from the health-food shop with some hard-looking bean and chick-pea pasties, Sophie was printing out a document.

'Didn't take long to find her.'

It was from Amazon.

Most popular results for Dr C. Winchester Sparke.

*Homing* (trade paperback, March 2004)

*A Healer's Diary* (with Declan Flynn, hardback, October 2001)

*Life-defining: a self-help tutor* (paperback, June 2000.)

*Legacy of the Golden Dawn* (paperback, reissued 2002)

'A writer,' Merrily said. 'It makes sense. I wondered what an American woman was doing living in the Malverns on her own. Kept meaning to ask people, but it never . . . A writer can live anywhere.'

'All her books appear to fall under the general heading of Mind, Body and Spirit,' Sophie said, with faint distaste, 'so I'm not sure how seriously we can take the *Doctor*.'

'New Age. She comes over as very . . . almost archetypally New Age.'

'Be careful,' Sophie said.

# 25

# Village Idiot

WINNIE SPARKE CUPPED HER hands, drank from the holy spring and then looked up at Merrily, holy water rippling down her face, hands pushing her wet curls back over both ears.

For a moment she looked stricken and feral, like some captured wood nymph.

'You have to help me. He'll die in there, I'm not kidding.'

Inside the nineteenth-century gabled building which enclosed the Holy Well, the once-sacred healing water ran from a thin plastic pipe into a stone sink. On the floor, a red cross was marked out in tiles. On the wall above the pipe someone had scrawled, in black, *The Goddess For Ever.*

Neo-pagan graffiti. Up in the wooded hills on the outskirts of town, it all seemed a little sad, a New Age fringe thing, no longer part of mainstream Malvern.

'You have contacts in the police, I know you do,' Winnie Sparke said. 'You have to get it over to them that Tim didn't do this thing.'

Like Wychehill on a grand scale, Great Malvern clung to the sides of hills, its houses and shops and public buildings like the seats in a long stadium with the vast Severn Plain as its arena. The difference being that the real action had been up here, where a village had grown into a fashionable resort town founded on a Victorian faith in the curative powers of spring water.

Now all that was long over, and Great Malvern was just a busy town with heavy scenery. Steep streets, an historic priory church built of exotically coloured stones, a good theatre and most of the wells and springs hidden away. Nowadays, if you wanted to drink the pure, healing water you were advised by the health police to boil it first, C. Winchester Sparke had said in disgust.

'Like, nobody understands any more. Nobody gets it about the energy of springs. The water's gushing and gurgling all through these rocks, like a blood supply, and nobody's *revelling* in it any more. It's become repressed, stifled . . . like the long-forgotten Wychehill well.'

'There was a well at Wychehill?' Merrily said.

'According to legend. Hell, more than that – according to *history*. There was this holy well at Wychehill that was supposed to have stopped flowing and nobody knows where it is. My theory is that it was blocked during the damn quarrying. Explains a lot about Wychehill.'

Winnie Sparke had said they had to meet here because Wychehill had too many furtive, prying eyes. Including Annie Howe's this afternoon, Merrily thought, so it wasn't a bad idea. They were lone pilgrims at the Holy Well. She'd found Winnie sitting on its steps, wearing a white summer dress and a cardigan decorated with ancient Egyptian figures making camp hand gestures.

'Why would they *think* he killed this man, Dr Sparke?'

Merrily stood in the doorway arch, looking down at the trees softening the vast green vista of the plain. Obviously, she couldn't tell Winnie Sparke about the text.

'Please don't call me Dr Sparke. People over here, an American called Dr Something, they think you purchased it off the web for like thirty dollars?' Winnie smiled wanly through the water-glaze. 'There's a public bridleway across there.'

'With a park bench,' Merrily said. 'Do you mind if we sit on the bench? I didn't get to bed until first light.'

'OK, we'll sit on the bench. Whatever. It's just I'm feeling like I need to move, make things take off . . . This is a very stressful time.'

In full daylight, Winnie looked older. A woman well into middle age but with good skin and good hair. They walked down from the Holy Well, across a small parking area and on to the bridleway, which sloped scenically away into the trees. They sat on the bench.

'I'm sorry, I don't really know . . . you and Tim Loste?'

'Friends. And fellow searchers. Tim came to Wychehill for a

purpose. He had an inheritance which allowed him to throw up his teaching job and pursue his ... calling.'

Merrily waited. The sun, hidden for most of the day, was now warm on her face.

'Elgar. People keep calling it an obsession – I hate that word, it implies a sickness rather than a penetrating, inspirational, creative *focus*. Is it so bad to be driven?'

'Depends what you're driven towards, I suppose.'

'Towards what drove Elgar. What made him into the greatest composer these islands ever had.'

'And does Tim Loste *know* what that was?'

'Oh, sure. I believe we've gotten close to that. The results will be Tim's own piece for orchestra and choir, with a divine theme, involving Elgar himself as a character. A major work about the stress and agony leading up to the realization of a great and beautiful mystery.'

'And your part is ... ?'

'I get to write the words, the libretto.'

Winnie looked away, at the view.

'And what *is* the mystery?'

'It's a *mystery*,' Winnie said. 'Hell, if we were in Wychehill, I wouldn't even be telling you this much. But, believe me, it's an awesome thing.'

'You don't like Wychehill?'

'I like my cottage. I like my views, I love the Malverns. No, I don't like Wychehill the way it is right now. I bought in a hurry after my divorce, and at some stage I'm gonna move on. I'm being frank with you. See, in Wychehill, they regard Tim not as a precious, fragile talent but as some kind of village idiot, a liability. You ask people there, like that asshole Holliday, if *they* think he killed the guy on the hill they'll go, sure why not ... look at the history.'

'I heard he ... smashed a window at the Royal Oak?'

'Oh wow, a window, yeah.' Winnie sighed. 'Sure, he did that. And got himself caught and beat up on by the muscle there. Who told you about that? Syd?'

A worrying idea settled on Merrily like cold air around her shoulders.

'Who exactly . . . who was it beat him up, do you know?'

'The muscle! They have these doormen who— Oh.' Winnie's head began to nod like a dog ornament on a car's rear-window shelf. 'OK, right, now I see where you're coming from. You think this guy, Roland . . .'

'Roman.'

'OK. Look, maybe it was him, maybe it wasn't, I wouldn't know. Only the cops could think that was significant. Truth of it is, Tim wouldn't even remember who it was beat up on him. The night it happened – two, three months ago? – he was up on the Beacon trying to puzzle something out in his work, and the wind was in the wrong direction, blew it up the hill, this techno, hip-hop shit – *barbaric*, he called it, like an invasion. He couldn't shut it out. It was filling up his head and he went a little crazy.'

'He'd been drinking?'

'I'm working on that.' Winnie Sparke looked down. 'I'm trying to clean it out of him with meditation.'

'What happened next?' Merrily said.

'He coulda just walked away. He can walk seven, eight miles up there on a clear night, I've known him do that. But . . . he stormed off down to the Royal Oak, took a rock out the wall, and he hurled it through a window. And then he like . . . he just stood there on the parking lot, screaming like a mad person. Like, if it was me, I'd've put the damn rock through the glass, run like hell. He just stood there screaming. Like he *wanted* them to come out for him. I guess he has a certain masochistic streak. And they obliged, my God, did they oblige . . .'

'He was badly hurt?'

'Those guys don't pull punches and they hit where it doesn't show. It was lucky Helen – the roving nurse? – was passing in her car, and she went to fetch Syd and they pulled him out, took him home. Didn't leave the house for five days. I wanted to have a doctor check him over, but he said . . . he refused. I guess the main damage was emotional.

Spiritual. He became depressed, couldn't work for maybe two weeks. But hey, *nobody* could think he'd take such an *extreme . . .*'

Winnie's dark eyes were shining hot and bruised under the heavy curls.

'I checked you out. On the Church of England Deliverance website. Also, some news stories. A lot happened to you, very quickly. Guess that was to do with being a woman in this job. Not too many women exorcists?'

'Not many, no.' Merrily anticipated the way this might be going. 'Maybe I'll write a book about it. In about thirty years.'

Winnie smiled ruefully in the shadows of her hair.

'Wicklow . . .' Merrily groped for a way of putting this without mentioning the text message. 'Roman Wicklow's body was found on what's called the Sacrificial Stone. Nobody seems to be sure whether it ever was that, but it's . . . obviously in a place immortalized in Elgar's *Caractacus*, as the site of Druidic blood rituals. It wouldn't be too hard for the police to see connections. I mean, the music Tim Loste puts on with his choir in the church. Obviously Elgar, but . . . ?'

'They did *Caractacus* once.' Winnie Sparke looked down at her hands, still wet, in her lap. 'OK. Tim is director of an amateur choir made up of men and women from all over the three counties. They did *Caractacus*, with incomplete instrumentation, and in spite of all of that it was pretty awesome. Tim wanted to stage it, open-air, on the Beacon, tap into that original energy, but the expense ruled it out. And the logistics. Getting an orchestra up there? And if it rained? And, worse than that, what if there was some rave thing on at the Oak, at the same time? Some nights, the amplified sound carries miles, drowns the valley.'

'I imagine it must've become the bane of his life, that pub?'

Winnie Sparke gave Merrily a hard look, like she was beginning to wonder if she wasn't talking to the wrong person.

'I'm just trying to look at it from the police's point of view,' Merrily said.

'That an artistic guy like Tim Loste could overpower some professional thug and then take out his throat?'

'I don't know . . . anything about him. I don't know how big he is or how old . . .'

'He's a creative person who hates violence, is all.'

They stopped talking while two women on horses clopped past.

'And he wasn't at the meeting at the church last night,' Merrily said. 'I would've expected him to be there.'

'Uh-huh.' Winnie shook her curls. 'I wouldn't let him near the church last night. I came on his behalf. See, when he heard about that meeting, he was scared you were gonna try to work some kind of exorcism . . . to dispel the spirit of Elgar? Me, too. I was just so mad at Syd for bringing in an exorcist, I wanted you to realize the hugeness of this thing you were being asked to do. Like if you'd jumped the wrong way in the church, I was ready to take it to the media – hey, here's the Church of England gonna drive the spirit of Elgar out of his beloved hills?'

'Nobody would dare consider anything like that. There'd be a national outcry.'

'Yeah, you say that now. But if you saw Tim, the state he was in, believe me, you might've been ready to look at something drastic. He needed . . . he needed to calm down some.'

'So *you* told him to stay away.'

'I was scared he'd start yelling, say something stupid.'

'Where did you find him, in the end?'

'The place I left him. The one place I could be sure . . . and I'm not gonna tell you, OK? You don't need to know that.'

'The police might need to. If you can prove he couldn't have been anywhere near the Beacon when—'

'I *can't* prove it, I wasn't with him, OK?' Winnie looked away. 'I can't talk to cops, their minds run on narrow rails.' She stood up. 'I'm sorry, I need to walk.'

Merrily followed her along the bridleway, thinking that the Malverns weren't exactly wild any more; few areas of this long, bumpy spine were unreachable by well-used footpaths.

'The gentle heart of England,' Winnie Sparke said. 'Miles of fertile, tranquil lowland . . . and then, suddenly, you have these volcanic rocks.

Like a long altar rising from the plain of the Severn. And, you see, *that* ... is precisely what it was – a place of spiritual significance since the Stone Age. To the early Christians, a dark place.'

'You mean a stronghold of pagan worship?'

'Still rich in stories of curses and the devil. So I guess what you had was a wilderness place for early Christian hermits to test their faith. A retreat for hermits and seers and prophets, riddled with springs – life-force. And I guess what you have now, Merrily – battered, hacked-at and under-esteemed – is the remains of an altar.'

'An altar to Elgar?'

'Sure, for some people. Hell, for a *lot* of people. But where was Elgar's altar?'

'I'm not sure what you mean.'

'He pulled music from out the air. He used to say that.'

'And he listened to the trees.'

'He had a thing going with trees,' Winnie said. 'This is true. I'll explain all this to you one day, but not right now. I ...' She took Merrily's arm. 'You're a spiritual person. Syd, too, but Syd was a soldier and he doesn't talk about it.'

'He's a priest. He *has* to talk about it.'

'He doesn't talk about himself. You don't know how he's reacting. Sure, he's helped Tim, but that doesn't mean he understands.'

'And you're a writer.'

'It's a living,' Winnie said. 'Just about. Listen, I ... Thank you for hearing me out. We can be friends, right?'

'I hope so.'

'I don't have too many friends in Wychehill. It's like I said about the rocks. Wychehill's built on a place hacked out from the rocks. A great open wound, prone to infection. Part of what Tim's doing at the church, with the music ... it's about that.'

'Healing the rocks?'

'As a priest, you should maybe think about that. Meantime, you remember what I said about Tim. And you tell ... whoever ... that wherever they're holding him they should look out for him, you know what I'm saying? Day and night.'

*

Merrily had just a few minutes to get back to Wychehill to meet Annie Howe, for whatever reason. Only about three miles, so no problem. She drove past the British Camp car park at the foot of the Beacon, where two marked police cars were on display. Also, outside the hotel across the road, a bill for the *Worcester Evening News* which read: HUNT ON FOR MALVERN RITUAL KILLER.

Maybe the holding of Tim Loste was not yet official. But he looked far more guilty to Merrily now than he had before she'd spoken to Winnie Sparke.

# 26

# Weight of the Ancestors

ON THE COMPUTER IN the scullery, Jane tapped in the URL that Eirion had dictated. She found, with an unexpected sense of shock and dismay, the picture of herself looking what he'd described as *pissed-off but sexy*. Behind her, Cole Hill was serene and enigmatic in its morning gauze of bright mist.

Oh God, *why* had she let him talk her into this? Probably all that stuff about the firm young breasts inside the school blouse. Underneath, she was just a whore.

'Yeah, got it,' she said into the mobile. 'What site *is* this?'

'EMA,' Eirion said. 'Earth Mysteries Affiliates. It's a campaigning outfit – kind of a mystical Greenpeace. Didn't waste any time, did they? But then it's probably the best story they've had all year.'

Under the picture, it said: *Jane Watkins – fighting for Alfred's ley.* Below that, the hand-drawn map that she and Eirion had scanned, showing all the points on the Cole Hill line.

'But it's only been up a few hours. How could the *Guardian* have got on to it so soon?'

'They wouldn't have. What's obviously happened is that one of the guys who runs the EMA site saw there was a potential news story here and scored himself a tip-off fee. I mean, *I* could've tried that, but the papers are never as interested if it comes from the people involved – just looks like you're desperate for publicity.'

Eirion was at home in Abergavenny. He'd left school early; you could apparently do that on the smallest excuse when your final days as a schoolkid were ebbing away.

'I'm not sure I am now,' Jane said.

'Not sure you're what?'

'Desperate for publicity.'

Feeling a little intimidated, to be honest. She told him about Morrell.

'Jane, you can't have it both ways. You *started* this. When are you going to call him back?'

'The *Guardian* guy? Don't know whether I am. I mean, the national press? Like, I thought it was OK pissing off the council, but that bitch can really damage me. And Mum, probably.'

'I doubt it,' Eirion said. 'She's only a councillor, isn't she? A servant of democracy.'

'*She* doesn't think she's a servant. Vice-chair of education? She thinks that's serious power. It's obvious she went straight to Morrell and told him that one of his students was making trouble for her mates.'

'It's the way they work. He's their employee. But she couldn't *really* threaten him. Least, I don't think she could.'

'Irene, Morrell is, like, insanely ambitious, and he's quite young. Moorfield's just a stepping stone. He's not going to offend a powerful councillor for the sake of one student ... who he hates and would really like to get rid of anyway.'

'You don't *know* that.'

'You've never seen him! All right ... what should I do?'

There was a silence.

Come *on*, there shouldn't be a silence! Eirion's dad was a BBC governor in Wales and he had a cousin who was news editor on the *Western Mail* in Cardiff. Eirion was, like, totally steeped in the media.

'I don't know,' Eirion said.

'Thanks.'

'Let me think about it. I'll call you back.'

'Soon?'

'Soon. I'm sorry, Jane.'

'It's OK.'

She sat staring at the screen, feeling terminally forlorn.

*Jane Watkins – fighting for Alfred's ley.* As Lol had pointed out, there was no proof that it was Alfred's ley. Alfred might not even have known about it. Or, worse, he might have discounted it. There could be some element here that totally disqualified Coleman's Meadow. Just because it *looked* right . . .

Could be she'd stitched herself up.

Jane couldn't face looking at that smug pout any more and switched off the computer. Just sat there waiting, dolefully stroking Ethel who was sitting in the in-tray. Best thing would be to leave it for a day or two, give the dust time to settle.

On the other hand, the planning committee would be meeting next week to make a decision on Coleman's Meadow.

Sure, she could leave it. She could walk away and spend the rest of her life regretting it, despising her own cowardice.

Or she could take some more time off school, in open defiance of her head teacher, and follow it through, because . . .

. . . Forget earth-energy, forget spirit paths; at the very least, whether Alfred Watkins had known about it or not, this was a rare alignment of ancient sacred sites which had somehow survived for maybe . . .

. . . Four thousand years?

Four thousand years of mystical tradition against one more year of schooling for somebody who wasn't sure whether she even wanted to go to university at the end of it.

Jane felt the weight of the ancestors on her shoulders.

This was probably one of those situations where Mum would go to the church and pray for guidance – Jane thinking that if she did that, after all she'd said over the years, it would at least give God the best laugh he'd had since he hit the Egyptians with a plague of locusts.

The scullery phone rang.

'Look, Irene,' Jane said, 'I've been thinking—'

'Jane, I'm really sorry . . .'

'Oh. Mum.'

'I'm also sorry for not being Eirion. Listen, flower, you can probably guess what's coming.'

'You have to go back to Malvern. Don't call me flower.'

'Right. I'm sorry. I'm there now, and I have someone else to meet. Will you be OK?'

'Sure. I've already fed Ethel. I'll get something for me later.'

'Is everything all right?'

'Everything's fine.'

'I won't be late. I promise I won't be late this time.'

'Honestly, take as long as you like,' Jane said.

She hung up and felt tearful. Felt like a stupid, ineffectual kid who got caught up in fads and crazes and thought she was so smart and spiritually developed but, faced with a crunch situation, didn't basically have the nerve to follow through.

# 27

# Bugger-All

TIM LOSTE'S HOUSE. The heart of the enigma.

A flat, grey Victorian or Edwardian town house that just happened to have been built in the country. A tiny front garden held in by iron railings. An oak tree that shouldn't be here.

Merrily stepped into the house called Caractacus with some trepidation and an uncomfortable sense of déjà vu. Well, not quite, because she knew where this feeling was coming from, remembering when Bliss had invited her to the home of a suspected serial murderer obsessed with the Cromwell Street killings. All black sheets and pin-up pictures of dead celebrities.

'Stay with me,' Annie Howe said, 'and don't touch anything. We've been over it forensically, but— *What?*'

'Nothing,' Merrily said.

In the dim, narrow, camphor-smelling hallway, she'd come face to face with a dead celebrity.

He was life-size, in bowler hat and hacking jacket. Standing there behind his black, yard-brush moustache and the high handlebars of Mr Phoebus, as if he was about to wheel the bicycle out of the shadows towards the front door.

'Yes, rather startling at first, isn't it?' Howe said.

The black and white photograph, massively blown-up, had been fixed to a wooden frame and propped up against the end wall of the passage so that it filled almost the full width, and when you came in by the front door you were looking directly into the grainy eyes.

Of all the pictures of Elgar, why this one? Merrily had the feeling that the huge, stately Mr Phoebus, important to Elgar, was also very important to Tim Loste: a bike that meant business, could take Elgar anywhere, a symbol of the mobility of the spirit.

It still didn't have a lamp.

'What are you thinking?' Annie Howe said.

'Just wondering what I'm doing here.'

Howe said. 'My understanding is that you've been here two or three times in the past few days.'

'I've never been *here*, before.'

'In the village, then. Before and possibly even during the murder of Roman Wicklow. So I thought I'd like to hear about the purpose of your visits.'

'Don't you know?'

'Well, frankly, the version of it that one of my officers was told seemed too ridiculous.'

'Even for me, huh?'

Merrily had come directly to Loste's cottage because this was where the police car was parked, along with a silver BMW, presumably Howe's. There had been a uniformed constable at the gate and Howe, in a mid-grey cotton suit, had been in the front garden, examining the oak sapling. Her fine, light hair was clipped close to her skull, her make-up minimal. Jane had once said she looked like a Nazi dentist. Unfair. Sort of.

Howe opened a panelled door to the right, stepping back.

'Living room. If you take a careful look around perhaps you could tell me if there's anything there that strikes as much of a chord for you as the Elgar blow-up evidently did.'

An atmosphere like a faded sepia photograph and more old photographs hanging from a wooden picture rail all around the mustard-coloured walls. Some of them were portraits of Elgar, some landscapes – Merrily recognized Stonehenge and Glastonbury Tor, but the rest were less easy: unknown hill scenery, might be Malverns, might not. Also churches, none of them obvious, no Hereford or Worcester cathedral, no Malvern Priory.

Over the tiled fireplace was a large framed photo of an obvious oak tree, a huge and ancient one, bulging black against the light. It was the only one in colour, but all the colour was in the sky. On the mantelpiece below it was a scattering of acorns and a bottle of whisky, half empty.

Howe looked at Merrily.

*When beneath the sacred oak.* Obvious where Howe was coming from. But what could Merrily, add to it? Nothing. She was mystified.

'Well, he ... clearly has a fascination with oak trees, Annie. But I expect your well-honed deductive skills had told you that already.'

On the way in, she'd spotted a line of what she'd thought were potted plants until she'd noticed the leaves. Somehow, she felt this was Winnie Sparke's doing, filling the place – filling Tim's life – with oak trees. Why? Druidry, *Caractacus*? What was this *about*?

'Maybe he can get some kind of weird buzz by smoking acorns or something,' Merrily said and then regretted it. Howe was in there.

'So what exactly have you heard about Mr Loste and illegal drugs?'

'*Nothing* ... I was being ...' Merrily sighed. 'Facetious. Something about you brings out the child in me.'

She looked around. There was a long writing desk with a musical score on it and an empty whisky bottle in the footwell. A bookcase, a CD cabinet. Two leather easy chairs but no television or radio.

'I mean ... what do you want me to say? He has a thing about oaks. How that ties in with the *Royal* Oak I have no idea. Is that one of the reasons you've nicked him?'

Howe said, 'Do you know of a connection between oaks and Elgar?'

'No, do you?'

Howe took down a book with pages marked by luminous Post-it stickers. It was a biography of Elgar, whose name, as far as Merrily could see, occurred on the spine of virtually every volume in the bookcase. Howe opened it out on the writing desk. A paragraph was marked by a pencil line.

*In July 1918, about two months after the Elgars had moved to Brinkwells, they were visited by their friend Algernon Blackwood, writer of ghost stories. Elgar took Blackwood to see a copse of, according to Alice Elgar, 'sinister' trees which were said – although Blackwood, may have invented this – to have once been Spanish monks punished for practising black magic. Elgar found them fascinating.*

Merrily looked up. 'Doesn't say they were oak trees. Where's Brinkwells?'

'Sussex.'

'*Sussex?*'

'Elgar lived there for a while before returning to Worcestershire.'

'So what does that tell us? Anything at all?'

'Evidently not.' Howe shut the book. 'But it was the only marked page in any of the books that wasn't self-explanatory.'

'I don't get it. What are you looking for, exactly?'

'Part of your . . . curious job, as I understand it, Ms Watkins, is to monitor the activities of religious cults.'

'Wouldn't put it that strongly.'

'Are there practising Druids in the area that you're aware of?'

'There are Druids everywhere. It's a popular form of paganism. No strict rules, no dogma, dress optional.'

'And the veneration of oak trees.'

'That's traditional. And still valid, sure. But if you want me to look around here and tell you that Tim Loste is an obvious Druid, I'd say it was far from obvious . . . and even unlikely, unless you've found robes and pentacles and stuff in his wardrobe.'

Howe said nothing. Merrily was reminded of those infamous satanic child-abuse investigations of the 1980s and 1990s when McCarthyite social workers would seize, as damning evidence, any fragment of conceivably occult paraphernalia, like a broomstick in the broom cupboard or a video of *Rosemary's Baby*.

'Also, modern Druids don't practise human sacrifice. They tend towards vegetarianism.'

'Not historically, however.'

Evidently still trying to stitch something onto that texted quote from the choral work after which this house was named.

'Have you asked *him* where this sudden interest in oaks comes from? Well, of course you have, but what did he say?'

'He said nothing. He froze up on me. Why do you think I'm here asking you?'

'I *dunno.*' Merrily shook her head. 'You've got bugger-all, really, haven't you, Annie? You're holding this guy on a few tenuous threads.'

'Let's go outside,' Howe said.

DCI Annie Howe: always a problem here. Howe was an ironclad atheist, therefore suspicious of the clergy and now clearly appalled that modern womanhood should also have descended, at this stage of human evolution, to medieval dressing-up games.

As for Deliverance . . .

There had been one surreal happening, in the heat of midday in a hop yard in the Frome Valley, when the reinforced walls of Howe's scepticism might have been badly breached . . . *if* she'd allowed it. If her reaction had not been flat denial, the whole incident apparently edited from her conscious memory.

Merrily followed her into the overgrown pocket garden, with its centrepiece oak sapling, thinking there was no real reason for Howe to have brought her here. It was as though she had to seize on any opportunity to look Merrily in the face and repeat, wordlessly, *Nothing has ever happened to dent my belief that you are wasting your intelligence on fairy tales.*

They walked to the rear of the house under the galvanized metal car port. Still no car in it. Presumably Loste hadn't got it back yet, after his crash. A small square yard ended at an iron gate opening to a well-trodden mud path leading directly on to the hill – the hill far closer here than in the Rectory garden.

'This is how Loste gets to the Herefordshire Beacon, or indeed into the whole network of Malvern footpaths,' Howe said. 'He spends whole days walking up there, and – I'm told – whole nights sometimes.'

'I think if I had to live in this house I might do that, too,' Merrily said.

'Never locks his back door. Seems to feel a certain . . . ownership.' Howe opened the gate and went through. '*His* hills.'

'Uh-huh.' Merrily shook her head. 'Elgar's.'

'Elgar's dead,' Howe said.

'In a manner of speaking.'

'The music lives on, I suppose. Loste sometimes takes the music with him. He has an MP3 player containing, I'd guess, everything Elgar ever wrote, some of it repeated with different orchestras, soloists, et cetera.'

'And that could be a bit mind-blowing, you think?' Merrily stepped onto the path. 'Up on the Beacon, head full of *Caractacus*, Druids chanting about human sacrifice? Something explodes in his brain and he goes for the nearest drug dealer with a knife he just happens to have on him?'

'You know *Caractacus*, Ms Watkins?'

'Sophie knows it. Sophie in the office.'

Howe deliberated for a moment.

'We have – and this is confidential – another link to Loste, relating directly to the concept of Druidic sacrifice as described in *Caractacus*.'

'What kind of link?'

Howe didn't reply.

'I suppose a lot of people around here are likely to know all the gory bits,' Merrily said.

'Not all of these people are as vocal in their opposition to the Royal Oak as Timothy Loste, or as . . . demonstrative.'

'As in throwing a stone through a window?'

'An act of wilful damage as a result of which several people suffered minor injuries. He would, if we'd known about it at the time, have faced charges.'

'If he hadn't been severely beaten up by the injured parties, making them less inclined to *press* charges.'

'One of the men forced to restrain him,' Howe said, 'was Roman Wicklow.'

'You know that for certain now?'

'We've spoken to both of the other doormen, who've signed statements to that effect, also providing us with a full and graphic description of Loste's behaviour that night and some of the threats issued by him during the struggle.'

'Oh.'

'So you see we don't quite have *bugger-all*.'

'No.'

Merrily looked away, up the steep path into the hills, soon barricaded by hard blue sky. It didn't look that good for Tim Loste, did it? No longer seemed like a case of Howe's people going for the easy option first, to save laboriously unravelling strands of rivalry in the West Midland drug community. She wondered how she was going to bring up the suggestion that the police should keep a serious eye on Loste for as long as he was in their care because of the risk of suicide or self-harming.

'What about blood on his clothes? Forensic evidence . . . DNA?'

'We should have some results tomorrow morning,' Howe said. 'I think it likely that they'll enable us to move on to the next stage.'

She stepped onto a small tump by a gorse bush, looked down to the road where another police car was pulling in. Looked down at Merrily.

'Right. I've been as open as I possibly can with you, Ms Watkins. I've put my cards on the table. I'd now like you to reciprocate. I'd like you to tell me – off the record for the present – exactly why you were called to Wychehill and what you know about the night Timothy Loste crashed his car into a telegraph pole.'

'I wasn't there.'

'*I* don't care if you were there or not – I'm looking for background information, not a witness statement. Gossip, if you like. I'm trying to get a picture of his mental condition, and my information is that he's so obsessed with the late Edward Elgar that he's seeing the man's ghost around every corner.'

'I'd say that's an exaggeration. And, as far as that particular ghost story goes, he's not the only one. At least, that's the basis on which I was asked to look into it.'

'Yes,' Howe said, 'we do know about the other one.'

'Also, you and I . . . we wouldn't necessarily agree on what claiming to have seen a ghost says about someone's state of mind.'

'I can think of very little that we'd agree on,' Howe said.

'And apart from anything, we're talking about an artist, a professional dreamer. Which, in his line of work, is not necessarily a pejorative term. *Elgar* was a dreamer, Loste is supposed to be writing a musical work *about* Elgar.'

'You know what? I'm getting bloody sick of this.' Annie Howe came down from the mound, her scrubbed face actually colouring. 'As if all so-called artists were wispy little tree-huggers. Have you ever *seen* Timothy Loste?'

'I've tried, Annie. God knows I've tried.'

'Then I'll describe him for you. Loste is forty years old and, despite his alcohol problem, extremely fit. Has been known to walk virtually the length of the Malverns and back within a day by a different route. Knows those hills like the back of his hand, every rock and cave and crevice.'

'Yes, but that hardly—'

'At the Royal Oak that night, as I may have implied, it took three experienced doormen to subdue him . . . as he's also about half a head taller than Wicklow was. And built, Ms Watkins, like the side of a house. Oh, and the rock he put through that window was, at a rough estimate, the size of a small television set and maybe twice as heavy.'

'Oh.'

'Now tell me again that we're talking about a harmless, inoffensive little dreamer with a natural abhorrence of violence.'

A buzzard passed silently overhead. A uniformed policeman appeared in the garden.

'They've been trying to get you, ma'am.'

Howe lifted her head. 'Thanks, Robert. I'm coming now.'

If she was going to be head of CID for the proposed new Midlands mega-force before turning forty she didn't have any time to waste.

Watching Howe talking tersely into her mobile, listening and nodding, *functioning*, Merrily felt useless, irrelevant. Chasing shadows, chasing lights. Sometimes it seemed that deliverance amounted to little more than this.

People nudging one another. *Who's that? What does she do? Oh, you're kidding* . . . Her role nebulous, her focus blurred. Why *was* she here? Who, in the end, would be healed?

What was clear, however, was that nobody else would try too hard to make sense of Loste, his obsession with Elgar, his oak-tree fetish.

Oaks. Sacred oaks. The Royal Oak. Too many oaks. Did any of this link into the history or even the folklore of the area? It wasn't as if there was some ancient resident whose memory she could tap into. Nobody had lived here longer than a quarter of a century.

Well . . . except for one person.

Not someone she particularly wanted to approach, but . . .

Merrily slipped away, knowing that Annie Howe, having failed to get anything useful out of her, would have forgotten by now that she'd even been here.

28

# Curse Came Down

THE NAME ON THE gate was *Old Wychehill Farm*, suggesting that perhaps this was what remained of the original hamlet, while the present village was just fragments of a repair job for a quarry-ravaged hill.

In fact, Old Wychehill Farm was big enough to have been a hamlet in itself. Sunk into its own valley, half-circled by mature broadleaf trees with the swizzle-stick profiles of pines and monkey puzzles poking out of the mix.

The farmhouse, at the end of nearly half a mile of private drive, turned out to be the turreted house in the valley which Merrily had noticed that first morning – the turret crowning a Victorian Gothic wing added to a much older dwelling with timbers like age-browned bones.

She parked in the farmyard – courtyard, really. No animals in view, no free-range chickens. The three-storey house was enclosed by outbuildings of the same grey-brown stone. Some of the more distant buildings had curtains at their diamond-paned windows.

*My lovely holiday lets.*

A black pick-up truck eased in behind her. A stylish truck with chrome side-rails and silver flashes on its flanks. Two men getting out, squinting into the sun, one of them strolling across.

'Help you?'

'Looking for Mr Devereaux.'

'Which one?'

'Preston Devereaux?'

The man stood looking her up and down, pinching his unshaven chin.

'Shame about that.'

Apart from golden highlights and a sharper jawline, he looked a lot like Preston Devereaux. Same narrow features, same loose, unhurried gait as he'd wandered over. Except this guy was over thirty years younger and the other one was the younger son, Hugo.

'Louis, this is Mrs Watkins,' Hugo said.

'*Merrily.*' The face of Louis Devereaux, former huntsman, alleged former substance-abuser, split into this voracious and undeniably attractive grin. 'And *we*'re stuck with Spicer. The injustice of it.' Louis turned to his brother. 'You better go and find the old man. No hurry. Want to come with me, Merrily?'

'Is it safe?'

'I'm a country gentleman,' Louis said, 'from a long, long line of country gentlemen. Of course it isn't safe.'

He strode past her across the yard, turning the handle on a plain door. It didn't open; it was jammed at the bottom. He gave it a kick.

'Whole place is seizing up.'

His accent was posher than his father's. Probably been away to public school. She looked up at him as he held open the door.

'I really won't keep him long.'

'He might want to keep *you*, though,' Louis said. 'I would. End of the passage, look.' He bent down, put an arm around her shoulders, pointing. 'The Beacon Room.'

Following her into the passage. There was an old manure smell, as if this entrance had been used for the changing of generations of farm boots. It was a rear hallway, low, earth-coloured, windowless, the only light funnelled down the well of some narrow back stairs to her left . . . until she pushed open the door at the end into lavish sunshine from a long window framing a *wow-gasp* view of the great tiered wedding-cake of Herefordshire Beacon.

The Beacon Room. Obviously built into the Victorian wing to accommodate this view. The hill was a couple of miles away, as if it had been aligned for maximum impact.

'Quite impressive, isn't it?' Louis said. 'As crime scenes go. Lit up like a housing estate last night. Cops swarming all over it.'

'Exciting?'

'Yeah, I guess it was. I suppose when it's somebody you don't know ... Well, I've probably *seen* him, if he's the one I think he is. At the Oak.'

'You go there?'

'Now and then. Not as often as I used to. Quite good for ... you know ... girls.'

'I can imagine.'

'And, of course, for pissing off Len Holliday and the Wychehill Residents' Action Group,' Louis said. 'One tries to sympathize, but that guy ...'

'Don't suppose you're really aware of the Royal Oak down here. Or the road.'

'Don't suppose we are, particularly,' Louis said.

She looked around the room. Lofty, wood-panelled, definitely a man's room, even a young man's room – minimal furniture apart from stereo speakers the size of small wardrobes. Racks of CDs and vinyl and potentially interesting framed photographs. Over the baronial fireplace was a period poster behind glass advertising The Pink Floyd and The Crazy World of Arthur Brown at the Roundhouse in London. The names were wreathed in coloured smoke from a pipe smoked by a reclining naked man like some stoned 1960s version of Michelangelo's Adam.

*I was a wild boy, too. Drove too fast, inhaled my share of blow.*

On the panelled wall over a writing desk with a worn leather top there was a framed black and white photo of a bunch of young long-haired men, one of whom was ... Eric Clapton? The lean, grinning guy on the end was also unmistakable. He looked like Louis Devereaux with longer hair and lush sideburns.

'Blimey,' Merrily said. 'Is that—?'

'Dad was very well connected. Once upon a time.'

'Images of a misspent youth, Mrs Watkins.'

Merrily jumped. Preston Devereaux was standing in the doorway, an older, duller figure than she remembered from the other night, a working man wearing a farmer's green nylon overalls and a nylon cap.

'Didn't know him well,' he said. 'But you don't throw away a picture like that, do you?'

'Were you in a band?'

'Never had the talent. Managed a couple, when I was up at Oxford in the late 1960s. Which meant carrying the amps, back then, and inventing light shows. I was good at that.'

'Oh Gawd, Memory Lane time,' Louis said. 'I'm out of here.'

He bowed to Merrily, made an exaggerated exit.

'Twenty-four next week,' Devereaux said. 'Going on ten.'

'If ten means pre-pubertal, I'm not sure I'd agree. What were you doing at Oxford?'

'Physics.'

'So ... what happened? I mean ...'

'What happened?' Devereaux walked over to the Beacon window. '*That* happened. History. Roots. No escape. You think there is, but there en't. Anyway ...'

He stood in front of Merrily, hands behind his back.

'No escape for me either, Mr Devereaux. What you said the other night about dealing with something in a discreet and dignified fashion ...'

'Have you?'

Merrily shook her head.

'Become too complicated. When you've had a man murdered, and when the local man under suspicion of having killed him—'

'*Local man?*' Preston Devereaux almost left the ground. 'There are no *local men* up there, Mrs Watkins. Why I was forced to come back.'

'I'm sorry.'

'No, *I'm* sorry. Continue.'

'I was just going to say that the man suspected of murder is also the man I most needed to talk to about ... the cyclist.'

'You *can* say Elgar in here, Merrily.'

'Thank you. Anyway, it means I haven't been able to get to Loste. And in the meantime, other questions have opened up.'

'Like?'

'He was the first to identify the image in the road as Elgar. He's obsessed with Elgar. He apparently hates what the Royal Oak has become.'

'So I understand, yes.'

'If his hatred of the Royal Oak has now led to a murder, I don't . . . well, I don't know how relevant that makes my idea of a requiem for two road-accident victims. And I do appreciate that one woman agonizing over the technicalities of a church service must seem entirely trivial to you . . .'

'So what do you want me to do?'

'You're . . . as you've just implied, you're the only person whose experience of this area goes back longer than about twenty years. I'd just like to get your opinion on a few things. Memory Lane, I'm afraid.'

'Memory Lane. With all its potholes and its road kill.'

Preston Devereaux went back and shut the door. Above it were three wooden shields, one bearing a coat of arms and a motto in Latin. Each of the others, on either side, displayed a fox's head, neither of them moth-eaten the way foxes' heads usually were in these displays. Mementoes, perhaps, of Louis's carefree youth.

Devereaux strode back to the Beacon window, pulling off his cap.

'Must be the most spectacular view in the Malverns,' Merrily said.

'Hated it, Merrily. With a vengeance. A forsaken stronghold, symbol of defeat. Turned my back on it and everything that the Malverns'd come to stand for, all the starchy gentility of it. And then my father died.'

'When was that?'

'Back end of '85. You learn that a farm that's been in your family since the Conquest, that's a family curse you can't lose. And periodically the curse strikes, giving you a little reminder that it *is* a curse. Like in the 1980s, when you had new patterns in farm subsidy, new regulations, the EC. Getting so a farmer didn't feel he owned his own land. My old man could see that was only the beginning. Which partly explains why he strung himself up in the tower.'

'Oh . . .' Merrily's gaze went instinctively to the ceiling. 'I didn't know. I'm sorry.'

'Which effectively did for my glittering future as a career scientist. Doing research at the time, bit of teaching. Having a good time. Had a smart city woman and a kid, and when I came home to bury the old man, everything in me was screaming, *don't look, don't look*. Don't look at the state of the place, just get it on the damned market. And then I found out, as I say, that there was not a single local family left in Wychehill. And the curse came down.'

'Your mother was still alive?'

'Moved my ma down to Ledbury – she wouldn't live here after that. Told her I'd take a couple of years off to pull it all together, before resuming the glittering career. Then we had Hugo. More roots.'

'What . . . happened to the boys' mother?'

'Left a long time ago. Wilful London girl, didn't get on with the country. Bit like Syd Spicer's missus. We weren't married, so no complications in those days. She went abroad, I got the boys. And we turned it around, by God we did, in spite of the shiny-arsed civil servants and the scum from Brussels. *Diversification.*'

'I remember that as a buzz word put around by the Min of Ag.'

'The pragmatic farmer's way out of the agricultural crisis. Thatcher's message. And, fair play, it worked for some of us. You felt a bit sick about it, but it worked. My case, luxury self-catering holidays. Not that they self-cater, they all eat out. But it works, and it provides employment locally. All nicely old-fashioned, and folks come back year after year, all the sad townies, and we charge 'em more every time and they still come.'

Preston Devereaux slumped into a wing-backed chair next to the big dead fireplace, smoke-blackened and flaked with log ash. He waved Merrily to a faded chaise longue.

'All the antique furniture from the house we put in the units – what do we need with antiques, me and the boys? Install a Queen Anne writing desk in your stone holiday chalet, that's worth an extra two hundred a week on the bill. You see the buildings out there?'

'Very classy.'

'Turned over all the old stone barns and stables and chicken houses to holiday units, added a few new ones in the same style. Put the farm, what's left of it, into new galvanized sheds painted dark green and nicely screened off. And the farm life, what's left of *that*, goes on around the townies. Give them an illusion of what it's like, let them into what country pursuits we're allowed to practise now – shooting parties and the like, hunting, before it was banned. Joining what they think of as the Old Squirearchy for a fortnight.'

'So the boys are part of that? Plenty for them to do. Don't want to move away like you did?'

'They won't leave. All changed since my day, look. It was either/or back then. Now you can take what you want from the city and come back next day. And growing up in the country hardens you. We can deal with the towns better than the townies can deal with us.'

'Only I heard that Louis . . .'

Merrily looked up at the foxes' heads above the door – the way their mouths were always forced open around their pointed canines, to make them look like savage beasts gloriously killed.

'Heard Louis what?' His voice spiking.

'Had some kind of breakdown? After hunting was banned?'

'Who told you that?'

'Can't be sure.'

'Selective memory you got there, Mrs Watkins.' Preston Devereaux, relaxed again. 'Aye, he loved his hunting. We ran the Countryside Alliance campaign in this area. *Fight the Ban* posters everywhere. Boy lost his rag at a demo, belted a copper guarding some Blairite toady. Weekend in custody. That's the state we're in – fight for our traditions, we're branded criminals. This government's scum. Anti-English. Don't get me started. We lost. You *move on*. You ask me a question? I can't remember.'

Merrily was confused by all the contradictions here. Trying to understand a man who, having been determined to escape his roots, came back to be driven by a born-again fervour fuelled by bitterness.

'Oak trees,' she said. 'Tim Loste has a lot of oak trees. Which, for a man with a tiny garden . . .'

'Does he?'

'Elgar and oak trees. Is there some connection I might not have heard about?'

'No idea. The only oak I know's the Royal Oak. Which is a pretty common name for a pub, relating, surely, to the tree where Charles II hid from his enemies.'

'No local legends about oaks?'

'Not that I know of. Can I get you a drink? Some coffee?'

'Thanks, but I'll have to be off in a few minutes. I shouldn't have come, anyway, without ringing.'

'Drop in anytime, we've nothing to hide.'

'Is there any kind of mystery ... legend ... rumour, connecting Elgar with Wychehill?'

'Only the church. Longworth and his so-called visionary experience.'

'What was that?'

'They say it's what he has on his tomb.'

'The angel?'

'Gruesome bloody thing, ennit? Not my idea of an angel. Story I was told as a child is that it appeared to the mad old bugger up on the hill, in a blaze of light, and drove him in a state of blind fear to religion.'

'And to Elgar.'

'Same thing. Elgar's become a religion now. I'm not a fan, Merrily, as you may have gathered. If he hadn't encouraged Longworth to build that bloody church there'd've been no Upper Wychehill for the townies to colonize. And what did Elgar ever do for the Malverns, anyway?'

'Massive tourism?'

Devereaux snorted.

'We've always had *that*. We got the scenery, don't need the bloody incidental music. Bugger always claimed he got his inspiration here but he cleared off soon enough when he was famous. And when he came back, as an old man, he came back as an *incomer*, that's what gets to me.'

'I don't understand. If he—'

'He'd *changed*. Starts out as a country boy, I'm not disputing that, even went foxhunting, according to some accounts. But then, soon as he makes it big, he's off ... big house in Hereford, then London, mixing with the nobs and the arty-farty veggies, George Bernard Shaw and the like. And when he finally returns, as this distinguished old man, he's turned into one of *them* – having places laid at the table for his bloody dogs. Likely, he thought the hills'd give him his inspiration back, but it never happened, did it? Closed door this time. Given up his soul to mix with the great and the good and – excuse my terminology – lost his balls. Never wrote another thing that was worthwhile. No wonder he's an unhappy bloody spirit. You believe that?'

'That he's unhappy, or that he's ...'

Devereaux leaned his head into a wing of his chair and looked at Merrily sideways through a bloodshot eye.

'That dead Elgar still bikes the hills.'

'I'm not sure.'

'Ha!'

'Sorry. I'm not usually so ... no, I suppose I am. I suspect there's something happening ... in the atmosphere. I'm just not sure it's anything to do with Elgar.'

'Well ...' Preston Devereaux smiled. 'If you ever decide it is and you want to exorcize the old bastard ... you can go ahead, far as I'm concerned. By all means. Wipe whatever's left of him off the hills for good and all. Just keep quiet about it.'

# 29

# Stoolie

THURSDAY BEGAN BADLY AND GOT WORSE. Just as Merrily was about to corner Jane on the Coleman's Meadow issue, Winnie Sparke was on the phone.

'Merrily, you talked to the cops?'

'Well, I have, but—'

'Only I've heard nothing. Last night I barely slept. See, the one time Tim called me, I wanted to fix him a lawyer, he kept saying there was no need. He said it was crazy they could think he did it. He said they'd know that soon enough.'

'Well, Winnie.' Merrily sat down at the desk in the scullery. 'Erm . . . I think there might be a need for a lawyer now.'

'I have to know. I have to call his parents in France— What did you just say?'

'Just that I think he may well need a lawyer. I've been trying to confirm the situation since last night but I'm not getting anywhere.'

She'd phoned Bliss, who'd come back to her late last night to say that Worcester were still holding Loste and studying lab reports, and that was all he could find out at this hour without inviting awkward questions.

'So, like, how long can they *hold* a guy without a charge?'

'No, look, Winnie, what I'm trying to say is—'

Merrily waved to Jane, hovering in the scullery doorway with her airline bag, meaning *hang on.* Jane raised a hand, smiled a worryingly wan kind of smile and was gone. *Bugger.*

'—What I'm trying to say is I don't know that there *hasn't* been a charge, in the light of new forensic evidence. I— This is confidential?'

'OK.'

'I talked at some length to the officer heading the inquiry, and frankly, after what she told me, even I'd have pulled Tim in for questioning. Even if it was only to have a look around inside his house. He comes across as a very strange person, Winnie, and he's clammed up on them and that makes it look worse.'

'And strange equals psychotic, right?'

'No, but—'

'Did you say you went into his house?'

'With the police. I was asked to take a look at ... some things.'

'What things?'

'Photographs, books ...'

'Why?'

'Because they're trying to get a handle on him, find out exactly where he's coming from.'

'They had no goddamn right. *You* had no right.'

'I tried to explain a couple of points, as best I could. I don't think I was very successful. There was just too much I didn't know. For instance, his background. I mean, how long have *you* actually known him?'

'Background? Background could not be more respectable. Parents are both professional classical musicians. He was a music teacher at private schools, ending up at Malvern College. Played rugby for a local team. How respectable do you want?

'This project of his,' Merrily said. 'The oratorio or whatever ...'

'OK.'

'He was working on that when you met him? Or was that your idea?'

'What's that matter?'

'We didn't go into this yesterday, but when he saw what he ... when he saw the figure he identified as Elgar, on his bike ... I'm just thinking of the big picture in the hallway ... Very much a presence in the house, you'll agree.'

'He's a presence in Tim's life.'

'And obviously a presence, on some level, in Wychehill.'

'What are you saying?'

'It's just that this seems to be the image of Elgar that Tim's ... carrying around with him. And it corresponds with the ... with the apparition that people – Tim included – appear to have been seeing.'

'What's that have to do with getting him out of gaol?'

'And you're a writer, specializing in books on mysticism, psychic studies, healing ... the occult? You said you were helping him with meditation exercises. To deal with his drinking and ... maybe to reach Elgar's level of creative inspiration. A man whose previous output, I understand, has been ... fairly ordinary. So he's living with Elgar's music, images of Elgar, in a place steeped in Elgar. He's immersing himself on a very intense level ...'

'You don't even wanna get him out, do you? All you want is to cover your own ass with the cops for whatever reason—'

'This has nothing to do with the cops.' Merrily felt a headache coming on. 'But if you want to deal with that first ... oak trees? Acorns? Little oaks in pots, the sapling that's going to be bigger than his house?'

'A symbol.'

'Of what?'

'A symbol from the natural world that he could use for meditation. He was drinking too much, I was trying to use meditation to give him a focus. And also to make him more ... receptive. Why are you asking me this stuff?'

'Because the police are linking oaks to Druidism and Druidism to blood sacrifice and ... you know?'

'*Oh, Jesus God* ...' Winnie's voice was suddenly perforated with panic. 'This is shit! This is so *wrong.*'

'Is it?'

'What?'

'I mean, why is it wrong? Elgar wrote *Caractacus* about Hereford-shire Beacon. Full of Druidism and magic and prophecy and people's throats being cut on sacrificial stones.'

There was a gap before Winnie's voice came back, the fissures hardening up.

'What are you, Merrily? Some kinda fucking stoolie for the cops?

Like I need to waste my time with a police snitch? I don't think so, lady. I think I told you far too much already, and all you did was you gave it to the cops.'

'That's not—'

'So from now on you can get off of my case, OK?'

'Look, I'm just trying to—'

'I'm gonna have a good lawyer I can't truly afford go see Tim right now, and I don't wanna *hear* from you again, so ... like when we get him outta there you just stay the *hell* away from the both of us.'

'Winnie, if you could just let me—'

'Goddamn fucking stoolie bitch.'

The phone went down hard.

At the start of mid-morning break, the sixth-form common room was like a call centre, a whole bunch of them switching on their mobiles to, like, maintain the temperature of their love lives.

When Jane switched on hers, just to be sociable, not expecting anything from Eirion this morning, it went directly into its tune. And, not recognising the number, it was like ...

'Jane Watkins?'

'Erm ...'

'Hi, Jane, this is Jerry Isles from the *Guardian*. I tried to leave a message on your voicemail yesterday – maybe you didn't get it?'

'Oh ... did you?'

'Never mind. Jane, I have to say it all sounds hugely fascinating. I used to be quite into leys a few years ago – we used to stay with friends in Cornwall, where you're practically tripping over megalithic sites, so I've read Watkins, obviously, and this really brought it all back. Are you running the campaign on your own?'

'Well ... you know ... me and a few friends, but—'

'But it was your idea.'

'Yes, only I'm not sure—'

'You seem to be wearing school uniform on the picture. How old are you, do you mind?'

'S— Eighteen.'

'Good. And your parents know about it?'

'My mother knows. I don't have a father any more. She, erm . . . My mum's cool with it.'

'Well . . . I took the liberty of checking your map with the Ordnance Survey, and the line certainly seems to work. Who did the pictures?'

'My . . . boyfriend.'

'They're good pix, on the whole. However, I think we'd like to do some of our own. We have a regular freelance photographer in your area, and the picture editor would like to send her along, if that's all right with you. How about . . . are you free this afternoon?'

Through the plate-glass window beyond the table-tennis table, Jane could see Morrell in his shirt sleeves jogging across the quad towards the car park.

'Look,' she said. 'I mean this is really good of you, but I'm not sure I want to go through with it now.'

'Oh? That mean you're no longer convinced?'

'Oh, no, it's true, it's all true. Even though when I went to see the local councillor, there were all these council officials there, and they were all, like, *Oh, it's all nonsense and Alfred Watkins was a misguided old man.* And the councillor was suggesting I was trying to mess up his plans for turning Ledwardine into some kind of town, which would be really crap. And I was warned that I should be careful what I said. I mean, I'm not worried about me that much, but my mum's the vicar there, you know?'

The line went quiet. If they'd lost it, Jane decided she wasn't going to call him back, at least not until tonight when she'd had time to think of a way he could maybe do the story but keep her out of it . . .

'The vicar,' Jerry Isles said. 'No, I *didn't* know that.'

Oh hell. Why, in this so-called secular age, were newspapers so fond of vicars?

Jerry said, 'Tell me again, Jane, what these people from the council said to you . . . ?'

'I don't think I told you the first time, did I?'

'About the councillor wanting to turn your village into a small town? That's what I've got.'

'You're writing this down?'

Morrell jogged back and went into the main building, his car keys swinging from a finger.

Jane began to sweat.

Merrily sat in the scullery, watching the play of morning light on the vicarage lawn, the clusters of yellow wild flowers in the churchyard drystone wall that bordered it. A whole ecosystem, that wall.

*What are you, some kinda stoolie for the cops?*

Going back over it, she could pinpoint the exact moment when Winnie Sparke's attitude had altered. It was when Merrily had revealed that she'd been inside Loste's house. Winnie had been afraid of what Merrily – not the police – might have seen in the house and been able to interpret for Howe.

Which meant there was something she should have spotted in there and hadn't.

She called Syd Spicer, not expecting him to be in. But he picked up on the second ring.

'You've offended Sparke, Merrily. Easily done.'

'She *told* you?'

'She's walking round wailing and gnashing her teeth. A woman who likes to be in control. And she can hardly control poor Tim at the moment, can she?'

'You think he did it, Syd?'

'I wouldn't have thought so, but time will tell.'

'I like an interventionist priest.'

'Yeah, well, I don't scale walls with pockets full of smoke bombs any more.'

It was the first reference that he'd made to his past, but this probably wasn't the time to follow it up.

'Loste and Winnie, Syd. What's that actually about? This musical work, this search for Elgar's source of inspiration. I mean, is there anything you haven't told me that might relate to that?'

'Lots, I imagine. I wouldn't know what was relevant. Equally, I can't betray a parishioner's trust. I can point you in a certain direction, which I've done, but I can't pass on what I've been told in confidence, can I? Would you? Maybe you would. Maybe you did.'

'Because I'm a police informer?'

'When Winnie Sparke takes offence, she doesn't hold back.'

'Why is Loste collecting oak trees?'

'I don't know.'

'OK, Joseph Longworth's vision. That sounds like a modern-day version of one of those old legends often connected to the foundation of churches. A vision indicating where to build.'

'There are some documents relating to that. It's in the parish records. Letters. Winnie has copies.'

'Could I have copies?'

'No reason why not, I suppose.'

'Could you send them? Email anything?'

Spicer sighed. Merrily persevered.

'Do you have any idea what Winnie Sparke might have meant when she talked about a great and beautiful secret?'

'No,' he said.


Merrily called the home of the dead girl, Sonia Maloney, in Droitwich. No answer. The Cookman number Syd Spicer had passed on turned out to be a spare line, which meant he hadn't even tried it.

She came to the third on the list.

'Who?' Stella Cobham said.

'Merrily Watkins. The deliverance woman?'

'Oh, yeah. Look, Merrily I was just on my way out. Perhaps I could call you back.'

'Won't keep you a minute, Mrs Cobham. I just wanted – before I make any specific arrangements – to find out if next Sunday would be suitable for you.'

'I'm sorry. What for?'

'We were discussing the idea of a Requiem Eucharist for Lincoln Cookman and Sonia Maloney?'

'Oh yeah.'

'It seemed to answer everybody's ... you know?'

'Yeah, well, look. I don't think we'll be coming.'

'But Mrs Cobham, it was your—'

'Things have changed. Change of plan. Change of future.' Brittle laugh. 'We're putting the barn on the market. I'm just off to the agent's in Ledbury now, actually.'

'Just like that?'

'It was a wrong move. Nothing's been right since we came here. We're probably going to America. Paul knows this guy in Naples, Florida. Anyway, all I'm trying to say is . . . it really doesn't concern us any more. Look, I've got to go, all right?'

Click.

Merrily threw the phone book at the wall.

# 30

# In Their Proper Place

IT HAD BEEN MERRILY's plan to go into her own church before lunch, when it was quietest. Find a cool place in the chancel and lay all this out, the whole Wychehill mess. To ask the question, *Is it time to leave this alone, walk away?* An in-depth exchange with the Management on this issue was long, long overdue.

So what was she doing in Lol's bed?

'Oh hell . . .' She gazed into his unshaven face. 'This is a bit like adultery.'

'In what way, exactly?'

Lol rolled off her. He looked almost hurt.

'*No, I* . . .' She trapped one of his legs between hers. 'I just meant . . . cheating on the Church. The parish. Sorry. All I need is to offend you, and that's virtually nobody left still speaking to me.'

He smiled. Maybe he hadn't looked hurt a moment ago. Maybe she'd conjured that out of her own hurt.

Lol's bedroom had a three-quarter bed in it. That was all. It was a very small room with no space for a wardrobe. He said he needed to sleep here because it had a view across Church Street to the vicarage – they could see each other's lights at bedtime. Which was nice. But she'd sometimes wondered if he wasn't just a little timid about using the bigger bedroom where Lucy Devenish had slept.

Whatever, this room was bare without being stark, a sanctuary, a space out of time. One day, perhaps, she might even get to spend a whole night here.

'Then, at the same time,' she said, 'I get the feeling that I'm neglecting you.'

'Some feelings you should listen to,' Lol said. 'This could be *God* telling you that you're neglecting me.'

'Dangerous to blaspheme in front of a vicar.' Her fingers paddling over his thigh. 'Especially when naked.'

He gripped her hand. They laughed, and when they stopped laughing she told him everything. About Winnie Sparke and Tim Loste and their beautiful secret and her own dismal morning.

'I'm tired. I can't get a handle on it any more. People's attitudes change overnight. They want me to do something, then they don't. They want to talk to me and then ... Winnie Sparke, particularly. It was as if she'd picked a fight just to wind up the conversation because I was asking the wrong questions. Like mentioning the blow-up photo of Elgar.'

'Let me get this right. Who's seen Elgar, other than Loste?'

'Stella Cobham. Who no longer wants to have anything to do with it because they've *suddenly* decided to move. Well, nobody just decides overnight to emigrate. Must've been very much on the cards when she came to the meeting in the church and poured it all out, thus burning her boats with Preston Devereaux who, according to Spicer, nobody likes to offend because he's Old Wychehill ...'

Lol sat up against the pillow, retrieved his little brass-rimmed glasses from the floorboards, and put them on.

'But for a couple of things,' he said, 'I'd be suggesting that Elgar might be a psychological projection by Tim Loste.'

'Well, me, too. Although, if we step over the threshold ... sometimes, if the personality behind it is strong enough, a psychological projection may be perceptible to a third party.'

'Musicians can be obsessive.'

'No kidding.'

'Um ...' Lol hesitated.

'What?'

'Anything I can do about this?'

'I don't like to interrupt your work.'

Lol laughed.

'What it comes down to,' Merrily said, 'is the only person I haven't spoken to, can't get at and may never get at.'

'Loste.'

'Who now seems to be the key to both mysteries, that is, the Elgar thing and the killing on the Beacon, whether he did that or not – and the circumstantial evidence is impressive. But the key to Tim Loste is Winnie Sparke, who isn't talking. I don't think she ever planned to say much, and yet she wanted to check me out. Why? I still don't really know these people or what they're doing.'

'There must be other ways in,' Lol said. 'For instance . . . a lot of singers in a choir.'

'You know any? I don't.'

'Not yet. But musicians can be obsessive. Leave this with me.'

'Thank you, Lol. And thanks for keeping an eye on Jane, which I . . . I'm not getting anything right, am I? I'm a lousy mother, a lousy girlfriend, an inept exorcist and an incompetent parish priest.'

'But at least you don't suffer from low self-esteem,' Lol said.

They went downstairs and shared half a loaf, a pot of hummus and a box of cress, and Merrily resolved to spend the rest of the day in penance, dusting and polishing the church furniture, finding sick parishioners to visit before . . .

. . . A last assault, tomorrow, on Wychehill. Or, more specifically, on Winnie Sparke.

'And I want to look at Coleman's Meadow.'

'Tonight?'

'Why does Jane think Lyndon Pierce has some secret scheme to expand the village?'

'Probably because he has. Don't worry. Gomer's looking into it.'

'That's reassuring.' Merrily sat on the sofa and smoked half a cigarette. 'Or maybe not. Pierce used to shoot blue tits, apparently. Nothing he could do for Jane to acquit himself after that. What if Sparke's right and Loste didn't kill that guy?'

'Then Annie Howe will find out for herself. She's not an incompetent detective, she just doesn't like you. And your mind's gone like a TV remote control switching from one channel to another.'

'Too many channels nowadays,' Merrily said. 'That's the problem.'

The grave was marked by a low wedge of sandstone and overhung by an apple tree from the old orchard over the wall. It was arguably the smallest, least ostentatious memorial in the churchyard.

Jane could have found it blindfolded.

*Lucy Devenish.*

The lettering tiny, and no dates. Lucy's will had requested no dates, and somehow Mum had been able to comply, probably against all the regulations. And if this wasn't a sign that Lucy had believed herself to be an eternal presence in Ledwardine, no date for her arrival, no date for her passing . . .

This always made Jane shiver, but with a kind of delight.

Underneath the name were the lines Lucy had chosen from Thomas Traherne (*his* dates were given: 1637–74), Herefordshire's greatest, most mysterious poet.

> *No more shall clouds eclipse my treasures*
> *Nor viler shades obscure my highest pleasures.*
> *All things in their proper place*
> *My Soul doth best embrace.*

*All things in their proper place.* That spelled it out, really, didn't it?

Jane placed her hands on the top of the stone for a moment. It always, even in winter, felt warm.

She stood up and looked back towards the church. Lucy's grave was at the very end of the churchyard, right beside the path which led, through a small wooden gate, to the orchard, which had once virtually surrounded the village. *Ledwardine – The Village in the Orchard –* some guidebooks still called it that. And this was the coffin track. No doubt about it.

Way back, corpses would have been carried in, ceremonially, through the orchard. There was a long, flat, backless bench, probably the successor to generations of wooden benches on which the bearers had rested the coffins. The lych-gate at the front of the church had been a comparatively modern addition.

Jane looked towards the steeple and imagined what Lucy might have seen – *might be seeing now*: the churchyard like a circular clearing in the orchard. Perhaps there'd once been a circle of stones around where the steeple now soared.

Jane remembered the day Lucy had cut an apple in half and showed her the five-pointed star, the pentagram at the heart of every apple. An indestructible symbol of the paganism at the heart of Ledwardine. In those days – the days when she'd painted the Mondrian walls – Jane had seen paganism as the *real* religion, Christianity as a pointless distraction from the Middle East, Mum as misguided.

It didn't seem as simple now. The church steeple was a powerful symbol and far more effective than a stone circle at indicating, from long distances, the alignment with Cole Hill. Now Jane felt – and arrangements like this underlined it – that paganism and Christianity had often walked together on the same straight path. She was sure that this was what Alfred Watkins had instinctively felt when archaeologists were slagging him off for including medieval churches in the otherwise Neolithic ley system.

*Have I done the right thing?* She still didn't know.

Jane walked through the churchyard, past the south door and out through the lych-gate into the market place. Perhaps an old cross or an outlying marker stone might have stood here.

Across into the alley, through the broken gate and into the derelict orchard behind Church Street, past the hump of the burial mound, if that was what it was. And so to Coleman's Meadow – the meadow of the earth-shaman – to Cole Hill, the sacred hill, the mother hill.

She felt choked up with emotion now, remembering the night she'd got drunk on cider with poor Colette and had started hallucinating in the orchard. *Cider's the blood of the orchard*, Lucy had said later, and Jane could still hear her sharp headmistressy voice. *It's in your blood now. I felt at once that it had be one or both of you . . . you and Merrily.*

This had to be the right path

Jane began to drift and, as on the night of Colette and the cider, could hardly feel the grass beneath her feet. When she stepped onto the ley it was as if she was floating on sunlit air-currents, and she saw Lucy waiting for her as she began to walk towards the steeple and the holy hill beyond.

'Hi,' Lucy said. 'Are you Jane?'

Jane stood there, blinking. The woman wore not a poncho but a kind of denim smock with lots of pockets, and there was a square metal case at her feet.

'Sally Ferriman. For the *Guardian*?'

'Oh,' Jane said. 'Hi.'

'You ready, Jane?'

Jane looked at Sally Ferriman, then up at Cole Hill, discovering that she had one of her own hands pressing down on top of her head as if she was trying to stop some part of it floating away.

'Yes,' Jane said. 'I think so.'

Merrily reached the church door and then turned back.

She wasn't ready. She went back to the vicarage and sat in front of the list of people whom she needed to tell about the idea for a requiem on Sunday. Crosses against Mrs Cookman and Stella Cobham. She tried the number for Sonia Maloney's parents: still no answer.

One more name on the list. She'd agonized about this one, had wondered whether to consult Syd Spicer – or even Bliss – about it first.

She rang Bliss's mobile. Switched off, but he rang back within a minute from outside the building.

'They've still got Loste, and they may make an application to hold on to him, but there's been no charge. They may still be waiting for forensics. However ... it doesn't look good from his point of view. They now have a witness who's identified Loste as someone seen conducting what may have been a transaction on the side of the Beacon with a black man in a woolly hat.'

'Loste bought drugs from Wicklow?'

'That's what it looks like. Usual rules, of course, Merrily.'

'Not a word to anyone.'

'So,' Bliss said, 'what do *you* have for *me*?'

'Erm ... another question?'

'Jesus, Merrily, I can't believe how one-sided this relationship's become.'

'I know. I'm sorry. This probably isn't something you can answer, anyway.'

'Fair enough. I'll see you around, then—'

'It's probably a Traffic matter.'

'In that case, all the abuse I've thrown at Traffic over the years, *no* chance.'

'It's my Wychehill road accidents. I just – this is stupid – just want to be sure they actually happened as they were described to me. Or indeed happened at all. Loste had a crash that wasn't reported to the police, so I can't do anything about that. But there was a lorry driver supposed to have gone into the church wall.'

'Name?'

'No idea.'

'Date?'

'Can't give you an exact ... Never mind, it was just a thought.'

'Merrily, even a brilliant investigator like myself ...'

'The only one where I do have a name, although I gather there was no charge in the end, so it may not be instantly accessible either ... Stella Cobham? And it was early this month. Could you possibly get anything from that ...?'

She heard the sound of grinding traffic and the gasp of air brakes.

'Frannie?'

'The doughnuts are on you, Merrily,' Bliss said. 'Probably for the rest of your life.'


And she'd forgotten to ask him about the final name on the requiem list.

But then, why *should* she ask him? Or Spicer. Spicer had unequivocally opted out of the requiem, and she wasn't a goddamn stoolie for the cops. Not officially, anyway.

Merrily switched on the computer to check the emails and, while it was booting up, stared at the phone. Should she?

Sod it. What was there to lose? She went into Yellow Pages for the number and then rang the Royal Oak at Wychehill and asked to speak to Mr Rajab Ali Khan.

Some guy said he wasn't there, mostly he worked out of his offices in Worcester and Kidderminster, and what did she want and could he take a message?

Merrily said yes, he probably could. No hurry. She merely wanted to invite Mr Khan to a church service.

The emails came up. Piece of spam offering her guaranteed penis enlargement and – wow – one from **Wychehill Rectory**.

*Dear Merrily*

*IN CONFIDENCE – you might find something here. Couldn't scan it – too faded – so I've copied it, for speed. It's in the parish records, a letter, dating back to 1926, apparently forwarded to Longworth, who seems to have preserved it as some kind of corroboration of his choice of site for Wychehill Church. I don't know who it's from or who he's talking about – in fact, for all I know, it could be a forgery – but Winnie was certainly impressed, so I'm guessing one of them's Elgar. Also note that Winnie changed the name of her house to Starlight Cottage.*

Spicer hadn't even signed the email. But then, what had she expected – *love, Syd?*

Merrily scrolled up the letter. It was something that he'd taken the trouble to send it.

*My dear Sirius*

*How are you? We seem hardly to have spoken since the utterly devastating loss of poor Electra, and so I was delighted to receive your letter ... and further delighted to confirm that your Hereford friend is absolutely right as regards the significance of the Wyche Hill site. My researches tell me this would be a most propitious place to build a church or temple. As we once discussed, there is a tradition of worship in the Malvern Hills long pre-dating Christianity yet absorbed by the early Church, and also, as recorded in the Triads of Wales, a most inspiring, long-lost tradition of sacred music-making.*

*It is my belief – and wonderful to think it could be so – that there may be no area of southern Britain more conducive to the creation and performance of music of the most exalted power than this. Your own work is surely ample testament to its extraordinary influence.*

*Please tell me if I can be of any further assistance to any of you, and I look forward to experiencing the church if ever it is built. But we must get together before that.*

*With every good wish,*

*Starlight.*

*PS. Some of my old, as Electra would say, 'out of the world' associates are inclined to think your friend's interpretations of his remarkable discovery tend toward the prosaic, but I suppose his provincial background is a bit of a constraint!*


That night, Jane went out with Eirion and Merrily went over to Lol's. They set off to walk to Coleman's Meadow, and she showed him the email.

'If one of them's Elgar, it's probably going to be Sirius.'

It was a warm night, the northern sky still a shimmering electric blue. Lol said that the weather forecast had suggested tomorrow would be the hottest day of the year so far.

'So Electra . . . ?'

'Would be Alice, who'd died some years earlier.'

'Music of the most exalted power,' Merrily said. 'What does that say to you?'

'I think it says, even with a Boswell guitar don't get any ideas.'

Coleman's Meadow was empty. Lol said there'd been Hereford cattle last time he was here, but now only a few rabbits bobbed around on the eastern fringe, by the thorn hedge.

The path through the middle of the meadow was strikingly evident, even among the shadows. Even when it disappeared through the gate and into the undergrowth, you could feel it burrowing like a live cable to light up the summit of Cole Hill, which, at nearly ten p.m. was ambered by an almost unearthly sunset afterglow.

'What do you think?' Lol said. 'Worth saving?'

# PART THREE

From chanting comes the word enchantment and it was largely by chanting that the Druids kept up the spell of enchantment which they spread across each of the Celtic kingdoms.

John Michell
*New Light on the Ancient Mystery of Glastonbury* (1990)

# 31

# On the Line

No POINT IN WORRYING. It probably wouldn't be in today's paper, anyway. After Jane had asssured him that no other media had been in touch, Jerry Isles had said they might well hold it over for a day. Later, media-savvy Eirion had explained that it was a *soft* story, therefore expendable.

Every time she'd awoken in the night, Jane had been hoping, increasingly, that they'd just dump it. After all, it wasn't much of a story in the great scheme of things, was it? And what, in the end, was it likely to achieve, apart from dropping her in some deep shit with Morrell?

Still, she was up before Mum and outside the Eight Till Late not long after it opened, this horrible queasy feeling at the bottom of her stomach. Despite the shop's name, Big Jim Prosser opened around seven, with all these morning papers outside on the rack – *Suns*, *Mirrors, Independents*.

No *Guardians*, however, this morning. Maybe not many people took it in Ledwardine, or they'd all gone for delivery.

The air was already warm, in line with the forecast on Eirion's car radio last night that this would be the first really hot day of the summer. Ledwardine looked impossibly beautiful, quiet and shaded and guarded by the church, with its glistening spire, and the enigmatic pyramid of Cole Hill. Everything serene and ancient and ... vulnerable. Jane felt as though she was carrying the weight of all that late-medieval timber-framing on her shoulders and was about to duck away, when Big Jim appeared in the shop doorway.

'Lovely morning, Jane. Looking for anything in particular, is it?'

THE REMAINS OF AN ALTAR

'No, I—'

'*Daily Telegraph*? *Times*?'

'Erm, it was just a *Guardian*, but if they've all gone it doesn't matter.'

'Just a *Guardian*, eh?' Jim Prosser had his hands behind his back, looking kind of smug. 'Oh, *they*'ve gone, all right. Every single one. Last one got snapped up five minutes before you come in. 'Fact, I just had to turn one feller away.'

'Oh.' Jane edged towards the door. 'Right. Never mind, then.'

This didn't necessarily mean anything.

'Lyndon Pierce, it was,' Jim said happily, the words coming down like the blade of a guillotine. 'I think he's driven over to Weobley to try and get one there. Didn't look a happy man, somehow. Can't imagine why.'

'Oh God,' Jane went hot and cold. 'They used it, didn't they?'

'Used what?'

'Don't make me suffer even more, Jim. What did it say?'

'Well, seeing it's you, Jane . . .' Jim brought a paper out from behind his back. 'I'll let you have a quick glance at my own copy, if you like.'

'You take the *Guardian*?'

'I do today,' Jim said.

He led her inside and spread the paper on the counter, folded at an inside news page, and, *Oh God, there it was*: in *Guardian* terms, a big spread, although – *Oh God, no* – most of the space was taken up by the full-colour picture.

The photographer had been standing on the stile at the bottom of Cole Hill, focusing down on Jane, and now you could see why she'd done it from that angle: Jane's face was in close-up, unsmiling, moody, with the path racing away over her shoulder, all the way to the church steeple. They'd done something to it with a computer, shading the edges so that the ley looked almost as if it was glowing.

Underneath, a second picture showed a section of Ordnance Survey map, with the ley points encircled, just like Alfred Watkins used to do it.

Altogether, not a story you could easily miss.

# Village future on the line, schoolgirl warns

Jeremy Isles

---

A schoolgirl is fighting county planners to defend the legacy of the man whose discovery of ley lines has been causing nationwide controversy for more than eighty years.

Planning officials in Herefordshire were ready to accept an application for new housing in the historic village of Ledwardine in the north of the county, when the vicar's daughter Jane Watkins, 18, accused them of destroying the sacred heritage of the community.

Ms Watkins says a proposed estate of 24 'luxury homes' would obliterate what she insists is a prehistoric straight track, or *ley*, linking several sacred sites including her mother's church and the summit of what she claims is the village's 'holy hill'. Ley hunters all over Britain are now set to join the protest.

The theory of ley lines was floated in 1925 by Alfred Watkins (no relation), a Hereford brewer and pioneer photographer in his book *The Old Straight Track*, which is still in print and something of a bible for New Agers and 'earth mysteries' enthusiasts. The latest theories suggest that Watkins's leys are lines of earth-energy or possibly spirit paths along which the souls of the dead were believed to be able to travel.

However, Hereford councillors and officials charged with implementing new government demands for more rural housing are taking a hard line on the issue.

At the end of the story, a council spokesman was quoted as saying, 'It's a storm in a teacup. We have consulted our county archaeologist who assures us that ley lines are simply a quaint myth. We applaud Jane Watkins's interest in local traditions, but consider this would be a very silly reason to forsake our commitment to allow quality new housing to be built on suitable sites.'

However, they also had a quote from J. M. Powys, described as 'an author specializing in 'landscape phenomena', who said, 'Although the concept of leys has been widely dismissed almost since Watkins first came up with it, he was definitely on to something, and his ideas have been powerfully influential. There's a lot about the ancient landscape we really don't understand, and I'd be interested in taking a look at this alignment – which looks like one that Watkins missed, even though it was virtually on his own doorstep.'

Earlier in the piece Jane had been quoted as describing council officials as ...

'Philistine morons?' Jim Prosser said. 'You actually said that, did you, Jane?'

'Oh God, Jim.' Jane covered up her face. 'I thought we were just having like a preliminary chat? He was really sympathetic, you know? I thought he'd come out with the photographer to interview me properly – I didn't realize that was *it*, he was doing it over the phone.'

Jim stood there, slowly shaking his head and smiling the smile of a man who couldn't quite believe this. He held out the paper.

'You wanner take this copy, show your mother before somebody else does?'

'*Christ, no* ... I mean, it's OK, she's going out early.' Jane felt clammy under her school shirt. 'Look ... what do *you* think, Jim? What have I done? Is this, like, going to cause trouble?'

'Hard to say, really. Twenty-four houses, that's another twenty-four bunches of papers and magazines for me. On the other hand, disturbing the spirits of the dead ...'

'You don't believe a word, do you? You think it's all total bollocks.'

'Well, you know us primitive, superstitious rural types, Jane ...'

'Do you think *anybody* here is going to agree with me?'

'Tough question,' Jim said. 'Go on, take the paper, you might need one.'

'Thanks.'

Jane went out and stood by the oak pillars of the medieval market hall. The brilliant sun was suspended over Cole Hill, as though it was either declaring its support or making some kind of ironic gesture. Jane screwed up her eyes and looked up, pleading.

It had been like a dream. Taking herself off to the end of the playing field yesterday lunchtime and sitting down and trying to see it from all sides. Mum's position in the village – no conflict there, she was supposed to be responsible for the collective soul of the community. And Morrell, always on about liberal causes and free speech and Amnesty International and stuff like that.

Once the decision had been made, it had been like being on a speeded-up escalator. A call to the photographer and then to Eirion on his mobile, and he'd blagged some time off and been waiting, parked down the lane, just out of sight, when she'd slipped away from the school soon after one p.m. Eirion finally dropping her off at the church so that she could walk the ley from there on her own, just to be . . . sure. And she *had* been sure.

Yesterday, the high. Today, the cold turkey.

Jane was getting a mental image, now, of Morrell with the *Guardian* on his desk – it was his favourite paper, normally. Folding it neatly . . . and then instructing his secretary to have all copies removed from the school library and the sixth-form common room before any of the students arrived. Then maybe a smarmy, self-defensive call to the woman on the education authority before sitting back to devise a suitable form of retribution.

Bloody unfair, really. Another couple of weeks and the term would've been over and she'd have been immune until September.

A few villagers were wandering over to the shop. Jane slipped behind a pillar of the market hall and didn't move. She felt disoriented and distanced from . . . from her usual self. Like she'd taken – beginning with that first small lie about her age to Jerry Isles – a decision to become a separate person, detached also from *The School* and *The Sixth Form*.

A slightly premature adult, in other words, and it felt lonely.

The sun was hot on her head and her arms. She felt as if she wanted to walk away and fade into the spirit path the way she almost had yesterday. Or was that . . . was she just going a little crazy, through stress and anxiety?

Across at the vicarage she could see Mum reversing the Volvo onto the side of the road. Looked like she was in a hurry. Well, good. But she wouldn't leave before she'd seen her daughter.

Jane raised a hand and wandered over, hiding the *Guardian* in the hedge. Best not to burden her with this.

Or the migraine.

Oh yeah, there was definitely a migraine coming on today.

32

# A Polka for the Loonies

THERE WERE NO CURTAINS at Lol's bedroom window. When he'd awoken, not long after dawn, the sky was slashed with red, bringing up ugly thoughts of the dead man on the stone in the Malverns.

Something Lol had not seen, but Merrily had, and Lol was lying there under the reddening duvet, thinking about all the times he'd sat fingering the frets of the graceful Boswell guitar, conjuring ephemera, while Merrily waded in spiritual sewage.

Increasingly, he worried about her. She was living much of the time on cigarettes instead of proper meals and sooner or later all this chasing around after madness – the kind of madness she'd never be able to validate – would start to take its toll.

Not many nights, lately, had passed without him waking in the dark or the early dawn, cold with this formless fear of losing Merrily.

And walking back in the late evening from Coleman's Meadow to the market square, splitting up to go to their separate beds . . . there'd been a disturbingly elegiac quality to that.

Recalling this, he'd felt a moment of anxiety that was close to panic and, turning it into determination, got up into the streaming red dawn and made some tea and a list of what he needed to find out.

Finding himself thinking about Winnie Sparke. The way she'd moved in on him: *Pardon me . . . but I think I know who you are?* The tumbling hair, the semi-see-through dress. Ready to come on to him that night, but now she wasn't talking. Not to Merrily. Protecting the enigmatic Tim Loste. So what was there to protect?

At around eight-thirty, Lol sat at his writing desk in the window

overlooking Church Street and rang Prof Levin at the Knight's Frome
studio.

'Five weeks,' Prof said. 'In five weeks, I have a window for
approximately ten days. If we can't break its back in ten days we're not
trying.'

'Sorry . . . ?'

'Your . . . second . . . solo . . . album?'

'Well, it's coming.' Lol could hear Prof pouring coffee from his
cafetière. 'I'm just . . . not there yet.'

'Shit,' Prof said. 'You haven't even started, have you, you useless
bastard?'

'No, I've started. I start every day. Except today. Today, I'm not
starting.'

'Because?'

'Tim Loste,' Lol said. 'What do you know about Tim Loste?'

The answer came back, sailing past on a breath like there'd been no
need for thought.

'Avoid,' Prof said.

'I see.' Lol inched his chair further into the desk, picked up a pencil,
gathered in his lyrics pad. 'Why, exactly?'

Prof said, 'Laurence, we're all mad, in our way, aren't we? Me, you,
Loste, Elgar.'

'Sorry, did *I* mention Elgar?'

'You mentioned Loste, which means that sooner or later we'd get
around to Elgar. And madness. Elgar grew up with it. Used to hang
around the local lunatic asylum at Worcester.'

'Yes, but that's because he was Director of Music there.'

'Yeah. Thirty quid a year, and five shillings every time he wrote a
polka for the loonies to dance to. But even then he's thinking, there
but for the grace of God . . .'

'You're saying Elgar was mentally ill?'

'But also, fortunately, touched with genius. Imagine what it's like if
you're mental and only touched with mediocrity.'

'Loste?'

'Terrific conductor, arranger . . . facilitator. Pure creativy? Nah.'

'You know him personally?'

'Mmmf.' Prof swallowing too-hot coffee. 'Laurence, mate, *everybody* knows him. If you're a halfway-proficient serious musician or a singer, the chances are he's been in touch at one time or another, offering you the chance to make your name. No money in it, of course, just the honour and the glory of working with the young master. This is in his manic phases.'

'In the clinical sense?'

'Whether it's been diagnosed I wouldn't know. But in his depressive phases, it's best to stay out of his way – and also in his manic phases, obviously. That's why I say just avoid. Tell you about me and him, shall I?'

It seemed that Loste, having heard about this new recording studio at Knight's Frome, had called Prof, introducing himself as a one-time soloist with the English Symphony Orchestra. Asking whether it was possible that Prof could put together a mobile unit to record his choir in Wychehill Church.

'Complicated job, Laurence, if you've never recorded a choir before, having to mike up this huge church on your own. So what's wrong with the studio? I'm asking him. Oh no, Loste insists it has to be the church. Not *a* church, *this* church. But . . . he had the money. *I* should argue.'

'*You* went to Wychehill?'

'Charming crowd, on the whole. The women worshipped Loste, this bumbling overgrown schoolboy . . . imprecise, incoherent.'

'You mean drunk?'

'Well . . . high, certainly. Or just, like I said, manic. And yet, in the end, unexpectedly, I was impressed. He's a bloody good conductor. He channels inspiration. Shouldn't've been any good at all, bunch of amateurs in a country church, but the atmosphere in there was . . . something else.'

'This was Elgar?'

'Ah, well, that's the point, you see. For Loste, it all comes through Elgar. Elgar was always moaning that nobody understood him; *Loste* understands him. Totally. And the combination of Elgar and Loste somehow brings something extraordinary out of amateurs. I remember the *Angelus*, particularly. Shivers-up-the-spine stuff. Or so it seemed to me whose skills have, for too long, been squandered on three-chord wonders such as your good self.'

'Four now.'

'Congratulations. Loste, meanwhile, his ambition is to do the full *Gerontius* with a choir and orchestra. On the strength of what we recorded already, it wouldn't be an embarrassment. Except he'll need to get somebody else to twiddle the knobs on it because *Gerontius* scares me. Too big, too complicated. Also, an attempted orchestration of the afterlife with angels and demons . . . am I going *there*? With Loste? I think not, Laurence. Definitely not with Timothy Loste.'

Lol said, 'Prof, was there a woman with Loste when you did the recording? A writer called Winnie Sparke?'

'Cheesecloth and glittery bits?'

'That would probably be her, yes.'

'All right,' Prof said, 'you remember Yoko Ono in the film they made of the session for *Let It Be*? Sitting there, watchful? More than a bit like that, only less of the inscrutable. Not a promising relationship, was my feeling. She looks at him, sees toyboy; he looks at her . . . mummy.'

'You know anything about her?'

'Not much. She's a writer. Does these Mystic Meg kind of books. What's your angle?'

'She's told Merrily that she and Loste are on the edge of the solution to a great and beautiful mystery.'

'Merrily?' Prof said. 'This is a *Merrily* situation? Oh, for fuck's sake. *A great and beautiful mystery?* Avoid, avoid, *avoid!*'

'Well, it's not too hard to avoid him at the moment,' Lol said. 'He's in custody. The cops are questioning him about a murder on Herefordshire Beacon.'

'*Loste?* This is the man found in the old fort, his throat cut from ear to ear? You're serious?'

'The guy worked at this hip-hop palace at the Royal Oak, outside Wychehill. Which Loste apparently believes is . . .'

'An evil presence sapping his creativity. I heard that. Only, he doesn't have any creativity. He's an interpreter. A facilitator. That's as far as it goes.' Bloody hell, Lol. I mean, *bloody hell.*'

Someone was knocking on Lol's back door.

'Do *you* see him as someone who could kill?' Lol asked.

'Loste?' Prof swallowed some coffee. 'Big bloke. Conducting, he snaps batons. But he— With a knife? Blood spurting everywhere?'

Lol heard the back door opening and shutting. The door of the living room opened, and Jane stood there in her school uniform. She wasn't smiling. She was unusually pale. When Lol pointed her to the sofa, she sat down with her hands clasped between her legs, biting her lip.

'Prof, can I ring you back?'

'Listen,' Prof said, 'if you really want to know more about Loste's games, I can put you in touch with one of the people in his choir. In fact, there's one guy might be more than happy to talk to you in particular. I'll call him, get him to ring you. OK?'

Lol saw that Jane had been crying.

'"Great and beautiful mystery",' Prof said. 'I'll tell you one thing about that. Like Elgar, Loste is obsessed with himself and his ideas. People, he can take or leave most of the time. Music is all. Nothing outside music, to Loste, could be both great and beautiful. Tell Merrily that.'

'Right,' Lol said. 'Thanks.'

'But, yeah. If there was some threat to his music, I suppose, when you think about it, he *could* kill,' Prof said.

# 33

# A Result, Anyway

THERE WAS A NEW sign and it said *Starlight Cottage*.

Of course. Winnie Sparke had told them how she'd changed the name from Wyche Cottage. Almost the first thing she'd said that evening with the choir laying its serene spell over Wychehill. This was what Lol had remembered.

The cottage was built of rubble stone and was not much bigger than Hannah Bradley's place, lower down the lane. Its back garden was formed around plates of rock and ended abruptly in a kind of cliff edge with an iron fence. Merrily looked down and saw the road.

*Yours etc., Starlight.* Winnie, according to Spicer, had *certainly been impressed* by the letter supposedly sent to Elgar and passed on to Longworth.

Which posed some interesting questions. But even at 9.30 a.m., with most of the cottage still pooled in shadow, the bloody woman wasn't around to deflect them. Frustrating, after an early night and only one remembered dream, which had been a dream of Cole Hill seen from Coleman's Meadow; the only detail that Merrily could recall was the sense of pain and the disembodied, breeze-blown voice of Winnie Sparke saying that the hill was hurting. Odd the way that view, once seen, nested in your mind.

Merrily peered through one of the small windows, but all she could make out was a dim wall of books. She'd left her car in the lane, right outside. She gave the wind chimes above the front door a final flick and went back to it and the copy of the weekly *Malvern Gazette* which lay on the passenger seat.

'RITUAL' MURDER –
LOCAL MAN HELD.

Tim Loste hadn't been named, which was normal if there were no charges yet. However, this was a weekly paper, printed yesterday, so if Loste had been been charged late last night it wouldn't have made the edition. The front-page story said the brutal killing on the Beacon had shattered a community already reeling from last weekend's double-fatal road accident (see page three).

On page three the rigid features of Leonard Holliday were in close-up against the blur of the road, under the headline:

'THIS CARNAGE WILL GO ON . . .'

The story said that WRAG, the Wychehill Residents' Action Group, was calling for the immediate closure of the Royal Oak pub as a music venue. Late-night traffic had increased dramatically on roads 'not much wider than bridleways' and 'inner city' nightlife had left residents living in fear. Mrs Joyce Aird, a widow living alone, said, 'It's terrifying. I'm a prisoner in my own home from Friday night to Sunday morning.'

The owner of the Royal Oak, promoter and gallery owner Rajab Ali Khan, had said, 'I have no intention of pre-empting the inquest verdict on these two unfortunate people, but I am anxious to cooperate fully, if Mr Holliday can provide me with any evidence at all of damage to the property or person of any of his neighbours.' It sounded like a quote that Raji had run past his solicitor.

Folding the paper, Merrily looked up to see a hare sitting at the top of Winnie's narrow, down-sloping driveway, its black-tipped ears seeming to quiver for a moment before it bounded away into the hedge. At the top of the lane, the Cobhams' tarted-up barn shone from its elevated site with an alien glamour, like some Pyrenean villa. It would look spectacularly seductive in the estate agent's window, where wealthy tourists would project upon it their doomed bucolic fantasies.

Meanwhile . . . Stella. When Merrily had stopped in Ledbury to buy the *Gazette*, she'd checked her mobile, and Frannie Bliss had called from home to say he had some information from Traffic about Stella. She'd called him back at once. What he had to tell her had made the air in the car seem stale.

Might as well get this over, then.

Leaving the Volvo outside Starlight Cottage, Merrily walked up to the barn. Ignoring the front door this time, going round the back. There was a low gate on a latch, and she lifted it and went through to where a paved area had been laid. There was a wooden table and a pink and yellow striped sunshade and a woman sitting there with a mug of pungent-smelling coffee and her back to Merrily, who coughed lightly.

'Morning, Mrs Cobham.'

Stella spun out of her chair, her red hair flaring up like a bonfire, the aggression emphasized by the kimono she wore, with yellow dragons on black and a hot slap of coffee, now, down the front.

'Yes?'

'Sorry to startle you.'

'You.' Stella subsided, pulling off her sunglasses and mopping at her kimono with a tissue. 'Didn't recognize you in ordinary clothes. What do you want? We've never encouraged people to just turn up.'

'Well . . . after the way you led me on and then did a neat U-turn on the phone, that really doesn't bother me too much.'

'How *dare*—?'

'And is this really a good time to be selling a house in Wychehill?'

Merrily placed the *Malvern Gazette* on the table.

'Makes no difference.' Stella barely glanced at it. 'None of the potential purchasers ever come from this area. Look, Paul's only gone into Ledbury, and he'll be back soon and the things I'm guessing you want to talk about, if they get raised again it's going to spoil his day, big time. And right now, our marriage, let me tell you, is hanging on . . . *that.*'

She held a thumb and forefinger about a millimetre apart.

'So this move's a new start, is it?' Merrily said.

'Darling, this—' Stella slumped back into her canvas-backed chair. '*This* was supposed to be the new start. He "retired". ' She did the quote marks in the air. 'Should've realized what a horribly ominous word that is for a man. Strongly suggestive of impending impotence.'

'What, these days, when everybody seems to be retiring at fifty?'

'With Paul, it means something to prove. We originally bought this place as just a holiday home – he was in wood stoves, British end of a firm in New England, so a lot of transatlantic travel. *He* wanted to move out there but I wanted to do this up as a permanent home. Disastrous idea. Flung together in isolation – for ever! – with a man you realize you really never properly knew because he'd spent so much time away.'

'Rows?'

'Lots.'

'Like on the night you crashed?'

Stella looked up at Merrily, squinting at the sun, fumbling her dark glasses back on.

'What are you after? I rather thought you'd had your money's worth the other night.'

'Just the truth, this time. Why you lied to the police and everybody else.'

'Fuck *off!*'

'Well, actually, it's fairly obvious *why* you lied. I'd just like to confirm it, and maybe ask a few supplementary questions. It won't go any further. And you're leaving anyway. You *are* actually leaving, or was that also—?'

'No!'

Stella peered into her coffee. It looked like the coffee you made after a long and sleepless night, its hours counted out on fingers of alcohol. She sniffed and stood up.

'I lie all the time, actually. Paul's not in Ledbury, he's in London and he won't be back until tomorrow. But, yes, we are leaving. You want some of this, or would you like to give me an excuse to open a bottle of wine?'

Stella was away in the house for some time. Merrily gazed at the wounded rocks behind the trees and smoked a cigarette and checked the vicarage answering machine on her mobile.

There were five messages.

At barely ten a.m.?

Oh, God.

First message: '*Hello, Mrs Watkins, you might remember me – it's Amanda Patel from* BBC Midlands Today. *Not about you this time, you'll be glad to know, but we've seen the story about your daughter in the* Guardian *and we'd like to follow it up for tonight's programme. I've been on to the school, but she's apparently not shown up, so I wonder if...*'

Not shown up at school? *Guardian?*

'*... So if you could call me ASAP. I'll probably be on my way to Ledwardine, so I'll leave my mobile number...*'

Merrily switched off the phone and put out her cigarette, trying to clear her head as Stella Cobham came out. Wearing a green silk robe, she was carrying an opened bottle of Chardonnay, the level already conspicuously down, and two glasses.

'What's *your* driving licence look like, Merry?'

'I can't remember.'

Stella peered at her.

'You all right?'

'Yes.'

'Well, mine's got enough points on it that I'm just barely on the road. Can you *imagine* what it would be like living here if you didn't have a car?'

'I ...' *Concentrate.* 'Yes, I can understand why you didn't need a conviction for careless driving.'

'I wasn't drunk. I was just in a blind rage.'

Stella pulled her robe closer to her throat with one hand and reached out with the other for her wineglass, picking it up and then immediately putting it down again, as if this was some kind of testament to her sobriety on the night.

'Then afterwards I was standing there in the road, with these whingeing bloody German tourists totting up the damage, and it was obviously my fault, and I'm thinking *Oh shit oh shit, what am I going to do? . . .* when it came to me. I'd heard about the mad Loste claiming to've seen Elgar, and I thought, what's to lose? And then . . . there was no going back.'

*Stuck to the story in every detail,* Bliss had said. *Wouldn't budge. Said there was this other bloke who'd seen it and she'd bring him into court. Report went to the CPS, and they don't get many like this – at least, not where it's an intelligent, eloquent, opinionated woman who's going to be red-hot in the box and get it all over the papers. So the CPS made what was considered at the time to be a cautious and sensible decision. No charge.*

'And I suppose,' Merrily said, 'that you repeated the story in the church the other night . . .'

'Because I was sick of the snide comments, and I suppose I felt a bit sorry for you. And I wanted to wipe the complacent smile off Devereaux's face because, in a way, if it hadn't been for him . . .'

'Devereaux?'

'The reason I was so mad . . . going like a bat out of hell . . . swerved too late . . . I . . . Paul had started going for long walks to "keep in condition". I figured it was long walks down the hill and back up again, and in through a different gate.'

'Sorry?'

'I thought he was shagging someone. That weird bitch with her cheap see-through frocks and her kittenish fawning and her *Oh, don't you look so cool today, Paul.*'

'*Winnie?*'

'Yeah, I accused him of having a fling with Sparke. I know he fancied her . . . and she was so blatantly available. You watch her. Any given situation, she'll home in on the nearest man. Which is interesting for a woman who goes on about goddesses all the time.'

Merrily recalled Winnie on the hill that first night, going straight to Lol. *Like, are you the exorcist?*

'And were they? Having a fling?'

'He *would've* done, no question. I mean, that was the point. And I was convinced she . . . I mean, she was *so* knocked sideways when she got dumped by Devereaux, so—'

'Preston Devereaux?'

'Sorry, I forgot you're not . . . It was fairly widely known in Wychehill. Nothing wrong with that, both single. I remember thinking it was quite nice, actually. She seemed genuinely besotted with the guy: Mr Countryman – wellies, cap, Land Rover, gun over his shoulder. Most of those types, they're a bit thick, no conversation, but Devereaux's educated, been around. And rich. Rich enough to rescue a poor woman washed up – and I mean *washed up* – in a foreign country.'

'But it didn't work out?'

'She came round here one night, she was gutted. Shocked and insulted. I was stupid enough to commiserate. Stayed half the night, couldn't get rid of her. Most of the people here don't want to know you, but she's all over you. When it suits.'

'So Devereaux dumped *her*?'

'Winnie wanted too much. He's been single for a long time, and that's how he likes it. I mean, *she* isn't normally clingy, far as I can see – too arrogant, had too many attractive men – but she was with him. Mr Darcy senior. The American dream. And she clearly needs a lot of money. She was married to some guy, brought her over to London and then pissed off. But does a man like Devereaux— I mean in the end, does he want crystal balls and Tarot cards?'

'When was this?'

'Few weeks ago. I mean, some people think she's got a thing going with Tim Loste, but it's clear to me it's not *that* kind of thing. He thinks it's for conducting his choir. She just dominates him and after Devereaux she's devoting all her time . . . no wonder he finally went insane. Mind you, that was a bloody shock, wasn't it?'

Stella nodded at the *Gazette* and took off her sunglasses. Her eyes were crimson-rimmed, almost the colour of her spiky hair. It looked like she'd been doing some crying.

'Drink and drugs. This place is sick.'

'Loste really was doing drugs?'

'Not heroin. More like LSD or something. Magic mushrooms? You see him coming down from the hill sometimes, he's all over the place, although that could be the drink. Once I came across him lying in the heather, mumbling stuff. You stop questioning it after a while. I can't wait to leave, now. Not that I'm saying that to Paul; he thinks he's dragging me away from my dream situation. There's no honesty between us any more.'

'Maybe it'll be different in America.'

'I don't know.' Stella shook her head in disgust. 'I think Sparke's doing the rector now.'

'*What?*'

'Now that he's on his own.'

'That's rumour, is it?'

'Who knows?' Stella flipped a hand. 'She's been seen going into the rectory more than once. People notice these things.'

'Which people?'

'Holliday, for one. He doesn't like the rector ... or anyone much. Well ...' Stella looked across at the hill, near-vertical here, because of the quarrying. 'Sorry to spoil your day. I suppose, people in your job, it must make you feel quite worthwhile when you think you've found a real one. Especially if it's somebody distinguished. Elgar. You've got to laugh, haven't you?'

'It's a result, anyway,' Merrily said tightly.

She stood up, and Stella Cobham swung round to face her.

'Who told you about that? Somebody obviously did.'

'I have a friend. At the CPS.'

What harm would another lie do, in a place like this?

# 34

# Don't Do Sorry

'Awful,' Jane said. *Barbaric*.'

She said there were three double rows of barbed wire, more than chest high and with new stakes. And like a plastic screen over part of it, so you couldn't even see through.

'Like some high-security . . . like Guantanamo Bay or something. Like Guantanamo Bay's just appeared in Coleman's Meadow.'

Lol said, 'You didn't—?'

'No. Well, I'd've had to go back to Gomer's for the wire-cutters. And anyway, it was very thick wire. Heavy-duty. A proper fence, like I say. Impossible. Plus there were these two blokes there, putting up a big sign.'

'I'm guessing it doesn't say *Welcome to The Coleman's Meadow Ley Line*.'

'It says *Private Land. Keep Out. Trespassers will be prosecuted*. And the word *will* is underlined in red. Like somebody's splattered it on in a rage.'

'*Can* they just fence it off like that, if it's a public footpath?'

'*Is* it a public footpath, though? I don't know.' Jane didn't look at him. 'I should've checked it out, and I didn't. It's not marked as any kind of footpath on the OS map. This is all so totally my fault, isn't it? You get carried away with the romance and the excitement and you don't check the basic nuts and bolts. Didn't even check whether it was a right-of-way and I ignored the fact that it wasn't in *The Old Straight Track*. I'm naive and immature. I'm an *idiot*, Lol.'

Jane punched her knee and winced and started to cry. The *Guardian* was crumpled up on the hearthrug. Lol thought it was actually a bit magnificent. Jane wouldn't look at it.

'Ever wish you hadn't started something?'

The warmest day of the summer so far and she looked starved. Lol eyed her, curious. He'd never before heard her wishing she'd never started something.

'When I first saw the fence I was shocked and then I was furious. And then I saw ... when you're right up to it, the worst thing is ... you can't even see Cole Hill. I felt just ... sick. I just walked away and sat down in a quiet part of the orchard and howled.'

'Jane ...'

Lol sat next to her on the sofa. This was the time to put a comforting arm around her, but he never had. They were close, but she wasn't his daughter and there was an old barbed-wire fence in his head that had never quite rusted away and probably never would.

'And you know what?' Jane said. 'When I stopped howling, I realized I was sitting right on the ley, and there was ... nothing. Nothing to feel. No ancient energy. No shades of Lucy.'

'Because they'd ... blocked the line, you think?'

'Oh, *Lol* ...' Jane squeezed his hand. 'There's absolutely no need to be kind. I just wanted ... just wanted there to be some magic left.'

'What's wrong with that?'

'It's naive. People like me who listen to Nick Drake singing "I Was Born to Love Magic" and go all shivery. See, what I should've done – what a mature person would've done – I should've just objected to the housing, got some backing for that. Kept quiet about the ley. But no, I'm too smart for that. I go doorstepping a bunch of council guys at Pierce's ... in effect, tipping the bastards off. Now they know what it's all about and they've turned it into some disgusting no-man's-land. So nobody will ever see the magic again.'

'Do you know who *they* are?'

Jane shrugged. 'This guy Murray, the owner? Lol, look, if—' She glanced towards the door. 'If anyone comes, you haven't seen me. Only, when I got back from the meadow just now, Jim Prosser's like, *Oh, Radio Hereford and Worcester are looking for you and some newspaper people, and they've all been ringing the vicarage and getting no answer.* So now I can't even go home in case anyone . . . I mean, I can't talk to them now – I'm supposed to be at *school.* And I haven't any evidence. They'd just walk all over me. I'm just totally *dead,* Lol.'

Lol stood up and went to the window. Saw two men and a woman walking up Church Street – people he didn't know, and it was too early in the day for tourists. He stepped back and saw his own shadowy reflection in the dark side of the pane and knew that it wasn't Jane who'd been stupid. She was a schoolgirl, below voting age, in no real position to object to a private housing plan or attempt to influence a local authority to veto it.

*He,* on the other hand . . .

. . . Had just stood and watched, perhaps only really concerned that Jane shouldn't do anything to embarrass Merrily as parish priest.

'You're right. Best if you don't talk to anybody at this stage. Best if you stay here while we work out how to handle this.'

'*We?*'

'If you have no objections.' Lol turned his back on the street. 'Interesting how fast this fence has gone up. They didn't even wait for it to appear in the paper. The cattle had already gone last night.'

'I noticed that. Jim said they belong to the guy who bought the Powell farm, rents the grazing from Murray.'

'So if the cattle were removed yesterday – before the story appeared – that suggests that it was set up as soon as they heard the media were on to the story. OK . . . I'll go and check it out. You stay here, don't answer the door and be careful who you answer the phone to.'

'You don't have to—'

'I do have to. Listen, while I'm gone, could you . . . My laptop's under the desk. Could you put Wychehill Church into Google, see what you can find?'

'What for?'

'Think of it as Brownie points with your mum. You might need them.'

Jane smiled. Bit watery, but it was there. He told her about Prof Levin and the recording of the choir that *had* to be made at Wychehill.

'You're looking for connections with music. Choirs. Singing. I don't know. Any link with Elgar in particular would be good. Use your intuition.'

'Don't you think that's caused enough damage?' Jane folded up the *Guardian*, put it behind a cushion, out of sight. 'I can't bear it. Why couldn't I have just smiled? The photographer was going, *no, no, don't smile*, but I didn't *have* to play along, did I? Now I totally look like some evil slapper. An ASBO waiting to be issued. Lol . . . ?'

'Mmm?'

'I'm sorry for getting you involved.'

'Pull yourself together, Jane,' Lol said. 'You don't *do* sorry.'

The men who'd put up the fencing had gone but it looked, as Jane had said, like a not-so-open prison. Lol was furious. The way governments, national and local, were operating now. Even the council had its *cabinet*, where iffy issues could be sorted in secret. Any hint of opposition, doors closed, locks turned, walls went up.

And barbed wire.

OK, there was no proof that anyone from the council was involved in this. But it was likely, at least, that the landowner had the support of the Establishment.

And they'd fenced off something they didn't believe existed. They'd blockaded an *idea*.

Standing on the edge of the old orchard, Lol began to sense some of Jane's feelings about Alfred Watkins, who stood for independence of thought. Well into his sixties, a respected local figure, when *The Old Straight Track* was published, and the archaeological establishment had immediately turned on him. A barrier had gone up, and it was still up.

Independence of thought. Always a crime in the eyes of the Establishment. Lol was starting to feel suffocated, as if the air had been turned into shrink-wrap, when Gomer Parry came ambling out of the orchard, an inch of roll-up gummed to his lips.

'Lol, boy . . .'

Gomer extracted his ciggy, blew out a grey balloon of smoke. Lol wondered if a disused orchard was now classed as a public place where, although it might be entirely legal to light a massively carcinogenic bonfire, nobody was allowed to smoke.

Gomer nodded at the wire.

'Janie seen this yet?'

'What do you think?'

Gomer said, 'What I think is, Lucy Devenish was still alive, she'd drag Lyndon Pierce yere by the scruff, make the bugger tear it down with his bare hands.'

Lol thought what a pity it was that this kind of organic, natural justice was purely the preserve of old ladies.

'You think Pierce had something do with this?'

Gomer's shoulders twitched under his summer tweed jacket.

'You know this guy Murray, who owns the land?'

'By sight. Never worked for him. Big farm, and does his own drainage.'

*Does his own drainage.* Lowest of the low in the plant-hire world.

'Knowed his auntie, though, Maggie Pole, her as left him the meadow. Nice lady. Always very fond o' that meadow.'

'I don't think I knew her.'

'Left before you was here, boy. Went to an old folks' home, over towards Hay. Hardwicke.'

'The Glades?' Lol smiled. 'I used to know somebody there. How do you mean, fond of the meadow?'

'Used t' be a bench near the gate, and her'd go and sit there sometimes on a nice day. Peaceful place, nobody disturbed her. That was all I remembered, but after Jane come over the other night, I went to see an ole boy name of Harold Wescott. Know him?'

Lol shook his head. Gomer pinched the ciggy from between his lips with his thumb and forefinger.

'Gotter be over ninety, now, has Harold, but still got his own house. Can't tell you what he had off the meals-on-wheels yesterday, but you wanner know about anything happened in Ledwardine fifty year ago, he's your man. Anyway, Harold, he knowed Maggie Pole pretty well, and he remembers her was real careful who her let the meadow out to, for grass. Wouldn't have no overgrazin', no ploughin' up. Said it was a piece o' history.'

'*Did* she?'

'Don't get too excited, boy, wasn't nothin' to do with ley lines, far as Harold knows. 'Fact, he didn't know nothin' about ley lines. Not many of the old folks does. That was harchaeology – not for the likes of we.'

'So why was the meadow a piece of history?'

'Dunno. Harold reckoned it was Maggie's mother used to go on about it. Maggie's dad, ole Cyril Pole, he was a bit of a rough bugger, but her ma was a lady – real cultured, read books, had her own wind-up gramophone. Point is, Harold Wescott says Maggie told him her ma always said Coleman's Meadow wasn't to be touched.'

'And it ... you're saying it was left to Maggie Pole on that basis?'

'Sure t'be. But things get forgot, ennit? No kids, see, Maggie, never married, so that's why it all went to the nephew and the niece. Niece got the money, this Murray had the ground.'

'Did anybody else know the meadow wasn't to be touched? Could be important, don't you think?'

Gomer put the last inch of ciggy into his mouth, took a puff.

'Hard to say, boy. Been all overgrown, round there, see, for a good while, since the orchard started goin' to rot. Hell, aye, I'm sure some folks knowed, over the years, but mabbe they thought it best kept quiet about, like all these things. I'll keep askin' around. Where's Janie now?'

'My place. Should be at school, really, but she's hiding from the papers and the TV. Not so sure any more that she's got it right, you know? What are people saying in the village?'

'Hippie thing,' Gomer said. 'That's what they're sayin', boy. Sorry.'

Figured. In this area, the antique term *hippie* applied to any incomer of relatively unconventional appearance who couldn't afford a luxury executive home.

'What about the housing scheme, the loss of the field, the view of Cole Hill?'

'Don't affect many folks, see. They'll do bugger-all, 'less it affects them personal. You listens to 'em, spoutin' off in the shop ...'

'What are they saying about Jane?'

'Leave it, Lol. These is just folks as don't know the girl. Not like what we does.'

'No, come on . . . what *are* they saying?'

Gomer squeezed his ciggy out.

'They're just ignorant people with too much time.'

'Gomer . . . ?'

'Ah . . . sayin' it's no wonder her's goin' off the rails when her . . . when her ma en't around half the time. And no wonder Janie's livin' in a bit of a fantasy world when the vicar spends her time chasin' things as don't exist.'

'Instead of looking after the parish.'

'Ar, more or less. Sorry, boy, but you assed.'

# 35

# Three Choirs

WALKING DOWN THE LANE towards the church, Merrily tried Lol's number again. Still engaged. Tried his mobile and Jane's. Both switched off. Left a message that just said, in a voice which she hoped did not sound over-hysterical, 'the *Guardian?*'

She'd asked Stella Cobham if they happened to take the *Guardian*. They didn't.

She replayed the message from Amanda Patel of *BBC Midlands Today*, watching Mrs Aird leaving the church with a shopping bag, crossing the road and becoming gradually shorter as if she was sinking into the green verge on the other side. Wychehill people disappearing into their homes like rabbits into burrows.

There were now six more messages on the machine about Jane: *BBC Hereford and Worcester*, *Central News*, *Daily Mail*, *Hereford Times*, *Hereford Journal*. And a clipped and icy Robert Morrell, school director, Moorfield.

'*Mrs Watkins, perhaps you can call me, ASAP.*'

No wonder the bloody kid was out early. Merrily walked into the churchyard. Where, for heaven's sake, was she going to get a *Guardian* in Wychehill? She was recognizing the onset of a cold sweat when a seventh message was delivered by a voice like suede and sounding close enough to lick her ear.

'Mrs Watkins. Khan.'

Quite a long pause, as if Mr Khan was used to people dashing to disable their answering machines and pick up once they knew it was him. And then he said, 'Call me back, would you?' A patina of impatience. 'I'm in my Kidderminster office.'

She plucked half a pencil and a cigarette packet from her shoulder bag and sat down on the steps of the Longworth tomb to write down the number. No hurry to call him back. It was probably going to be a courtesy call, apologizing for bothering him. Any requiem now was likely to be a cosmetic exercise.

She ought to call Morrell. At least he'd be able to tell her what was in the *Guardian*. On the other hand, if she revealed to Morrell that she didn't know, what was *that* going to look like?

Leaning her head into the still-cool shadow of the stovelike tomb Merrily found herself staring up into the grotesque inverted rictus of the Angel of the Agony.

Purgatory. *I think we can deal with purgatory right here,* Winnie Sparke had said.

How true that was.

*It's as good as over.* Directing this thought at the Angel of the Agony. *I expect you know all about being burdened with crap.*

She'd knocked on Hannah Bradley's door. No answer. Probably one of her days at the Tourist Office in Ledbury. The mountain bike wasn't around. If Stella had lied and Loste was delusional, how likely was it that Hannah had told her the truth?

But she'd been so convincing. It had been like a breath of pure air. Who *could* you trust?

Merrily stared at the writing on the tomb.

'ALL HOLY ANGELS PRAY FOR HIM
CHOIRS OF THE RIGHTEOUS PRAY FOR HIM.'

So the quarry owner, Joseph Longworth, had seen an invented angel in a blaze of light and built a huge and costly church?

Wondering if Tim Loste's choir was praying for *him*, she heard not prayer but laughter and, peering around the tomb, saw two people walking into the church drive.

One of them was Winnie Sparke in her long, pale, flimsy dress. Winnie was laughing, her good and abundant hair thrown back.

Merrily slid down behind the tomb.

The man with Sparke was a very big man. Overweight, but with the height, almost, to carry it. Wide-shouldered, wearing a flannely sort of shirt outside his trousers. His dark hair was long and brushed back, and he had a moustache – not Lord Lucan, not Freddie Mercury, but a wide, black, *muscular* kind of moustache, like the one on the face on the back of a twenty-pound note.

Jane had washed her face; her eyes were bright but a little wild.

'I can't find the printer.'

'Haven't got one.'

Lol shut the front door and, for some paranoid reason, barred it. Although Church Street was deserted, there would be eyes at windows. This was Ledwardine.

'Lol ... you've got a laptop but no printer?'

'Just an oversight. I'll get one sometime.'

'Jeez.' Jane stood up. 'Did you see anybody?'

'Gomer. The fence guys've gone now. Gomer's not sure what's happening there either, but he does know a lot of people.'

'He's still on our side, though?'

'Jane, this is *Gomer Parry*. Anybody rung?'

'Bloke called Dan. Friend of Prof Levin's. I said you'd call him back. Then I had to go on-line. You ought to get broadband.'

'Don't use it enough. What did you find?'

'I was going to print it out when you got back, but under the circs I'd better give you the basics.'

Lol sat down on the sofa. Jane had the laptop on the desk, with a curtain half-drawn.

'Wychehill Church. Dedicated to St Dunstan, who's one of the patron saints of music. He was Bishop of Glastonbury in the eleventh century, and he played the harp or something. But the church was only dedicated in the 1920s. Built in the Victorian Gothic style by Joseph Longworth, quarry owner, after his conversion which – get this – was said to have followed a visionary experience on the hill.'

'What kind of visionary experience?'

'Haven't been able to find out. This was a boring ecclesiastical website, mainly dates and architectural features. All it says is that Longworth was stricken with remorse at the damage his quarrying had done to what he now realized was "holy ground". And so he went to Little Malvern Priory and prayed for forgiveness and was subsequently directed to this spot.'

'By God?'

'That's all it says about that. But something must've directed him because when he got there he found the remains of what was described as "a single-cell rectangular building" which was thought to be the remains of a monk's cell or a hermit's sanctuary.'

'Next to the road?'

'There wasn't a road there in those days, just a quarry track, and that was a few hundred yards away, so the road must've been put in later, probably after Longworth was dead. So he built his church on top of the foundations of the single-cell rectangular building – you could get away with that kind of thing in those days. It says he built a church big enough to take a full choir and orchestra.'

'Interesting.'

'And then he built the rectory and houses for the church warden and the choirmaster. And then other people built houses there, as the Malverns had become fairly sought-after with the spa and everything. So Longworth is actually credited with establishing what is now considered to be Wychehill. Lol – is all this anything to do with that guy getting his throat cut on the Beacon?'

'Anything's possible,' Lol said. 'It's a holistic world.'

'You want me to keep searching?'

'No, give it a rest. I'll ring this bloke. Thanks, Jane.'

'Took my mind off things a bit.' Jane closed the laptop. 'Feel like a ... fugitive.'

'We'll deal with it.'

'It's not your problem.'

'I suppose I'd like to think it was,' Lol said.

'Sorry.' Jane smiled. A strained kind of smile. 'I'd be honoured to be your problem. Especially if you can restrain Mum.'

*

The choir guy said his name was Dan and he lived up near the Frome Valley, which was presumably how he came to know Prof Levin. He also knew . . .

'Lol Robinson! I was at your concert at The Courtyard. Amazing. Shit hot. I mean it, man. A comeback in the truest sense.'

'Well . . . thank you. That's very kind.'

'Best tenor in these parts, me,' Dan said. 'But I'd give it all away for a croak if I could write songs like you. Seriously, I'd rather be in a band – Robert Plant, or something, big-voice stuff – but if you've got the finest tenor in Much Cowarne you're expected to use it. Cross to bear, man. On the plus side, you get to work with some unexpectedly wild people.'

'Tim Loste?'

'Yeah.' Dan's voice came down like he'd been unplugged. 'Prof told me. It's crazy, man. You *look* at Tim Loste, you think, yeah, wouldn't like to meet him on a dark night in a back alley. You *talk* to Tim Loste . . . no way. With a knife? Utterly out of the question. Problem is, the police talk to him . . . different wavelengths, you know?'

'Can you tell me a bit about his . . . wavelength?'

'Oh man, I could bend your ear for hours about Lostie. Only, I'm still in the choir, in a loose way, so none of this came from me, right?'

'Count on it.'

'Well, it's a big choir. The Loste boys – and girls. Drawn from maybe a fifty-mile radius. And you don't have to totally love Elgar, but it helps. Me, I like him better than I used to – when you're born in this area, you get the guy shoved down your throat from an early age. You live in *Elgar Country*. It's an honour. Yeah, thanks.'

'So you sang at Wychehill Church?'

'St Timothy's. As we call it. Acoustics are amazing. The quarry tycoon who had it built . . . Longthorne? You know that story?'

'Longworth?'

'That's the man. Venerated Elgar, saw himself as like Gerontius, from the oratorio, an ordinary man who'd sinned a bit, and now he's facing the final judgement and he's shitting himself. So the guy builds a bloody church. Stairway to heaven or what?

'A very big church designed for sacred music.'

'I think he wanted to buy into the Three Choirs.'

'Right. That would be The Three Choirs Festival? Gloucestershire, Worcestershire and Herefordshire?'

'Oldest fest of its kind in the country. Dates back to about 1700. But it's a cathedral thing, mainly, so I don't suppose Wychehill was much involved. The road wouldn't've been much more than a quarry track in those days. But it obsesses Tim. I don't get too close, to be honest, you get ... roped into stuff, and for every one that works there's a lot of time-wasters. He's inclined to exploit people – fair enough, he is a bit inspirational, and the women fancy him, not that they can get too close with the Witch of Endor around.'

'Winnie?'

'Spooky.'

'Why do you say that?'

'Just is. She gets the ideas. There was one where we were divided into groups of twelve, and Tim fixed up for us to use three different churches – Wychehill, Little Malvern Priory and St Bart's at Redmarley D'Abitot. We had to go to these separate churches and sing a set programme at the same time. I copped for Little Malvern – the parish church now, it is – and we had mobile phones connected with Tim and Winnie at Wychehill. And he'd give the word, and we'd all start singing simultaneously.'

'Singing what?'

'Gregorian chant, to start off, the warm-up. Then Elgar's *Kyrie Eleison*. These solid C of E establishments reverting to their Catholic roots. Strange at first but quite ... moving. The other thing I remember is how weird it felt, but I don't dwell on these things.'

'Weird how?'

'I dunno ... unexpectedly exciting, really. We did it by candlelight – that was Winnie's idea, too. Dunno whether you know the Priory church, but it's quite small and narrow. And it was, you know, quite a thrilling experience. I was a bit cynical about the whole idea at first, taking the piss, as you do, but ... I'd do it again tomorrow, I mean it, I'd travel a long way to do it.'

Dan sounded like he'd surprised himself, saying that. Lol waited. He was fascinated. He sometimes thought about playing in a church, not in some dumb happy-clappy band, but ... he didn't know; he just wanted, sometimes, to put himself into a situation where his music might find a different level.

'It was the things that were happening in my head,' Dan said. 'And my whole body, really. A vibration going through you, like wiring, and it's like different parts of you are lighting up in sequence. Can't explain it. I mean, all right, the chant usually gives you a bit of a lift. But this time the interconnectedness thing ... it wasn't just three churches coming together, it was like being inside a big ... orb of sound. Like we'd broken through to another place. I mean it. More than that, really, I ... bugger me, I sound like I'd taken something, don't I?'

'Why those particular churches?'

'Well, Tim never explained, he never does. He's an inarticulate bugger at the best of times; you think if he could talk in notes and chords, instead of words, he would, you know? They say he was a useless teacher. But we worked it out, kind of. Comes down to the three churches being in the Three Counties – Wychehill in Hereford-shire, Little Malvern Priory in Worcestershire and Redmarley D'Abitot in Gloucestershire. So what he'd done, he'd assembled his own Three Counties choir ... the Three Counties united in sacred chant. Weird.'

'And he never tells you what's behind all this?'

'Not talked about, Lol. We're all a bit funny about that kind of thing, en't we? One woman – this is just one woman, mind, and I don't know her very well, but she was white as a sheet when we come out. Said that when we were doing the Mass, she seen like a figure, up at the altar. Tall hat. Well, a bishop's mitre. And he's standing there with his arms raised. Like ... like a bishop, I suppose. She was pretty shocked, but it might've been just the state we were all in.'

'This happened when you were singing music from the Mass – Elgar's music?'

'Well, yeah, but I later found out there was a famous photo taken in there where you're supposed to be able to see the ghostly shape of a bishop with his crozier. So she may've come back down with that in her head. You're a bit high with the singing and you find you're focused on the same spot that you've seen in the picture, and it's all candlelit. When she told us, she wasn't frightened exactly, it was more white with awe. And I remember thinking, *Yeah, we woke him up, and he's celebrating the Mass.* And suddenly the idea of *celebrating* the Mass made sense to me for the first time.'

'Well,' Lol said. 'Thanks.'

'You should write a song about him,' Dan said.

# 36

# The Dream

STASHING AWAY THE NOTEBOOK and the phone and shouldering her bag, Merrily walked directly over. But Winnie was already blocking the porch, her hands out, long nails, and her eyes almost black in the full sunlight.

'No way.'

'They let him go?'

'I'm asking you, Merrily, with civility, to back off.'

'That was him, wasn't it?' Merrily said.

'*Whaddaya* think, it's Elgar's freaking ghost?'

Tim Loste had vanished into the church and the oak doors were shut. At the porch entrance, Winnie Sparke didn't move. Her arms were slim but unexpectedly muscular, tanned and taut.

'And this is just as close as you get today, lady. He's in a delicate state. You need to show some respect.'

'You were laughing.'

'I'm laughing, he isn't. I'm happy he's out.'

'I need to talk to him.'

'Some other time. Jeez, he was accused of *killing* a guy ... with a knife? They had him in some interrogation cell, threw the whole damn package at him, hour after hour, different cops, good cop/bad cop, all that shit. How they make you confess to what you didn't do. Come at you and come at you till you don't know whether it's night or freaking day.'

'Bad experience, Winnie, but *I* didn't get him arrested. My business here's road accidents. And that's as good as over. I'm just drawing lines under things.'

'Well, you go draw your lines someplace else.'

'Why don't you want me to talk to him?'

'That's how you choose to see it, you go right ahead. You put it all on me.'

Unbelievable. Was this really the same woman who, a couple of nights ago, in this very spot, had been all let's-get-together and explaining how the rocks were in pain, telling Merrily how cute she was?

*... And her kittenish fawning and her, Oh, don't you look so cool today, Paul.*

'All right,' Merrily said. 'How about I just talk to you?'

'Later.' Winnie Sparke's eyes were like smoked glass. 'I have to take care of Tim.'

In the church, the organ started up, low and growling chords. Winnie smiled.

'Giving himself a fix.'

'He'll be OK on his own for a while, then.'

'Look, I'll call you sometime. OK?'

'It's a public place, the church. I often go into other churches to pray. I think I feel the need—'

'No . . .'

Winnie's hands were out, clawed again.

'You really going to scratch my eyes out? Winnie, I've been messed about for days, and my daughter's got some problems and I need to go home. I'm asking for a few minutes of your time. Or if you're determined to have an unseemly cat fight to prevent me entering a church . . .' Merrily unslung her bag, dropped it at her feet. 'Then let's *do it.*'

The sun burned down and the church shimmered.

'OK.' Winnie Sparke's hands fell, her shoulders slumping. 'But give me three minutes to go talk to him.'

'I expect there's a back door, right?'

'You have my word,' Winnie said.

Merrily sighed.

'Save me some time, Frannie,' Merrily said into the phone. 'Just tell me why he's out.'

Bliss left the line open while he went downstairs to the car park. '*Yeh*, it's true.'

'I know it's true. I've just seen him. When did they let him go?'

'Your friend Sparke collected him from Worcester about an hour ago. The DNA evidence was, to say the least, inconclusive. But, mainly, other developments have altered the focus of the case in a way more meaningful for me, as an observer.'

'Can you tell me?'

'With the usual proviso. The murder I told you about in Pershore – the drug dealer tortured and shot in his car, Christopher Smith? We may have his killer.'

'In custody?'

'In a manner of speaking, although he won't be signing a confession. What happened, two mates of Smith's, encouraged by a modest reward and considerably emboldened, no doubt, by news of Roman Wicklow's death, have now come forward to say that they saw Mr Smith leaving a nightclub in Worcester on the night of the killing, in the company of Mr Wicklow. Mr Wicklow being, as we've learned, a man who inspired considerable fear in his community.'

'Wicklow murdered Smith?'

'It begins to look like it.'

'Do you know why?'

'Apparently we do not, at this stage. But it's usually a simple territorial dispute.'

'So if they were both dealers and Wicklow was working for Khan, who was Smith working for?'

'*Dunno*. It was part-time with Smith, he had a day job in an abattoir. Maybe he was also working for Khan. These situations get complicated. Maybe Smith had been unreliable and Wicklow was assigned to take him out. We don't know, Merrily, that's the honest answer.'

'But Loste is off the hook.'

'*Course* he isn't. They just had to let him go for the moment. No

DNA pointers, and the CPS advised that there was insufficient evidence to support a murder charge.'

'So they could have him in again?'

'He's a big lad, Merrily, and clearly three sheets in the wind.'

'But surely the idea of a former music teacher killing a man who's now emerging as a cold and practised assassin . . .'

'Look,' Bliss said, 'I agree with you. Like I said *I* think it's drug-related and even though there's evidence of Loste trading with Wicklow on the Beacon, if it was me I'd be looking to talk to the friends of Mr Smith – the ones we *don't* know about yet. And Raji, naturally. But it's not me, it's Annie Howe, and Howe's still keen on Mr Loste. On the points scale, one nice, educated, upper-middle-class killer is worth at least five street urchins.'

Surprisingly, Winnie Sparke came out of the church. Alone, but it was a start.

Merrily guided her to Longworth's tomb under the Angel of the Agony. Winnie seemed uneasy about this, glancing up a couple of times before perching on the edge of a step. The Angel's half-spread wings were shielding them against the sun, but in a predatory way.

The hell with him. Merrily sat down and leaned a shoulder into the lower folds of his marble robe.

'Sometimes this job can be quite damaging to your faith, Winnie.'

'I don't care for faith. Faith is intellectually lazy.'

'OK, skip the theological debate.'

'It's your show.'

'Until I ask you something you don't want to answer.'

Winnie shrugged. The organ started up again, something that Merrily half recognized. Not Elgar, too clipped, like fine topiary. Bach?

'Bottom line, here?' Winnie said.

'Bottom line is the ghost of Edward Elgar. It's the only reason I'm here, and I've wasted enough time on it. And I'm fed up with being circuitous. Did Tim make it up, or did he, in some way, conjure it up? Is he disturbed, sick or just a drunk?'

'You want me to place a tick against one of the above?'

'Or if a fourth possibility got missed out along the way . . .'

'And what if I was to tell you . . .' Winnie looked down into her lap '. . . that I didn't know?'

'I thought you'd at least have an opinion, all the esoteric subjects I assume you've studied.'

'In order to write books, it helps to study.'

'Is that still what you do?'

'It's an income. Not a good one. Better in the States. Life is more expensive here, and Mind, Body, Spirit books don't sell so many.'

'Are you doing a book on this?'

'Maybe.'

'Is that why you're playing it close to the chest?'

Winnie didn't answer.

Merrily said, 'I don't write books. Sometimes I have to make reports, but they're internal. Say, for the Bishop, or as a safeguard against comebacks, or background notes for my successor in the job.'

'This may be the book I get remembered for,' Winnie said.

'Not just another New Age paperback.'

'No. I came over ten years ago on account of an English guy who was . . . who proved to be not Mr Right. Not even Mr Halfway Right. Couple years ago, I realized that if I was to stay – and I kind of like it here – I needed a project that would turn over some bigger money. I conceived the idea of a book that would explore the spiritual roots of musical creativity, through Elgar and the Malverns. I have a degree in ancient history and anthropology, although I knew I was gonna need some help with the music.'

'You had a new angle on this?'

'I visited here, found Longworth's church and also this cottage that was proving hard to shift off the agent's books on account it was too small and the quarrying had left no place to extend and it was dangerous for kids and stuff like that. I could afford to buy, if I sold my apartment in London, which was what I did. And then, at a conference on Elgar at the Abbey Hotel in Malvern, I met Tim.'

'Someone who could help you with the music.'

'More than that. A whole lot more. Tim grew up in Sussex, near

Elgar's home there, Brinkwells. He'd always felt there was something between him and Elgar that was . . . going someplace.'

'Creatively?'

'Creatively, yes. Which basically was how *he* wound up in Malvern. In most other areas, around this time, I should tell you, his life was a mess. He'd split with his girlfriend, he was starting to drink too much and he was pretty close to getting fired from his job at the college.'

'When was this?'

'This would be just over a year ago.'

'So you and Tim . . .'

'Began to work together. To get this out of the way, I need to tell you that there's no physical relationship. Situation was, there was someone else in my life at the time.'

'Preston Devereaux?'

'Stop.' Winnie's expression didn't alter.

'Don't go there?'

'On no account.'

'OK.'

'Tim's parents live in France, and he was closest to his grandmother. When she died, he inherited a substantial sum of money. By this time, I'd researched the situation here, pertaining to *this* gentleman.' Winnie gently tapped the tomb. 'I drew Tim's attention to a house that'd come on the market in Wychehill.'

'Caractacus.'

'It seemed too perfect. It's an ugly house, but it's in the right place, and I . . . I should've explained that Tim's primary problem was an inability to reach the heights as a composer. He'd always written music, his knowledge and his technique were never in doubt. He taught with flair and sympathy. His original work was . . . of a standard. There was a barrier between him and . . . what I call the sublime. The fact that he could never get beyond that caused him intense emotional pain.'

'But he bought the house . . .'

'He didn't want to *know* about the house. He didn't want to see me. I gave up on him. A week later, he swallowed a bottle of pills with most of a bottle of whisky, walked out in the street and collapsed. I didn't know about this, I'd been down in London, tying up the ends of my divorce and seeing friends. I didn't know how close he came to death. I didn't know anything about it until he showed up at my door, couple of weeks later, and said he'd had a dream, while they were fighting to save him in the hospital. Like *The Dream of Gerontius*. You listened to all of that yet?'

'Twice. In my uneducated way.'

'Gerontius dies. He's an old man, not a young man like Tim, but no matter. Gerontius either dies or he's in a deep coma. Whatever, he sheds the body load and loses the weight of his pain. And he meets with his guardian angel.'

'A woman, in my version.'

'It's always a woman. So Tim arrives at my door – a moment I relive quite frequently – and he tells me that he now understands that I am his guardian angel.'

'And how does he know that?'

'From his dream. He says he awoke in hospital knowing it. And now he goes along with me. He buys the house and we meet with the rector and Tim starts to play the organ in church – there was an old guy who fumbled his way around the keys, he was happy to let it go. And then, quite quickly, the choir was formed. People love to sing. They love to have the music drawn through them, like silk. The choir comes out of the three counties, building its reputation, refining its membership. It's a fine choir, growing toward the sublime.'

'So Tim has died and come through to a new level? His old life has dropped away, he's in a new place, with a new—'

'Yeah, maybe.'

'This was what you meant when you said you believed that purgatory could be dealt with in this life. Tim is physically purged, with a stomach pump, and then—'

'Gradually, I became aware of a pattern. A grand design of cosmic proportions. And I can see from your eyes, Merrily, that you're sorry we got here.'

'No, I— He hasn't exactly stopped drinking, has he?'

Winnie Sparke stood up. Her face and neck shone with sweat.

'Go deal with your kid, huh? You're Episcopalian, and this is Catholic theology. You have an inbuilt antipathy.'

'That's not fair.'

'Women priests . . . that's a political thing. I'm not being . . . I mean, there's no spiritual basis to it, right?'

Like she was the very first person to say that.

'Is it part of your image, to come over as mercurial, Winnie?' The heat was getting to Merrily's patience. 'Or are we simply approaching another area that you feel it would not be advantageous to get into?'

'You're not ready. You need to go away and consider this. I don't believe you're ready, spiritually, emotionally or intellectually, to feel the heat of the sublime.'

'Whereas . . . you are?'

'You have to excuse me,' Winnie said. 'I have things to do.'

# 37

# Spiritual Malnutrition

A TRACTOR AND TRAILER were rattling past, down the lane from the track which led into the hills. Merrily climbed into her boiling car in front of Starlight Cottage and slammed the door, the mobile clamped tight to her ear.

'Sorry, couldn't hear for the traffic.'

'I just said, she's here,' Lol said.

She closed her eyes and tipped her head back, the direct sun making a pulsing orange light show on her eyelids.

'Thank God for something.'

'And the piece in the *Guardian* . . .' Lol said. 'I'll read it out to you.'

When he'd finished, she asked him if he'd mind reading it again. He read it again, slowly, while Merrily was opening all the car windows.

'It could be worse, couldn't it? She lied about her age.'

'To make her an adult,' Lol said.

'And obviously her terminology – *Philistine morons*, for heaven's sake. But the worst thing—'

'She should have told you.'

'That's the worst thing, yes.'

'It all happened so quickly, and you weren't around. But she *should* have told you, and she knows that.'

'I'm a lousy mother.' Merrily leaned out of the window for more air. 'I'll come home. I'll be home in an hour.'

'No,' Lol said. 'Don't.' ·

'Don't— *Ow!*' Merrily pulled her bare forearm away from the Volvo's scorching bodywork. 'Sorry. Don't come home?'

'I mean not yet. There's a TV crew around, and they'll doorstep you, and you won't know what to say.'

'You're right, I suppose.' Merrily ran fingers through her hair; her head felt full of swirling fragments. 'It's just—'

'Better to wait until late afternoon, when they've all filed their pieces – and without Jane they won't be able to do much. Most of them might even drop it. It's not a huge story, after all. And it's Friday, and ... How are things over there?'

'Well, since you ask, it's starting to seriously piss me off.'

It was good to unload it all on someone entirely non-judgemental. She told him everything, from Stella Cobham to Winnie Sparke who was all over the place.

'First she's doing the New Age paganism bit – springs and water goddesses – and then it's High Catholic theology and getting lofty about women priests! It gets very hard to listen politely to this crap.'

'I talked to an interesting guy.'

Lol told her about Prof Levin and a chorister called Dan who, working with Loste, thought he'd broken through to a higher place.

'That must have been nice for him. What a dismal life of spiritual malnutrition we lead in the Anglican Church.'

'But at least you never become bitter and cynical.'

'Sparke ...' Merrily wiped sweat off her forehead with the back of her hand. 'Winnie Sparke virtually accused me of not being equipped to grasp the profundity of it. Not equipped to feel *the heat of the sublime!*'

'The bitch,' Lol said.

'Time to talk to Syd Spicer. And I mean *talk*. You'll look after Jane?'

'Merrily, you sound like—'

'And I also need to ring Morrell.'


Morrell. What was it about Morrell? You *tried* to like these people – as a priest, you tried to like virtually everybody, but ...

'Before you say anything else, Mr Morrell, it's my fault entirely. *I* kept her off school. I decided it wasn't fair to inflict this situation on you, and as it was near the end of term ...'

'But surely,' Morrell said, 'you must realize the normal procedure would have been to consult me first. I might well have agreed.'

'Well, yes, but there wasn't really *time*. I mean, there it was, in the paper . . . and I had an appointment.'

'You didn't *know* it was going to be in the paper?'

'Well . . . not this particular *day* . . .'

'But you evidently knew, Mrs Watkins, that she was embarking on this madness—'

'Madness? What's so mad about—?'

'—Under the pretext of an A-level project, and didn't think to inform me.'

'According to Jane you already knew.'

'One thing I most certainly did *not* know was that she'd taken this unscientific nonsense to the media. But I *had* warned her that repeatedly playing truant in order to pursue some misguided campaign against the local authority was going to get her into seriously hot—'

He must have heard Merrily catch her breath.

'Did I surprise you there, Mrs Watkins?'

'Well, I—'

'Could it be that you didn't know about Jane's recurrent *migraine*?'

'Migraine.'

She shut her eyes against the sun. Even with all the windows down it was getting unbearable in here. *Migraine?*

'I gather your curious job keeps you away from home quite a lot these days.' Morrell's voice was plumped out with satisfaction. 'But you must know this is not something I can be seen to overlook. Yes, I value my reputation as a liberal, even radical school director, but if I allow students to come and go to pursue their whims I'm undermining my own authority. So I have to tell you that what I'm looking for now is Jane Watkins outside my room on Monday morning, with a full explanation, an abject apology and a readiness to accept whatever retribution I consider necessary.'

'I see.'

'And if that isn't forthcoming, I also have to tell you I don't expect to see her at all.'

'You're talking about suspension?'

'Oh, I'm talking about a bigger word than *that*, Mrs Watkins. And also, in line with the usual procedure, I'm talking to the governors about it. I'm sorry, you'll have to excuse me, I have another call waiting.'

'*No*,' Merrily said. 'If you hang up on me now, I'm—'

Jesus, *what*? She was sweating. He'd have the governors in his pocket.

Dead noise. He might have gone; you could never tell with a mobile. Or he might just want her to think he'd gone.

'If you hang up on me, Mr Morrell . . . or take any extreme action against my daughter until I've had a chance to sort this out . . . Heaven's sake, you've got kids dealing drugs, assaulting teachers, here's one, all she's doing is making a stand against something in her own village – not even in the school – that she feels is wrong? OK, something that you, as an atheist and an arch-sceptic, probably wouldn't understand. And, yes, she's never exactly tactful, and she gets up people's noses. But if you go to the governors with this – some of whom are bound to be on the bloody council – I'm going straight to the national press, and I'll make it my business to ensure that everybody knows what a pompous, smug, self-seeking, hypocritical prick you've become.'

Merrily cut the line, dropped the mobile on the passenger seat.

She was shaking. Her sweat was turning cold. She fastened her seat belt, fumbling with it, started the car and drove down to the church parking bay. Stared for a moment through the windscreen, past the church entrance to the gables of the Rectory, its windows smoky-black against the sun.

Not many people left to antagonize.


Spicer wasn't answering the bell and she couldn't hear it ringing inside the Rectory. Merrily banged on the front door, stepped back, scanned all the windows for movement.

Nothing. She went round the side of the house – like her own rectory, too damned big – and hammered on the back door, then walked away onto the lawn that rose into the forestry, a screen concealing quarrying scars and who knew what else.

So many screens in Wychehill, but the afternoon sun was high and hot and relentless and drove her back into the shade of the open back porch, where she stood beating one last time on the back door. Leaning on the lever-handle in frustration – and the door opened.

It swung back with no creak, and she was looking into a utility room with a Belfast sink, a pair of Wellingtons standing underneath it, a balding Barbour on a peg.

Merrily said, 'Syd?'

No reply.

'Syd, are you in?'

She was experiencing an unseemly urge to search the house, find the secret photos in the drawers, uncover Syd Spicer's hidden history. The door at the end might not be locked, but she was reluctant to approach it. Afraid to? Maybe.

For reasons that she was reluctant to examine, she backed away, closed the porch door and went down the drive to the roadside.

Back in the car she rang Rajab Ali Khan's office in Kidderminster, returning his call to her answering machine.

'If that's Mrs Watkins,' a woman said, 'Mr Khan said to tell you he'll be at the Royal Oak for the rest of the day. He says if you can spare the time he'd like to see you.'

# 38

# Local Democracy

JANE HAD FOUND REDMARLEY D'Abitot church on the OS map, ringing it in pencil.

'This is interesting. Look . . .'

'One second . . .'

Lol peered around the curtain. Mid-afternoon, and the tourists were out on Church Street, the camera-hung carousel with its tape-loop of soundbite conversations. Only today, some of the visitors would be media and they knew, from the *Guardian*, what Jane Watkins looked like.

'Go on . . .'

He polished his glasses on his T-shirt, put them back on to examine the map folded on the desk. Redmarley, on the other side of the M50 motorway, just over the Gloucestershire border, was almost due south of the Malvern range.

'I know I'm obsessed with leys at the moment,' Jane said. 'But it's almost like there *is* one, going up from Redmarley, interlinking the three counties, the full length of the Malverns. See?'

Jane had drawn in the line. It wasn't connecting ancient sites as much as hilltops. Lol counted five: Midsummer Hill, Hangman's Hill, Pinnacle Hill, Perseverance Hill, North Hill.

'And look at this . . .'

She'd also marked the two major Iron Age hill forts, Herefordshire Beacon and Worcestershire Beacon. But the line didn't go through the middle of either – it skirted the first to the right and the second to the left.

'That's not a problem, it's how it seems to work,' Jane said. 'Alfred Watkins noticed that leys almost always cut along the edge of a hill fort rather than through the middle. If you look on the map, it's the same with Cole Hill – although when you're actually on the line it looks as if you're looking directly towards the summit.'

'What does that mean?' Lol said. 'Cutting to the sides.'

'Simple. Iron Age people lived in the middle of those hill forts. There were huts and things. You don't want powerful spiritual energy in your actual home, do you? You'd go slowly insane with the intensity of it. So you live to the *side* of the ley. Churches built on sites of ritual worship are something else, obviously.'

'Being places you actually go to for a spiritual buzz?'

'Uh-huh. So Redmarley Church is right on the line. Now, the other church where they had a choir going, Little Malvern Priory, that's *not* on the great north-south ley. It is on *a* ley, though, another one that's cutting left to right, across the north-south line. Now here's Wychehill . . .'

'Where the two lines cross.'

'Cool, huh?'

'You may be on to something here,' Lol said. 'I just wish I knew what.'

'We're looking at a whole *range* of holy hills. That would make this a massively important area, geopsychically.'

She looked up at Lol and sighed softly.

'You know, I love this. It reinforces your sense of . . . I dunno . . . Like, you just put your pencil on the map, and it's like the choir guy said, you're suddenly at the centre of something immense. Almost like you're making a personal connection with . . .' Jane shook her head rapidly '. . . bollocks.'

'Maybe all great ideas start off as bollocks,' Lol said. 'It's the way—'

'Oh hell, who's this?'

Jane snatched a quick glance around the curtain and then moved away from the window, her head down. Someone was knocking on the front door.

'Go upstairs,' Lol said.

'Mr Robinson, is it? Sorry to bother you, but I understood you might know where the vicar is.'

He was wearing a suit and a wine-coloured tie which – first thing Lol noticed – matched his plump lips. Swaying a little, rattling small change and keys in his pockets. It seemed so not his generation, rattling your keys. He couldn't be more than thirty.

'Sorry,' Lol said. 'I'm not really sure where she is. Her work takes her all over the diocese.'

'Daughter with her, do you know?'

'Wouldn't imagine so. It's, um, Mr Pierce, isn't it?'

'Lyndon Pierce, that's right.' Gelled hair glinting in the sunlight like the roof of a black cab. 'Sure we must've met sometime or other. Been trying to get around to see all the newcomers to the village, one by one.'

'I've been here a few years now, actually,' Lol said. 'You probably didn't notice me. Is there . . . anything I can do? Any message I can pass on?'

'That's very possible, Mr Robinson, yes.'

Lyndon Pierce's local accent seemed to have acquired a transatlantic roll. He glanced meaningfully over his shoulder at a Japanese dad photographing his family on the edge of the square.

'You want to come in?' Lol said.

'Thank you.' Pierce rubbed his hands. 'Won't keep you a minute, Mr Robinson, but there *are* some things that I think Mrs Watkins should know about, if you happen to be in . . . contact with her.'

Letting him into the living room, Lol felt unexpectedly nervous. The guy represented aspects of life he'd avoided: never needed to consult a local councillor, never earned enough to need an accountant.

Pierce was standing on the hearthrug, taking in the orange ceiling that Jane had recommended, the crystals that Jane had positioned in the window, the Boswell guitar. No doubt thinking, *neo-hippie.*

'Lot of people're looking for Mrs Watkins today, Mr Robinson. And . . . Jane, of course. Girl seems to have started something she'll likely live to regret. Her mother, too, mabbe.'

He must have figured, from the contents of the room, that the chances of ever getting the occupant's vote were remote enough for him to skip the niceties.

'Unfortunate, but people do tend to blame the parents for the behaviour of the child, don't they, Mr Robinson?'

'You'd call Jane a child?'

The door to the hall and the stairs was not quite closed. *Please don't let her be behind it.*

'Likely not to her face.' Lyndon Pierce laughed. 'Look, all right, Mr Robinson, I'll come directly to the point. We got quite a serious problem yere. I was phoned up a few hours ago by Gerry Murray – owner of Coleman's Meadow? Not a happy man, as you can imagine. I went to check out the situation for myself and then I gave him my suggestion, which was to get the police in.'

Lol blinked. 'To arrest Jane?'

'I'm sure a lot of folk would think that wasn't a bad idea, actually, Laurence.'

Using *Laurence* now, in the power-trip way of young policemen when they pulled you over for speeding.

'I'm sorry, Lyndon,' Lol said. 'I don't get out much. Something's happening in Coleman's Meadow?'

Pierce sniffed. 'All look the same to me – green activists, animal liberationists, ragbag of scruffs from God knows where. *They* say it's a demonstration . . . we might consider it threatening behaviour.'

'You mean . . . there's a protest?' Lol was fighting a smile. 'About the ley line?'

'You're telling me you didn't know? Very, very stupid people, Laurence. 'Bout a dozen of 'em. Posters, placards. Trying to protect something we all know *don't exist.*'

Lol saw Pierce taking in the OS maps on the desk with the ancient sites ringed and the pencil lines connecting them. He began to fold them up as Pierce smirked.

'Yes, I can see you didn't know a thing about it.'

'It was in the *Guardian.*'

'And who put it there, Laurence? I'll admit I'm having difficulty with this, see. Why you and that girl and those cranky sods out there wanner put the mockers on a much-needed development in an otherwise-useless, derelict area.'

'But . . . isn't there a statutory notice posted at the site for the actual purpose of inviting objections?'

'Aimed at local council-tax payers with a legitimate viewpoint, not sad buggers with nose rings who come from miles away 'cause they feel lost if they en't got a protest to go to. And not adolescents getting above themselves and trying to cause trouble. In fact . . .' Pierce looked down at his shoes and then back at Lol. 'I think I should tell you that people are beginning to feel it's time that girl's mother did something to curb her behaviour before—'

'Before the community does? A curfew? Court order banning her from going within half a mile of Cole Hill?'

'Don't get silly, now.'

Lol raised both eyebrows. 'All because she feels strongly about preserving the village heritage?'

'Laurence, that's *balls*. One of our experts says it en't even in that feller's book. She made it up. It don't exist. It never existed. It's a bloody joke. It's . . . flying-saucer stuff. Me, I'm simply trying to be reasonable, here, see both sides of it. When she's a bit more mature, she'll likely realize that, like all these villages, Ledwardine has to grow or die.'

'Grow into what?'

'All I'm saying . . . if people consider we're now within commuting distance of London, then we got to run with that. Home Counties overrun with asylum seekers, decent hard-working folk gotter move somewhere. If they wanner sell up and bring their money here, who're we to—?'

'Grow into an extension of London suburbia? Three hours is now commuting distance?'

'Or quicker, with a fast car.'

'Jesus,' Lol said.

'You people . . .' Lyndon went back on his heels. 'You really make me laugh. You're living in the bloody past. I'm an accountant, boy, we're the first to see the signs. I see the farmers' profits going on the slide, year after year. It's patently clear that agriculture can't sustain the county any longer and the county can't sustain agriculture. If cheap imports are killing farms and the government don't want 'em growing food n' more, there en't nothing we can do about that. Farmer wants to survive, he sells what ground he can for quality housing at the best price he can get. Our job's to support the farmers.'

'That's a very twisted kind of logic, Lyndon.'

'And I'll give you some more. City people, weekend folk, are used to more sophisticated facilities than we've been able to provide, and if they wants 'em on the doorstep we gotter give them that in Ledwardine itself – more shops, proper supermarkets, and at the same time—'

'Jim Prosser know about that?'

'Jim Prosser'll be retired soon. And we can catch up on what the rural areas've been missing all these years. You don't think local people should have sophisticated facilities, Laurence? Decent leisure centre?'

'Has anybody asked them?'

'Laurence . . .' Lyndon Pierce blew air slowly down his nostrils. 'That's why you elect councillors. It's called *local democracy.*' He beamed, case proven. 'Anyway, if you do hear from Mrs Watkins, put her in the picture, would you? If she wants to speak with me about this matter I'll be available.'

'Are these . . . ?' Lol heard the stairs creak. 'Are these protesters still there?'

'Not for long. New legislation's made it easier to deal with time-wasting scum. Likely we'll have it sorted before teatime without any arrests.'

'What with, water cannon? Rubber bullets?'

'People like you worry me,' Pierce said. 'Vicar be back home tonight, will she?'

'Far as I know.'

'Only, folks keep saying to me as how she spends so much time out of the parish these days we might as well not have a vicar at all.'

'Who would that be, specifically, Lyndon?'

'Pretty hard, seems to me, for a parish vicar to win back support once it starts to slip, Laurence. Specially if her daughter's setting a bad example to other kids, skipping school, making trouble. I'll leave you to think about the implications of that.'

Pierce placed a hand on the living-room doorknob, then turned back to Lol with a minimal smile.

'Oh . . . and if certain people who en't local don't like the way we do things around yere, seems to me they might think about moving on? Knowing they can always get a good price for their period cott—'

The door opened, pushing Lyndon Pierce back into the room. Jane was standing there, face as white as her school shirt, gazing at Pierce with all the warmth of a November twilight.

'You mean if people don't like things being run by bent councillors?'

Pierce's smile was history. Lol watched, with a horrified kind of fascination, as the man tongued his full lips as though he was trying to tease it back.

'Or maybe,' Jane said, 'maybe if they don't like bastards who used to shoot blue tits off the nut-containers with their airguns?'

'You . . .' Pierce's forefinger came up '. . . had better watch your mouth.'

'Lyndon,' Lol said softly. 'She's just a *child*.'

Pierce spun round at him.

'As for you . . . vicar know you've had her daughter upstairs? 'Cause it looks like she's gonner find out, ennit? But don't you worry, Laurence, it won't be from me. Not directly, boy, not *directly*.'

Lol had to grab Jane and hold on to her to stop her going for Pierce. Or maybe it was the other way round.

Whichever, them holding one another like this, he knew as soon as Pierce stepped briskly outside and all the heads began to turn that it wasn't going to look good from the crowded street.

# 39

# Temple of Sound

IN THE COPY OF the *Malvern Gazette* open on Raji Khan's ebony desk, there was a hole where the face of Leonard Holliday used to be.

Mr Khan stabbed it again with his Gold Cross pen.

'Why are they doing this to me, Mrs Watkins? Can *you* tell me that?'

He was wearing a cricket shirt and cream slacks and white shoes. His black hair hung beyond his shoulders, cavalier style. In his left ear he wore what might have been an emerald. Merrily sat on the other side of the desk in a dark wood chair which was meaningfully lower than his.

'Probably just that . . . this is not what they expect to find,' she said carefully, 'in a place like this? Have you tried inviting the Wychehill Residents' Action Group up here to discuss it?'

Mr Khan's office, upstairs at the Royal Oak, was like something out of Sherlock Holmes: drapery and brass standard lamps, deep maroon walls and a grey picture-rail. Didn't really work in summer, but with a coal fire on a December day it would be awfully cosy. A middle-aged Asian woman who dressed like Sophie had shown Merrily up. No doormen apparent on the premises, no DJ Xex.

'You know, I once did invite them,' Mr Khan said. 'They wouldn't meet me. I am, it would appear, the very spawn of Satan.'

'And I left the holy water in the car.'

Mr Khan beamed. At first, she'd been thinking how surreal all this was, how unlike anyone's idea of a drug baron's lair. But it was, in effect, like a *traditional* drug baron's lair, and Mr Khan was behaving curiously like the kind of urbane, educated executive criminal you saw in old films. While she didn't feel uncomfortable here, it might have made sense to tell Bliss she was coming.

'Now.' Mr Khan was leaning back in his leather swivel chair, hands behind his head. 'Tell me again. You are planning to hold . . . ?'

'A requiem.'

'A *requiem*?'

Repeating it in the manner of Wilde's Lady Bracknell, disarming young fogey that he was. An expensive education hadn't quite ironed Wolverhampton out of his accent.

'Requiem Eucharist, Mr Khan. A Holy Communion for the dead. I wasn't sure whether your own faith might present some—'

'Oh, not a problem at all, Mrs Watkins. In my capacity as a patron of the arts and popular culture, I've attended no small number of Christian funerals. My initial problem, however . . . is the fact that I simply didn't know these poor people as individuals. Many hundreds, thousands, now frequent Inn Ya Face and travel many miles to do so. Did *you* know the late Mr Cookman?'

'No, I didn't.'

'And yet you're proposing to conduct a service in his memory and that of his girlfriend.'

'Not exactly that. Or rather, not *entirely* that. It also relates to the circumstances of their deaths and the effects all of that has had on the community.'

'*All* of that?'

'There have been a number of other accidents. Very minor, in comparison, but there's a general atmosphere of . . . discomfort.'

'*Discomfort.*'

'I'd like this to be a service of closure. Of healing. Which, in my experience, can be quite . . . all-embracing. Which is why I thought it would be appropriate for you to be there.'

'And why is it being conducted by you, rather than by Mr Spicer?'

'Because . . .' Aware of painting herself into a corner. 'Because I specialize in this kind of healing.'

'You're a spiritual healer. A faith healer.'

'That would not be a description I'd welcome.'

'And what would be?'

Mr Khan waited, his prominent chin uptilted.

'I'm the Deliverance Consultant for Hereford Diocese,' Merrily said. 'I suppose I should explain what that—'

'You think I don't *know*? It certainly suggests that your earlier reference to holy water was not entirely in jest.'

'It was *entirely* in jest, but I can understand your ... misgivings.'

'We hear so much nowadays about so-called deliverance.' Mr Khan frowned. 'Children and babies being exorcized to the point of abuse and beyond, because they are believed to be harbouring evil spirits.'

'Not us. If we're ever invited to exorcize a young child, the social and psychiatric reports come first. And the situation in Wychehill, fortunately, is nothing to do with kids. We're looking at the relatively high incidence of problems on the road and other ... problems. Which have been linked to experiences of a possibly paranormal nature.'

'I can't wait to hear this, Mrs Watkins.'

'People say they've become aware of a figure on a bicycle. In the road. Before an accident. That's it, basically.'

Coming out with this kind of stuff cold was, Merrily often thought, the hardest part of the job. Sometimes you could almost feel the derision on your skin.

'How extraordinary, Mrs Watkins. And did the civilized Mr Devereaux witness this apparition?'

'We haven't yet discussed it in any depth. But it seemed to me that a Requiem Eucharist for two people who'd recently died on the road would be a calming influence, as well as bringing together the local community in a spiritual way. I think I'm right in saying that Islamic theology accepts that social and atmospheric disturbances *can* be caused by various discarnate ... presences.'

'Oh, very much so. *Very* much so.' Mr Khan stood up and moved to the window. 'So this has absolutely nothing to do with the murder of my employee Mr Wicklow.'

'Not directly,' Merrily said. 'But I'm sure he'll be very much in our minds.'

He smiled. 'What diplomacy.'

'It seems he was a violent man, Mr Khan.'

'Yes, apparently he was. But still a man. And still, in the end, a victim. Who is mourned. Look...'

Mr Khan beckoned her and she walked over to the window. Down in the courtyard, a man was adjusting the driving seat of a bright orange sports car with an ENGLAND sticker in the rear window. Two women looking on, the older one clutching a tissue.

'His family?'

'They've been here most of the day, to attend the opening of the inquest and collect his personal possessions – his car, his clothing, his jewellery. His mother's taken it very badly. He was her only son.'

Merrily said nothing, wondering about the mothers of dead junkies whose habits had been fed by Roman.

'Perhaps I was naive,' Mr Khan said, 'in watching my head doorman walk out onto the hills with his knapsack and his binoculars and being gratified by his seeming appreciation of the natural world. It's been a sobering experience for all of us.'

He turned away from the window.

'And you don't really believe me, do you, Mrs Watkins? You don't believe I knew nothing about Roman's enterprise. Perhaps you even think I'm involved in it myself.'

Hadn't been expecting that.

'Well...' She went back slowly to her chair. 'I don't think you're naive. Not all your regulars like to keep going all night, unassisted. It's a chemical culture. If you were widely known for taking a hard line against drugs, this wouldn't be considered a very cool venue, would it?'

Khan gave Merrily a sharp look which, she thought, was close to conveying respect.

'I'll tell you one thing.' He sat down again and prodded the newspaper on his desk, opened at 'THIS CARNAGE WILL GO ON...' 'This is a quite ludicrous exaggeration. A couple of weeks ago, I made a point of parking my own car in Wychehill early on a Sunday morning to see for myself the alleged havoc we were wreaking. No one, in the course of an hour and a half, seemed to stop there, and there was no noise. And although we sell alcohol, like any other country pub, I'm aware of no drink- or drug-related convictions, so far this year, that are connected with Inn Ya Face. And the traffic police *do* target us – they'd be foolish not to.'

Merrily chanced her arm. 'But not the drug squad?'

'Why are you—?' He spread his arms. 'Mrs Watkins, why are you pursuing this? The police aren't. The media are still calling Roman's death some sort of ritual murder. The police have been inclined to view it as an extreme reaction to something considered . . . culturally alien to the area. While you . . . is this a holy war?

'Do you know DCI Howe well?'

Khan's eyes narrowed, for just an instant, and then he smiled.

'She's a fine officer. Her record on community relations is impeccable.'

'Clearly going right to the top,' Merrily said.

And wondered what their relationshop was, Annie Howe and Raji Khan. He'd surely be an informer to die for.

'I do hope so,' he said. 'The police service needs more people like Annie.'

'And I hope you'll able to attend the service.' She stood up. 'Erm . . . if you don't mind me asking, how did you get into this business?'

'This *murky* business?' He laughed, a yelp of delight. 'This world of gangland rivalry and territorial wars? Mrs Watkins, you have such a . . . a darkly romanticized view of the nightclub scene.'

'I tend to watch a lot of trash TV. To unwind from the pressures of the job.'

Raji Khan came around the desk.

'I shall tell you why, rather than how – despite coming down from Cambridge with a moderately acceptable second – I got into this business. I came into it, Mrs Watkins, because I *absolutely love it*. I love it to death . . . the music, the atmosphere, the *milieu* . . . have loved it since escaping from my dormitory at fourteen, with a friend, to attend my very first rave on a hillside in Wiltshire. Electrifying. Pure, ecstatic, naked *vibration*. You leave everything behind . . . your mind, your body, your— I'm sorry, was that *your* generation – acid house, drum-

'n'-bass – or did you miss out? Do you know what I'm talking about? Or are you persuaded, like Mr Holliday and his cohorts, that we are demonic?'

'Well, I . . .'

'I am a Sufi,' Raji Khan said. 'Music is a sacred form to me. I tell people that Inn Ya Face has been transformed from a common drinking den into a temple of sound.'

'Yes.'

Two wires connecting in Merrily head with an almost audible fizz.

'Have I said something, Mrs Watkins?'

'Mmm, I think you have. Have you got something on tonight?'

'Of course. It's Friday. We have an old friend of mine, the good Dr Samedi.'

'From Kidderminster? Jeff?'

Khan looked startled.

'He was hired for a party in our village, a couple of years ago. With his voodoo hip-hop show. He still doing that? Not so famous then, of course.'

'My, my,' Raji Khan said.

He escorted her to the car park. Roman Wicklow's family had gone. Two white vans were arriving.

'Well,' Khan said, 'I'm not sure whether I shall be able to attend your *requiem*. But I do hope that you can help to stop the carnage.'

40

# Netherworld

ALL JANE WANTED WAS to leave, go running back to the vicarage, bar the doors and spend the night slapping tin after tin of white paint on the Mondrian walls. But Lol said that leaving now would only make it worse, like they actually did have something to hide, so she just kept walking round and round the little front parlour like a caged tiger – hamster, more like – ending up face-down on the sofa, beating the cushions in blind despair at a world where the scum always came out on top.

And at the bottom of it all, like a cold stone in her gut, was the knowledge that this was *all so totally her fault.* This half-arsed venture had been cursed from the start, and the curse was spreading and, of all the people she never in her life wanted to harm, of all the people who didn't deserve it . . .

Lol was always tethered to his past, that was the problem. He'd stretch it just so far and then something would send it snapping back, old rope twisting itself into a new noose.

After the disgusting Pierce had gone, Lol had sat at the desk assuring her that this was really not a problem, and the kind of people who'd believe someone like Lyndon were the kind who were not worth worrying about.

But he must be worried, terribly worried about the damage Pierce could do, with a word here and a word there, scattered like rat poison over all the places he went in his capacity as a democratically elected member of the Herefordshire Council. Democratically elected, Lol said, because nobody could be bothered to stand against him.

Lol's personal history, however, would always stand against *him.*

She'd been called Tracy . . . Cooke? Jane had known all about this for a couple of years now. Anyway, her name was Tracy and she'd been aged about fifteen at the time.

Lol would have been only eighteen or so himself when he was set up by the bass player in his band who'd wanted Tracy's mate and had got them all, Lol included, hopelessly drunk . . . and then had decided he was having both girls and had crept into Lol's hotel room and virtually raped Tracy while Lol was sleeping it off. Slipping away and leaving Lol – who knew nothing about it, hadn't even had sex with the girl – to face the police investigation that would crush his career, turn his loopy, born-again Christian parents against him and tip him down the chute into what he'd called in a song *the medicated netherworld* of psychiatric so-called care.

Taken years to drag himself out of the System and, while he wasn't exactly on *that* register, he must still have a record for a distant sex offence. An offence that never was, but which explained everything about Lol: all the caution, the timidity, the fear of facing an audience which he'd seemed finally to be leaving behind.

Did Lyndon Pierce know about this, or was it just a lucky stab? Villages were such *evil* places.

At least *she* wasn't under-age, just the bloody vicar's bloody daughter so, even if anyone believed it, the worst they could say . . .

Oh *God, God, God* . . .

Harsh colours collided behind Jane's eyelids, a small universe exploding.

When she eventually opened her eyes, she saw that Lol was looking surprisingly calm – a danger sign, surely? Sitting there at the desk in his black T-shirt with the alien motif, his little round glasses on his nose, fine slivers of grey in his hair, and the phone at his ear, and he was going 'Yes, thank you . . . Look, I wonder if it's possible to speak to Mrs Pole.'

Jane scrambled to her feet. 'Lol?'

Lol was saying, 'Margaret Pole, yes . . . Oh . . . Oh *no*. I didn't know. I'm so . . . I'm really very sorry . . .'

Jane didn't know what was happening. She wanted to snatch the phone out of his hand and start shaking him.

'No,' he said. 'Just a friend of the family. I came to visit her once, a few years ago. I've, um, been abroad. It's just that I'm not far from Hardwicke, and I was thinking . . . I had some flowers and chocolates and . . . Well, never mind. Sorry you've been . . .'

Lol's face tightening in concentration. Jane felt almost panicked now. Why was he trying to reach a woman who was evidently dead? What if something had gone wrong in his head? Or hers.

'Unless . . .' Lol said. 'Look, she had a friend there, I remember, we got on very well. Miss White. Athena White. I expect she's dead, too, by now.'

Lol listened. When he put the phone down, he was looking kind of excited.

'She's still there, Jane. When I said I expect she's dead, too, the woman said, *No, I'm afraid not.*'

'What are you talking about?'

'Miss White. Athena White is still a resident at The Glades Residential Home at Hardwicke.'

'So?'

'Maybe you never met her. I don't suppose Merrily would have gone out of her way to introduce you. Not then, anyway. Jane, will you do something for me?'

'I'll do bloody anything, Lol, if you'll just tell me what's *happening?*'

'If I give Gomer a call, will you go down to his place and stay there until Merrily gets back?'

'Why?'

'Because, under the circumstances, I don't want you on your own. And if we're seen driving out of here together – and we *will* be seen . . .'

'Where are you going? This is not funny, Lol – we've got to warn Mum about Pierce.'

'I'm just following up something that Gomer told me. Won't take long. I'm going to try and find out about Coleman's Meadow.'

'Does that matter any more?' Jane said bleakly.

Lol pulled his old denim jacket from the back of the chair.
'Oh yes,' he said.

Merrily drove away from the Royal Oak still undecided about Raji
Khan. It could be that Bliss, for once, was entirely wrong and that
Khan was no more than what he seemed: arrogant and pompous in a
way that was almost engaging because you could detect, behind it,
something young and almost naive.

Mr Khan was delighted with himself and a system in which an
enterprising Englishman from an Asian family could capitalize on his
cultural roots to an unprecedented degree.

On the way out, he'd shown her how the Royal Oak had morphed
discreetly into Inn Ya Face. It was not a listed building, and so it had
been possible to remove internal walls, creating a series of archways
and turning two ground-floor bars and a restaurant area into
something cavernous. Black-painted wooden shutters had been
installed at the windows. Although it was at ground level, with the
shutters across it would be like a cellar. Yes, it did now resemble a
temple, and the stone-based stage, built out from a big fireplace, was
its altar.

And it had a feeling of permanence that belied Preston Devereaux's
insistence that Raji Khan wouldn't be here long.

Would Khan risk destroying all this by involving himself in the
wholesale distribution of illegal drugs? Or did he have relationships
inside West Mercia Police permitting a certain ... freedom of
movement?

Whatever you thought about Annie Howe as a human being, it was
hard to imagine her operating on that level.

Not exactly a deliverance issue, anyway.

But *this* was ...

Driving past Wychehill Church, Merrily braked hard, drove across
the road into the Church Lane cutting and turned the Volvo around,
swinging back into the parking bay in front of the lantern. By the time
she was running through the gates, he'd gone into the church. If it *was*
him.

In the porch, getting her breath back into rhythm, she hesitated, the way she'd done at the Rectory.

Dealing with eccentrics ... fruitcakes ... imaginative and inspired people – whatever they were, it was important to keep reminding yourself that it was not about what you believed could happen so much as what *they* believed could happen. And it was about accepting that, when someone believed strongly enough, *something* could happen.

There was a lot she didn't know, but she was getting closer.

She pushed at the double doors into the body of the church. The doors resisted her.

Locked?

He'd locked himself in?

Merrily rapped on the bevelled glass.

'Syd?'

She could hear his footsteps on the flags. Then they stopped and she sensed him staring at the doors from the other side, the one word she'd spoken insufficient for him to identify her.

'It's Merrily. Are you going to let me in?'

He must have kept her waiting for a good half-minute before she heard the key turning, and then his footsteps going away again.

When she pushed open the doors and entered the vast parish church, Syd was standing in front of the chancel with its capacious semicircular choir stalls. He was wearing his cassock, and she thought what a particularly constraining garment it must be for a one-time man of action.

He looked around, with his arms out, at the empty pews, the oak-framed pulpit, the organ pipes like giant shell-cases.

'Can *you* do anything about this?'

There was nothing to see. But Merrily could smell the incense.

41

# Protect the Memory

THERE USED TO BE a setting sun on the sign, Lol recalled. But it had been replaced now with less scary white lettering on a sky-blue background.

The Glades Residential Home: a one-time Victorian gentleman's residence at the end of a drive close to the border with Wales. Wide views of the Radnorshire hills. Big, long sunsets.

Lol sat in the old white Astra in the car park, knowing he was here at least partly because, after shutting the door on Lyndon Pierce, he'd needed to be somewhere else – and fast. Him rather than Jane.

He'd watched her walking with Gomer down the street to Gomer's bungalow, in her school uniform. Girls in uniform: always suggestive of sexual impropriety? Ironic, really: he wasn't at all fond of uniforms, especially nurses' uniforms. Kissing a woman in a dog collar had taken an act of will, the first time.

When he left the car, a mantle of heavy windless heat settled around him. A woman came towards him out of the stern gabled porch, a big woman in a light blue overall, late fifties, bobbed blonde hair.

'Brenda Cardelow,' she said. 'Mr Robinson?'

The situation at The Glades had changed. The proprietors Lol remembered, the Thorpes, had left over a year ago, Mrs Cardelow had told him on the phone. *Burn-out.* She'd laughed.

'You're a lucky man, Mr Robinson. She appears to remember you. She's usually inclined to deny all knowledge of visitors.'

'One of the privileges of age,' Lol said, but Mrs Cardelow looked unconvinced.

'I tried to persuade her to come down to the residents' lounge, but

274

she insists on seeing you in her room, so I hope you're prepared for that.'

'I've never been in her room. But I've heard a lot about it.'

'I'm sure you must have,' Mrs Cardelow said.

The old woman wore a black woollen cardigan and a black wool skirt. A fluffy scarf, also black, was around her neck. Her eyes were hard and bright like cut diamonds. Nestling in the window seat, among the cushions and the books and the Egyptian tapestries and the wall-hung Turkish rugs and more books and more cushions, she was like a tiny, possibly malevolent story-book spider.

'Robinson.'

Crooking a finger with a purple-varnished, finely pointed nail. Same sherbet-centred voice. The air in here was tinged with incense.

'Miss White,' Lol said.

'Of *course* I remember him.' Miss White flung a brief, barbed glance at Mrs Cardelow. 'Nervous, would-be paramour of an unusually attractive little clergyperson – quite a curiosity at the time, amongst all those horse-faced lezzies in bondage clobber. How goes it, Robinson? Been inside the cassock yet?'

'Anthea!' Mrs Cardelow turned to Lol. 'They've all read that damned poem that goes on about "when I'm an old woman I shall dress in purple". They think that shedding their inhibitions will keep senility at bay, but in my experience it only hastens the onset.'

'You'll be demented *long* before me, Cardelow,' Miss White said in her baby-kitten voice.

'Yes,' Mrs Cardelow said sadly. 'I'm afraid she could be right.'

'Mind's on the blink already. Keeps calling me Anthea.'

'That's what it says on your pension book.'

'Then it's a misprint. Go away, Governor. Lock us in the cell if you must, but kindly leave us alone.'

Mrs Cardelow raised a martyr's eyebrow at Lol on her way out. Lol settled himself on a piano stool with no piano.

'Still demoralizing the screws, then, Athena.'

'Passes the time. Where are the chocolates? She said you'd brought me chocolates.'

'Sorry, left them in the car. Black Magic still appropriate?'

Miss White giggled. Lol remembered how Merrily had reacted when she'd first encountered her – called in within weeks of being appointed Deliverance consultant to look into claims by elderly residents that The Glades was being haunted by a handsome man of a certain era. Treading on eggshells in the big shoes of Canon Dobbs, Hereford's last Diocesan Exorcist. On a later occasion, knowing that Merrily needed help but was afraid of what Athena White might represent, Lol had gone on his own to tap into her knowledge of forbidden things.

Finding he got on rather well with this one-time highly placed civil servant who'd decide to devote her retirement to the study of the complex esoteric disciplines popularized by Madame Blavatsky, Rudolf Steiner and Dion Fortune. Maybe a stretch on psychiatric wards had helped.

'So?' she said. '*Have* you been inside the cassock?'

'Never really been turned on by women in uniform.'

'Don't be evasive.'

Miss White used to say she'd foregone the high-maintenance, roses-round-the-door cottage to set up what she called her *eyrie* in a old people's home because it gave her *more inner space*. Lol had no idea how old she was, but, like an elderly radio, all her valves still appeared to be glowing.

'OK. Out of uniform, it's much easier,' he said, and Miss White clapped her tiny hands.

'Splendid! And you needn't explain why the clergyperson isn't with you. I always felt she regarded me as a potential patroller of the Left-Hand Path, with whom it would not be *at all* appropriate to be publicly associated.'

'I'm the go-between,' Lol said.

'You lied to Cardelow. Told her some frightful porkie about first meeting me when you came to visit poor Pole.'

'That was because I wanted to talk to you . . . *about* Maggie Pole,' Lol said.

'She died.'

'I know.'

'In her sleep. And in the middle of a quandary. She thought I was a spiritualist, you know. A medium. Some of the inmates do. Frightfully insulting, to be lumped in with the pygmies. But I tend not to disabuse them – they wouldn't understand the distinction.'

'Mrs Pole asked you to help her, as a . . . spiritualist?'

Athena White didn't respond for a while, exploring him with her eyes.

'Robinson, are you still working with that dreadful shrink in Hereford?'

'Dick Lydon?'

'So-called psychotherapist.'

'No, I gave all that up. It didn't seem to be actually curing people.'

'Good,' Miss White said. 'Psychoanalysis was the great folly of the twentieth century. Leads nowhere except up its own bottom.'

'In what way did Maggie Pole ask you to help her?'

'Robinson, I know the woman's dead, but there *are* certain proprieties to be observed. Why do you want to know?'

'All right,' Lol said. 'When I first came to see you . . . you remember? We talked about about Moon, the archaeologist, and Hereford Cathedral and its connection, along the ley line, with Dinedor Hill?'

'Ley lines?' Miss White placed a purple-tipped finger on her chin. 'Watkins? Your friend's called Watkins, isn't she?'

'So's her daughter. Jane. I don't think you've ever met Jane, but she . . . Jane feels very strongly about things, and she doesn't give up. And she's only seventeen and still at school, and she's thrown herself into something which is backfiring on her. And I'm feeling guilty, because I didn't get involved and she's vulnerable and I'm not . . . well, not in that way.'

'Oh, I think you are, Robinson. You didn't want to interfere in case it should harm your relationship with her mother, which you appear to value above life itself.'

'You ought to be—'

'Don't you *dare* tell me I ought to be a psychologist. How does this connect with Margaret Pole?'

'Jane's found what she thinks is a forgotten ley line, which somebody wants to build across. In Ledwardine. It's called Coleman's Meadow. We're told that Margaret Pole's mother left it to her, having apparently said she didn't want it touched. I wondered what had made Maggie Pole change her mind. When I heard she'd been at The Glades I thought if anyone might know something about this it would be . . . you?'

Miss White withdrew into her cushioned grotto like some little English guru.

'Ah . . .' It came out like a tiny puff of white smoke. 'A ley line. Could *that* have been what it was about?'

'This makes sense?'

'She wanted me to contact her mother.'

'You mean on the . . .'

'In the land where the dead sit in an eternal garden among eternal fountains, discussing trivia and eating fairy cakes. Wanted me to contact her mother to ask if she was doing the right thing. A man kept coming to visit her – all too frequently in her last year. Well, you see this all the time. You don't have to be here very long to recognize a vulture in a suit. He was . . . some relation.'

'Nephew?'

'I listened to Pole talking to the inmates – sometimes sit in the lounge, pretending to be asleep. She'd ramble on about how worried she was that he was going to have to give up his farm – the last farm in a farming family, for umpteen generations. Falling prices, imports, the usual problems. I was thinking, what does he want from her?'

'Maybe a piece of land that he knew he could sell for a lot of money, for housing? Which she'd promised not to sell.'

'Yes. On which basis, I think he wanted her to *give* him the land. As a way of saving his farm. Trying to persuade her it was futile to preserve it as . . . I don't know, some sort of memorial? Do *you* know what kind of memorial?'

Lol shook his head.

'Rather intriguing. Pole used to talk of her mother as some frightfully elevated creature with aesthetic sensibilities far beyond those of her slug of a husband. Perhaps she'd met a lover in that meadow. That would be nice, wouldn't it? Pole never told me.'

'But she came to you . . . eventually.'

'A dilemma. Said she was sure the last thing her mother would have wanted was for her grandson, or whatever he was, to lose everything. Keeping her awake at nights – well, you know how old people dwell on these things. So yes, in the end, after much heart-searching, she came to me.'

'And what did you do?'

'Oh, we had a seance. *Great* fun! Most of the old dears were absolutely terrified – they do so love to be terrified. And then Cardelow appeared in the middle of the proceedings like some great dollop of rancid ectoplasm and broke it up.'

'And did you . . . ?'

'Of course I didn't. Never been drawn to necromancy . . . well, not in that way. The seance was a sham. My attitude was to take the path of least resistance. If Pole's mother was such an elevated soul, she'd hardly be worried about the loss of one field. Obvious way to go was for Pole to keep her promise not to sell it in her lifetime and simply agree to leave it to the sod. I said an angel in Grecian attire appeared to me in a dream and passed on that little snippet.'

'So, um . . . the fate of Coleman's Meadow is probably your fault.'

'I suppose it is, yes. But you know, Robinson . . .' Miss White smiled sweetly. 'We really aren't meant to have much of an effect.'

'And I suppose we'll never find out what Mrs Pole knew about the significance of that field.'

'What does the *girl* think is significant?'

'Jane? She thinks it more or less holds the secret soul of the village. It connects the church and a few other sites with Cole Hill, which Jane thinks is the village's holy hill – like Dinedor is to Hereford. She's at a . . . an intense age.'

'A *perceptive* age,' Miss White said. 'Although they often need assistance in decoding their perceptions. What are yours?'

279

'Oh, I . . . just think a particular councillor has a stake in it.'

'Hmm.' Miss White kicked off her slippers. She wore a black bow around one ankle. 'There is a niece, you know. Elizabeth . . . Kington? Kingsley?'

'Who got the money.'

'And the memories. In two suitcases. She came to collect them. I made a point of beckoning her over. I said *protect the memory*. As if I knew what I was talking about. She knew who I was – or *thought* she knew *what* I was. She said, If you get any more messages – oh dear! – and left me her address. I have it somewhere.'

'Yes, that might . . .'

Not once had Athena White stopped looking at Lol. Or through him. Eyes like miniature fairy lights. If he hadn't been feeling so empty inside, it might have been disconcerting.

'What else?' she said. 'Come on, Robinson, you must make the most of me before I'm called away to spend whole aeons in atonement. What ails you? Can't get it up?'

'Something like that,' Lol said.

42

# All the Time in the Worlds

GOMER'S KITCHEN WAS THIS cheerful but fading memorial to Minnie, full of bright, shiny, literal objects like biscuit tins with BISCUITS printed on the side in crumbly brown letters. The letters on the bread bin were badly worn; time after time, when Jane looked up she read 'bread' as DEAD.

Even Gomer seemed jittery, unsteady. Around six, he agreed to go and monitor the situation at Coleman's Meadow, and Jane switched on her mobile to check the answering service. Couldn't put it off any longer. Supposed if it was all too heavy to handle – follow-up calls from Jerry Isles, threats from Mum – she could always pretend she'd left the phone at home.

Didn't remember the last time she'd felt this low, this useless.

'*Where the hell are you?*' Eirion was demanding, on voicemail. '*We're getting masses of emails referred from the EMA site. Have you any idea at all what's going down here?*'

She called him back. She told him she knew exactly what was going down. Told him about Pierce, how she'd played it all wrong, couldn't restrain herself, ended up shafting Lol.

'The *Meadow*,' Eirion said. 'What's happening at the Meadow?'

'Fenced off.'

Jane told him about the ragged protest, and how terrible she felt that she hadn't been there supporting them. But she didn't dare show her stupid, notorious face, and at least it sounded like it was all over for tonight.

'Over?' Eirion said. 'I don't think so.'

'They got the police in. I'm dead in the water, Irene. I haven't been

281

to school again. I'm *stuffed*.' Disgusted at how she must sound, how *waily*. 'I'm probably going to have to leave, as from like now, get a job or something. Grow up, you know?'

He'd been talking; she'd only half-heard.

'. . . The Deathroad Society, of Antwerp? Conservers of coffin tracks in the low countries. Particularly pissed off. Their chairman, Ronald Verheyen—'

'All right.' Jane sat down. 'I'm sorry. What are you on about?'

Eirion laid it out for her. If Alfred Watkins wasn't much honoured in his home town, it looked like there were thousands of people all over the world to whom he was some kind of minor deity, and earth-mysteries geeks and landscape anoraks from the US, Canada, Australia, Germany, wherever, were now blasting Herefordshire Council with electronic hate-mail. Far as Eirion could make out, just about every department in the authority – planning, health, chief executive's, trading standards – they'd *all* been getting it.

'It's somehow got tied into the whole international Green politics thing. These guys are picking up email addresses wherever they can find them. Apparently, individual councillors have even been targeted at home.'

'How do you know all this?'

'Because the EMA have had an approach from the council's lawyers. Jesus, Jane, if the council hated you before . . .'

'Irene . . .' Jane swallowed. 'You're joking aren't you?'

She felt hot and swollen all over, like she'd invaded a wasps' nest and been multi-stung. Gomer's phone started ringing just as he came in and he hooked it from the wall by the fridge.

'Gomer Parry Plant Hire yere.'

'The EMA guy says if it gets too hot he'll have to pull the story,' Eirion was saying. 'I mean, *they* haven't got any lawyers or any money, not to speak of. But it's too late, anyway, now it's been picked up by the general media. You watching *Midlands Today*?'

'I don't want to know.'

'Well, I can't see it either, in Wales, but I gather—'

'I don't *care*! Oh shit, Irene. This explains Pierce. What do I *do*?'

282

'Just keep your head down, I suppose. I'd come over and try and take your mind off it, but it's Gwennan's birthday, and Dad's got this surprise party, where we all have to pretend nobody speaks English.'

'Her's on the mobile right now, boy,' Gomer said into the phone. 'I get her to call you back?'

Jane said, 'I'll call you back, Irene.'

Clicked him off and went over to secondary-smoke Gomer's ciggy.

'All right,' Gomer said. 'Will do, boy.' Handed the phone to Jane. 'Lol.'

'Look, what Pierce said before— I didn't—'

'Doesn't matter,' Lol said, 'I'm over that. It doesn't get to me any more. Can you write something down?'

The very fact that he knew instantly what she was talking about showed he was far from over it. Jane made scribbling motions to Gomer and he brought her a pen and a receipt book with *Gomer Parry Plant Hire* billheads. Lol said that if she and Gomer wanted to get out of the village for a while there was a woman they could check out. It might be something or nothing, Lol said. She needed to be polite. *Thanks.*

'Where are you?'

'I'm still at The Glades.'

'I'm bad news today, Lol. Nothing works out for me. Can't you do it?'

'No, I'm . . . I think I'm getting into something else,' Lol said.

His voice sounding disconnected, like he was with someone, or his mind was already working on the something else.


'Sholto.' Lol folded up his mobile. 'I think that was his name.'

'Frightfully good-looking. Essence of Ronald Colman.' Athena was gazing wistfully into a corner of the room. 'So few of us remember Ronald Colman any more, even here.'

'I bet they all remember Sholto, though,' Lol said.

'We needed him, Robinson. As I think I told your paramour at the time, who among the living could we attract any more?'

The alleged haunting of The Glades, as described by Merrily, had involved a languid shadow on the landing, blown bulbs. Hadn't there been a smell of cigarette smoke, the flicking of a lighter?

'The point being,' Lol said, 'that Sholto had no history at The Glades. He was just a face from an old photo album. Someone whose image you'd somehow contrived to . . . appropriate. And insinuate into people's consciousness.'

'What *fun* he was, though.'

'But he was a . . . a product of persuasion?'

'If you say so.'

'Oh, come on, Athena.'

'Well, it's all so devalued now.' She looked cross. 'The techniques of projection. Used to be frightfully effective, but since that annoying young man on the television, Derren Somebody-or-other . . .'

'Brown?'

'Derren Brown, yes. Little twerp. Makes a point of insisting that it's all psychology and suggestion, because it makes him look cleverer and the whole business less metaphysical and out of his control. Deserves a good spanking.'

'Can I describe something to you?'

'Why not?' Athena stretched like a small cat, purple claws extended. 'I have all the time in the worlds.'

Still unsure where he was going with this, Lol told her about Tim Loste and Sir Edward Elgar and Wychehill.

'I'm afraid it's a very, very different situation,' Athena said.

She'd made some fragrant Earl Grey tea. They drank it out of small china cups. The teapot had a Tarot symbol on it – the Hanged Man, dangling from a tree by one foot.

'You see, this place is ideal for it,' Athena said. 'Old women living for much of the time inside their own heads, inside their distant memories. Hothouse of hopeless fantasies. *Frightfully* easy to insinuate an image.'

'And how exactly would you . . . ?'

'Beyond that . . .' Athena lifted both palms '. . . I'm revealing no tradecraft. Except to say that it soon begins to generate its own energy. Now, the village you're describing seems far from a hothouse. If the dwellings are well separated and the residents have little in common and don't mix socially . . . hopeless.'

'It was only an idea,' Lol said. 'I was just—'

'Being a little helpmate?' Athena squealed. 'Robinson, you infuriate me! She is a lowly . . . parish . . . priest. In the *Church of England* – half-baked, miserably unfocused, spiritually stagnant and led by a dithering Welshman who thinks that looking like an Old Testament prophet is half the battle. Now— Sit down, I haven't finished.'

Athena White stood up, plumped out her cushions and curled up again in the window seat.

'You've intrigued me now. Mentioned Elgar. Now *there's* a man with problems. Repressed, frustrated . . . trapped, for much of his life, inside petty conventions and constraints. A spirit yearning for a freedom which he was foolish enough to think was only granted to children. Do you know *The Wand of Youth* – piece he wrote when young himself, about children and fairyland?'

'Only read about it.'

'He kept trying to revive it at various times, as if he could rediscover the oneness with nature that he believed he had possessed as a child. Now. If you were to ask me if Edward Elgar could be summoned back to his beloved hills, I would say that it was quite conceivable that much of him never left. In other words—'

Athena's head came forward, like a tortoise's from its shell. She seemed quite excited.

'. . . A man who indeed might *haunt*.'

Not what Lol had wanted to hear.

He watched Athena placing both her hands on top of her head, as if to prevent significant thoughts from fluttering away like butterflies.

'Elgar's biographers, you see, tend to be terribly highbrow music buffs with too much academic credibility to lose. His esoteric side is usually glossed over.'

'You've read the biographies?'

'Robinson, I spend at least seven hours a day reading. I've also known several people – some of them in this very mausoleum – who met him when young. Not always the most delightful of experiences, I'm afraid: he could be a rather negative presence.'

'Someone said manic-depressive.'

'There you go *again* with your silly psychiatric generalizations. Stop it.'

'Sorry. What did you mean by his esoteric side?'

Lol was feeling confused. Everybody seemed to have a piece of Elgar, and all of them with jagged edges. He was a kind man, an inconsiderate and self-obsessed man; he was arrogant, he was insecure; he was a no-nonsense, self-made, practical man, and he was a mental case; he was a patriot and he was an artist resentful of the taint of patriotism. He was a staunch Catholic, and yet . . .

'He was, like so many prominent figures of his time, drawn to the otherwordly,' Athena said. '"Fond of ghost stories" is what the books usually say. But it was clearly more than that. His intermittent Catholicism was never enough to satisfy his curiosity. What do you know about The Hermetic Order of the Golden Dawn?'

'Top people's magical club,' Lol said. 'Aleister Crowley, W. B. Yeats . . .'

'They all began there, certainly. Yeats was prominent in it, and Elgar worked with Yeats. But his favourite was Algernon Blackwood. Did the music for Blackwood's play *The Starlight Express*, and the music contained elements of *The Wand of Youth*. About children and the otherworld. Bit of a disaster, but they had fun. Blackwood was a likeable cove. Met him once at my uncle's house – my Uncle Thomas was a latter-day member of the GD. Left me all his "secret papers". Which was what started *me* off, I suppose.'

Athena smiled at the memory. Lol drank what remained of his Earl Grey.

'But Elgar wasn't a member of the Golden Dawn, was he?'

'I think he might well have joined if it hadn't been for his wife and her top-drawer conservative family. Alice, to whom he owed so much. Fortunately, however, Alice liked Blackwood and Blackwood liked Alice. She wrote in her diary of the "out of the world" conversations Elgar had with Blackwood. *Blackwood* . . .'

Athena pursed her lips.

'I may have read one of his stories once,' Lol said. 'When I was a kid. "The Haunted and the Haunters"? Very scary.'

'No, that was Bulwer-Lytton – ah, *there*, you see, Elgar liked *his* stories, too. Was said to have based one of his piano pieces on a novel of Bulwer-Lytton's. Oh, Robinson, how intriguing ... what *is* happening here?'

'I don't know.'

'I'm trying to *think* ...' Athena pressing fingertips to her temples. 'Yes ... now ... Blackwood wrote a strange novel about music, *The Human Chord*. It's about a group of people – singers – brought together by a retired clergyman to intone the constituent notes in an archaic, mystical chord that will allow them to sound the secret names of God and thus draw down immense power from the heavens. It's a mad, romantic book but – as with all Blackwood's fiction – was drawn from his personal experience, in this case with The Golden Dawn. Now ...'

Athena rose and went to one of the floor-to-ceiling cupboards. When she opened it up, Lol saw that its sagging shelves were bulging with books. Athena knew what she was looking for, however, and brought it back to her window seat.

'We're looking at Plato. And, of course, Pythagoras. And probably some forgotten ancient Egyptian before that. We're looking at a time when music was not "a branch of the arts" but a medium of construction ... the construction of the universe itself. Pythagoras saw an exquisite mathematical harmony in the universe, and the harmony was held together by music. Music was formed upon strict laws ... music *was* the law. Can you comprehend any of this?'

'I'm trying.'

Lol wondered what time it was, if Jane and Gomer had gone to find Margaret Pole's niece, if Merrily ...

'Keep going, Athena,' he said.

'Oh, I could go on all night and all through tomorrow. But I think what you need to know is that the planets were said to vibrate and respond to one another in a musical sequence – the Music of the Spheres. You've heard the term?'

Lol nodded. 'But I always imagined that as a poetic . . . metaphor?'

'It *is* a metaphor, like all these images, for an internal process. As above, so below. A connection between our inner selves and God, forged through the power of music. This was studied in some depth by The Golden Dawn, and Blackwood used some of what he'd learned there in *The Human Chord* – Blackwood being a writer first and foremost, rather than a true seeker after cosmic consciousness. A romantic, if you like.'

'Like Elgar.'

'Absolutely like Elgar. And for Blackwood *not* to have seized the opportunity to discuss what he'd learned about the origins of music with the most famous composer in the land is . . . well, so unlikely as to be not worth consideration.'

Lol said, 'The play – musical, whatever – that Elgar and Blackwood worked on. You said it was called *The Starlight Express?* The house where Winnie Sparke – Tim Loste's mentor – lives, at Wychehill, is called Starlight Cottage.'

Athena White squeaked in delight.

'Starlight, as it happens, was Elgar's nickname for Blackwood! They used nicknames as a kind of code.'

'There's a letter,' Lol said, 'in the Wychehill parish records from someone signing himself *Starlight* . . . suggesting Wychehill as a highly suitable place for a church because no area of southern Britain was more conducive to the . . . to the creation and performance of the most spiritually exalted music . . . does that make any—?'

'Sounds like something Blackwood would write and if he signed himself Starlight he could only have been addressing Elgar.'

'The letter's to "Sirius".'

'The dog star?' Athena's eyes glittered. 'Yes! Elgar was frightfully fond of dogs. That would make absolute sense. Oh, Robinson, I wonder . . . I wonder . . .'

Athena began leafing through the book she'd brought from the cupboard, a fairly slim hardback with a plain green cover, called *City of Revelation*.

'I think where this brings us,' she said softly, 'is to the Whiteleafed Oak.'

# 43

# The One Per Cent

Syd Spicer looked like a priest feeling unwelcome in his own church and uncomfortable – or was she imagining this? – in his own cassock.

'So he's out, right?'

Spicer looked pale. Few people, in the current weather, looked pale. Regiment men, always getting dispatched to sun-kissed hell-holes, never did; only their wives. That was the standing joke in Hereford: foolproof way of recognizing an SAS man – suntanned bloke, pale wife.

'He was released this morning, without charge,' Merrily said. 'But I gather they haven't lost interest in him.'

'Who could?'

But, for some reason, he looked relieved. Merrily sniffed the air.

'He burns incense in here?'

'Not when I'm here, he doesn't. But, yeah, who else? Or Winnie.' He sat down in one of the choir stalls, looking down the aisle with distaste. 'It's got to end.'

'What has?'

'I don't like this church much – have I indicated that?'

'A few times.'

'Sometimes there's a peculiar energy in here. You can feel it on your skin, abrasive, like on a cold morning when you've cut yourself shaving. And sometimes you can still smell the incense when Loste hasn't been in for days.'

Merrily looked around. With the afternoon sunlight in free fall through the diamond-paned windows, it was like being inside a great stone lantern.

'Something's needed doing for a while, but I couldn't do it,' Spicer said.

'Couldn't do what?'

'What you do. Maybe that's another reason I called you last weekend. Maybe I couldn't admit it to myself, but something needs sorting here.'

She sat down next to him. 'You trying to make me feel worthwhile or something, Syd?

He was still gazing down the nave, his eyes like currants. She could feel him becoming quiet. The screen-saver routine. She looked at him, saying nothing, trying to be as still as he was. But she couldn't manage it.

'It's a technique,' he said. 'That's all. Makes me look heavy. On nodding terms with minor seraphim. I'm just a fucked-up old soldier, Merrily, and coming into the Church was a mistake. I can't hack it.'

'What?'

Spicer pulled a box of matches out of his cassock, followed by a packet of cigarettes. He flipped it open, offered it to Merrily. She blinked.

'We're, erm, in church.'

'Don't go spiritually correct on me, Merrily. You think *he* cares? It's smoking, not sex.'

'You're right, but I don't think I will right now, all the same.'

'Fair enough.'

He lit up, the striking match a sacrilegious gasp. He stretched out his legs in the direction of the central aisle, watching the smoke float up and dissipate at pulpit level.

'At the core of the Special Air Service, there's a harsh kind of mysticism. Kind you won't find in any other area of the armed forces. Connected with survival. I used to think survival was ninety per cent training and preparation, nine per cent luck, and one per cent . . . one per cent something you could call on when you were at breaking point.'

'I can imagine the closer you get to—'

Merrily shut up. She didn't know. How could she possibly know?

291

'I'm not gonna tell you when and where this happened to me,' Syd said. 'But there's always one time when it all drops away – all your training and your discipline – and your insides turn to water. At first you're just afraid of dying. Not death, dying. The way it's gonna happen. The fear of . . . of fear itself, I suppose. Of giving in to fear. Of dying in it. Dying as someone who you can only despise. And when you're suddenly confronted with that sorry person – with the sight and the smell of your own terror . . . that's a big, gaping moment, Merrily.'

She nodded. She kept quiet. They didn't know one another, not at all. All they had in common was the one per cent.

'So I started to pray,' Spicer said. 'Prayed the way those poor buggers probably prayed when they jumped off the twin towers, out of the flames.'

Merrily nodded.

'And something happened. Not a flash-of-lightning kind of thing . . . just a bloke behaving in a way he wouldn't normally behave in the circumstances, and me finding a sudden unexpected strength. I won't go further into it . . . except I thought, afterwards, *I can respect this.* A source of strength infinitely greater than your training's ever gonna give you – and in the Regiment, training's all, to a level of aptitude and precision that you believe makes you equal to anyone. Any*one.* But in that moment, the one per cent had become a hundred per cent. And I suppose it still is.'

'Yes.'

'What I'll admit to being good at,' Syd Spicer said, 'is helping the dying. Having been there, very close, twice, I can find them strength. I know there's gonna be help for them, and I can take the weight off just enough for them to feel it. The way you help your mates in a shit situation. So the dying . . . they're the only people I tell exactly what happened at *my* times. Times and places, nothing concealed. It's me passing on something precious, and they value it, and I think they take it with them.'

'Syd,' Merrily said, 'how on earth can you say you can't hack it?'

'Because I could do that without being a priest.'

*

The phone was ringing when Lol got home. He caught the call just before the machine lifted it.

'Lol, Dan.'

'Sorry?'

'From Much Cowarne?'

'Sorry . . . out of breath.'

'Me too, I expect, by the end of the night. Look, when you talked to Mr Levin, did you know something was about to happen?'

'Like what?'

'Just had a call from Tim. I'm glad to say they let him out – did you know?'

'I'd heard. But I don't know much more than that.'

'Reason he was calling . . . I'm one of the three coordinators of the choirs. I told you about the three choirs, who did the three churches simultaneously?'

'You did.'

'OK, well, there's a pool of about sixty of us, right? Three coordinators who can each pull twelve compatible choristers together at short notice. Twelve out of twenty's usually a safe bet. Tim called me about half an hour ago. They're trying to arrange Redmarley and Little Malvern Priory to join in with Wychehill again. Another simultaneous chant.'

'When?'

'Tonight. Like we did before, only longer. It has to last, somehow, from nine tonight until three a.m. Luckily, it's Saturday tomorrow.'

'Why?'

'That's what I'm ringing for, Lol. I wondered if *you* knew.'

'He won't tell you?'

'He *never* tells you. He rambles. He gets incoherent. You stop asking because you think maybe he doesn't know the answer anyway, but it don't matter, you know you're gonner get something out of it. Bit of a coincidence, though, ennit?'

'I don't know. Honestly. You going to be able to organize it in time?'

'Won't be too much of a problem,' Dan said. 'After last time, nobody's going to want to miss it. Even the ones who went home scared.'

A priest could go through his entire career without facing this kind of situation. That was the irony of it.

'Not a lot frightens me. I can deal with most physical pain, emotional pain, stress. I can achieve separation from the weakness of the body. But there are leaps I can't make. Aspects I can't face.'

'You're worried by the non-physical?'

Syd leaned back and took a deep pull on his cigarette.

'Samuel Dennis Spicer,' he said. 'Church of England.'

'Because you can't resist it, overpower it . . . *slot* it? Is that what you mean?'

'Samuel Dennis Spicer. Church of England.'

Merrily smiled.

'You talked about any of this to Winnie Sparke?'

'Winnie?' He'd been about to bring the cigarette back to his mouth. He brought his arm down. 'Why would I?'

'They're saying in Wychehill that you're seeing a lot of her.'

'Told you.' He leaned his head back over the chorister's stall. 'Didn't I?'

'You told me about the Ladies of Wychehill.'

'I assisted Winnie Sparke with her researches into the origins of the church. Parish records. And a few other things. Anything else . . .' He squeezed out the cigarette between finger and thumb. 'Anything else, my wife really wouldn't like.'

'Your—?'

'In essence, stories of our separation are overstated. Having three parishes can be an advantage, Merrily. You go missing for a while, they all think you're in one of the others. Fiona took the kids down to Reading to get away from a difficult situation. We have a house, and her family's down there, so it seemed expedient. I go down every week, or we meet somwhere. Yesterday it was in Berkshire. Hungerford.'

'That *works*?'

'Separation – she's used to that. Least I'm less likely to get killed as a clergyman. Seemed easier to let people think we'd split, otherwise there'd be three restless parishes wondering how long before the new guy.'

'But why didn't you? Why didn't you just leave? Go for a new—'

'Because I was sent *here*. Never yet failed to complete a mission. One way or another.'

Like God was his field commander. But obviously Merrily understood.

'And the difficult situation . . . that would be drugs?'

'Partly. Emily's been a problem. Shrinks say she has an addictive personality. As a kid she overate. You tried to cut down the Mars Bars to three a day . . . tantrums. Cold turkey on Mars Bars, you believe that? With adolescence, it stopped, all the weight dropped away, and we were so relieved that it was quite a while before we realized what'd replaced it. The shoplifting conviction was a clue. Then robbing the offertory box.'

'She was in rehab?'

'Joyce told you all this, I assume. Joyce, the parish talking-newsletter.'

'And then the Royal Oak changed hands,' Merrily said. 'And suddenly it was all on your doorstep. Like a sweetshop.'

'Yeah. There's a group of us, county-wide – parents of kids with drug problems. We attend briefing sessions with the police, regional seminars. We learn what to look out for.'

'Like Roman Wicklow? Did you know about him?'

'Suspected.'

'But you didn't tell the police.'

'One man with a rucksack?' Spicer snorted. 'Take Wicklow out of the picture and there's another one in place by next week, in a different beauty spot. Better the devil you know.'

'If they'd arrested him, he could've fingered others . . .'

'His sort don't finger people.'

'What about Raji Khan?' Merrily said.

'Raji Khan—' he looked almost amused '—is a very clever boy. Somebody like me says a word against him, it's like the Crusades are back – I must be starting a holy war. Anyway, not your problem. Your problem's more ethereal. It's my problem too but . . . we've been into that.'

'What are you asking me to do?'

'Your requiem should be broadened. I was thinking a wider brief. For a start, you might give *this* place some attention.'

'What are you trying to lose?'

'Longworth, for a start. I don't know what his problem was, but I reckon St Dunstan's only compounded it. You look at the records, you find that what existed on this site could have been no more than a single monk's cell. A Celtic hermit's primitive stone hut. So he builds a pseudo-cathedral. Look—'

Spicer sprang up, walked into the nave, pointing out empty stone ledges, blank areas of wall.

'When I first came, there were terrible pictures on these walls, of saints and angels . . . figurines in niches.'

Merrily looked around. Light oak furniture, a marbled font. He was right: there was little of the period clutter that even churches less than a century old accumulated.

'They're in storage. None of them great works of art. No treasure. Phoney High-Church iconography, reeking of . . . hierarchy. Grotesque, to me. Forbidding – like that hideous angel on Longworth's tomb. When we had one small statue nicked, I talked the parish council – well, Preston Devereaux – into *safeguarding* the rest. He didn't need much encouraging. His family always found Upper Wychehill an intrusion. His grandfather's on record as having attempted to stop Longworth building.'

'You've virtually . . . stripped the place?'

'Best we could, bit by bit, over a period. They're all newcomers here, nobody missed anything. But I didn't get rid of it. It's as if it's built into the stone.'

'What is?'

'Longworth's grandiose concept. Longworth himself. He brought something here that's caused an imbalance. This church is disproportionate to its surroundings and to the community. It's a big stone ego-trip, and it's like the houses are hiding away from it . . . below the road, over the road, squeezing into the rocks. It explains a lot about Wychehill. I found a journal kept by one of my predecessors, thirty, forty years ago. Even then, the population was unstable, people buying and selling, coming and going.'

Syd Spicer's voice was crisp and carried across the body of the church with hardly an echo. Whatever you thought about Joseph Longworth, he'd known who to consult about acoustics.

'I know a bit about geology,' Spicer said. 'Rock-climbing used to be my specialist skill. I was an instructor some of the time, so I know about rock. There's a small fault through Wychehill, did you know that? I mean, the whole of the Malverns, that was volcanic, but a long time ago. The shifts in *this* area – there's been more recent action here. I say recent – eighteenth, nineteenth centuries.'

'A history of earth-movement and *then* quarrying?' Merrily followed him down the central aisle. 'No wonder Winnie Sparke says the hills are in pain.'

'She's not a stupid woman,' Syd Spicer said. 'She gives you all this fey stuff, but that's her screen. If you think she's more gullible than you are, you start to lose your inhibitions, tell her more than you intended to. C. Winchester Sparke – former professor of anthropology, back in the US. Did you know that?'

'Yes.'

'Specializing in ancient history, comparative religion, philosophy, anthropology. Smart woman. Don't be fooled. We had a serious talk about this once. Her theory is that the whole of the Malvern range was one huge ritual site . . . *because* it was so volatile. People didn't live here, they came here to experience transcendence . . . to have visions. That's the pagans *and* the early Christians.'

'The hermits in their cells and their caves. Like in Tibet.'

'Presumably. That's not the point of Christianity, though, is it? That's smoke. Smoke and . . . incense.'

'Wasn't Longworth supposed to have had a vision?'

'I have a theory about that.' Spicer sat down on the edge of a pew. 'Well, it's not *my* theory, but it fits. You mess around on volatile rocks, on operations or just on exercises, and you become aware of occasional phenomena, linked particularly to fault lines and places where the Earth's crust has been been disrupted. Lights, usually. Balls of light.'

'You've seen it?'

'Couple of times. It's like ball lightning. Might have *been* ball lightning. Gets people excited about UFOs, but it's natural, I think. The Ministry of Defence knows about it. I think that's what Longworth saw.'

'Preston Devereaux says the story is that Longworth saw the Angel of the Agony in a blaze of light. Which, presumably, is why there's a representation of it on his tomb.'

'I'd go for just the blaze of light.'

'Is there any actual *record* of what Longworth believed he saw? Did he ever describe it?'

'If he did, it wasn't around this locality. Maybe he told Elgar. It's all smoke, Merrily. And I'd like to get rid of it. Starting with the music.'

'I'm sorry – which music?'

'Loste's music. His lush, extravagant choral works. It's become clear to me that that's part of the problem. It's not the place for music like that. And certainly not the place for experiments.'

'I know what you're saying . . .' And it was odd, Merrily thought, that a man inclined towards a blanket rejection of the numinous should be saying it. 'I think you're saying that, for sacred music to be effective, it needs a strong, *working* spiritual foundation – an abbey, a cathedral. Like the difference between a puddle and a well.'

'And if you're being literal about that, the Wychehill well disappeared with the quarrying.' Spicer shrugged. 'I might be wrong. If I am . . . But I thought about it all the way back from Berkshire and it was the only conclusion I could reach. Which means that as from next week Tim Loste and his choir can go and look for a new home.'

'You mean you're . . . ?'

'Evicting him. I'm within my rights, as priest in charge – I checked. What's more, I think it's for his own good. He's being drawn into an unhealthy fantasy.'

'When are you going to tell him?'

'I've already told him, Merrily. I went in the back way from the rectory while you were talking to Winnie Sparke. I told him there were probably dozens of other churches and halls that would be overjoyed to have him and the choir. I said he might want to think about moving. That this place wasn't good for his ... health.'

'That must've sounded like a threat.'

'Not the way I put it, I assure you.'

'What did he say?'

'He said ... he said he didn't know how he was going to tell Winnie.'

'Syd ...' God almighty, no wonder Spicer had needed a cigarette. 'She'll go completely bloody berserk. This – whatever she's trying to reach through Loste – this has become the central focus of her life.'

'Merrily, if the central focus of her life is producing a bestselling book on the secret source of Elgar's inspiration ... well, she can do that anywhere, can't she?'

'I'm not sure she can. Not the way she sees it. And I'm not sure that's the entire—'

'She needs to get out of here, too, the quicker the better. Out of the area.'

'What are you saying?'

Spicer stood up and stepped out of the pew.

'And, of course, this had to be done before Sunday evening.'

'Oh, I see. Jesus, Syd ...'

'You have a problem with that?'

'You mean so that, on Sunday evening, we can solemnly invite God to wipe away every last taint of Longworth and Loste's brand of Anglo-Catholicism?'

'Think about it. It makes sense.' He walked towards the main doors. 'Maybe you should stay for a few minutes on your own, get the feel of the place?'

Merrily sat down in a pew, the confluence of at least three sunbeams.

Spicer probably didn't want them to be seen leaving together. People might talk.

What a *total bloody* . . . It wasn't quite a sectarian isssue, but it was close. She wondered if he'd served with the SAS in Northern Ireland and something had left a bad taste.

No, that was ridiculous. His decision to stop the choral singing could be justified purely on the basis of what they'd said about puddles and wells.

But there was already a bad taste in her own mouth.

And Spicer still hadn't told her everything he knew, of course. Merrily was sure of that.

PART FOUR

'On our hillside night after night looking out on our "illimitable" horizon ... I've seen in thought the Soul go up and have written my own heart's blood into the score.'

Edward Elgar
from a letter (1899)

'For some, it is the living on after the action that requires the final reserves of courage.'

Tony Geraghty
*Who Dares Wins:*
*The Special Air Service,*
*1950 to the Gulf War*

# 44

# The Plant-Hire Code

JANE THOUGHT, THERE ARE still women like this?

'My husband's out,' she'd said. 'You should really come back when my husband's in.'

It was a detached bungalow on an estate on the wrong side of Hereford – not that there was a right side any more, with all the roadworks connected with the building of new superstores that nobody wanted except Lyndon Pierce and his power-crazed mates. Taken Jane and Gomer most of an hour just to get here, and Jane wasn't planning on moving without some answers.

'Mrs Kingsley, it's you I wanted to talk to. If that's all right.'

Mrs Kingsley was a tired-eyed woman in an apron, sixtyish, with a resigned sort of look. She didn't seem like a *Guardian* reader.

'But I don't really understand what you want,' she said. 'As I say, my husband deals with our finances.'

OK, wrong approach. Stupid to say it was about her inheritance. Stupid to try and sound mature and official. Shouldn't have nipped home to change out of the school uniform. Start again.

'My name's Jane Watkins. And I'm doing a project. For ... for school. I'm a ... you know ... a schoolgirl?'

'Oh.' Mrs Kingsley looked happier. 'Which school is that?'

'Erm ... Moorfield? It's near—'

'Yes, I know it. I had a nephew there.'

'Well, I probably—'

'He's a bank manager now, in Leominster. Now, what did you want to know again?'

'Well, it's this project on ... on my great-grandfather? Alfred

303

Watkins? You know who I mean? He was a county councillor and a magistrate, back in the 1920s and . . .'

'Mr Watkins?' Mrs Kingsley smiled at last and nodded and came down from her front doorstep. 'Yes, I know about Mr Watkins. And his photography, and his ley lines. And he was . . .' She looked suddenly uncertain. 'Your great-grandfather?'

*Oh no.* 'Sorry . . .' Jane did some rapid arithmetic. 'I always get this wrong. *Great*-great-grandfather. It takes me ages to trace it back through the generations. We're all over the place now, you know, the Watkinses.'

Jane glanced back at Gomer, sitting at the roadside in the old US Army jeep he was driving now. He'd said he probably wouldn't be much use, not knowing Mrs Kingsley, only her late aunt.

'Of course, it was my grandmother knew Mr Watkins, not me,' Mrs Kingsley said. 'I'm not *that* old. My grandmother, you see, was *very* well connected, that was what I was always told, although I was quite small when she died. I imagine she could've told you some marvellous stories about Mr Alfred Watkins.'

'Really . . . ? Well, that . . . that's what I heard,' Jane said. 'You see, we live in Ledwardine—'

'Yes, that's where my aunt—'

'And all the main people in Ledwardine told me the person I could've spoken to, if I wanted to know about Alfred's connections with the village, was Mrs . . . Pole.'

'Do you know Mr Bull-Davies?'

'James Bull-Davies! Absolutely. James said Mrs Pole was, erm . . . he said she was a real lady.'

'Oh, she was. I'm so glad Mr Bull-Davies remembers her.'

'They all do, Mrs Kingsley. Ted Clowes, the senior churchwarden? Ted said, Jane, you want to be sure and get Mrs Pole into your project. And her family. Which, erm, could eventually be published, of course, by the Ledwardine Local History Society.'

'So that was what you meant when you mentioned my inheritance,' Mrs Kingsley said.

'Well, it . . .'

'You meant Coleman's Meadow,' Mrs Kingsley said.

'I think that was what it was called.'

'Well, I'm afraid I didn't inherit the land, dear. That was my cousin. He's the farmer.'

'Well, yes, but—'

'As you'd probably have known if you'd seen the local television news tonight,' Mrs Kingsley said. 'Where he was interviewed.'

'Oh.'

*Shit.*

'The reporter did say they'd tried to find the instigator of the protest, but you were keeping a low profile. Although they did have quite a good photograph of you, from one of the newspapers.'

Just when you thought you were being *so* smart.

'It was strange, though,' Mrs Kingsley said, 'that they didn't mention you were the great-great-granddaughter of Alfred Watkins.'

'Well, it's not something I . . .'

'Talk about,' Mrs Kingsley said. 'No. I don't suppose you do, you silly little girl.'

Which was when Gomer came over.


He wasn't even smoking, and he'd buttoned his tweed jacket.

'Gomer Parry Plant Hire.' Handing one of his cards up to Mrs Kingsley. 'Once put in a new soakaway for your auntie, but I don't suppose her'd've talked about it much at family gatherings.'

For a man of seventy-odd he moved fast. Must have seen Jane's face folding up, and he'd been there before she reached the bottom of the steps.

Mrs Kingsley stood on the top step, holding the card. The ambering sunlight flashed from windows all over the estate and boiled in Gomer's bottle glasses.

'Brung Janie over on account o' the importance o' this, see. Good girl, means well, but her gets a bit . . . emotional. Takes things to heart.' Gomer took off his cap. 'Got herself in a real state over this argy-bargy, missus, as you can likely see.'

Mrs Kingsley looked at the card, said faintly, 'Plant hire?'

Gomer looked solemn. It was touching, really. The words plant hire, for Gomer, represented some old and honourable tradition of saving the countryside from flood and famine, bringing mighty machinery to the aid of the needy. A plant-hire code of decency was implied and it shone out of Gomer's glasses.

'You see much of your cousin Gerry?' Gomer said. 'Gerry Murray, Lyonshall?'

'No.'

'Ar,' Gomer said. 'What I'd yeard.'

Jane looked at him, curious. He'd had very little to say in the jeep on the way here. But Gomer knew about the local network, its grudges and its feuds, and what he didn't know he'd find out.

'*You* know him?' Mrs Kingsley said.

'No. But I knows *of* him. If you see what I mean.'

Standing there with his hands behind his back, not pushing it. Little and lean, the cords in his neck like plaited bailer twine.

'Gerry . . . knows what he wants and makes sure he gets it,' Mrs Kingsley said. 'One way or another.'

'Yeard that, too. And your Auntie Maggie . . . seems to me her was a bit like Janie, yere – worried too much about what was right and what was wrong, kind o' thing.'

Mrs Kingsley looked down, brushing her apron. It was beige, with black cats on it.

'My aunt *did* talk about you once or twice, Mr Parry,' she said. 'You're making this very difficult for me.'

'Ar?'

'I have some letters . . . and photographs.'

'What Mrs Pole left you.'

'You obviously know about them.'

'Mabbe.'

'I was going to offer them to the Hereford Museum. Or perhaps the Woolhope Club.'

Gomer looked blank.

'The naturalist and local history club that Alfred Watkins belonged to,' Jane said. 'It still exists.'

'Mr Watkins *was* a member, yes. Among other important people. The photographs belonged to my grandmother, Hazel Probert. I think it's what she would have wanted, after all this time.'

Mrs Kingsley looked out over the housing estate. You could hear lawn-mowers and strimmers and a few children shouting. Across the estate and another estate, on higher ground, you could see the top of Dinedor, Hereford's own holy hill.

Jane found she was holding her breath.

'After the TV item, I brought them down,' Mrs Kingsley said. 'On television, it didn't look like the same place – all that fencing and the signs.'

'That's nothing to what it'll look like when it's covered with executive homes,' Jane said.

'Well,' Mrs Kingsley said, 'I can't let you take the photographs. But I can let you see them. I suppose they explain why my grandmother might not have wanted someone like Gerry Murray to have the meadow.'

# 45

# Of Great Renown

MERRILY GOT IN, AND there was nobody there except Ethel. Forking out a tray of Felix, drifting through to the scullery, it felt like weeks since she'd last been in here, doing ordinary things. The answering machine was overfed, no longer accepting messages. The air was stale and stuffy, and there was the rattle and hum of a bluebottle in the window.

She opened the window, sat down at the desk with a bag of crisps and rang Lol: no answer. Rang his mobile: engaged.

She needed advice, wanted to pray but wasn't sure what she'd be asking for. She'd never felt so confused. Laying her head on the sermon pad, she closed her eyes. Forget the answers, some coherent questions would help.

Despite the open window, the bluebottle wouldn't go out, as though it was determined to tell her something. All the buzzing things that wouldn't go away.

Merrily jerked upright. The phone was ringing right next to her ear. Last birthday, Jane had bought her another old-fashioned black bakelite phone with a real ring, loud and warm and thrilling, like the church bells which had once peeled across the land from steeple to steeple to warn of impending invasion. She grabbed the phone in a panic, something quaking in her chest.

'Merrily?'

'Frannie?'

'You all right?'

She shook herself, blinking, rubbing at her eyes.

'Sorry, I was . . .'

'I don't know why I'm calling you, really,' Bliss said. 'I didn't plan to. I was just tearing through the CID room with no time at all to spare – not now, no bloody way – but a little voice is going *ring Merrily.*'

'You're not a man who responds to little voices.'

'Nah, you're right. You been listening to the local radio at all today, Merrily?'

'Haven't even had it on in the car. Probably afraid of hearing people talking about Jane. Just tell me this isn't about Jane.'

'Not unless she's shot somebody.'


'The problem was my grandfather,' Mrs Kingsley said. 'It seems Mr Watkins turned up at the door this day – quiet sort of chap, my grandma always said, according to my mother. Very polite, and could he have a look at their bottom meadow?'

Jane clung to an arm of the sofa. *He came? He knew? He really knew about the Ledwardine ley?*

'My grandma was all of a flutter, of course, that such a man as Mr Watkins should be calling on the likes of them. She was quite young at the time, not so very long married. They'd all heard of Mr Watkins, quite a public figure by then, though not because of ley lines.'

'This was . . . when, exactly?' Jane asked.

'About 1924, I would guess. *The Old Straight Track* hadn't been published, I'm fairly sure of that, so not many people knew what it was all about. To be told you had an ancient trackway across your land which had been used by Stone Age people . . . well, it didn't mean anything. Certainly not to my grandfather.'

Gomer said, 'He'd've likely been in the First World War, then, your ole grandad?'

'Yes, he was, Mr Parry. And came back a different man. Not the man Grandma married, my mother used to tell me. He just wanted a quiet life surrounded by his own land. Positively antisocial. It wasn't a very big farm, even if you included the orchard, and he was determined to hold on to it. My grandma liked to go to concerts and the plays, but he would have none of it. Wouldn't take a holiday. And was suspicious of anyone who appeared on his land. Particularly someone with strange equipment, like Mr Watkins. I expect you can guess what *that* was, Jane.'

'Didn't he sometimes use, like, surveying tools?'

'Surveying tools?' Mrs Kingsley laughed. 'Good heavens, he wouldn't have got as far as the gate. No, his *camera* . . . that was enough. Aunt Margaret, who would have been a very small child at the time, thought she remembered some of this, but I suppose the details were filled in for her later. As she described it, Mr Watkins stood for a while at the field gate then walked the length of the meadow to the other gate, near the foot of Cole Hill, and then he came back, and he said, "Mr Probert, would you permit me to take some photographs?"'

'I suppose his camera was . . . pretty big.'

'And on a tripod. In those days, there weren't that many cameras in Herefordshire. Having your photo taken was a big occasion. Almost ceremonial. It was a matter of taking your place in history and you had to look your very best. And, of course, that field didn't. Despite all Grandad's efforts, it was still poorly drained and there'd been floods, and so Grandad says "No, absolutely not." Because it would be a permanent reflection on him, you see, the state of that field, and he was a very proud man.'

Mrs Kingsley held out a faded sepia photograph of a couple standing in front of a fairly run-down-looking cottage. The man wore a tie and a waistcoat and a bowler hat, and he wasn't smiling.

'Well, Mr Watkins tried his best to explain that the field was very important, archaeologically, and he wanted to include it in a book . . . and of course this made things worse. A book! The state of that field preserved for all eternity, to be sniggered over by farmers all over the county. My grandad took what he believed to be the only reasonable action open to him and respectfully ordered Mr Watkins to leave his property at once. Mr Watkins appealed to him to think again and said he would call the next time he was passing. And he did call again, but in the meantime my grandad had been talking to some other councillor who told him not to worry as Mr Watkins's ideas were nonsense.'

'Nothing changes, does it?' Jane said bitterly.

'Mr Watkins said *please* could he just take some photographs if he promised they wouldn't be used in his book or published in any way at all. Just as evidence of what *was*. But Farmer Probert, I'm afraid, refused to believe him. He couldn't get his head round the idea of just *taking* a photograph and not doing anything with it. He didn't think Mr Watkins would be so wasteful of an expensive plate, and he turned the poor man away *again*. Of course, my grandma was *deeply* embarassed by now. She was, as I say, quite a refined lady, with her books and her wind-up gramophone.'

'Not many folks yereabouts had a wind-up gramophone back then,' Gomer said.

'Definitely not, Mr Parry. And, do you know, I think it was that gramophone that saved the day.'

Mrs Kingsley rose and went over to a sideboard under a framed colour photo of some children and a horse.

'I've done quite a lot of research on all this since it came into my possession. As you'll see, it's our family's claim to fame. Our small place in history.'

Gomer looked at her shrewdly.

'Wouldn't reckon Gerry Murray be all that interested in hist'ry?'

'Nor as hard-up as he led my Aunt Margaret to believe.' Mrs Kingsley snorted. 'Bringing his accountant to convince her of the parlous state of his finances.'

Jane looked at Gomer.

'Brung his accountant, did he, missus?' Gomer said.

Mrs Kingsley didn't reply. She unlocked the top section of the sideboard and took out a stiff parchment envelope.

'Mr Watkins was always very polite but he was ... canny, I think the word would be. The next time he came back, it was market day, when he knew my grandad would be in town and my grandma would be on her own. And this time ... he had a friend with him.'

She brought the envelope back to the sofa where Jane and Gomer sat. It had a wing-clip which she undid.

'A titled gentleman,' she said, 'of great renown. *Great* renown, and

311

not only in Hereford. I should imagine my grandma was practically on her knees, when she saw who it was.'

Jane said. 'The Prince of Wales?'

'I'll show you in a minute. But first I'll tell you the result of it. Mr Watkins offered her a deal. If my grandfather let him take pictures of the meadow, for the record, he'd take some other pictures – of grandma and the distinguished gentleman, together. And he would give her the pictures to keep.'

Cool, Jane thought. The man was a true Watkins.

'Well, there was absolutely no way that Hazel Probert was going to turn Mr Watkins away. Certainly not with his distinguished companion, and the promise of the souvenir of a lifetime. And so the photos were taken that very day, while Grandad was at the market.'

'Brilliant,' Jane said.

'And – do you know? – I don't think they were *ever* shown to him or even mentioned from that day until the day he died. She kept them secret for the whole of her life. You can imagine her hiding them away in her bottom drawer and only bringing them out when her husband was at market. Sharing her pride with no one.'

'Then how—?'

'And they were only entrusted before she died – the *week* before she died – to Aunt Margaret, the eldest daughter. Her mother thinking she was the only one who would understand.'

Mrs Kingsley handed the opened envelope to Jane. Jane looked at her hands to make sure that they were clean.

'Don't worry, I checked when you came in,' Mrs Kingsley said. 'We'll have a cup of tea when they're safely away again.'

Aware that her breathing had become shallow, Jane carefully slid out the pictures. There were four of them, in cardboard frames, each one protected by tissue paper. She was going to be the first outsider to see original and almost certaintly historic photos taken by Alfred Watkins himself. She could almost feel him bending over her, with his pointed beard and his glasses on the end of his nose. She shivered slightly.

'Go on,' Mrs Kingsley said.

The first one was a bit faded but, like all Watkins pictures, nice and sharp. Jane saw a woman she guessed to be in early middle age, but could have been younger – hard to tell, the severe way they had their hair in those days. She was dressed in a long skirt and she had a little handbag and a bashful smile. And she was standing...

... *On the ley*...

... The trackway even clearer then than it was now. And this...

... This was just *everything* Jane could have wanted: incontestable proof that the great Alfred Watkins had photographed Coleman's Meadow.

The picture had been taken from the Cole Hill side, with the steeple of Ledwardine Church soaring above the woman's head and the head of the man who Jane hadn't really noticed at first. Quite an ordinary-looking elderly guy. Serious-looking, with a big white moustache, a hairy jacket and a trilby hat.

Jane thought she might've seen him somewhere before but ... well, she hadn't really expected to recognize him, anyway. There were two other pictures of the couple and a third taken from the other side, the old guy on his own pointing towards Cole Hill and he was kind of smiling, and he...

Hang on...

'Gomer...?'

Jane showed the photo to Gomer.

He scutinized the picture very carefully, holding it up to his glasses. Then he lowered it slowly.

'Bugger me, Janie ... that's ole wassisname, ennit?'

# 46

# Black Vapour Trails

BLISS SAID IT WAS nothing fancy, this one. Not some ritual-looking killing in a beauty spot that Annie Howe would take away from him for the headlines.

'This is an old-fashioned, down-home, nasty, sordid, backstreet— I woke you up, didn't I?'

'I'm not in bed,' Merrily said. 'I just . . . go on.'

'Malcolm France. Forty-six years old. Independent security adviser. Know what that means, do we?'

'Minder?'

'Partly. Also a private inquiry agent. Which wasn't attracting enough business for a full-time occupation, so Mal did everything from following wives, to recommending burglar alarms on commission and guarding the rich or the famous when necessary. It was a living. It's where a lot of us go when they kick us out.'

'I'm sorry, Frannie. I hadn't realized he was an ex-colleague. What happened?'

'Not a colleague, no. I knew him, but not well – all that animosity between cops and private eyes, that's for the story books. We keep in with them now, with an eye to the future. He was found early this afternoon, back of St Owen's Street. Broad daylight, Merrily. Not a robbery. I hate that kind of thing. Makes me angry. A crime committed with never a thought that they aren't going to get away with it. We think they were even on view. Two men in white coveralls – familiar sight nowadays, with all the health-and-safety regulations – were seen by a number of witnesses to walk into the building carrying a paint spray. Nobody saw them come out, which suggests that the coveralls were packed away in a case, and the fellers who came out were wearing nice suits.'

'In Hereford?'

'That didn't use to happen in Hereford, did it?' Bliss said.

Merrily heard a car pulling into the vicarage drive. The bluebottle was still making hysterical circuits of the window, or maybe it was another bluebottle. She was very tired of people buzzing her and then flying out of range.

A key turned in the front door. Thank God.

'And did you ... explain why you're ringing me?'

'I said it wasn't robbery, but we think his laptop had been taken and some disks. No sign of case notes or files lying around the office, anyway. So we got permission from his family to check out his bank accounts. Discovering that, among recent payments, was one from a Ms C.W. Sparke, of Wychehill, Malvern.'

Merrily's body jerked; the chair legs scraped the thinning carpet.

'That's a surprise, then, is it?' Bliss said.

'What was he doing for *her*?'

'I don't know. All we have is a receipt for £250, including exes.'

'Winnie Sparke paid this man £250?'

'Peanuts, Merrily. He'd get more than that for finding a lost dog. Most clients, it runs into thousands. Anyway, there it is. She's among a dozen or so of his customers we're checking out. Although it may have nothing do with his current business. However, what do you know about her?'

'She's a writer. From California, but she's lived here quite a few years. Divorced.'

'I was thinking more about her links to our friend Mr Loste, actually. She paid for his lawyer and she collected him from Worcester nick. It might be just a coincidence, but it's interesting.'

'She's working on a book with Loste. He's probably very important to her career at this stage.'

'Any indication she might not trust him, might want him checked out?'

'It's possible, but unlikely. She told me stuff about his origins that

she might not have . . . I don't know, Frannie, that's the truth. I mean
. . . Loste? Even *you're* thinking Loste? Knifes a man on the Beacon and
then . . . You did say this was a shooting?'

'Head and chest. Pistol. Looks like the gun got completely emptied
into him – more enthusiastic than efficient.'

'I saw Loste go into the church, late morning. That rule him out?'

'Hard to say yet. You going back to Wychehill tonight?'

'Hope not.'

'Only, there'll be some uniforms keeping tabs on tonight's young
persons' social event, at the Royal Oak. You haven't seen the TV?'

'Haven't seen anything.'

'Me neither, but it seems there's trouble following press and TV
items with a bloke called Holliday who reckons inner-city trash
elements have turned his village into an apocalyptic battlefield. Mr
Holliday's now saying that he's received personal threats.'

'From whom?'

'From anonymous supporters of the Royal Oak, presumably. It's not
significant enough to worry us, but I thought I'd pass it on.'

Merrily turned at a shadow and saw Lol in the scullery doorway.
They had one another's keys now.

'Well,' she said. 'If I come across anything—'

'Don't worry about it. It's possible that Mal's murder is linked to his
former occupation, in which case I'll probably be sidelined again.
Look, I've gorra go—'

'What *was* his former occupation?'

'Like a number of local security advisers in this general area who
weren't formerly in the police, until six years ago, he was a serving
soldier.'

'In . . . Hereford?'

'Thereabouts,' Bliss said.

It was clear that Lol had a lot to tell Merrily, but there were things that
needed to be dealt with first. Fears racing like black vapour trails across
an already darkening sky.

Before she could think about any of it, there was Jane to deal with.

'Jane's with Gomer,' Lol said. 'They've gone to check out some details about the history of Coleman's Meadow.'

'She's OK, though?'

'She's fine. She's with Gomer.'

'And under the circumstances, *that's* OK? I mean, Gomer has no axe to grind here.'

'I ... I'm pretty sure it's OK.'

'All right. Look, thanks for ... It must've been ...'

'I'll put the kettle on.'

'I'll do it. Need to keep moving. There are some things I want to run past you, and if you tell me it's all crap, I just might not go insane.'

Merrily filled the kettle and plugged it in. The clock said 7.01, and the light on the cream-washed walls was beginning to weaken.

'I don't know whether you got any of that, but Bliss is investigating the murder of a security consultant and private investigator. Who was a former member of the SAS. As was Syd Spicer.'

'And a few hundred other blokes in this county,' Lol reminded her.

'I was told that Spicer's marriage had broken up, but he tells me today he's just sent his wife and daughter down south while he stays here. Because, he says, his "mission" is not yet over. The daughter, Emily, became a serious user in Hereford and he was worried about the proximity of the Royal Oak.'

'Heroin?'

'I don't know. He doesn't tell you a lot. And, although he's with an anti-drug group in Herefordshire, he doesn't involve himself in the campaign by the Wychehill Residents' Action Group. Neither does the chairman of the parish council, Preston Devereaux. Whose eldest son appears to have had similar problems and, I'm told, went out with Spicer's daughter. Devereaux – a man who is conspicuously sitting on a lot of bitterness and rage about the government and the way the countryside gets treated – becomes curiously blasé when you mention the Royal Oak. It won't last, he says. Raji Khan will move on. *Move on* is Devereaux's favourite expression.'

Merrily put tea bags in the pot, thinking this out.

'Although the anti-drugs group works with the police. Spicer admitted tonight that he suspected Roman Wicklow was dealing on the Beacon and didn't see the point in telling the police.'

'OK, that's odd,' Lol said.

'So ... Spicer and Devereaux. Two strong, self-sufficient, arguably dangerous men, who know each other well but don't conspicuously hang out together. Two men in public positions locally who, nonetheless, keep low profiles.'

'You're suggesting they don't trust the police to do a proper job? They've got some vigilante thing?'

'Bliss thinks Raji Khan is behind the influx of heroin, crack and whatever sells ... into the market towns. Bliss suggests that Khan, with his social position, his connections, has a bit of a charmed life. I met Khan this afternoon and – just a feeling – wondered about a special relationship with Annie Howe. He's very cool. Far less wary than ... than Spicer, for heaven's sake.'

'I don't know what to say.' Lol paced the flagged floor. 'SAS men are well trained in the use of knives to dispose of people without any fuss. But Wicklow – that wasn't exactly discreet, was it?'

'God,' Merrily said. 'Spicer's a—'

'But you don't really have anything other than conjecture, do you?'

'Nothing at all. He's also a *priest*...'

'Priests have done worse,' Lol said, 'even in *your* limited experience. Well, one priest. And he wasn't even trained to kill. Look, why not just unload it all on Bliss?'

'But if it turns out it's nothing at all to do with Spicer, a fellow priest, what does that make me?'

'Cautious. How does any of this tie into the killing of this guy in Hereford?'

'Turns out that Winnie Sparke was one of his clients – Bliss doesn't know why.'

'*You* have any ideas?'

Merrily shook her head. 'But Spicer and France had to know each other. They're about the same age – they must've served together.'

'Well ... yes ... but what does that ... ?'

'I don't *know*. I'm just a humble bloody vicar. What do I do with this, Lol? Do I call Bliss back?'

'I don't know, either.' Lol said. 'But I can give you a very good reason to call Winnie Sparke.'

# 47

# A Perfect Universe

'THIS IS STARLIGHT COTTAGE,' Winnie said. 'Who is that?'

'This is Merrily Watkins, Winnie.'

'What do you want?'

When it came to it, nobody could do cold better than someone from the Sunshine State.

'I wanted to talk to you about the Whiteleafed Oak,' Merrily said.

Pause.

'Whiteleafed . . . ?'

'Oak.'

'I don't know what you're talking about.'

'I'm sorry, Winnie, but I think you do,' Merrily said, gripping the big bakelite phone for some kind of support. 'Whiteleafed Oak is a hamlet at the southern tip of the Malverns. It seems to be the joining point of the three counties: Worcestershire, Herefordshire and Gloucestershire.'

Winnie was silent.

'The three counties that come together every year for what seems to be the world's oldest music festival, the Three Choirs. Which, although it only officially dates back to the eighteenth century, reflects something a lot older. I mean, the concept of . . . perpetual choirs?'

It had taken most of an hour to become basically conversant with this from the information that Lol had picked up from Athena White *(Oh God, Athena White?)* and it was coming up to eight p.m., and half of the churchyard wall was in shadow.

At one stage, Merrily had gone up to Jane's apartment in search of books which might illuminate the subject, coming down with a paperback entitled *Sound and the Shaman* and not discovering, until she'd laid it on the desk in front of Lol, that it had been published by an American company called Taliesin and written by one C. Winchester Sparke – the name appearing in small, perfunctory lettering under a picture of an Irish bodhran drum with feathers attached to its frame. One of those books which sold purely on subject, and the author's identity was of little significance.

*In the beginning,* the book began, *was – and is – the sound.*

'The idea of perpetual choirs seems to have begun as a Druidic concept. It also seems to link into the theory of the Music of the Spheres, attributed to Pythagoras, way back before Christ. In which the planets are believed to resonate according to a musical pattern that maintains celestial harmony. A perfect universe.'

Merrily paused, looking at Lol. Felt like she was in the pulpit. Lol was nodding.

'The Perpetual Choirs – stop me if you start to lose interest – were supposed to have maintained that level of harmony on earth. As above, so below. Each choir would have at least twelve members – monks in Christian times, bards or whatever before that. Singing in shifts so that it never stopped. And the choirs were said to have been set up in churches or temples on the perimeters of huge circles in the countryside.'

*But where did this idea come from?* Merrily had demanded desperately, watching Lol spreading out an OS map on the carpet. A map with black lines and circles drawn on it.

He had, after all, obtained the information from Athena White, a little old woman whom Merrily had encountered perhaps twice, in those scary early days of Deliverance. A long-retired civil servant with a child's voice and a child's instinctive, remorseless cunning. A repository of arcane data who'd made that intimidating new assignment seem even more like a journey to the centre of the Earth. Merrily had been slightly afraid for the woman's soul, whereas wary, tentative Lol could casually approach Athena – real name Anthea, it helped to keep reminding yourself of that – and emerge ... enlightened?

Or at least slightly infatuated. The musician lit up by this beautiful but possibly apocryphal concept resurrected in the early 1970s in England by the earth-mysteries scholar John Michell, who had suggested that maintaining the perpetual chant was how the Druids kept control over the Celtic tribes – presumably because nobody would risk breaking the sonic connection between heaven and earth. And then it was absorbed by Christian communities, perhaps using Gregorian chant, and . . .

'Only fragments of knowledge seem to remain. Apparently it was thought that there were twelve choirs in a circle, like a big clock. But, as I say only fragmentary . . . Three Choirs. Twelve choristers. The figures one and two adding up to—'

'Who told you all this?'

Winnie Sparke's voice was distant, as if she was looking away from the phone, into space.

'Of course, you can explain anything with numbers. Biblical scholars do it all the time, but . . . chanting, in any religion you can name, is designed to induce a higher state of consciousness. And something – psychological or whatever – something certainly seemed to work when Tim Loste put choirs of twelve into three churches, one in each of the three counties. Two ancient churches and Wychehill, which was built on an ancient site.'

'You did some homework.'

'I had help. We . . . don't have a record of Druidic chant, but Gregorian chant goes back a long, long way. And Elgar . . . while Elgar's music is modern, it arose from his grounding in the Catholic church and I think much of it was nurtured and developed by the Three Choirs Festival.'

*The festival rotates among the cathedrals of Hereford, Worcester and Gloucester, right?* Lol had said. *All of which are at least medieval. Obviously, Loste doesn't have access to cathedrals, but little-used ancient parish churches are easier, and the three he chose are roughly equidistant to Whiteleafed Oak, where the counties converge. And there's more . . .*

'Over the years, Elgar wrote a lot of music for the Three Choirs, I believe,' Merrily said. 'Having been connected with the festival since, I understand, the age of nine. Or, if you want to be esoteric about it, that would be three times three.'

'Listen.' Winnie Sparke's voice was higher now, and sounding satisfyingly abraded. 'I don't have time for this right now.'

'You keep saying that.'

'You don't understand. I have to go collect Tim.'

'Where from, his self-defence class?'

'Goddamn you, Merrily—'

'I'm sorry, that was— You have something planned for tonight, don't you? Choirs singing in the three counties from nine p.m. till three a.m. Is that because this is the last chance you'll get to approach what you—?'

'That your doing?' Winnie's voice was like cracking ice. 'Getting us kicked out of the church?

'No, of course it isn't. It had already happened when I . . .'

Merrily waited, the big phone clammy against her ear.

'OK, listen,' Winnie said, 'I spend all of Friday and Saturday evenings with Tim. When the Royal Oak starts up. He'll go crazy, else. I get down there well before dark and sometimes we have to get out of Wychehill. We go . . . we go someplace.'

'Like Whiteleafed Oak,' Merrily said. 'Was that where you sent Tim when the parish meeeting was on in Wychehill?'

'Why can't you just leave us *alone*?'

'I wish I could, but I can't.'

'*Why* can't you?'

'Because nobody tells me the whole truth. And when so much is being hidden—'

'Sometimes things *have* to be hidden, you stupid woman. For the sake of preservation.'

'I didn't mean that. This is—'

So difficult. So easy for the cops, but a priest had no right to demand answers and you were on shaky ground even asking questions.

'Malcolm France,' Merrily said. 'Do know about that?'

'Who?'

'Malcolm France was found dead this afternoon, at his office in Hereford.'

Two seconds of silence almost sizzling on the line.

'What are you doing?' Winnie screamed. 'Why are you *lying*? Why are you giving me this shit?'

'France was murdered. He was shot, repeatedly. I'm sorry if—'

Winnie's breathing was turning to panting.

'I want to help,' Merrily said. 'I would like to help you.'

And then she kept quiet, not wanting to give away how little she knew.

'France was killed?'

'In his office.'

'Listen ... this is crazy. That was a personal thing. Nobody was supposed to ... I got fucking *human rights*...'

And this was a terrible mistake. How could Merrily possibly know about Winnie being a client of France's? If Winnie chose to push this, it would rebound heavily on Bliss.

Winnie said, 'Who else knows this?'

'Probably half the county – it's been on the radio.'

'No, the oak. The *oak*.'

'Just me. And my friend Lol, who you met last Monday night. The guy you thought was the exorcist.'

'OK, listen,' Winnie Sparke said. 'You wanna talk about all of this, we'll meet you. We'll meet you there in an hour. Give me time to talk to Tim. We'll meet you there. But you have to promise to leave us when I say. Before nightfall. OK?'

'Sure ... OK.'

'Park where you can and go through the five-bar gate and keep walking. You won't miss it. Nobody could.'

'Won't miss what?'

'It's about the only goddamn place I feel safe.'

'Winnie...'

'One hour.'

'Where?'

'The *oak*.'

# 48

# Neighbours

GOMER AND JANE DROVE to the east of the city, down the deep
shadow of St Owen's Street, with its heavy, brooding Shirehall, where
two police cars and a van were parked.

'Small town, see, Janie,' Gomer said when they stopped at the lights.
'Calls itself a city, but it en't like Worcester and Gloucester. Small
town, out on its own on the border. Even smaller back in the 1920s. So
everybody of a partic'lar class knowed each other. And them bein'
neighbours for years . . .'

'It could make a difference,' Jane said. 'Couldn't it? In Ledwardine?'

'Mabbe. But mabbe not. Don't get your hopes up. Still don't prove
that ole line's any more'n a bit of a sheep track.'

'Yes, but now we can show that Alfred Watkins knew about it, and it
was really important to him . . . and he wasn't the only one.'

'Dunno, girl. Comes down to it, it's just a couple ole boys helpin'
each other out.'

They rattled through the lights to the Hampton Bishop road where
Jane had come with Eirion the other day in search of Alfred Watkins.
This fairly pleasant tree-shaded suburb, and the river wasn't far away.
Gomer turned the old jeep left into Vineyard Lane, where they'd
looked for Alfred's house, and then they got out into the smell of rich
mown grass and walked back to the main road, towards the setting
sun.

The big white Victorian house was on the corner, converted into
flats now. The usual plaque revealing its historic importance. Jane
hadn't even noticed it the other night with Eirion, although it had been
mentioned a few times in school, over the past couple of years.

Plas Gwyn. The white place.

For nine or ten years, these two men had been close neighbours, even if only one of them had been famous at the time.

It wasn't really Jane's idea of a nice house, although back in Edwardian days she supposed it must have looked really modern and flash. It had four floors and a verandah. It was ... well, functional.

In those days, Mrs Kingsley had told them, there weren't many houses around here, and Plas Gwyn had had major views across the river and the water meadows to the Black Mountains ... across the border country to Wales, and Elgar had loved the idea of that when, newly knighted, at the height of his fame, he'd moved here in 1904 with his wife Alice and his daughter Carice.

*Wow.*

Mr Alfred Watkins and Sir Edward Elgar. It made total sense that they should've been mates. Elizabeth Kingsley had drawn up a chart showing that they'd been almost exact contemporaries – Elgar had been born in 1857 and had died in 1934, Watkins was born in 1855 and died in 1935.

And so much in common.

Both of them photographers – Elgar was said to have had a darkroom here at Plas Gwyn, where he also, like Watkins, invented things.

Both of them members of the Woolhope Club.

Both them fascinated by the landscape.

And most of Elgar's Hereford years had been kind of slow and uninspired where music was concerned. He hadn't composed much here at all, Mrs Kingsley said, leaving him time to spare for his other interests. The council, in search of some reflected glory, had even offered to make him Mayor of Hereford, but he'd politely – and wisely, in Jane's view – turned it down.

Jane remembered Mrs Waters, the art teacher at Moorfield, talking about this, when the Elgar sculpture was being planned for the Cathedral green. And how Elgar got disillusioned because, although he was this mega-celeb, he thought nobody really understood his music.

Elgar at low ebb in Hereford just as the great revelation was coming to sixty-ish Alfred Watkins, billowing towards him across the humpy fields in great waves of vision.

Of course, by the time *The Old Straight Track* was published, Elgar had left this house. But he loved the city, Mrs Kingsley had said, and he was always coming back to stay, especially when the Three Choirs Festival was held here. Used to meet his old friends, like the playwright George Bernard Shaw, who was always trying to encourage Elgar to get back into some serious composing after the death of his wife in 1920.

'So he and Alfred Watkins stayed in touch, obviously.'

'Sure t'be,' Gomer said.

Jane getting a picture in her head of these two elderly guys, Alf and Ed, standing on Dinedor Hill with the city's churches aligned below them in the vastness of the old-gold evening. The air filling with ancient energy and orchestral murmurings.

Alf going, *Bit of a problem, d'ye see? Best ley I ever found and I en't allowed to go in there with my camera.*

*Something I could help with, you think, old chap?* Ed tilting his head to one side. *People seem to think a lot of me these days . . . for all the wrong blasted reasons, of course.*

*Well . . . mabbe.* Alf's beard splitting into a slow grin. *Mabbe you could, too.*

'It's weird, Gomer,' Jane said. 'How things happen, kind of simultaneously. Mum's into this ridiculous situation over at Malvern where some people think that, like . . . Elgar's ghost has returned?'

She stood on the pavement in front of Plas Gwyn and checked for messages on the mobile.

*'Jane, I'm so sorry.'* Mum sounded . . . upset? What? *'I've come home, and obviously there's a lot we need to . . . only I've got to go out again. With Lol. Shouldn't be too late. Could you stay with Gomer? Please?'*

The sun was dropping like a great molten weight into Wales, and the air was warm and airless. Jane's bare arms, for some reason, were tingling.

# 49

# The Lesson

THERE WAS, AT FIRST, a cramped, dead-end kind of feel, as they edged out of the Volvo. Merrily had had to squeeze it onto a rough verge, one wheel partly overhanging a ditch. Might be somebody's parking place, but there was nobody about in the hamlet of Whiteleafed Oak to ask. A few bungalows, cottages, and nowhere to park because the lane was so narrow.

But it was wooded, sun-dappled, intimate. It didn't have the wide-viewed isolation of Wychehill. Locking the Volvo, Merrily could hear a radio from an open window, and there was a small trampoline and a yellow bike in one of the sloping front gardens. Whiteleafed Oak was lived-in.

The sun was burning low in a sky like tarnished brass, the air was heavy and humid, and the only sacred sound was placid evening birdsong.

Merrily looked around. There were no directional signs, no indication of where to find whatever was to be found.

Lol opened out the OS map on the bonnet of the Volvo. There were several pencil lines drawn on it, one of them, lengthways, more defined than the others.

'This is what Jane found. A north-south line along the spine of the range, touching all these hills – Midsummer Hill, Hangman's Hill, Pinnacle Hill, Perseverance Hill, North Hill – on, or at least close to, their summits. Cutting along the side of Herefordshire Beacon and passing through Wychehill Church.'

'You can't fault the alignment,' Merrily admitted. 'Not without a bigger map, anyway.'

'And if we extend the line south . . .' Lol continued it with a thumb
'. . . we can see that it begins at . . .'

*Whiteleafed Oak.*

'Obvious when you know,' Lol said.

'Is this a ley line?'

'I don't know. Most of these are natural features. But they were probably all ritual sites.'

'Or part of one huge ritual site,' Merrily said. '*Moel Bryn.* The sacred Malverns.'

She was quite glad to see Whiteleafed Oak marked on the map. Didn't even recall seeing any road signs pointing to it. Although it was only a few miles out of Ledbury, past the Eastnor Castle estate and into a twisting single-track lane, this was a place you would never find by accident. Nor particularly search out. Nearby villages like Eastnor and Eastwood were picturesque in the traditional sense, Whiteleafed Oak was not.

Lol folded up the map.

'Better find this place before it gets any darker.'

*Still be light enough to find your way. Park where you can and go through the five-bar gate and keep walking.*

'Which five-barred gate?' Merrily opening out her hands. 'Over there? Along there?'

'It's apparently the hamlet itself which marks the point at which the three counties merge.'

'Nothing obvious here. Not even a church.'

'Only a possible Druidic processional way.'

This was what Athena White had told Lol although she hadn't been here in many years.

The fact that they'd been directed here by Athena White was why Merrily was wearing, under her thin sweatshirt, her pectoral cross. Why she'd slipped a pocket Bible into her jeans and taped to the Volvo's dash the text, as if she could ever forget it, of St Patrick's Breastplate.

Merrily said, 'What on earth *happened* here?'

Thinking, And why didn't I know about it?

With the hamlet of Whiteleafed Oak out of sight, nearly half a mile behind them, she was standing on what might have been – might *still* be – a processional way.

Looking around in the calm of the evening. Finding that the place was instantly familiar and perceptibly strange. Familiar because of well-known landmarks, like the stone obelisk, projecting like a stubby pencil from Eastnor Park in Herefordshire. And May Hill, in western Gloucestershire, identifiable from the Black Mountains to the Cotswolds by the stand of pines on its summit.

At the tail of the Malverns, three counties were drawn together by landmarks and legend. The closer countryside was scabbed with odd mounds before it scrolled out into low hills, woods and copses and isolated clumps of conifers, all of it textured like velvet in the softening light.

And it was strange because none of this seemed random. It was as though each feature of the landscape had a special significance, a role to play in some eternally unfolding drama. And if they carried on walking into the arena – and it did feel like an arena – they'd be given their own parts to play.

Perhaps this was the great lesson to be learned about all of nature, although there were only certain spots where you could receive it with any intensity. Places of – *oh God, wake me up before I turn into Jane* – palpably sentient scenery.

They were alone in the landscape but, as they followed a vague path over a shallow rise, the sunset turning flat fields into sandbanks, she couldn't lose the feeling that something knew they were coming.

*You won't miss it*, Winnie Sparke had said. *Nobody could.*

She was right.

Merrily saw that Lol had stopped about twenty paces away, as though he was wondering how best to approach it, if he should take off his shoes.

'Nobody said it was still here.' His voice quite hoarse.

'Nobody said it was still in use,' Merrily said.

330

OK, it probably wasn't the original one, after which the place was named, but it had to be many centuries old. Even without white leaves, it had grown into the heart of an earlier belief system which conspicuously lived on.

There were several other oak trees nearby, young satellite churches around this ancient, ruinous cathedral.

'Venerated,' Merrily said. 'Still. On a serious scale.'

There was enough veneration to cover several Christmas trees, but the great oak, with its enormous swollen bole, had easily absorbed it all.

Offerings. Ribbons tied to twigs, fragments of coloured cloth, foil, labels with handwritten messages, flowers, balls of wool. Tiny intimate, symbolic items stuffed into folds and crevices, snagged in clawed branches. Hundreds of them, some fresh, some decaying, some fusing with fungi on the blistered bark.

Small sacrifices. People were still coming here – now – to make small sacrifices. Immense in the muddied light, the oak represented an everyday, naked paganism.

'You uncomfortable with this, Merrily?'

Lol walking softly all around the oak – considered steps as if he was moonwalking or something.

'I don't know,' she said. 'I just ... It's very ... human. All these people making their pilgrimages, leaving their small offerings in ... what? A celebration of survival?' She dared to touch the tree with one hand. 'What about you?'

'To be quite honest, it kind of excites the hell out of me.'

'Mmm, thought it might.'

'Like, you read about ancient theories on music, and it seems so remote and ... theoretical. But when you actually find a link with a bit of landscape only an hour or so from where you live. And then you come, for the first time, and it's ...'

'It's a tree, Lol.'

'Merrily, it is so palpably *not ... just ... a ... tree.*'

'Well, it ... it's certainly the oak in the big picture over Tim Loste's fireplace. I'm sure of that.'

It was all rolling at her like the ball lightning that Spicer had talked about, connections forming: all the saplings in the pots outside Loste's house and the one planted in his garden ... had they been grown from acorns picked up here, descendants of the Whiteleafed Oak?

It was as well to keep reminding yourself that the central reason you were here was finally to get to meet Tim Loste, without whom ...

Lol stepped back, as if the atmosphere was too charged so close to the massive tree. You brought a blocked musician to what was alleged to be the most powerful source of musical energy within his ambit, you had to expect a certain ... fascination.

'If a few white leaves appeared on your oak tree, it was taken as a sign of major change.'

'Athena?'

'So if there was a tree here that was full of white leaves, maybe it was seen as a place where you could find transformation.'

'That figures. Winnie's blueprint for Tim Loste seems to be all about transformation. Like *The Dream of Gerontius*. The processing of the soul.'

'You mentioned there were some other pictures on Loste's walls,' Lol said.

'Mostly, they were places I didn't recognize. Hills. Churches. But some were well known.'

'Stonehenge?' he said. 'Glastonbury?'

She stared at him.

'What the hell *else* did that woman tell you?'

Lol sat down in the grass, outside the growing shadow of the oak.

'I didn't want to confuse you with the bigger picture before you rang Winnie. The Three Choirs is only the local part of the story.'

'I'm not sure I can handle this.'

Merrily sat next to him and he told her, his face shining in the blush of evening, about the big picture: twelve of them. A dozen perpetual choirs in south-west Britain, on the perimeter of a vast circle – supposedly. Their locations including Stonehenge, Glastonbury and Llantwit Major in South Wales, site of an ancient monastic college.

Not exactly recorded history. *Poetic* history. It could be valid, but scepticism, Merrily thought, might be safer at this stage.

'If you plot the big circle,' Lol said, 'you find Whiteleafed Oak is the centre – equidistant from Stonehenge, Glastonbury and Llantwit. The pivot.'

'But these – Stonehenge, Glastonbury, et cetera – were the only *known* sites?'

'The only ones actually named in early Welsh literature. The others have been identified in places like Meifod, near Welshpool, Llandovery in west Wales and Goring-on-Thames – the word Goring comes from Cor, which means choir.'

'So we're ... sitting at the centre of ...'

'... Arguably *the* most important focus of musical energy in Britain's oldest established culture. A culture in which music was not *one of the arts*, part of *entertainment* ... but a crucial element in the structure of life. An element in religion but also part of science and mathematics. And all the more spiritual for that.'

'So all these offerings ...'

'Oh ... I should've mentioned that some people visiting the presumed sites of perpetual choirs have said that they can still be heard. As a kind of droning, like distant bees. But then ... people are impressionable.'

'Erm ... ?'

'Just the birds,' Lol said.

'Thank God for that. So, we're assuming that Elgar knew this place.'

'Elgar said there wasn't a single lane in Worcestershire that he hadn't been down. Would've been an easy walk from Birchwood. Where he was living when he composed *Caractacus*. Is *this* his sacred oak? Look.'

Lol stood up and walked down below the tree where, guarded by younger oaks, there was a depression in the ground, a hollow. Merrily looked down at a charcoal stain near its centre. Fires were still being lit here. Worn bits of branches were lying around in the shallow pit like discarded bones. So much here suggestive of bone. A knobbly outgrowth at the base of the great oak itself was like a big bovine skull with one jagged eye socket.

'Everything has its dark side,' Lol said.

The last segment of sun went into the ground like a household fire collapsing in a shower of bright red sparks.

'So this,' Merrily said, 'is where New Age paganism meets High Catholicism.'

'This very spot.'

'The Three Counties, though . . . I mean, the Three Choirs Festival is this posh, prestigious . . . the sort of thing that *Sophie* attends. Are we really looking at something distantly descended from some folk memory of pagan chanting?'

'The official version is that it was set up as a clerical charity about three hundred years ago. Religious music performed – Handel and Purcell. But who knows? Be interesting to hear what Loste has to say.'

'Except they're not here.' Merrily stepping away from the edge of the pit, looking all around. 'She said an hour.'

'Or they might be waiting for darkness,' Lol said. 'According to Dan, the choirs start at nine. Until three in the morning. Would they really be here, rather than with one of the choirs?'

'Maybe Loste standing under that tree, remotely conducting his three choirs from the centre of the circle?'

'Maybe we'll get to see.'

'Don't build up your hopes. Between us and him there's Sparke.'

The western sky was like dull copper and the air was heavy with stored heat. Merrily noticed that she and Lol were almost whispering, as if the oak might be absorbing it all, to be replayed to future generations.

Lol said, 'You want to go back to Wychehill, see if she's around?'

'What if they come here while we're gone? They won't necessarily come the same way we did. Loste knows the hidden paths.'

'I'll stay, if you like.'

'On your own? *Here?*'

He shrugged. Merrily tried to make out his expression, but it was too dim now, veils of mauve and sepia.

'It's less than ten minutes away,' Lol said, 'and we've both got mobiles. I'll walk with you back to the car and when you're on your way back you call me, so I can be waiting for you. If they turn up, I'll call you straight away.'

'OK. Just . . . you know . . .'

'Don't do pagan things? Merrily, I'm not Jane. I don't even *know* any pagan things.'

They walked back, hand in hand, towards the hamlet of Whiteleafed Oak. The night was warm and the air smelled like a wholefood shop. Only a few weeks to the first hay harvest and that rich caramel scent which Merrily would always associate now with the Frome Valley and the first night she'd spent with Lol.

Some things were not worth risking.

'They'll come back,' she told him.

'Loste and Winnie?'

'The songs. Your songs. They'll come back. You know they will.'

She looked back at the oak, a fat old open-air preacher. Or maybe a conductor, the branches like a blurring of arms, summoning and gathering in three hundred and sixty degrees of sacred sound.

The trees are singing my music . . . *or am I singing theirs?*

Jesus.

Merrily was quite glad to be leaving. But not glad that Lol was staying.

# 50

# In the Country, After Dark

TRAVELLING BACK TO LEDWARDINE in the open-top jeep, the thoughts blowing through Jane's head were exhilarating and bewildering. Couldn't wait to tell Mum and Lol, get some idea of where this could take them.

She was on firm ground at last. She could speak out. The council guys had made so much of the fact that the Coleman's Meadow ley wasn't in *The Old Straight Track*. Now she had proof that Watkins had known about it and seen its importance, and...

... And so had *Elgar*.

Britain's greatest composer? This figure of serious international distinction, whose involvement *nobody* could ignore?

It was just a question of getting one of those incredible pictures photocopied – and, although they hadn't pushed it at all, it had seemed like Mrs Kingsley was well up for that. Clearly no love lost between her and Murray.

And this breakthrough was entirely down to Gomer.

Ciggy between his teeth, glasses like goggles, his cap in his lap and his dense white hair like smoke in the dusk. Driving like he was really concentrating on the road, but he was clearly concentrating on something else.

About three miles from home, he slowed.

'This new leisure centre. What you reckon o' that, girl?'

'Came out of the blue, didn't it? Nobody ever said we needed one. Mum doesn't know where it came from.'

'Ah, well,' Gomer said. 'Where it all d' come from, I reckon, is Stu Twigg.'

'Huh?'

'He owns the land what the village hall's built on. ' 'Herited it off his ole man last year. Gwyn Twigg? No? Had a petrol station over towards Monkland. Supermarket opens up at Leominster, cheap petrol, Gwyn shuts down, but he's got these bits o' ground all over the place, worth a good few hundred grand, so he's all right, ennit? When he dies, Stu's in the money. Lazy bugger, though, Stu Twigg. Calls hisself a mechanic, all he does is messes around soupin' up ole bangers and scarin' the life out o' folks in the lanes.'

'Got him now,' Jane said. 'I think. White Jaguar?'

'That's the boy.'

'Came round a corner once, had Irene in the ditch. He's insane.'

'Not insane enough he don't know the value of land,' Gomer said. 'Ground rent on the village-hall site, that's peanuts, see – only public-spirited gesture Gwyn Twigg ever made. Mabbe owed somebody on the parish council a favour. Anyway, word is, Stu's been talkin' serious to one o' the supermarket chains.'

'You mean with a view to . . . ?'

'Only one suitable site for a supermarket in Ledwardine, they reckons. Only it's got a village hall on it.'

This didn't take a lot of thinking out. The village hall was 1960s and a bit run down. Not exactly a listed building.

Jane said, 'So if there was a *new* village hall . . . like one that was built somewhere else . . . ?'

'Or a posh new leisure centre with playin' fields, what'd need a bigger site. Mabbe a greenfield site, outside the village kind o' thing. If you had some'ing like that . . .'

'Stu could could flog the village-hall site to the supermarket and clean up. And we'd have a big flash superstore dominating the bottom of Church Street like a . . . a shrine to commercialism.'

'Ar. Some'ing like that. You wanner take a guess who Stu's accountant is, Janie?'

'Wow.' Jane lurched forward against her seat belt. 'You are *kidding*.'

'Open secret, girl. Like I tole you, startin' off thinkin' your local councillor's bent always saves a bit o' time.'

'Gomer, that is just so—'

'En't even the whole story, girl. Supermarket chain, they got a limit, kind o' thing – what I mean is, a place needs to have a partic'lar head o' population to make it worthwhile movin' in. And Ledwardine's borderline. Needs mabbe a hundred or so new houses to qualify. See where I'm goin' yere?'

'Luxury . . . executive . . .' Jane lost her breath '. . . homes.'

'It's a start.'

'That's—'

'And it don't stop there. I been talkin' to Jack Brodrick, see. Jack was a surveyor with the ole Radnorshire Council. *He* d'reckon Coleman's Meadow's *a key strategic move*. Strategic, see. His word. What it means is this: you got housing on Coleman's Meadow, you gets to put a road through the ole orchard as was. Which opens up the whole of the east side o' Ledwardine. And then you're *off*, and big time, Janie. More new estates up the back of Ole Barn Lane, out towards the bypass, and all the way to . . .'

Gomer gave Jane a sideways glance and crushed out his ciggy.

Jane pictured it. The back of Old Barn Lane? That would take the housing to . . .

'The bottom of Cole Hill, from the other side?'

'Sure t'be.'

'Which would mean . . . with Coleman's Meadow built on, Cole Hill would be totally boxed in.'

''Course, this is only what Jack Brodrick reckons.'

'*Christ, Gomer!*'

'Shrewd ole bugger, Jack, mind.'

'Pierce is quietly stitching up the whole village! We'll be like . . . like a new town.'

'Looks that way.'

'How long have you known?'

'I *don't* know, Janie. It's all guesswork, ennit?'

'It's not.' Jane leaned back against the passenger door, her head out of the jeep, as if this would blow away the images of black and white houses crushed by an avalanche of pink brick.

Gomer drove on towards the Ledwardine turning.

'*Is it?*' Jane screamed against the slipstream.

'Mabbe not,' Gomer said.

As Gomer slowed for the Ledwardine turn, Jane checked her mobile, found the message from Mum. So what was new? Maybe Mum and Lol would be home by the time she got in. Anyway, she didn't want to call back now. There was just too much to say. And she was too angry.

They came into the village. Ledwardine in the smoky dusk. The black and white houses timeless and ghostly in the fake gaslight from the square and the orange and lemon light spilling from the diamond-paned windows of the Black Swan. No neon.

Outside the Swan, the high-powered cars and SUVs of smug diners. A few young guys of fourteen or so with lager cans on the square.

Imagine it in five years, with twice the population.

Two ways it could go: either a refuge of the rich with high gates and burglar alarms and suspicion and unfriendliness. Or teeming streets, vandalism, drunkenness, fights, burglaries and gutters full of infected needles and crack pipes.

Not that there was anything *new* about all that, even in Ledwardine. In centuries past, the gutters would probably have been overflowing nightly with blood and vomit. And, like . . . well, everybody got drunk sometime, it was just . . .

. . . Just that the kind of *mass* drunkenness you got in the cities now was symptomatic of something scary: an almost suicidal hopelessness seeping through society. Jane had done this really heartfelt essay on it for the school magazine. The attitude was: the world is made of shit, the politicians of all three major parties are clueless tossers on the make, the country's already more than halfway down the toilet, so if you don't get pissed tonight, tomorrow could be too late.

There'd been times when she'd felt that way herself, obviously. And although she hadn't used the words *pissed* or *shit* in the essay, it had still been censored. Good old Morrell. Good old *Rob*. Maybe it *was* time to leave, make her own way. Somehow.

'Home, is it?'

'Huh? Sorry, Gomer, I was . . .'

'You wanner check if the vicar's back, Janie?'

Gomer had stopped the jeep at the edge of the market square, engine clattering.

'Actually, Gomer, I wouldn't mind – like, now there'll be nobody about – checking out Coleman's Meadow? See if they've taken the fence down or anything.'

'They en't gonner do that, girl.'

'Only . . . I feel bad about just going to ground all day. Not having the courage of my convictions.'

'Wisest thing. You hadn't got no proof.'

'Yeah. And now we have. *Can* you take me back to Mrs Kingsley's in the morning? Get those pictures photocopied?'

'I'll do that.'

'You're a star, Gomer.'

But still tomorrow morning seemed a long way off. What if – call it paranoia, but anything could happen in this sick world – what if Mrs Kingsley had changed her mind? What if Lyndon Pierce and Gerry Murray had found out and persuaded her to hand over the photos, and by tomorrow morning they were ashes?

'Best to stay away from the meadow, I reckon, Janie. Don't invite no trouble till you're ready for it.' Gomer pulled the jeep onto the square, switched off the engine. 'I'll come over the vicarage with you. If they en't back, mabbe get some chips?'

'Brilliant. See, all I was thinking . . . maybe more protesters might've turned up. I've got this fantasy of . . . like one of these old peace camps? Where people come and occupy the site?'

'Got new laws to prevent all that, now.'

'They're stifling everything spontaneous, aren't they? Free speech. Whatever happened to that?'

'En't gonner stifle me, girl,' Gomer said. 'Too old to be stifled, see.'

They walked across the square and under the market hall. It was around ten p.m. and the only light was in the northern sky – a strange light, with swirls of white, like cream in dark coffee.

There were no lights in the vicarage.

'Chips then, is it?' Gomer said.

'Yeah, why not? My treat. You've done a great job tonight, Gomer. All we have to do now is make sure everybody knows . . . and about the leisure centre and everything. We've got to wake up the village.'

'Easier said than done, Janie. Thing is—'

Gomer froze.

'What?' Jane said.

'Y'ear that?'

All Jane could hear was the sound of a distant engine, like a lorry or something, carrying the way sounds did in the country after dark. Gomer stepped back onto the square, his head on one side.

'It's a JCB, ennit? Gimme a couple more minutes, I could mabbe tell you what size and how old.'

Jane smiled. Gomer Parry Plant Hire never sleeps.

Gomer wasn't smiling. He stood hunched, looking down at his Doc Martens, listening hard.

'Comin' from the orchard, it is.'

'I don't—'

'Seems to me there en't many places back there where you can manoeuvre a JCB. Specially at night, see.' He looked at Jane, and there was no light in his glasses. He took the ciggy out of his mouth and coughed unhappily. 'You know what they're doin', don't you?'

51

# The Blade

OF COURSE, LOL HAD half-lied to Merrily, and he hated that, but now he was compelled to go through with it.

By evening light, the sacred oak had seemed inspirational – its weight, its setting. The glow of sunset had instilled a transitional tension which was unsettling. And he needed that. Badly needed to be unsettled again. Have something reawoken in him, even if it was through fear of the unknown.

It was odd. Since the sun had gone down, the sky seemed brighter. The landscape, as he neared the oak, had the eeriness of a vast attic lit by a single candle. The voice of Dan the chorister was crackling behind his ears like tinnitus: *I was a bit cynical about the whole idea at first but . . . I'd do it again tomorrow, I mean it, I'd travel a long way to do it.'*

Maybe the words of Dan the chorister had been quietly playing at the back of his mind for hours.

*. . . Vibration going through you, like wiring . . . different parts of you lighting up in some kind of sequence . . . wasn't just three churches coming together, it was like being inside a big orb of sound. Like we'd broken through to another place.*

Lol was wondering when, since the terror and adrenalin rushes of the comeback concert at the Courtyard, he'd last experienced anything approaching that level of connection. What use was he to Merrily or Jane if he couldn't feel their level of commitment? The way both of them, from their different directions, were driven, while he was just the hanger-on, the timid inhabitant of the witch's cottage who hadn't been able to construct a serviceable song for over a month.

Night had widened the landscape. Nothing visible between Lol and

342

Stonehenge and Glastonbury Abbey. Two tawny owls conversed across the valley.

He stopped and looked up: stars ... planets ... spheres.

And then, as the naked, dead, topmost branches of the sacred oak appeared over the nearest horizon like a claw, he was shaking his head because this was faintly despicable. He should have gone with Merrily.

But Lol kept on walking until, at some point, the whistling arose.

Jane followed the tiny beacon of Gomer's ciggy through the churchyard, through the wicket gate and into the orchard, which had once encircled the village. All that was around her now was the sluggish sound of the JCB flexing its metal muscles.

A friendly sound, normally. She'd always associated JCBs with Gomer. Gomer Parry Plant Hire: drain your fields, clear your ditches, lay your pipes, dig your soakaway.

Now it was a grinding headache, maybe the fantasy-migraine she'd invented coming back to haunt her, karmic retribution: clanking, dragging, ripping, an organ of destruction. Darkness closing in on mellow old Ledwardine.

'Slow, Janie,' Gomer said.

They were beyond the church, into the patch of ground where Jane had found the circular bump that might be a Bronze Age burial mound. Too dark now to make it out. There was a moon somewhere, but its meagre light wasn't getting in here, and the nettles were high; she must have been stung a dozen times already, but that didn't matter. Sweating, grit in her eyes, she stopped at the sound of a heavy blade on stone, raw friction, a pulling back, a meshing of gears.

'Careful, girl – wire.'

Gomer, breathing hard, was feeling his way along an old barbed-wire fence, not the kind of fence you tried to climb over at night without a torch. He'd wanted to go back to the jeep for his lambing light, but Jane had been frantic by then, and anyway ... there were headlamps on the JCB. She could see them at last through the trees, and the shape of the big yellow digger itself, monstrous now and brutal, an implement of scorched earth.

Gomer found the stile and tested its strength with both hands before climbing over and waiting to help Jane down. But Jane didn't need any help and she hit the ground running, ripping the back of a hand on the bottom of the sign on which she could have read, if there'd been any light, *Herefordshire Council Planning Department*.

'*Bast—*'

'Janie—'

'Stop it!' Jane screamed. 'You total *bastards!*'

Bursting into Coleman's Meadow where they'd taken down a section of the new fencing to let the JCB in. The JCB that was approaching the middle of the meadow along twin bars of yellow-white headlamp beam. Moving in for another attack.

Jane ran out towards the digger – and hands grabbed her. The JCB reared up like a rampant dinosaur and its mud-flecked lights went spearing across the meadow towards Jane as she wrenched herself away, and then ricocheted from the yellow hard-hat worn by the man who'd held her arms.

'Health and Safety regulations are very explicit,' he said. 'That's as far you go.'

Jane backed away, coughing, pulling hair out of her eyes, as he bent and picked up a lamp, throwing the beam full in her face.

'Might've known,' he said.

'This is . . .' She could hardly speak for the rage and the shock. 'This is *wrong*. This is *illegal*. This is a crime against—'

'Not wrong at all,' Lyndon Pierce said, 'and certainly not illegal. This is private land, and the man in the digger is the owner of the land. And also of the digger, as it happens.'

The lamp beam swung to one side to find Gomer. He was panting and his ciggy had gone.

'By God, you en't bloody changed, Lyndon, boy. En't changed one bit.'

'Not your problem, Mr Parry. I don't know what you're doing here.' Pierce's tone was remote; he didn't look at Gomer. 'But I strongly suggest you leave immediately and take this . . . girl with you before she gets into any more trouble. It's *not your business*.'

'En't your business, either. You're supposed to be a councillor, boy. Supposed to see both bloody sides.'

'I'm not taking sides. I'm observing. I'm here as a member of the Herefordshire Council Planning Committee. An official . . . observer.'

He looked out across the meadow, and Jane followed his gaze. The digger had reversed back into a corner of the meadow, its blade up and retracted, its headlights illuminating what it had already done to Coleman's Meadow, revealing the extent of the massacre.

'Here I go now, in fact,' Lyndon Pierce said. 'Observing.'

Jane was too shattered to cry. It looked like pictures she'd seen of the Somme. More than half the central track had been dug up, ripped away. The surface turf torn off and dumped in rough spoil heaps, and deeper, more jagged furrows dug out where the ground was softer. Water coming up from somewhere, pooling in the glistening clay-sided trenches.

They'd systematically destroyed it. They'd all but obliterated the ley. They'd waited until it had got dark and the few protesters had gone and then they'd opened the fence and let in the JCB. Like letting a hungry fox into a chicken house, to do its worst.

The enemy was pointing at them across the meadow and Jane could see the shape of its driver, hunched behind the levers in the reinforced glass cab. Gerry Murray, presumably. Sitting there watching them now, waiting, an agent of the darkness.

'*Stop him.*' Jane's fingers were sticky. 'Stop him while you can. While there's still some of the track left. Because it's not going to look good for you tomorrow when . . . when the truth comes out.'

'Truth?'

Pierce laughed. Jane felt the delta of blood washing down from the back of the hand she'd slashed on the sign, oozing between her fingers.

'Jane, the only truth that's coming out is the kind of truth that'll be damaging to you and your mother and your mother's hippie boyfriend. Now go home quietly before you make things worse.'

'Like I'm really going to let you destroy an ancient monument?'

'We've been there, Jane. This is no more an ancient monument than your friend Mr Parry.'

'You're just ... you're just a scumbag and a ...'

All the names she wanted to spit at him, but that would just be abuse and childish, like the sad underage drivers you saw howling *wanker* at the traffic cops in all those cheap TV documentaries.

'Why do you—' She stared up at him, and then turned quickly away, feeling tear-pressure. 'Why do you have to do this?'

'I'll remind you one more time,' Pierce said, 'that you're on a development site and you're not wearing protective clothing. If you don't go, I'll be calling the police to have you removed, and we'll see how good *that* looks in the papers. Now be a good girl and let Mr Murray finish the preparation of his ground.'

'*Preparation?* He hasn't even got planning permission yet, even if it's as good as a done deal. This is just sick, mindless ... *peevish* ... destruction. *Why do you have to do this?*'

'Because of *you*, you stupid little—' Pierce's face coming at her, dark with evening-stubble. 'What do you think all this fencing cost, to keep those cranks out? Eh? What if they come back tomorrow and there's even more of them? What then?'

'Well, good ...'

'No. *Not* good, Jane. Bad for all of us. Costly. So, to forestall the possibility of further public disturbance, Mr Murray took the entirely sensible decision to remove what our county archaeologists have formally confirmed was *never there in the first place.* And invited me, as the local representative, to come along and observe that no regulations were breached, and that's what I'm doing. That's it. All right?'

He turned away, adjusting his hard hat. He was wearing a khaki-coloured shirt and cargo trousers, like he was in the SAS or something, on a special high-risk mission.

'So *he* invited *you*, is it?' Gomer said.

'I gotter say everything twice for you, is it, Mr Parry?'

'Sure you din't invite yourself? Strikes me this is just the sorter thing you'd think of all by yourself, that's all.'

Lyndon Pierce didn't reply.

'Because, like, all you care about,' Jane said, 'is protecting your corrupt schemes and the bungs you're getting from the guy who's flogging his land to the supermarket firm, and the bungs you're probably getting from the developers of the *luxury, executive...*'

Pierce turned slowly. Too late to stop now.

'You're just ... totally fucking *bent.* Just like your dad. With your crap Marbella-style villa and your naff swimming pool and your ... You couldn't lie straight in *bed.*'

Gomer said quietly, 'Janie...'

'Right...'

Pierce turning to Gomer, the lamp under his face, uplighting it, the way kids did to turn themselves into monsters.

'Now, I want you to remember this, Mr Parry. First off, I don't give a fig what this nasty little girl says, on account she's too young to think of any of it for herself—'

'Like fuck she is!'

'Janie—'

'So I'm holding *you* solely responsible for that actionable shite. Even though nothing you say counts for a thing round yere and never did. Never did, ole man.'

Jane kept quiet. Stopped breathing.

Because Pierce had lost it. His accent had broken through again, and his language had broken down. Gomer went silent, too. This was, like, confirmation. Well, wasn't it?

Pierce shone his hand-lamp from Gomer's face to Jane's face and back again.

'You're halfway senile, Mr Parry. You and your bloody *plant hire.* You don't even know what bloody plant hire means. You're a joke, ole man. You en't even *safe* to climb into one of them no more.' Pierce jerking a thumb at the JCB, his words coming faster. 'And everybody knows ... *everybody* knows you always got it in for farmers like Gerry, does their own drainage rather than paying good money, out of pity, to a clapped-out ole fart like you for half a fuckin' job.'

Gomer didn't say anything, but something tightened in his neck and he went rigid, the lamplight swirling like liquid in his glasses. For a terrified couple of seconds, Jane thought, *Oh Christ, he's having a stroke.*

Wanting to kill Pierce and only dimly aware of the JCB's engine revving up, until Pierce turned to the meadow, his hard-hat tipping back as his arm came up like the arm of some petty Roman-emperor figure.

'You wanner watch?' he said. 'All right, *you watch.*'

'No!' Jane screamed. '*No!*'

Pierce brought his arm down, a chopping motion.

On the other side of Coleman's Meadow the big digger rocked, its blade lowering. And then it began to roll on its caterpillars towards the last, pathetic piece of old straight track.

'Oughter be in an old folks' home, you ought, Parry,' Pierce said as he walked away. 'I should think about that, I were you.'

He'd been blocking the long view of Cole Hill, which never entirely faded away on summer nights. A lick of moon had risen behind it like a candle on a coffin. Down below, the last four or five metres of track made a perfect shadow.

'Stop him! Please stop him!' Jane arching forward, screaming at Pierce's back. 'You *shit!*'

He was gone. He'd walked casually away into the orchard, and all there was left was the yellow lights and the roaring, and Jane looked back at Gomer. But Gomer wasn't moving, he was just standing there, a bit bent now, like one of the old, dying apple trees in the derelict orchard behind him.

It was almost over.

Jane was on her own. She'd failed. She'd mishandled everything, through immaturity, her eagerness to do something, *be* somebody. She couldn't live with that.

She was only half aware of running blindly towards the digger's bobbing lights. Running out, sobbing, into the meadow, where the ruined ley carried what remained of the ancestry of an historic village.

Oh, not historic in the sense of having kings or dukes living there or battles fought on its soil. More important than that.

She heard a shout from behind her, glanced over her shoulder and saw Gomer stumbling after her, and she shouted back at him, '*No ...* '

But he was already slipping sideways into a new-made trench, sinking down on his knees, and her heart lurched and she desperately wanted to go rushing back to help him, but she was too far now, too far gone.

And convinced, despite the savaging of the meadow, that she could still see the mystic line, glowing and alive and fresh with the clean, crisp scent of apples . . . sharp with the cool, dry tang of the cider . . . hardened by the hooves of Hereford cattle with hides the colour of the soil . . . marked out by the shadow of the church, where the bells had called generations of farm workers to prayer . . . still walked by the sombre shades of Alfred Watkins and his distinguished musical associate and the spirit . . .

. . . The sad, sepia spirit of Lucy Devenish herself, hiding her anguish in the folds of her poncho as Jane threw herself into the gutted ground and rolled in front of the blade.

# 52

# Remembering the Hurt

Half past ten and no signs of apocalypse.

Parked alone in the bay outside Wychehill Church, with the window down, Merrily could just about hear the choir. Not what she'd expected, not the fulsome, floating sound which had gilded the air last Monday night when she and Lol had arrived in Wychehill. This was low-level and travelled in pulses.

She'd walked quietly down to the church, some of whose windows were quietly aglow. Sliding into the porch with the idea of inching open the doors to see if Loste or Winnie was in there. But the doors were locked. No audience for this choir tonight.

She'd crept outside again, found a metal bucket and positioned it upside down below one of the clear windows and stood on it.

'*Ave Mary*,' she heard. Low and liquid. '*Ave Mary*.'

She saw a group of heads in the chancel, in a nest of candlelight. A candle in a pewter tray on the lectern, a candle on the pulpit, eerily Dickensian.

Also *workmanlike*. Not a performance.

Anyway, the conductor was bald. Merrily had fled back to the car.

Two police vehicles went past slowly: a lurid traffic car and a dark blue van. Perhaps the action wouldn't start until the early hours. Perhaps it wouldn't start at all. Perhaps Khan was right and what worried people like Leonard Holliday was not so much the reality of the Royal Oak as the idea of it, any challenge to the idyll. Hard, however, to imagine Holliday ever experiencing an idyll.

She lit a cigarette, looked across at the Rectory. Like everywhere else, it was in darkness. Ledwardine Vicarage was never entirely in darkness.

If there was no light on in the house, a low-powered bulb would be burning in one of the outside lanterns. The light of the world. The glow of sanctuary.

No sanctuary here.

She got out and locked the car and walked up through the cutting into Church Lane, saw a TV flicker in Hannah Bradley's cottage and thought about knocking. No time. Stay focused.

She walked on up the lane, surprised at how bright the night was with a moon that was far from full. There was a single guiding lamp at the top of the steep path down to Starlight Cottage, but the place itself was unlit and clearly deserted, even the windchimes unmoving in the herb-scented silence. Wind chimes: part of the illusion of innocence.

If Sparke had deliberately misdirected her, neither she nor Loste were going to be easily discovered tonight. Merrily didn't hang around, walked quickly back up to the lane and down the hill towards the church.

A bulkhead light blinked on across the lane and a door opened.

'Hey, I thought it was you,' Hannah said. 'Is there something wrong?'

'Looking for Winnie, that's all.' Merrily walked across the road. 'You haven't seen her?'

'I never look out for her.' Hannah was standing by her gate. She wore a Keane T-shirt and shorts. 'She looks out for herself.'

'How do you mean?'

'Nice bloke, Tim Loste. Used to be. I don't know what he's like now.'

'I wouldn't know, either,' Merrily said. 'I haven't been allowed to talk to him.'

'Join the club. Phew, it's hot tonight, innit? Yeh, I do a bit of running on the hill, you know, and I ran into a Tim a few times. I thought he'd be all up in the air and highbrow, but he wasn't. Not like that at all. Quite uncomplicated, really. We went to the theatre in Malvern once. Matinée. It had some quite famous actors in it, from TV. It was a laugh. Then *she* found out.'

'Winnie?'

'And that was it. Our paths, as they say, stopped crossing. And not for want of me going out of my way, I'll tell you.'

'When was this, Hannah?'

'Few months ago. I think he's back drinking now. She won't stop him. She'll bloody kill him before she's done, and that's a shame.'

'Go on. Tell me.'

Merrily leaned on the gate. Hannah looked up and down the lane and then lowered her voice but not much.

'When we were in Malvern, right? We ran into this old mate of Tim's, from when he was a teacher. And I remembered his name after and I rang him up to ask him, like, you know, what's the situation with Tim. And *he* said the Sparke woman was the reason his engagement was broken off . . .'

'Tim's? What, you mean she—'

'Oh, nothing like that. She'd eat him for breakfast. She just tells him he's a genius. She's good at making people feel special. *I* don't know if he's a genius or not, but what's it matter if genius is being miserable all the time? You know he tried to top himself? If you see her, you can tell her what I said. I don't care any more. I wish I could get between them, but he won't listen.'

'And how are things with you?'

'I just don't go that way any more on the bike,' Hannah said. 'You getting anywhere with it?'

'To be honest . . . don't know.'

Back at the car, Merrily lit another cigarette, brought out the phone, watched it flare up, singing in her hand, and called Jane again. Her call *could not be taken.* Left another message on the voicemail and then called Gomer's landline – Gomer's partner Danny Thomas kept the firm's only mobile, as Gomer had never been known to charge it up.

No answer.

At least this was likely to mean that wherever Jane was, Gomer was also there. Made no difference; *she* should be there. There was nothing much to be done here. If Loste and Winnie were doing a *Last Night of the Proms* before they were barred from Wychehill Church, it was perhaps none of her business.

On the other hand, when somebody had deceived you . . .

She rang Bliss: voicemail.

'Frannie,' Merrily said, 'I don't really know what to say to you except that something's not right here. Which of course you— Oh, sod it, just call me back.'

She killed the connection and her cigarette, leaned back into the seat. Time to go and collect poor Lol. Drive back to Whiteleafed Oak hamlet and then call him on the mobile, call him away from the perpetual choirs.

Nice concept, lovely imagery. The great and beautiful mystery: how Elgar tapped into the music of the spheres. The ultimate unprovable theory. But also un*dis*provable. Clever Winnie.

She decided to drive back to the Ledbury road by the slightly longer route that would take her past the Royal Oak which, after all, she'd never seen fully operational – the moral cesspit, the gateway to hell. The road taking her past the gaunt Edwardian home of Tim Loste, which she hadn't yet checked. She made out its wall and its peeling railings. No lights on here either, and she hadn't expected any, but, as she accelerated away, something did catch her eye. Not a peeling railing, but . . .

*Oh hell.*

Merrily braked, lowered her window, looked behind her for oncoming headlights and, when it was clear there was nothing, reversed along the road to the front of the house and switched off the engine.

She couldn't see it from here and had to get out. The narrow house rose up against the hill like an upended domino, double blank, and, halfway into Loste's cramped driveway, she was able to confirm what she'd seen from the car.

It was the oak sapling planted in his tiny front garden, the tree which eventually would have crumbled his foundations and fused destructively with his supporting walls. The oak which she now knew represented something infinitely bigger. *A symbol of something, is all,* Winnie had said. *A symbol he could use for meditation.*

THE REMAINS OF AN ALTAR

Merrily walked up to the front of the house and held the sapling in both hands, halfway up, where it was gleaming white.

Not white leaves. Somebody had snapped its trunk.

Jane tasted the earth.

It was cold and gritty and bitter, and her ears were full of roaring night.

'Get up.'

'Nergh.'

Jane rolled away from the blade but kept on hugging the earth.

'Get up out of there before I pull you out.'

A voice she didn't know. Then a voice she did.

'Don't touch her, Gerry. You must never touch them these days.'

'I'd *like* to fucking—'

'I've already called the police,' Lyndon Pierce said. 'Jane, you know what'll happen if the police have to move you. You'll be arrested. You'll be charged. You'll appear in court, and when you've appeared in court once, at your age, that's the slippery slope.'

Jane dug her fingers into the soil, opened her eyes slightly and saw the white eyes of the JCB, heard its engine idling. She saw the boots of Gerry Murray, heard the voice of Lyndon Pierce again.

'—Mother won't survive that. Be on your way, the pair of you. No skin off my nose. Women vicars, that was always gonner be a mistake.'

Jane concentrated on the roaring of the engine in her ears and gripped the earth, one hand aching where the grit was in the bleeding cut. The earth smelled rich and raw and warm, now. Warm as the grave.

'I been talking to Tessa Bird, in Education,' Pierce said. 'Looks like you're finished at the school anyway. You're maladjusted, Jane. Always been a problem child—'

'*What the fuck—?*'

She heard the change in the engine's tone. A gear change like a huge throat-clearing. When she opened her eyes, the digger's lights were receding.

Murray screaming, 'Get the fuck out of there, you mad ole bastard!'

354

Swallowing wet clay, Jane saw the swirl of the digger's lights, and then the night went mad.

It wasn't the wind; there was no wind. It wasn't an accident, either. The sapling was too thick in its lower trunk for Merrily to clasp a hand around.

Someone had bent it over until it split. It wasn't quite severed but the top three or four feet of it were hanging off.

She felt the violence still in the air, could almost smell someone's sweat. It was, in some indefinable way, like when she and Syd Spicer had been standing by the remains of Lincoln Cookman's car. As if the violence had been inflicted on the atmosphere itself and the atmosphere wanted you to know that it was remembering the hurt.

She went around the path to the back door to see if the oaks in plant pots had been damaged. They seemed to be intact, although one was knocked over. But the back door, which Tim Loste was said never to lock, was ajar, and the bar of pinkish light down the side was, amidst so much darkness, a lurid shock.

Merrily took a step back and waited. No suggestion of movement inside. She didn't go in, but she prodded the door a little wider open and called out.

'Mr Loste?'

Not really expecting an answer. But from out on the hill behind the house she could hear a distant sound, both explosive and staccato, like duelling machine guns: dance music from the Royal Oak somehow deflected from the hill, bouncing back toward the house and the road.

*I spend all of Friday and Saturday evenings with Tim. When the Royal Oak starts up. He needs me – he'll go crazy, else.*

If they weren't here and they weren't at Whiteleafed Oak, where were they?

With her left trainer, Merrily pushed the door further open, saw into the kitchen, which she hadn't really taken in when she was here with Annie Howe. It was basic but not small. Pine units and cupboards up to the high ceiling. A microwave, a dishwasher, a coffee-machine.

An empty pizza packet on the worktop near the microwave. All of this lit by one long, thin peach-coloured strip light.

No conspicuous damage, no sounds of intrusion. So who had left the door open? Had the sole objective been the killing of the oak tree?

Who would have known its importance? Presumably, only Winnie Sparke. And Merrily, now, and Lol.

She stepped cautiously over the threshold.

'Mr Loste?'

It seemed so unlikely that she hadn't met this man she knew so much about. Or did she? Like all the impressions you received of Elgar, the individual portraits of Tim Loste didn't quite match. He was inspired and inspirational; he was crazy and manipulative.

There was certainly nothing of him in this kitchen. Opposite her, the door to the hall was wide open. The hall was in darkness. She started thinking about the big framed photograph of Whiteleafed Oak over the mantelpiece in the living room and all the other pictures of the sites of the perpetual choirs. Obvious and easy targets if someone *really* wanted to upset him.

She went into the hall. Always hated being inside someone else's house when they weren't there.

Especially in the dark. Merrily felt around for a light switch, and as soon as her hand found it – one of those little metal nipples – the light from a white crystal bowl in the ceiling sprang into the otherworldly eyes of Edward Elgar, urging Mr Phoebus out of the shadows towards her.

It also fanned unevenly into the living room, where the glass protecting the photo of the whiteleafed oak had indeed been smashed, the picture tipped so that it looked as if the whole room was awry . . . as if a sudden gust of wind had rushed into it, tossing Winnie Sparke's slight body back into the bookshelves in a hot shower of blood.

53

# Unseeingness

THE LINE WAS OPEN, but there was no voice. Then the signal cut out and the screen went dark and the music from Inn Ya Face was going *whoomp, chissa, hiss, whoomp* like machinery deep inside the hill.

'Frannie?' Merrily said urgently. *'Frannie.'*

She looked up in blank despair from the lawn behind Caractacus. The moon was high but the house was in the shadow of the hill.

All right, she'd try *him.*

She went back to the path, opening up the phone again, illuminating the screen and scrolling down the list to bring up Bliss's mobile number.

*Sorry,* Bliss said, *I'm norrin. Leave me a message.*

'Frannie. *Please.'* Letting some very real distress come through – like she could prevent it. 'Get back to me. Get back to me *now.'*

When she snapped the phone shut, her hand was shaking. She could see this in the peachy glow from the kitchen door. She squeezed the phone hard, gripped the shaking hand with the other hand. Tried to pray for self-control. Couldn't.

She didn't have a choice any more. She had to go back in there. Make sure. Merrily felt the tautness of impending panic in her chest, turned away and saw a glinting from the edge of the lawn, where it met the path.

Knife?

Merrily walked around it, the hill going *whoomp, chissa, chissa, hiss, whoomp,* the perpetual techno-choir from hell. She bent down and found the remains of a Bell's Whisky bottle, possibly smashed against the wall of the house. Tim Loste's whisky. Smashed on his way out, after he . . .

She shook the phone.

*Call me. Lol . . . Frannie . . . call me . . .*

What if they didn't? What if Bliss didn't call back for an hour or more? She should go back to Whiteleafed Oak. After . . . after she'd been back in there. After she'd gone back and checked once more. Made, dear God, absolutely certain that there was going to be no need for an ambulance.

*Calm down. This can't be done without calm.*


It definitely *was* the *Cello Concerto*. But where a cello was veined and richly visceral, the whistled theme was faint and remote and fusewire-thin and painfully isolated.

It was as if, Lol thought . . . as if this was how it was *meant* to be heard, to convey its meaning.

In which case, its meaning was: *solitary.*

The sky was clear and starry and smeared with a buttery northern light, and the whistling made slow, luminous coils and lonely whorls on the silence.

Twice it had stopped and then started up again from a different direction, the way tawny owls might answer one another across the vastness of the valley.

The oak tree was flat and featureless, like a massive spidery blot of Indian ink. Lol kept on walking towards it.

A joke. But who, in this situation, wouldn't be unnerved? It would be eerie enough after dark outside your own front door on Ledwardine market square – one reason being that nobody *did* this any more. Nobody seemed to whistle. No window cleaners, no butchers' boys with baskets. And *nobody* whistled this achingly sad, regretful . . .

As he approached the oak tree, the whistling seemed to develop a slow and rolling rhythm, like the breath-pattern induced, Lol caught himself imagining, by even, heavy pedalling on a gradual incline.

*Only me . . .*

He'd thought it was coming from under the tree, perhaps from the hollow that looked like a sacrificial pit. But when he reached the oak, the whistling was still some distance away, across to the right.

It stopped again. Lol crept up to the oak and lowered himself between two of its varicose roots, pushing himself back into the bole, spreading out his legs against the roots, gripping cakes of bark in his palms and staying very still, just another part of the tree, an offering of himself in return for shelter – shelter against madness – as it began again.

The moon was higher now, with an amber cast, and he saw, over to the right – the east? where the distant Eastnor obelisk was, anyway – he thought he saw a movement. He kept still, and the tune continued, fluidly, long beyond the point where his own version might have feebled out. Under the circumstances, with your own breath coming faster, all rational judgement in suspense, it was impossible not to imagine for one thought-dissolving moment . . .

This time, when it was over, Lol spent some seconds with his eyes closed, trying to breathe evenly, before lifting his hands and beginning – with as lazy and relaxed a rhythm as he could summon – to applaud.


Merrily took three or four long breaths before stepping into the kitchen.

Walking directly through to the hall, this time touching nothing. Activating the living-room light by brushing the metal switch with her sleeve.

Last time, she'd seen it only by the light washing in from the hall. Now, two big white wall brackets were flaring theatrically, scattering shadows, and it was so much worse: blood on the books, blood on the pictures, blood on the walls, blood on the writing table, gouts and drips and smears, and Winnie Sparke in silent freeze-frame.

Winnie wore one of her long filmy dresses which seemed now as if it was hanging together in threads of blood and tissue. Her arms spread out across the bookcase, with books pulled out, and the empty fireplace. Her buckled bare knees, touchingly girlish. A breast partly exposed, cut into like a flaccid fruit. Her face ripped in several places, top lip joined to her nose by strings of blood and mucus. Her throat slashed many times.

But the worst of it was never the gore. It was always the unseeingness of the eyes and the open mouth through which no breath passed.

The room was hot and clammy and stank and, worst of all, it was so waxily still. Merrily swallowed bile, and then something overtook her and she was just standing there raging.

'You got him *out* . . . You brought him home. Keeping your secrets, playing your cards— Why couldn't you just talk to me? Talk to *anybody?*'

She froze. *What if he's still here? What if he's upstairs? What if he's halfway down the stairs and listening?*

Not likely. Believe it. Seriously not likely. He was long gone. He'd gone lurching out with his whisky, draining the bottle and smashing it against the wall in his agony and self-hatred – *please God, let it be self-hatred and repentance, let there be no more of this* – and then he'd gone walking out on to the hill.

*Why?*

'I mean why, for Christ's sake, has he done this to you, Winnie? His saviour, his mentor, his—?'

There could be no halfway-rational explanation, not this time, not like the disposal of the drug dealer on the Beacon. This was frenzied. This was full on, the killer looking her in the eyes, as it was being done. This screamed *insanity.*

Merrily looked into Winnie Sparke's last frozen cry. Could only see one eye through the blood and the hair. Winnie Sparke's good hair. And the eye was a dead eye. It had been floating in blood and now the blood had congealed around it like a stiff collar.

'*Why couldn't you talk about it?*'

Letting the sob empty itself out of her, as she did all there was left to do.

Pray.

Her job.

*Take her and hold her and calm her. Take her from this place now. Take her into light.*

Following this with the Lord's Prayer, the oldest exorcism.

' . . . *Power and the glory, for ever and ever, amen.*'

Quelling the dread, she opened her eyes.

And was able, for just a moment, to hold herself in and remain calm in the presence of a new shadow in the room.

Winnie Sparke hung there, no less dead. It was not Winnie Sparke who was breathing, who said, 'Amen,' softly from the doorway behind her.

# 54

# Snaps Batons

'Shouldn't have done that,' he said sternly. 'You broke the vibration.'

Looming over Lol, nodding his head as though it was too heavy for him. He wore baggy grey sweatpants and a white singlet with dark stains and smudges on it.

'Percussive noises . . .' Clapping his hands clumsily; sometimes they missed. '. . . Break the connection. Gone.'

He moved in his bent, shuffling way over to a half-collapsed bale of straw, flopping down on it with his legs apart, his hands clasped between them, his body rocking slowly.

'Take a pew, old cock.'

Lol found another damaged bale to sit on. There was a lamp on the floor between them, one of those battery-powered lanterns with a blue plastic shade, spraying a light like watered milk over the long shed that was either an open-fronted barn or a horse shelter.

Whatever, it was a walk of only a minute or so from the oak, and he'd come wading out of it soon after Lol had started clapping. Staggering behind his lantern, dazed survivor of some Iron Age tribal skirmish. Lol had recognized him at once from Merrily's brief description and his accent and the way his words came blustering out as if his lungs were organ bellows.

'Wasn't working anyway, tell the truth. Ran out of puff. You need to do the whole jolly thing. All the way through until you become—'

He stopped, blinking slowly. Sliding back along his bale, bringing down a straw-storm from another, his mouth slack.

'Really don't know . . . wassa matter with me tonight.'

What was obviously the matter was coming sickly sweet and sour off his breath. Lol didn't get too close. It was as well to remember this guy was only here because of a shortage of evidence.

His weighty, ragged moustache hung down either side of his mouth, more Mongol warlord than Victorian composer, his stomach over-hanging his sweatpants, like a bag of sugar under his singlet.

'I look all right to *you?*'

'I suppose,' Lol said.

Aware of Tim Loste really looking at him now, trying to focus over the moist pink bags under his eyes.

'Trying to remember ... where exactly are you from?'

'Me? Led—' Lol thought about it, changed his mind. 'Knights Frome.' He paused. 'Mate of Dan's?'

'Dan?'

'Dan from Much Cowarne?'

'*Dan!* Good Lord, yes.' Tim made to clap his left knee, missed and clapped the hay, tumbling sideways, kicking over the lantern. Lol caught it. Tim pulled himself upright. 'Super chap. Just ... you know ... went into it. Didn't inter ... inter ... lectulise ...'

'Finest tenor in Much Cowarne,' Lol said.

'Absolutely. Wherever the fuck Much Cowarne is.'

They both laughed. Lol looked out of the open front of the barn across the moonlit landscape. It was like being in a grandstand. The field seemed luminous, and there was another oak tree with two dead branches, bleached like bones.

'You on your own?'

Tim squinted up at the wooden rafters and the flaking galvanized roof. The light was fanning out from the circular lamp like a merry-go-round with moths riding it.

'For the moment,' Tim said.

'Where is she?'

'She?'

'Winnie Sparke.'

Tim let his head fall forward into his big hands, began breathing hard into them, like some kind of exercise to head off an asthma attack. Lol saw dark stains between Tim's fingers.

He said, 'Are you . . .'

Tim's shoulders were heaving.

'Are you hurt?'

'I'm . . .' Tim peered out through his fingers. 'I think I'm in a bit of mess, frankly, old cock.'

'You walked here?'

'Don't remember.'

'Where's Winnie?'

Tim looked at him silently through those discoloured fingers.

'Winnie said you'd meet us here. She talked to my friend. On the phone. She said you'd meet us here.'

'Winnie? I . . .' His voice dropped. 'I don't remember.'

'Did she walk over with you? From Wychehill?'

'No. Just the two of us.'

'But you're alone.'

'I think . . . think something happened.'

Lol felt a small abdominal chill. His glasses kept misting. He took them off, rubbed them on his sleeve, put them back quickly.

'On the way here?'

'Don't remember,' Tim said.

'Look . . .' Lol brought out his mobile, flipped it open. 'I think we could do with some help here.'

'Help,' Tim repeated. Vaguely, like he was recalling something. 'Help me.' His voice melting into a wail, as he came to his feet. '*Help me, I'm*— Who're you calling, old cock?'

'Just a friend.' Lol brought up Merrily's number. 'She'll get us some help.'

Peering at the keys through misting glasses, he sent the call, listened to Merrily's phone ringing.

And then Tim lurched at him, ramming him off the bale, snatching the phone as it flew up. Lol leaping up, making a grab for it, but Tim was taller and fumbled it well out of his reach.

Lumbering out of the barn into the night, twisting around, his arm going back, this monstrous baby throwing something out of its pram.

Lol saw his phone disappearing into the night like a tiny silver spacecraft.

For a while, in the red-spattered white room, neither of them spoke.

Syd Spicer was in dark jeans, black clerical shirt, dog collar. His small eyes were flat and unmoving.

'Well done,' he said.

Merrily came shakily to her feet, her jeans damp at the knees. Didn't even remember kneeling down.

'Not many of us would've done that, Merrily. Not alone, in a situation like this.'

Neither of them spoke again until they were on the back lawn and the air was the kind you were prepared to breathe.

She waited while Spicer shut the back door. He was, she noticed, wearing black gloves.

'I was once,' he said, 'in another life, given some crude medical training. I think what you need is a hot, sugary brew and a sit-down.'

'I'm all right.'

'Of course you're not all right. Who could be?'

'Can you get the police? I need to go somewhere. Right away.'

'Merrily—'

'I have to collect Lol. I'll come straight back.'

'Where is he?'

'Just bear with me.' She prodded Lol's number into the mobile. It rang and rang. *Christ.* 'Call the police.'

'That's in hand. Merrily, you can't go anywhere.'

She walked away down the side of the house. It had gone too far, now. She was in over her head, just wanted to get over to Whiteleafed Oak, find Lol. Patch things together, make sure Jane was all right and *then* go to the police and, if necessary, answer questions until the sun came up. She looked back at Spicer.

'What about Tim Loste?'

'He can take care of himself, I hope.'

365

'I mean, what's he going to do now? Where's he going to go?'

'Merrily—'

'He'll have gone out on the hill.' Stopping next to the brutalized oak, failing to prevent her voice rising to an unnatural shrillness. 'He always does. He has a place he goes to. Where he went to with Winnie. Which is the place where I left Lol because Winnie said they'd meet us there. And Lol's not answering his phone. And there's a man out there fresh from . . .' pointing wildly at the house '. . . *That!*'

Spicer stepped back, shaking his head. Merrily walked down towards the road, feeling in her left-hand hip pocket for her keys, aware that he wasn't following her. At the bottom of the drive, she realized the car keys weren't in her pocket.

Must have left them in the ignition. She'd only got out to look at the sapling.

She stopped at the side of the road, looked from side to side. Couldn't take it in at first. She turned on Spicer, bewildered. He shrugged.

'I meant to tell you. That was why I came in. Only it got . . . superseded.'

'Someone's nicked my car.'

'Yeah. I saw you drive past. About twenty minutes later, the car comes back the other way, couple of kids in it. I didn't figure you'd have asked them to go down the shop and get you some cigarettes.'

She leaned against the railings. Closing her eyes.

'A gift is a gift,' Spicer said. 'Sadly, for what it's worth, I reckon you've just become the first genuine victim of the notorious criminal element frequenting the Royal Oak.'


Suddenly, without preamble, like a baby, Tim was howling. Crashing back and flinging himself face down into the rotting hay and straw, beating his fists into the broken bales. Lol ran past him into the open, saw how long the grass was and the nettles. Saw that the chances of finding the phone before the morning were remote, and even then . . .

Better to take off fast, get away, run back to the centre of the hamlet, wait there for Merrily. Bang on someone's door and ask to use the phone. He started to walk away.

'Don't . . . go.' Sour whisky-breath on the air. Tim Loste standing very close behind him. 'Think I need help.'

It was as if throwing the phone out of the barn had expelled what remained of his energy. Blown out his candle. He went back and sat down meekly on his bale, looking at the baked mud floor, then up at Lol in the lamplight.

'*I* remember Dan. Dan's got a beard. Tall as me. Bald.'

Lol stood in the open mouth of the barn, considering the options. He could probably walk out of here now and keep walking and Tim wouldn't necessarily follow him. But what would that achieve?

'You're not Dan, are you?' Tim said.

'I'm Lol.'

'Kind of name's that?'

'Short for Laurence.'

'Lol.' Loste sounding it like a bass note.

'And who are you?' Lol asked him.

'Me?' Tim Loste leaned back into the hay. 'I'm the chap who's come here to see God.'

# 55

# Build a Cathedral

MUSTN'T PUSH IT. MOVE yourself into deep shadow, introduce the subject of Edward Elgar and watch it forming in the milky lamplight ... what your old boss, Dick Lydon, the Hereford psychotherapist, would have called an elaborate fantasy structure.

Except maybe it wasn't.

There was clearly something wrong with Tim Loste. No question there, except *what was it?* There was whisky breath, but this wasn't normal intoxication. For long periods, his thoughts would appear fluid. Usually when he was interested in the subject under discussion.

Elgar. Anyone who didn't understand what Elgar was about, Tim had no time for them. Fortunately, he hadn't had to mix with many people like that. The only child of orchestral musicians, he'd grown up in Sussex, not far from Brinkwells, Elgar's house when the composer was living down south.

The place where he'd met Algernon Blackwood, writer of ghost stories and sometime-magician.

Lol came back to sit on the bale. He said he knew about Brinkwells.

'Ah ...' Tim beaming whitely in the lamplight. 'So not like most of the airy-fairy types who come out here.'

'Friend of Dan's,' Lol reminded him.

'Dan ... ?'

'Finest tenor in Much Cowarne?'

'Good old Dan.' Tim's eyes were cloudy again. 'Often meet people here, all times of the day and night. Disappointing. Wispy types. Never want to talk about Elgar.'

'Brinkwells,' Lol said. 'You were at Brinkwells.'

'I was drawn to it from an early age. Six? Maybe earlier. Had a nanny, for when the parents were on tour. Used to take me to Brinkwells until I could go on my own – just the fields around there, you know? Better when I could go alone. We'd go for walks, and he'd be pointing out things. *Look at this, young 'un.*'

'Your nanny was a bloke?'

'Not the *nanny*, old cock.'

Tim leaned forward, hands on knees, his big face uptilted, summoning memories. Or the ones he'd fabricated earlier?

'Used to wait for him. Or he'd wait for me. There were some old trees – bit like this. You could stand by the trees and he'd be there. He loved those trees. There was a legend that they were supposed to have been monks who got bewitched. When Blackwood came to visit, he took him to see the trees.'

'Were they oaks?'

'Suppose they must've been. *What do you make of these, young 'un*, he'd say. *Can you see the monks?*'

Lol wondered how much of this Tim had blocked in, years later. It wasn't unusual for an only child to have a famous imaginary companion. Even one who must, even at the time, have been dead for over forty years.

'He loved all trees, didn't he?' Lol said.

'I'll say.'

'What about the Whiteleafed Oak?'

'Well, of course. This was his favourite walk. This was where *Caractacus* was formed. And then *Gerontius.* Everything leading up to *Gerontius.* But he kept jolly quiet about Whiteleafed Oak. People do. It's a place of powerful initiation.'

'Elgar said that?'

'Did he?'

'No, I mean was that Elgar or ... Winnie Sparke?'

Tim looked away.

'That lamp getting fainter, do you think, Dan? Need to bring some new batteries. Should we switch it off?'

'You keep the lamp here?'

'Under the hay. With this.' Tim tugged out a stiff-backed folder covered in brown leather and opened it up on his knees. 'Don't always need light here, though, if there's a moon.'

'You come here a lot?'

Lol leaned into the light so that he could see what was on the pages. Tim closed the book quickly. It was musical manuscript. A score.

Tim leaned over and switched off the lamp, inflating himself into this hulking shadow against the chalk-dust night.

'Tim . . .' Lol hesitated. 'Do you think Elgar knew about the idea of the perpetual choirs?'

Tim looked for him.

'Who did you say you were?'

'Friend of Dan's.'

'Yes, but . . . were you in my choir once?'

'Dan talks about you. You made a big impression. He told me about the night you divided them into three and sent some of them to Little Malvern Priory and some to Redmarley D'Abitot.'

'Hmm, yes.' Tim seemed to relax. 'Redmarley – that was terribly significant, you see. Elgar's mother's family came from there. His mother carried the strand. A countrywoman. *My* mother – bit of a townie, didn't like me to go out without a mac or walk on the wet grass. But Elgar's mother encouraged her offspring to go out in all weathers, so that they were always at home with nature whatever the conditions. So they were, you know, *part of it*. Yes, Ann Elgar's family were actually from Redmarley.'

It was like talking to very old people. Ask them what they had for lunch and their minds went opaque, but talk about the past and the stories came spinning out, green-mouldy tape gliding smoothly past still-keen magnetic heads.

'What about Little Malvern?'

'Well, that was important because it's where Elgar's buried – at the Catholic church there, St Wulstan's. Didn't *want* to be planted there – didn't want to be buried *at all*. They had to talk him into it, and I suppose he agreed for the wife's sake. Terribly proper, Alice, a traditionalist. What Elgar really wanted was for his ashes to be scattered where the River Severn meets the River Teme.'

Lol gazed out between the uprights supporting the open front of the barn at the secondary oak tree with the white, dead branches.

'And when you separated the choirs, it was important that the three churches were in the Three Counties.'

'It was just an idea,' Tim said. 'Played around with different permu— permutations. Different churches. Winnie . . .'

'It was Winnie's idea?'

'It was all Winnie's idea, at first.'

Tim's voice down to a whisper.

'Dan was telling me about Wychehill Church,' Lol said. 'St Dunstan's. He was a patron saint of music, wasn't he? Was that the quarry guy, Walter Longworth's idea? He was paying for it so he got to choose?'

'St Dunstan was an Abbot of Glastonbury.'

'Where one of the original perpetual choirs was said to be.'

'Yes. Winnie . . . spotted that at once. She always says that once something is put in train, all sorts of wonderful coincidences occur in a pre-ordained sort of way.'

Tim fumbled around in the straw and then looked up, dismayed.

'Didn't bring it, did I? I always bring water from the Holy Well. Can't understand—'

'Maybe you dropped it somewhere.'

'No, I—' Tim was clenching and unclenching his fists like the grab mechanism on a crane. 'Must've left in . . . in a hurry.'

'Never mind,' Lol said. 'Why did Winnie want you to come to Wychehill?'

*I'm the chap who's come to see God.*

'Well . . . the church had been built for the performance of choral music. Longworth wrote to Elgar asking what he could do to make amends . . . having heard that Elgar and Bernard Shaw were jolly miffed about the damage caused by the quarrying. Elgar . . . not in the best of moods at the time . . . wrote him a cursory reply saying something like, Oh, go and build a damn cathedral! Winding

371

Longworth up, really. Quite surprised when Longworth wrote back saying, where do you *want* your cathedral, then?'

'Where did you find out about this, Tim?'

'Parish records. It's all documented. More or less. So when Elgar realized the chap actually had a few quid to spare, he decided that he'd better give it some thought, and he consulted some people. Blackwood and a chap he knew in Hereford. Watson. Ley-line man, you've probably heard of him – all you Whiteleaf Oakies, as Winnie used to call them, are into . . . all that.'

'You mean Watkins? You mean *Alfred* Watkins?'

'I . . . sure. Yah. Watkins. Friend of Elgar's when he lived in Hereford. He'd been doing some work around the Beacon, mapping out his lines, and he'd come across the foundations of what appeared to be an ancient chapel or a monk's cell at Wychehill and told Longworth that if he built his church there it would be a very significant thing to do.'

'So what you're saying . . . Watkins and Elgar advised Longworth to build his church on the ley from Whiteleafed Oak along the Malverns. Was Blackwood involved in this, too?'

'Winnie was sure he must've been. Former member of . . . something or other . . .'

'The Golden Dawn.'

'That's the outfit. Studied magic.'

'Blackwood wrote a novel, *The Human Chord*, about a man's attempt to recreate celestial music. Call out the secret names of God.'

'You really know your stuff, don't you? Glad we met. But you know, I don't think I'm even supposed to talk about this.'

'Tim, is it possible that Elgar – in later years, perhaps by talking to Blackwood – *did* know about the supposed significance of Whiteleafed Oak?'

'Winnie thought he must have been at least instinctively aware of— Why am I here? Do *you* know? I don't remember. I don't—' Tim began to tremble like he'd been hot-wired, his engine coming alive. 'What am I doing? Can you help me?'

Lol bit his lip, hands pressing into his knees.

'God?'

Tim's eyes filled with panic.

'Ed,' he said. 'Where's Ed? Can't do it without Ed.'

# 56

# Tennis Courts

No choice. Merrily had to go with Spicer.

And she was close to frantic.

'It'll take twenty minutes. *Please.*'

They were getting into Spicer's Golf outside the rectory. His car, he could call the shots.

'Merrily, if there was one thing I learned in my former life it's that preparation and intelligence are invariably more important than skill, technique and courage, all that stuff from the comics. There's something I need to know before we go anywhere. Something I need to check before we pick up your Mr Robinson. It won't take take long, and it won't wait.'

'Are you going to phone the police, then, or shall I?'

'I told you, it's in hand. I made a call while you were screaming at poor Winnie. Thought you needed to get that out of your system.'

'Good of you.'

'I've a trusted friend who'll contact the right person in the police and explain it fully. Otherwise it could get messy. And another thing you need to know. Tim Loste didn't kill Winnie. You got that? He didn't kill Wicklow and he didn't kill Winnie.'

She stared at him, his face flecked with the colours of the dashlights.

'On what basis can you *possibly*—?

'Oh, and *I* didn't either, in case you were considering that possibility. This is not what you thought. There *is* evil here. On an almost unimaginable scale. And we do need to collect your friend at some point. Right now, though, there are things I need to know that could save us all some grief.'

'Grief?'

'I blew it, Merrily. I left things too late. If it's anybody's fault, what's happened to Winnie, it's mine. Should have got them out of that church a week ago. Should never have let them *in.*'

'I don't understand.'

'Nor me, yet. Not fully.'

Spicer turned left.

'This is the road to—'

'Old Wychehill Farm.' He put on the headlights. 'Now listen to me. We're going to be quite open about this. If Preston's here, it's best you stay in the car, and I'll run some parish business past him. It'll be unconvincing but it doesn't matter a lot at this stage. I don't *think* he'll be here, but I need to be sure.'

Spicer drove carefully into the valley, on full beams, and pulled up conspicuously in the centre of the courtyard, gravel spurting.

There were lights in the big house and a couple of wrought-iron lanterns twinkling romantically among the stone holiday units. But the outbuildings themselves were in complete darkness and there were no other cars around. No signs of holidaymakers in residence. The Victorian turret, the pines and the monkey puzzles were stage-set silhouettes against the pale, powdery night.

The idyllic effect spoiled only by the figure, naked from the waist up, legs braced, the shotgun levelled at the windscreen of the Golf.

'*You fucking stop there!*'

Spicer kept the engine running.

'Best if you don't get out just yet, Merrily.'

'You really think . . .' Merrily was sinking slowly down the passenger seat. '. . . I'm going to get out?'

'*Get fucking back! I'll take your fucking head off!*'

Spicer lowered his window.

'Hugo?'

'*One more step I'll blow your fucking windows out!*'

The twelve-bore vibrating, shards of moonlight on the twin barrels.

'Kid's a bag of nerves,' Spicer murmured. 'Something took him over the edge.' Shouting out of his side window. 'Syd Spicer, son. Come for your old man.'

'You're fucking lying!'

'Been a bad night, ain't it, Hugo? Don't make it worse. I'm coming out. All right? I'm gonner walk under the lamp, to your left, so you can see it's me. Promise you I won't come any closer. Just under the lamp, yeah, so you can ID me?'

'You keep back . . .'

A jerk of the shotgun.

'No worries.' Spicer got out of the car, walked across to a wrought-iron lamp projecting from one of the buildings. 'Now. See?'

'Who's that with you?'

'That's Mrs Watkins. The lady vicar? You're making her nervous, Hugo.'

Finally recognizing Spicer, Preston Devereaux's younger son lowered the gun just fractionally. Through the car window Merrily could smell fumes like a smouldering bonfire or an incinerator.

'Sorry to scare you, son,' Spicer said.

'I wasn't—'

'Nah, nah, you got good reason to be wary, way things've been lately. Louis with you?'

'He's with Dad. They're meeting a guy about . . . installing tennis courts.'

*Tennis courts?*

'Tennis courts, eh? Smart move.' Spicer walked up to the boy. 'Be having an eighteen-hole golf course next.'

'Yeah. Look, I'll tell them you—'

Spicer's back blurred across the windscreen. Merrily didn't see how it happened, but it happened in near-silence, and when Spicer stepped aside he was holding the shotgun and Hugo Devereaux was writhing on the lamplit gravel.

She gasped, sat up, springing open the car door and rolling out to find Spicer breaking the shotgun, taking out both cartridges, putting them one by one in his pocket.

He looked down at the boy. 'God have mercy on you, son.'

But she saw that he'd taken off his dog collar.

What followed was surreal and desperately chilling. Reality distanced, like she was watching down the wrong end of a telescope. The mind's way of handling an experience that was both alien and vividly shocking.

They'd followed Hugo Devereaux into the house and Spicer, still wearing his black gloves, was opening doors and cupboards like a burglar. Seemed to know his way around as well as if he had the layout in his head.

Kicking open the door of the Beacon Room with its long window, the British Camp like a high altar, hard under the haloed moon. Syd stopping to listen in the churchy stillness.

'Cellars, Hugo?'

'By the back stairs.'

'Keys?'

'I'll get them. But there's nothing down there.'

'Good. You go first.'

Spicer no longer had the shotgun with him, just a bunch of keys on a ring. Merrily followed them, hanging back, trying to filter out what was most important: primarily that, if Spicer was correct and Loste hadn't murdered Winnie or Wicklow, Lol was in no direct danger at Whiteleafed Oak. It was something.

Spicer had followed Hugo to the top of some stone steps going down. Curving. No handrail. Fluorescent lights were stammering on. Hugo – couldn't be more than eighteen or nineteen – was stumbling in front of Spicer without argument, his head bent, his body occasionally twitching in pain. Merrily staying well back, a hand on the wall on either side. Not trusting Spicer, not by a long way.

The cellars at the bottom had strip lights at crazy angles on the low ceilings. There were several rooms and Spicer checked them all before motioning the boy into a square and windowless cell where wooden crates and cardboard boxes were stacked.

'Can I ask you to do something, Merrily? Could I ask you to go back to the car and, if Mr Devereaux or Louis or both should happen to appear in their new Land Rover – or, indeed, if anyone appears in anything – drive out past them and blow the horn, once.'

'And what will you be doing?'

'I'll be talking to my friend Hugo, and if he helps me, as I'm sure he will, I'll join you in a very short time.'

'Why have you taken off your collar?'

'I was hot. I swear to you before God that I'm doing the best I can to spare lives, prevent violence. I might be proved wrong, and that's my responsibility— *No!*'

Hugo had been edging towards the door.

'Don't, son,' Spicer said wearily. 'Please. I can hurt you very badly in a very short time, and if you insist on making me prove it we'll both be very upset. No shame in this. In your place I'd cooperate fully because I'd realize the situation was seriously weighted against me. We understanding one another, Hugo?'

Hugo's narrow face was white under the striplight, except for eyes which looked hot and red. His cheek was grazed and flecked with grit from where he'd fallen outside.

Spicer said, 'I'm sure Mrs Watkins would be more inclined to do what I'm suggesting if she thought you weren't going to get hurt.'

'Fuck off,' Hugo said.

It had never sounded feebler.

'Man's world, eh, Hugo?' Spicer said. 'Was that what it felt like when you were dealing with Winnie? That wasn't like Wicklow, was it? Wait in the cave or somewhere out of sight, then a quick bang on the head and the rest is just . . . well, just basic butchery, piece of cake for a country boy. Done some slaughtering, have we? Pigs, maybe? Enjoy that, did we? Made us feel like a big, grown man? Power of life and death?'

Hugo sniffed hard, wouldn't look at Spicer.

Spicer said, 'Maybe Wicklow was even easier than pigs.'

He glanced at Merrily. She didn't move, avoiding eye contact. In the blueish, gassy light, Spicer's face was flat, like his voice.

'But when they're in front of you, facing you full on, and they know it's coming and they're fighting to stay alive, that's not so easy, is it?'

He took a step towards Hugo who edged himself into a corner, stumbling over a crate.

'I mean, that is *unbelievably* more difficult. Even when it's two of you, hard boys against one little woman.'

Merrily's mouth was suddenly dry.

'Amazing how long the life stays in them, isn't it?' Syd Spicer said. 'You slash and you slash and they're all over the place – wouldn't have believed it, would you, how much *life* there is to deal with when they're determined to keep it. Hacking it away, bit by bit, but it still clings on, and you start to panic, too, and she's screaming and crying and flailing and spitting just to hold on to that precious God-given gift of life. So precious to her and so cheap to you, up to now. And maybe this is when you realize for the first time what a *huge* item life is. But you can't stop now, and you just keep slash—'

'*Stop it! Fuck you . . . !*' Hugo running at him, face red and wet and twisted. '*Just*—'

Syd Spicer sidestepped and tipped him almost gently to the stone flags. He said over his shoulder, '*Would* you do that, Merrily? Wait in the car. Keep a lookout?'

'No,' Merrily said. 'I don't think so.'

# 57

# Difficult Times in Old England

'THE LINE,' LOL SAID. 'The line from here, from Whiteleafed Oak through all the hilltops and Wychehill Church . . . how does Winnie see that? An energy line or a . . . spirit path?'

There was silence, except for an owl somewhere. Lol was thinking about Jane and Coleman's Meadow.

'Where the dead can travel,' he said. 'I'm just trying to help you to remember.'

Tim began to rock backwards and forwards, his bulk alternately blocking out the moon and then exposing it. He'd gone soft and rambling again.

'Exercises to do.'

'Winnie gave you exercises?'

'Breathing and meditation. Pretty hard at first, but I kept on. I persevered and then it . . . I had to visualize him walking. And Mr Phoebus. We had a photo enlarged to life-size and put it in the hall, so it looked as if he was there, waiting to . . . to ride out.'

'And you visualized this . . .'

'Yes. Sometimes, when I was walking the hills at night, I . . . felt I was able to hear what *he* could hear . . . the hidden themes in the whistling of the wind. I'd just start walking, and he'd bring me here. *Come along, young 'un.* He loved to come to Whiteleafed Oak. One of his favourite walks when he lived at Birchwood. When he was working on G—, on *Gerontius*. When his mind was hovering between life and death and . . . whatever comes. He was walking this path in his dreams. And he still does.'

'Yes. So you visualized Elgar . . .'

'Coming along the path, to and from Whiteleafed Oak. Or along the road with Mr Phoebus.'

'To Wychehill Church.'

'Or the other way.'

'So, earlier on, when you were whistling the *Cello Concerto*...?'

'Sometimes, when you do it properly, all the way ... it's as if there are two of you whistling it. It's ... very weird. And thrilling.'

Lol succumbed to a small shiver.

'And is that where *you* walk ... along the spirit path, from hilltop to hilltop, by the Iron Age sites and the monastic chapels and shrines, from Wychehill ... to the Beacon ... Hangman's Hill ... Midsummer Hill ... Whiteleafed Oak.'

'Yes.'

'That's the way you came tonight?'

Tim's face contorted.

'To escape from the demons.'

'I'm sorry ... ?'

'Just when you think you've come through it all, the demons are there.' Tim swung round. 'It's the price you have to pay.'

'For what?'

'For daring to reach for the Highest. You have to get past the demons first.'

'And who are the demons?'

Tim stood up, moved to the open front of the barn, holding on to one of the supporting uprights, began to beat his head against it.


In the end, Merrily had agreed to go out and move the car out of the yard into a space suggested by Spicer behind one of the barns. She'd just had to get out of there.

She took the opportunity to try again to get through to Lol: *voicemail.* Jane: *voicemail.* Gomer: endless ringing in an empty bungalow. And now it was late, getting on for eleven, surely. She didn't try Bliss again.

As she stood in the yard, breathing in the soft, sweet summer air, a different countryside lay revealed. The moon was high now, and white and hard, less of a security lamp than a hunting tool. Owl sounds flickered through the woodland, a screen for shadowy slaughter. Owls hunting, talons out. Jets of blood and small lives taken, big lives too, and God looking diplomatically away, supervising the sunrise in another hemisphere.

Merrily felt numb, isolated. Cored by outrage and horror. Also, starved of light, starved of knowledge. A spectator who didn't even understand the game.

When she went back, the atmosphere in the cellar was tight with a stripped-down harshness. Syd Spicer's sleeves were rolled up.

The Reverend S. D. Spicer. Try to imagine him celebrating communion, visiting the sick, organizing a donkey for the church nativity play.

'The gullet,' he was saying, nodding. 'Yeah, that makes sense. I should've thought of that.'

Syd and Hugo were sitting on upturned crates. Hugo looked up when Merrily came in, then looked away. Merrily noticed a new bruise just below his left eye. But, more than that, he looked emotionally beaten, dulled by defeat. He sniffed occasionally, his eyes watering, his thin face bony in the purply fluorescence. Resentment there and self-pity. The sullen ugliness of corrupted youth.

She looked at Syd, at his still, small eyes.

*The gullet.*

'Hugo is on his gap year, Merrily,' Syd said. 'He was going to spend it with the West Malvern Hunt, but of course the ban put a stop to that. They're not even doing drag hunts, Hugo?'

'What's the point of that?' Hugo said. 'It's a joke.'

'A lot of disappointment in your family, then.'

Hugo snorted.

'And a lot of rage,' Syd said. 'To understand this, you need to understand the rage, the way it ferments. The ingredients. Remember when the MP for Worcester was in the forefront of the campaign for a total ban? Must've seemed like a betrayal from within.'

'Yeah.'

'Betrayal upon betrayal. The hunting ban was just the final insult.

Years before that they'd killed your grandfather, turned your dad's life around. The government. The EC. The way the farmers in every other European country seem to ignore the new rules, but Britain's farmers got away with *nothing*. And then the great plagues: Mad Cow Disease and the ban on exports. Foot and Mouth. When the countryside smelled of smoke and burning flesh.'

'It'll never be the same,' Hugo said. 'We built this country. We made it what it was, and now they've giving it all away to the scum. Eating their cheap foreign meat from supermarkets owned by foreigners.'

'And the one law they pass that isn't crawling up the Euro-arse, it's a ban on hunting. They'll be coming for your guns soon. Land of hope and glory. Mother of the free.'

'Joke.'

Syd said, 'You know, sometimes – thinking back to the Regiment – it was hard to work out who you were fighting for. Had to come down to values in the end. You start thinking you're doing it for Blair and Brown, it don't work *at all*. Luckily, we still got Her Maj.' Syd smiled. 'Obviously it's worse for an old family. Came with the Conquest, the Devereauxs? 1066?'

'Bit later.'

'Good long time, though. Longer than the Windsors. A long and glorious history going down the pan.'

'We're not the only ones.'

'No, I appreciate that,' Syd said. 'Difficult times in Old England. Tell me about Wicklow.'

'Came to my father for a job.'

'*Did* he? Cheeky.'

'It was a bit like . . . close to blackmail. Thought he was clever, but he didn't know anything really. Thought he was hard and we were middle-class and soft. They don't know what hard is.'

'The city boys?'

'Strip off all the bling and boasting, take their guns away, they're weak. Thick as shit. It's why they always get caught. You don't need scum like that.'

'And was I right?' Syd said. 'You waited for him in the cave.'

'No, *he* was using the cave. Dealing out of there. Thought that was smart. We waited for him to come *out* of the cave. We were in the trees then the rocks behind the cave.'

'You and Louis.'

'Yeah.'

'Bang. Pro job.'

'Then Louis sent the text to Khan.'

'Text? What was that for?'

Hugo shut his mouth. Syd put his head on one side, looking sorrowful, his fingers flexing slightly. It was enough.

'Louis had these lines about Druid sacrifice from an Elgar CD,' Hugo said. 'We put it in the text to Khan from Wicklow's phone. Louis said it was like a warning of what he was taking on.'

'Old England showing its teeth,' Syd said. 'How dare these lowlifes pollute the Malverns with their noxious substances. And the Elgar – that would also be why the police pulled Tim? Neat. Double whammy.'

'Dad didn't think so. He didn't think it was cool doing him on the stone, either. He's like, *You don't get flash. You don't get cocky. And if it looks a bit intelligent the police can narrow it down right away.* But Louis'd done it by then. And it did work. Nearly.'

'But then someone else figured it out. Someone your ole man really did underestimate for a while.'

'Yeah.'

'Your dad know what you did to her tonight?'

Hugo stared at the stone flags.

'Does now.'

'He was here when you came back?'

'Yeah.'

'Mad?'

'Pretty pissed off.' Hugo's head jerked forward. 'He'd've wanted it done, though. He said he—'

'Pissed off that you couldn't handle it? Or that Louis made you go with him?'

'Mainly...' Hugo found a sickly smile. 'Mainly, he was mad that Loste wasn't in the Gullet.'

Merrily said, 'The gullet?'

Syd ignored her. 'So where's he now, your old man? And Louis.'

'Out there. He—'

'Finishing the job?'

'Maybe.'

'Where?'

'I don't know.'

Syd tilted his head, put his hands on his knees as if he was about to get up. Terror bloomed in Hugo's eyes. Merrily went cold.

'I *don't* know. *Please!*' Hugo rolled off his crate onto the flags, putting his hands up. 'Honest to God!'

Syd stood up.

Hugo rolled away. He was weeping.

'I'm locking you in, son.' Syd stepped away from him. 'At some stage, the police'll be told where you are. When they arrive, I'd cooperate fully, if I were you.'

Hugo nodded, sagging, not trying to get up.

'It's completely finished, Hugo. But I'm guessing you knew that in Loste's back room. There's a point where you cross a barrier, and Louis led you right to the wire, and you didn't go over. It's a life you didn't quite take, and you'll be grateful for that.'

Hugo said nothing. Syd motioned to Merrily and followed her out of the door. The door was oak and reinforced and not very old. Syd tried various keys until one of them locked it.

'I hope you didn't want to pray with the boy, Merrily, but I'm afraid that would've conveyed the wrong message.'

'Unlike hitting him again . . .'

'Once. God forgive me, but experience suggested it needed underlining, or he might've thought he could get away with lies or half-truths. Intelligent lad, and he'd've been able to string the cops along. For a while. But we don't have a while. We did the best we could. We hit on the weak link. That was the easy part. I suspect we've exhausted our quota of good fortune for one night.'

Merrily went ahead of Spicer up the stone steps into the manure-smelling back hall, with its coat hooks and its wellies, and waited for him by the door to the courtyard. She felt reduced and dirty and a long and twisted way from God.

'What's the gullet?'

Syd Spicer hung the bunch of keys on one of the coat hooks.

'The Gullet is this deep pool, flooded quarry, up near the Beacon. People get drowned there sometimes. Kids thinking it's safe for a swim on summer nights like this. Only it's very, very cold.'

'And?'

'It's on Tim Loste's regular route – they knew this; they'd followed him enough times – takes him close to the Gullet. The plan was to mess him with Winnie's blood and turn him loose and catch up with him near the Gullet, and then *oops*. Only, what happened with Winnie, Hugo couldn't take it, he's only a boy. Hugo went badly to pieces and Louis had to take him outside, case he left vomit anywhere. And of course by the time Louis'd slapped some sense into Hugo, Tim was away. Not quite on the usual path, either, which was understandable under the circumstances, and they couldn't find him.'

'They were going to . . . ?'

'Toss him in the Gullet. Drown him. Nothing easier. So many accidents there, but this would be suicide. Louis's scenario ends with the recovery from the Gullet, maybe tomorrow, of the body. Winnie's blood not quite washed away. Murder and suicide. Case closed. Only Tim had wandered off. Can't trust drugs. Where did you put the car, Merrily?'

'What drugs?'

'Where's the car?'

'In the Dutch barn, like you said.' Trying to keep pace with Spicer across the yard. 'What am I not getting? What crucial piece of information have I been denied?'

Spicer kept on walking, pointing around the courtyard, building to building, the density of it, row upon row, nicely leaning stone and timbered alleyways reaching back into the fields and the woodland.

Merrily persisted. 'Drugs?'

'They'd spiked his Scotch. Roofies.'

'What?'

'Rohypnol. Know what that is?'

'The date-rape drug?'

'Compliance. Do what you want with them. Softened up. Plus, it causes short-term memory loss, which is useful. Tim habitually leaves his door unlocked, for Elgar or whoever. Hugo comes in earlier in the day, spikes his whisky with Rohypnol. Tasteless, odourless. Works well with alcohol, as we all know. On men as well as women. If you get the dose right, the effects are usually predictable. Can be used in combination with certain drugs to improve the high.'

'Hugo told you this?'

'Emily, once.'

'Your—'

'Don't ask. But whether that means Loste was sitting there with a vacant smile on his face when they were killing Winnie—'

'Oh my *God*.'

'We don't know that. We don't how much he had, but that sounds likely. It can take hours to wear off. Maybe he's asleep somewhere on the hill, maybe . . . I don't know. Time he comes out of it, blood on his hands and his clothes, he may even think Winnie *was* down to him. But . . . the plan was he wouldn't come out of it.'

They reached the car, and Merrily handed Spicer the keys. Glad she wouldn't be driving.

'Syd, what *is* this?'

Thinking what Bliss had said about outrage killing. *Fight for our traditions, we're branded criminals,* Devereaux had said. *This government's scum. Anti-English. Don't get me started.*

Rage against the system? Little Englander vigilantism gone mad?

Winnie. Hacked to death by the sons of a former lover, like the climax of some old and bloody folk-ballad.

'We could spend all night going over the farm,' Spicer said, 'and I could doubtless show you signs – things that are obvious when you know – but it would take a long time and I'm afraid we don't have that kind of time. Whiteleafed Oak, you said. That's where he goes.'

'Loste?'

'Loste, yes.' He was gripping her shoulders. 'You're sure about this.'

'We were supposed to meet them there tonight, Loste and Winnie. Lol's waiting in case case he—'

'They'll find him, then. Maybe they already have.'

'What about Lol?'

'I don't think we should hang around, Merrily.'

'What will they do to Lol? They surely—'

'Why don't I drop you in the village, give you the keys to the rectory?'

'Don't even think about it.'

'All right.' Spicer opened the passenger door for her. 'Perhaps a serious prayer wouldn't come amiss. I can never seem to do it when I'm driving.'

# 58

# Mr Phoebus and the Whiteleafed Oak

TIM LOSTE AND THE oak stood together under the moon with its acid-green halo.

'Tell me about the demons,' Lol said.

He'd followed Tim out of the barn, leaving the lamp behind in the hay. Tim no longer staggered, as if beating his head on one of the uprights had unblocked something. He looked slowly around the whitewashed wooded valley and finally up at the great oak, its branches laden with dark foliage and glittering things like some weird midsummer hoar frost.

'A living symphony, this tree. Look at the complexity of it. We're old mates now. I'm bringing up some of the children.' Tim started to laugh. 'Sat here, meditating for hours. All weathers. Freezing cold. Snowed on, soaked to the skin.'

'Elgar's mother would have approved.'

'Yes.'

'Was nobody curious about what you were doing?'

'The few people who come here, if you're meditating they leave you alone. They understand that much.'

Lol tried again.

'The demons. That *is* the Royal Oak? The demonic counterpoint to what you're doing. Like when the demons come for the soul of Gerontius ... they're discordant. They're taunting him.'

'Didn't really notice it,' Tim said. 'Not at first.'

'You didn't hear the noise?'

'I could block it out with headphones. Put on the old cans, close my eyes and I'm in a concert hall. Or a cathedral. Or when I'm writing just put them on, unplugged, and it's a blank canvas. But she made me take them off. She said it was meant.'

'Winnie?'

'Made me take my headphones off while I was writing, to experience the violence. Suppose I didn't react strongly enough. So we walked down the hill one night, a Saturday night – we'd been drinking ... well, I'd been ... and she said, this is evil. It's deriding you. And it was filling the valley, terribly loud and I was getting pretty sick of it and I said, can't we go? And then she took me to where there was a loose stone in the wall.'

'*She* made you throw the stone through the window?'

'Had a few drinks. And you learn not to make her annoyed.'

'And then ...'

'Just stood there, thinking, what the bloody hell have I done now? Next thing, they're all on me. Big chaps. Beat the shit out of me.'

'And where was Winnie?'

'Gone for help.'

'She let them beat you up.'

Tim sat down under the tree.

'She's a writer,' he said.

Driving through Wychehill, picking up speed but not too much, Syd Spicer said, 'You understand about Louis Devereaux, now? Loves to kill.'

Merrily fumbled out a cigarette, both hands shaking. Once you sat down, it all caught up with you again.

'Odd thing was, Emily was always anti-hunting till she started going out with Louis. And then it was, *Oh he just does it for the riding and the excitement.* I wasn't too happy about a teenage kid going out with a bloke six years older. So I asked around. There's a few hunting types in my other parishes. Some of them *very* doubtful about Louis.'

They passed the gates of Wychehill Church, with its cracked lantern alight.

'Can't you go any faster, Syd?'

'Too many traffic cops. They'll stop anybody tonight.'

Merrily had rung Bliss again and left a slightly hysterical, urgent message on his voicemail. Now she was even wondering about trying to get Howe. Meanwhile, groping for self-reassurance. *No way anyone's going to mistake Lol for Tim Loste. Not even in the countryside in the dark.*

*Please God.*

She lit the cigarette.

'Let's have the worst, then.'

'I'm telling you this in case we run into him. Heroics are inadvisable. Louis will kill anything. Example: when the hounds start to slow up in the chase, they get shot, a side of hunting seldom advertised. Louis would volunteer to do it. For other hunts as well, which made him popular with kennel men, who mainly dislike that side of it. There's more, of course, mostly hearsay. Essentially, people who love to kill will find or create a need for it. Justification. What it tells me is that killing Wicklow, after Louis justified it to himself, would have been an act done in a frenzy of pure excitement.'

'You *understand* that feeling?'

'I understand the rush you get when you convince yourself that, in the great scheme of things, it's not only justified but necessary. When you know that a difficult situation can only be resolved by an act of swift, efficient, intense and quite colossal violence.'

'And to a woman?'

'No,' Spicer said. 'No, I could never see that far.'

Merrily thought, irrationally, of Lyndon Pierce and the blue tits: tiny, mean, cowardly violence, with no risk to self.

For the Devereaux boys, something far bigger. A war.

But *Winnie?*

'Sometimes it's a fine line, Merrily. Luckily, in the armed forces, especially the more hands-on areas, there's also a very thick line, and it's called training.'

'And without that?'

'Without training there's no efficiency and no safe judgement. In this instance, we're looking at a perceived justification gone wild.'

'Your daughter had a relationship with Louis.'

'Wouldn't hear a word against him. Well, he's a charming boy. OK, he was arrested for attacking an MP's minder during a pro-hunt protest – well, a lot of strong feelings at the time. OK, he went to pieces when the ban went through – poor boy, his life dismantled. Goes off to the city at weekends to work off his frustrations ... nicked for possession of coke, gets a caution. Well, he was chastened by that. And look how he's changed.'

Merrily was thinking about the five minutes or less she'd spent in the company of Louis Devereaux: posh, educated, good-looking, flirtatious.

'He was one of the reasons you wanted Emily out of Wychehill?'

'He was one of the reasons I wanted *Winnie* out of Wychehill.'

'So stopping them using the church—'

'Partly.'

'Syd ...' Merrily gulping smoke. 'I still don't know why they did this. Wicklow, yes, an invader from the hated cities. But Winnie ... I'm not getting it.'

Syd swerved into the Ledbury road under the ramparts of Herefordshire Beacon.

'Take too long, Merrily, and I'm still not totally sure of my facts. And your bloke's out there. And he doesn't know what else is, does he?'

At first, seeing the curious white clouds in the northern sky, Lol had thought for a moment that time itself, at Whiteleafed Oak, was unreliable and this was the dawn. But the visible landmarks had told him the lights were in the wrong part of the sky; these were just unusually pale clouds over the southern Malverns, gassy, white and luminous, as if they were chemically producing their own glow.

It lit up the valley like a vast sports stadium, and Lol was starting to see the pattern ... the structure.

This much was not fantasy: Tim Loste *was* working on a piece of music, in the dramatized, semi-operatic style of *The Dream of Gerontius*. And it was *about* Gerontius. Or rather, about the spiritual and emotional challenges, for Elgar, of composing what was regarded as his greatest work: orchestrating a metaphysical world.

But it was also about Loste's own links with both Gerontius and Elgar. Some perceived by Loste, some perceived – or constructed – by Winnie Sparke. Bizarre. But art was allowed – even expected – to be bizarre.

'When you came to Wychehill, it was as if you were entering a different world. Elgar's world. And Winnie's your guardian angel. That really came to you in a dream?'

Tim's eyes widened. There was enough light now to see that they were not yet normal. Like an owl's eyes.

'Had a horrible, ghastly dream. Dreamed that Winnie was bleeding. I heard her screaming her heart out. I saw . . . the shadows of demons. But I couldn't do anything. Why couldn't I *do* anything?'

Lol looked at the stains on Tim's singlet.

'When was this?'

'I don't know. Last night? Gha . . . ghastly.' He stared at Lol, his eyes still too wide. 'Look, I don't . . . How do you know all this about me?'

'Just know people who've worked with you. Whose lives you've changed.'

'What are you doing here?'

'I think I . . . wanted to learn. I'm a musician. Of sorts.'

'Yes.' Tim seemed to accept that, his mind veering off again. 'Used to walk the hills night after night. Listening to G along the path.'

'*Gerontius.*'

'Wanting to die because I knew I was never going to be as good as that. I was engaged, and she wanted us to go to London – chance of a teaching job with some conducting, on the side, with a jolly decent choir. But Winnie was on the scene by then, said I mustn't leave Elgar. Got the ring thrown back at me. Pretty bad times at work. All got too much. Kept on listening to G, over and over. Got drunk. Embraced death.'

'But then Winnie told you that you didn't have to die. She rescued you. You called her the guardian angel.'

'She said the journey could be accomplished in this life through the use of symbolism. With great art as a by-product.'

'What's it going to be called?'

Tim looked blank for a moment. The white clouds were like pillows on the lumpy mattress of the hills.

'*Mr Phoebus*,' he said at last. '*Mr Phoebus and the Whiteleafed Oak*.'

'I like it. It's a wonderful title.'

'Winnie's doing a book, too. All about me and Elgar.'

'Elgar's biographer, Kennedy, says Elgar scored *Gerontius* in a kind of trance,' Lol said.

'Yes. Composing G, he said he could look out from Birchwood and see the soul rise. Tremendous emotional experience. State of near-ecstasy when he'd finished it. That was the summer he'd learned to ride a bike. In his element, laughing and joking . . . and then . . .' Tim's chin sank into his chest.

'Then it all went wrong.'

'First performance in Birmingham . . . complete disaster. Chorus was under-rehearsed and performed badly. The chorusmaster had died suddenly and the man they brought in to replace him wasn't up to the job. All went to pieces. Elgar was suicidal.'

'*Actually* suicidal?'

'It brought on the most dreadful depression. *I wish I were dead*, he kept saying. He wrote, *I've always said God was against art*. Swore he'd never again attempt to write religious music. Closed his mind against the spiritual. 'Course, in later years G would be beautifully performed, its genius exalted, but in the early days . . .'

'Elgar thought it was cursed? Why?'

'Because he thought God was punishing him for overreaching his . . . mere humanity. For daring to approach . . . to approach God, I suppose. Head-on.'

'You mean through the music.'

'After the soul has withstood the torments of the demons, after his encounter with the Angel of the Agony, as he approaches judgement . . . he's given one glimpse – sudden, cataclysmic – of the Holiest.'

'God.'

'A glimpse of God, yes.'

'And Elgar had to convey that in music.'

'Couldn't do it,' Tim said. 'Or wouldn't. Shied away from it. As a Catholic, he was afraid it might be approaching blasphemy. Anyway, thought he'd finished – *I've put my heart's blood into the score*, he said, and sent the manuscript to his publishers. Thought he'd got away with it, but his friend there – friend and confidant – August Jaeger, accused him of bottling it, running scared of the big moment. Jaeger's saying, *you're not doing* enough *with this. You're not* showing *us God . . . you're not giving us* the moment. Pushing him. And Elgar, the timid Catholic, going, *Can't. Not humanly possible, almost blasphemous to try to convey in music the ultimate blinding light.*'

Tim's deceptively warlike face glowing now with sweat in the unnatural night whiteness.

'And this, you see . . . in my own work, this is Elgar's most agonized solo. We agreed, Winnie and I, that it should contain elements of foreboding . . . perhaps a premonition of that disastrous first perform-ance in Birmingham.'

'Nice touch,' Lol said.

'Jaeger was joshing him, knew exactly how to handle the poor chap. He said something like, *Of course, conveying the full glory of God, that would take a Wagner . . .*'

Lol nodded. Elgar's major influence had been Wagner.

'So Elgar goes back? To try again?'

'Looks like muso-banter to us now, Jaeger winding Elgar up. But it would have cut him to the quick. Yes, of course he went back.'

'Back here. To Whiteleafed Oak?'

'Where else?'

'And . . . what happened?'

'On a basic level, I suppose you'd say he . . . simply restructured some chords to manufacture a climactic moment. This short series of swiping chords, and then . . . Do you know G?'

'To a point.'

Certainly this point. The Guardian Angel had warned the soul that the momentary vision would blow him away with its power. When it finally happened, it was barely flagged-up and it went through your spine, that single chord, every time you heard it, like a razor-edged, shining scythe.

'You see, my job here . . . I have to capture the moment it came to Elgar. Or *Mr Phoebus* fails.'

'That's why you're here?'

'Have to catch the moment, and more.'

'More?'

'No good just *copying* Elgar, Dan. You have to try to take it further or what's the point?'

'Further than Elgar?'

'Winnie believes that whatever happened to him was so personal and terrifying that he was still afraid to orchestrate the full intensity of it. Clearly, the build-up to that one frightening, revelatory *slashing* chord was enough to convince Jaeger. Winnie – God knows, Dan, I'm not the bravest chap on the block either – but Winnie believes I can widen the crack in the door.'

'That's . . .' Lol stepped back. 'That's a big thing, Tim.'

'The biggest.'

'That's what the preparation's all been about? Those three simultaneous choirs in the three churches?'

'Yes. And the . . .'

'She's not without ambition, is she, Winnie?'

'And the exercises. The meditation and the visualization. Endless. And the need for Elgar to be part of it. I just couldn't hack it at first. Too much of an ordinary bloke, Dan.'

Tim sighed, sat down on the grass.

'There was a girl. On a bike. Legs pumping up and down. For a while we . . . *No!*' His voice going shrill and transatlantic. '*Don't you realize you will never have a chance like this again? You gonna throw it all away?*'

'Winnie.'

'I owe her so much, you see. Saved my life. *Made* my life.'

Lol said nothing. Tim blotted the sweat from around his eyes with the heel of his palm.

'Yes, we had a practice, in the three churches. Would have been wonderful to have the three cathedrals, hundreds of choristers, but even Winnie's energy doesn't extend that far.'

'And did you come here – to Whiteleafed Oak – when the choirs were in the three churches?'

'No, I was at Wychehill, then drove to Little Malvern. It was a run-through. Only a run-through.'

'Did Winnie think it was going to be just a run-through?'

'Dan, I was *scared.* Quite often scared. *Gerontius* has always scared me. You think it's easy to live with something so . . . cosmically huge? Day in, day out? And the nights. Tried to psych myself up, on the quiet. Booze wasn't doing it. I even went up the hill one night, scored a few – not my thing at all, normally – few grams of coke off— They said I'd killed him, did you know that?'

Lol nodded.

'I was scared, Dan. This hallowed place. I don't know. *Is* it hallowed? Are we fed – *still* – by the old choirs? Help me.'

'Would be good to think so.'

And Lol saw it all now. The psychology of it. *She said the journey could be accomplished in this life through the use of symbolism. With great art as a by-product.*

All it needed was for Tim to believe in it strongly enough, through months of meditation, visualization, conditioning, and the magic would happen.

'Are you frightened?' Lol said.

Tim covered his face with his hands for a moment and then tore them away and looked all around at the strange, blanched landscape, a winter landscape in the heat of June. Looked up into the northern sky where the white, gaseous clouds hung like smothered lamps over the southern Malverns.

'A great orchestral slash of light, Dan. His one shattering glimpse of God. And Gerontius sings . . . worshipful submission as a kind of triumph . . .'

Tim stepping away from the tree, raising his arms, releasing this vast torn and piercing tenor.

'*Take me awayyyyyyyyyy!*'

Tim sank to his knees, kept his eyes down.

'Think it's time for you to bugger off, Dan.'

'You need to be alone for this?'

'Otherwise there's no courage required,' Tim said. 'Is there?'

'Suppose not.'

'What are you going to do?'

Tim placed a hand on his chest, over the stained singlet.

'All happens in here.'

'Right.' Lol turned and walked away from the oak. 'Just ... be careful.'

Tim grinned.

After a few paces, Lol looked over his shoulder to see what he knew he was going to see: what the combination of the moon and those northern clouds had done to the leaves of the oak.

59

# Life-Force

A PAINFULLY SLOW AND twisting half-mile short of Whiteleafed Oak, Syd Spicer asked Merrily to feel under her seat for a small leather case.

'Night glasses. High-tech.' He cleared his throat. 'We all loved our gadgets, the Hereford boys.'

'The Hereford Boys.' She found the case. 'Look, there's something I should've mentioned, but with Winnie—'

Merrily gripped the sides of her seat. Every time she thought of the name, she saw the breathless mouth, the unseeing eyes. The body ripped up like old clothes. A woman who was sometimes a life-force and sometimes a vampire.

'We can see this place from some distance, right?'

'Reasonably well. But there's lots of cover when you get there. Dells, copses.'

Within a minute, a small green area came up in the headlights. A display case for local notices.

'This the village?'

'Yes.'

'And the five-barred gate?'

'End of that little lane, but you can't get . . . I mean you'll just block the track.'

'I'll pull in here, then. Close your door quietly when you get out.'

At the five-barred gate, Spicer pointed ahead of them. He was still wearing his thin black gloves.

'Know what that is?'

'Shiny white clouds. Weird.'

'Noctilucent clouds. Quite rare. Sometimes caused by chemicals, sometimes natural. Second night this week we've had them. Maybe a good thing, maybe not, but something to be aware of. What were you going to tell me back there?'

'When you mentioned the Hereford Boys . . . I don't know whether you heard this on the news. A former SAS man's been shot. In Hereford.'

Spicer kept on looking over the gate, but he'd gone still.

'A security consultant,' Merrily said.

'Do you know his name?'

'Malcolm France.'

He went on watching the bright clouds.

'Bliss – the detective I know – called me about it. His records had been stolen, but they found out from the bank that he'd once been paid two hundred and fifty pounds. By Winnie Sparke. Syd . . .'

He was standing so still you'd swear he wasn't breathing.

'Just tell me,' Merrily said.

'My mate. We were working together. Until a few seconds ago. I thought we still were.'

'Oh God, I'm—'

Syd Spicer held up his palms for silence.

'I'll give you the basics. Winnie's convinced she's going to be the next Mrs Devereaux and all her money problems are over. When he dumps her, she starts obsessing over whether there's someone else. Kind of woman she is. Life on the scrap heap, not for Winnie. Comes to bits on my kitchen table. I tell her there's this mate of mine could check him out. She doesn't have much money to spare, and there're things I want to know, too. It was expedient. I put up some of the fee. On the side. Cash in hand.'

'I should've told you about him ages ago, but it . . . circumstances intervened.'

'How were you to know?'

'I did know. I knew Winnie had been his client.'

'Yeah, well, another thing you should know,' Syd said. 'He was the guy I rang. Back at Wychehill, soon as I saw the body. I left a half-coded message. I told him to go to the police with everything he knew. Mal always checked his messages very assiduously every hour. I was about to call him back, bring him up to date. He has ... *had* police contacts and credibility.'

Merrily felt light-headed. Now nobody in the police could know they were here. She watched Syd Spicer opening the gate.

'He was a bloody good guy. Went through the first Gulf War. Did Bosnia.'

Syd kicked the five-barred gate, hard, once, until it jammed against the long grass and quivered.

'We're on our own,' he said.

'And your training says go back, phone for help.'

'Except your bloke's ...'

'Yes, he is.'


Lol didn't go far. How could he? Where was he supposed to go?

Was he going to leave a damaged man to wait, like some half-demented hermit in the rocks, for God?

Elgar had been right, it was a kind of blasphemy, or at least arrogance. Not really Tim Loste's arrogance; he was the tool of someone's else's ambition.

All he was going to face tonight was the cold, unredemptive shining of his own madness. His own *induced* madness.

And yet ...

Lol walked away over the rise and followed a slow arc back towards the open barn, went down on his knees as he approached it, patting the grass in search of his phone.

And yet he understood. He understood the desperation of Elgar who had done it before, made art, and was afraid – as you always were, every time – that you were never going to be able to do it again, that your best had gone.

And he knew that what Elgar was drawing from the landscape was not – like his contemporary, Vaughan Williams – inspiration from an English rural tradition, because Elgar's style was influenced more by German music ... Wagner.

No, this was about pure, electrical energy. Energy was what Elgar, with his daily walking and his fifty-mile bike rides, was all about. What *he* was tapping from the countryside was its life-force.

*The trees are singing my music or am I singing theirs?*

What happened when the trees stopped singing? Or, in Loste's case, never had sung much. How far would you go?

Lol looked into the sky where strange white lights were kindling pale sparks in the springing antennae of the ancient oak. He imagined Tim Loste huddled like a goblin into its bole.

The difference was that Elgar had been a natural. He didn't need photo blow-ups or three choirs singing *Praise to the Holiest* at the stroke of midnight or whatever kind of Golden Dawn ceremonial magic they were planning. *He didn't need a structure.*

This was wrong. Lol, on all fours, felt his heart beating and discovered one hand was embedded in a patch of nettles.

It came out stinging like hell and holding the mobile phone.

Still switched on, and it still had battery life. Lol let out a long breath, stumbled to his feet and took it into the barn. Crouching in the hay, he found three messages, the last of which ended, '... *Winnie murdered. Keep away from it. I love you.*'

He'd started to call her back when he heard a voice.

Tim's voice, conversational. If he was talking to God, it hadn't taken long to break the ice.

Lol moved out of the barn, up the rise. He saw Tim, with roots humped around him like serpents and, across his knees, the leather-bound book open to the score of *Mr Phoebus and the Whiteleafed Oak*.

The man sitting next to him handed him a hip flask and Tim drank.

# 60

# Into the Pit

MERRILY WATCHED PRESTON DEVEREAUX screw the top back on his hip flask and stow it inside his dark green overalls. She slipped back behind Syd Spicer, with no idea how to play this.

Looking at Lol coming up the rise and willing him not to move, not to speak. Looking across at Syd and realizing he had no idea how to react either.

Seeing Preston Devereaux coming slowly to his feet among the roots of the sacred oak. Tim Loste huddling into the tree.

Nobody spoke. Syd was watching Devereaux. The vapour trail of a plane you couldn't hear was like a chalk scribble on the shiny sky.

It struck Merrily the chances were that none of them could be entirely sure what the others were doing here or how much each of them knew.

In which case, go for it.

She walked up to the base of the tree, put out a hand.

'Mr Loste? My name's Merrily. I've been trying to talk to you for days.'

Relief was amazing. At first it weakened you, and then it flung you back into life with an unexpected strength and a vividly heightened sense of reality. Suddenly, there was nothing you couldn't handle.

Which was probably dangerous, but what the hell?

Tim Loste was on his feet now, his back to the bole of the oak. His hand felt like soft cheese.

Merrily glanced at Lol, gave him a half-smile, her eyebrows slightly raised, and then turned back to Tim.

He had Winnie's blood all over him. She wondered if he'd even noticed it. Without Syd, the chances of him talking his way out of this one would have been remote. Annie Howe would have him charged by daybreak and a press release put out.

Merrily wondered how long the effects of Rohypnol lasted.

Wondered what was in Preston Devereaux's hip flask.

How much of it Tim had drunk.

'I'm sorry we had to meet like this, Mr Loste, but we heard you were coming to Whiteleafed Oak and Syd very kindly offered to show me the way.' She looked up at Devereaux. 'Of course, we didn't expect ...'

'I like to walk,' Devereaux said slowly, 'when the tourists have gone home. Don't get many nights like this, where you can see for miles.'

'Syd said it's ... what did you call it?'

'Noctilucence,' Syd said. 'Happens more often in ... other countries I've spent time in.'

'Quite an intimate place, really, the Malverns.' Merrily looked at Lol. 'I'd imagine it's hard to go anywhere without running into people you know. Sorry, you are ...?'

'Dan,' Lol said. 'I'm in Tim's choir.'

Merrily nodded, chanced her arm again.

'We thought Winnie might be here. Didn't meet her on the way.'

'We haven't seen her,' Lol said.

'On your own, Preston?' Syd walked across and stood with his back to the tree. 'Only thought I saw one of the boys. Possibly Louis.'

He hadn't, had he?

'Yes, I'm on my own tonight, Syd. Nice to get away for a while.'

Merrily's relief twisted into tension as she moved close to Lol.

'Well,' Devereaux said. 'If you've come all this way to talk to Tim, Merrily, I should leave you to it. I don't know what the subject of your discussion's going to be, but if it's what I think it is ... well, you know my views. I'll say goodnight to you.'

He walked away, Merrily whispering to Lol, 'Did you get my—?'

'Just.'

'Does Loste know about Winnie?'

'No.'

'What's he doing here on his own?'

'Long story. Basically, he's come to expose himself to the blinding light of God. Like Gerontius. *Take me away.*'

'*What?*'

'Yeah, 'night, Preston,' Syd called out. 'Careful of the Gullet.'

Preston Devereaux walked no more than forty paces before he stopped and shrugged and turned back.


Four of them sitting on the ridged and knobbly earth at the edge of the sacrificial pit, like some surreal midnight picnic party. Tim Loste hadn't moved from the oak. Syd Spicer was hunched between Devereaux and Merrily, his legs overhanging the hollow as if he was conducting a confirmation class at the front of his church.

*Careful of the Gullet.*

He'd wanted this confrontation. Some payback for all those weeks without his family. Or something. Merrily was furious and anxious. If this was an example of the benefits of *training*, the bastard hadn't left the Regiment a day too soon.

'I suppose we're people who know each other, mostly,' Syd said. 'And what we are.'

Preston Devereaux had his cap tilted over his eyes. Reluctant returned exile, begetter of murderers.

'You, for instance, are such a *clever* man, Preston. With such stupid sons.'

Devereaux didn't look at him.

'Should've stopped when you were ahead. All you needed was to sit tight and do nothing.'

Devereaux slipped him a look.

'Yeah, that's what I thought,' Syd said. 'That's exactly what you *were* doing. Nothing been shifted through Old Wychehill for quite a while, or Mal would've known. You should've ignored Wicklow, too. Somebody else would've had him sooner or later. Maybe you *were* ignoring him. But not Louis ... Louis's a real hard man. Louis has to act.'

Merrily sat with goose bumps forming on her folded arms, unsure of the sense of this. Fears over Lol had blocked all meaningful consideration of what might be happening, the phrase *outrage crime* covering all.

'Family. You always reckoned it was a curse.' Syd turned to Merrily. 'The boy Louis likes to show off. Show how inventive he is. For a long time, I was thinking, *I wonder if Preston knows. Do I have a word?* But sometimes God saves us from ourselves. You noticed that?'

Preston Devereaux said, irritably, 'All the conversations we've had, Syd, you never brought God into it, not once. This is not a good time to start.'

'Fair enough. To answer your earlier question, Merrily, Winnie gave Mal two hundred and fifty quid, up front to find out if Preston was seeing another woman – Winnie, against everything she stood for, being crazy about Preston. On a whim, I bunged Mal a quiet grand to extend the inquiry.'

'Into—?'

'Not that he wouldn't've done it anyway, purely out of interest. Maybe a bit bored with the work he was getting. This was the real thing again. We sat up late one night at the rectory and planned it like an operation – the Hereford Boys ride again. Winnie was Mal's cover story, if they rumbled him. He liked that. We both liked it, I'm afraid.'

'Am *I* supposed to know who you're talking about?' Devereaux sounding bored.

'Oh, I'm very upset about Mal, Preston, and – God help me – very angry. My guess is it was someone came in from Wales rather than Louis, but that changes nothing. It still all comes back to Old Wychehill.'

Merrily coughed. 'I'm not . . .' Badly wanting a cigarette. 'Not really getting this.'

'Diversification, Merrily. Preston decided to follow the government's advice to the letter. Government helps destroy the basis of traditional agriculture, farmers complain, government says, Use your heads, be adventurous . . . *diversify*. Preston Devereaux, a deeply embittered man, full of hatred – some of it justified, fair play – says *Thank you for the advice, I'll do just that.'*

'Putting words into my mouth, Syd.'

Merrily realizing, even as Devereaux spoke, that there was no need to.

*And we turned it around, by God we did, in spite of the shiny-arsed civil servants and the scum from Brussels.*

She gazed into the pit. *Dear God.*

# 61

# Trying to be a Priest

'MAL TAILED PRESTON DAY after day,' Syd Spicer said. 'Into Worcester, Gloucester and Cheltenham, parts of Birmingham. Finally, down towards Tregaron, near where the old acid factory was, back in the 1970s. The only deals Preston cuts in Wychehill at the moment are with people who come to stay in his holiday apartments, but I'm guessing that in the early days it was buzzing.'

Preston Devereaux slid his hand into a pocket of his overall. Syd moved closer to him. Devereaux brought out a packet of cigarettes, held it up. Syd nodded.

'But Preston's still got to be directing the business, else why would he be making the visits? Sometimes, he goes alone to Worcester or Cheltenham, sometimes it's him and Louis. Mal had to lie a bit to Winnie, because occasionally they'd drop into clubs and massage parlours as well – sampling the pleasures of the cities they were poisoning. But mostly it was private houses, or the offices of an independent cattle-feed dealer, or a couple of family-owned abattoirs. The service industries.'

'Victims of Blair's slow demolition of England's oldest industry,' Devereaux said.

Merrily shifted on the baked earth, still resisting the urge to smoke.

'How long since Mal France told you all this, Syd?'

'Over a period. Up to last night, on his way back from the West Wales coast. Had to leave in a hurry to lose someone on a motorbike. Seems to be a string across the border counties and down through Mid-Wales. Couple of coastal landowners. Some of it, mainly smack, comes in that way, all courtesy of selected tight-lipped farmers. And no profession has tighter lips than farming. Inbred silence, inbred resentment. Watertight. Supplemented, in this case, by people who lost jobs after the hunting ban. A feudal thing, really. Old feudal instincts. Almost – God forbid – a crusade.'

Devereaux lit a cigarette. Syd moved away from the smoke.

'Not quite sure know how long it's been going on, maybe two years, maybe four. It only starts to make serious sense when you look back to Preston's formative years. His university years.'

'Oxford?' Merrily said. 'Balliol?'

'In the 1960s. Wasn't that guy, the Welsh guy, Mr Nice . . . ?'

'Howard Marks?'

'That's him. World-class dope dealer. Living legend in his field. And, as it happens, a student at Balliol College in the 1960s. You knew him, Preston?'

'Before my time.'

'Not that much before, by my reckoning. Maybe you just had some of the same contacts – I'm guessing here, you understand, I'm just a simple cleric. But where Mr Marks stuck with dope – marijuana-based goods . . .'

'Evangelical, with him,' Merrily remembered.

'Yeah, a real calling. So he's always maintained. The fact that he also made a few fortunes before he was nicked and banged up in the States . . . Preston, it's different. Different background *altogether*. And different attitude. Fuelled by this self-righteous, blind resentment. Powerful. It's in his Norman blood. Blood of the Vikings.'

Devereaux smiled. Merrily saw Lol stand up and wander over to the oak tree.

'Mal reckoned it probably wasn't as difficult as you might think,' Syd said. 'Just a question of renewing old student contacts and making connections with new ones. Cultures have changed, of course. Would've taken patience at first, convincing the sources. But when they know you're a safe pair of hands, and that you mean it – that's the important thing. Showing them that just because you come from money, that doesn't mean you're soft.'

Merrily said, 'Wicklow . . . ?'

'Would reverberate nicely. But the way it was done ... stupid. Attention-grabbing. But, like I say, Louis's immature. He thinks it's hugely clever. The sacrificial stone.'

'He sent a text about human sacrifice to Raji Khan. From Elgar's *Caractacus*. Whether that was *intended* to point to Tim ...'

'Whatever, it came off. When you're arrogant and cocksure and on a high, things often do come off. For a while. But it's clever-clever and so immature. Preston knows that. Anybody in their right mind, if it was really necessary to get rid of Wicklow, they'd do it the way someone got rid of that guy in Pershore ... forget his name ...'

'Chris Smith. Which the police think was Wicklow. Smith worked in an abattoir.'

'Ah. One of your boys, Preston?'

Devereaux said nothing. Not once had he admitted to anything specific.

'Farms, abattoirs, feed merchants. Little crack labs, some of them. The stuff moved in cattle transporters, feed trucks. The kind of country-road vehicles the police were never going to search in a million years. Shambolic but also very neat. I believe we might also be looking at secret compartments in the SUVs and people-carriers of the holidaymakers coming to stay in Preston's luxury units. Bet you'd find some of those holidaymakers had only just *been* on holiday. Some to Spain, some to less-favoured resorts like ... which is it these days, Rotterdam?'

'Be more than happy,' Devereaux said, 'for the police to search all my buildings. I'd challenge them to find a trace of anything.'

'Lying fallow at the moment, are we, Preston? Movable feast, innit? What – a dozen farms? More? Whichever way you look at it, this has to be the most successful farmers' cooperative since the first Iron Age village.'

'What about Raji Khan?' Merrily said.

'Still a bit of a mystery there,' Syd said. 'He's not clean, obviously. But he must be a very small player by comparison. Can't be involved, or he'd never have been allowed to move in so close. What was that like, Preston, Raji moving in? You must've been awful nervy. Did he know, or didn't he? If he ever found out, that could be tricky – and always a possibility with ambitious little men like Wicklow around. And do you officially support the opposition? Leonard Holliday and WRAG? Difficult one.'

'Especially if it attracted too much publicity,' Merrily said. 'Thus engaging the attention of hundreds of thousands of Elgar enthusiasts, all over the world. You really had to curb Mr Holliday, didn't you?'

'And maybe do something about Tim Loste,' Syd said. 'Very much a wild card. And supported – *more* than supported – by your former good friend but not any more, Winnie Sparke. I tried to warn her, best I could. She wouldn't buy it. *Syd*, she said, *this is* England.'

Lol didn't do drugs. The only reason he had to be grateful to his psychiatric hospital: a sojourn in Medication City and you never wanted to swallow so much as an aspirin ever again.

The white in the sky had dulled, the oak was going grey. A great and beautiful mystery had shrunk to something squalid. Lol sat down next to Tim, whispered to him.

'How much did you drink from the hip flask?'

'Chap offers you a swig, not the thing to decline, Dan.'

'Depends who's offering.'

'Raised it to my lips. Faked it.'

'Oh.'

'If he brought it back now, I'd drink the lot. Elgar was right, old cock. God's against art.'

'May just be,' Lol said, 'that artists don't have mystical experiences. Artists are a medium. Think of it as an internal process you're not aware of. *You* don't have to see blinding light and the heavenly host. You might sit down tomorrow and it'll all come out in the music.'

'You're full of bullshit, Dan. Anyone ever tell you that?'

'Never,' Lol said honestly. 'I'm normally a low-key sort of bloke. But it did seem to me as if the leaves had turned white. Don't give up. Give it a try.'

'For Winnie?' Tim said.

'Tim—'

'Thought it was a dream. Thought it was a fucking *dream.*'

'I didn't know, either. I'm sorry.'

'Blocked it out. Why didn't I stop them? Why couldn't—?'

'Because, somehow, you were drugged. Sedated. I've been there. Seen it happen. I can tell you for certain there was nothing you could've done.'

'It's a sick fucking joke, Dan. I've been sitting here all this time, waiting for—'

Tim's hands squeezing the roots either side of him.


'As a gentleman, I'm listening to you,' Devereaux said. 'Just not talking to you.'

'A gentleman?' Merrily sat up. 'A gentleman who kills kids? Teenagers with infected syringes? Teenagers who murder old ladies in their own homes to steal enough to keep them going for another week?'

Preston Devereaux stared into the shadows below his feet.

'The cities are a lost cause, Mrs Watkins. Reinfecting themselves on their own sewage. Nothing to be done about that. The road to ruin. No doubt the two of you can find Biblical parallels.'

'And out of the ruins will rise ... what?'

'Better government,' Devereaux said.

At first Merrily thought he was coughing over his cigarette. But he was laughing. She looked at Syd Spicer. Where was he going with this? Did he have some plan that she couldn't see? Why hadn't he just let Devereaux walk away? Why did he have to throw out that remark about the Gullet?

'Why did you kill Winnie Sparke?' Syd asked.

'I didn't.'

'Whoever murdered France took his files,' Merrily said, just wanting to end this. 'Presumably that's where they found Winnie's name. Who would recognize that but you?'

'Winnie's name's on Mal's books,' Syd said, 'so it must be Winnie who's paying him to look into the drug operation. And Winnie being Winnie, a loose cannon— My fault. Should've been my name.'

'Syd, this is not something you could ever have predicted.'

'Who rumbled Mal?' Syd said. 'I'd like to know that, Preston.'

Devereaux tossed his cigarette end into the pit.

'Who told you about the Gullet?' he said.

'You were going to take Tim back that way, right? You waited for . . . Mr Robinson to leave, and then you were in with the spiked Scotch and time to go home, Tim. How desperate was that?'

'Who told you about the Gullet?'

'Hugo, actually.'

'*Hugo?*' Devereaux looking at him at last.

'We have to get our information where we can.'

'Where is he? Syd, he's a *boy*.'

'He's no more a boy than half the drug barons in Birmingham. And if you tell me he hasn't killed anybody, I wouldn't be sure and neither could you. Can't control these boys like you used to, can you? Let them go too far down the road. Maybe that's another reason Old Wychehill's been fallow for a bit, you trying to rein Louis in before it's too late. Tell me who rumbled Mal.'

'Or what?'

'Or tell the police when they get here, I don't mind. It'll add to what they'll have learned from Hugo, already naming names faster than they can write them down.'

'Hugo doesn't know any names.'

'Boy goes around with his eyes shut, does he? It's over, Preston, it's disintegrating as we speak. That's what I'm trying to get across to you.'

'You've told me some far-fetched theories, that's—'

'*That's* because I'm not trying to trick you, mate. And because I've been trying, maybe not too successfully, to be a priest. Sometimes, especially lately, I have to keep reminding myself that that's what I am now. I can look at this situation and see clearly what would be the best way of dealing with it if I was still in the Army.'

'The situation being?'

'The situation being a dangerous young man out there, and probably more dangerous because he's frightened and not really, with his background, the big gangster he thinks he is. He's clever, but clever's not the same as smart. Police see what Louis did, it's an Armed Response Unit. Marksmen all over the hills. The soldier in me would take him out ASAP. Expedience. But the priest doesn't want another death. Not even Louis's.'

'And how would the priest avoid that?'

'I think . . . by letting you walk away like you did a short time ago. You presumably know where he is, so you can explain to him what I've just explained to you, and then the two of you can walk into a police station of your choice.'

'Or leave the country.'

'Leaving young Hugo to take all the weight? Nah. You've got *some* honour left. It's the best thing you can do as a father and a clever man. Exercise some control over your boy. Tell him it's pointless.'

Preston Devereaux straightened his back, hands on his knees. There was a glaze of sweat on his forehead under the line of his cap.

'Where's the point in that, Syd, when you've already told him?'

Perhaps Louis Devereaux had been there the whole time. Plenty of cover. Coppices and dells.

Perhaps Syd had known this. He half-turned and looked up at Louis with no surprise.

Merrily was on her feet, backing away, instinctively looking for Lol, but seeing only Louis Devereaux, a half-silhouette in the grey light, as still, for a moment, as any of the oaks, arms extended, rigid as dead branches, both hands clasped around the pistol.

'Where'd you buy that, Louis?' Syd said mildly. '*Very* professional. They say you can get them in Hereford these days. Glock?'

The gun twitched.

'Move away from my father, Rector.'

'What for? Which one of us you planning to shoot to prove your old man isn't in control any more?'

'And shut up.'

'Shouldn't that be shut *the fuck* up? Got to get the tone right, the correct phraseology.'

'*Shut the—*' Louis's hands jerking around the pistol. 'I could kill you now.'

'Or blow me away, even. Blow all of us away. That'd simplify things a lot. Like that feller in Hungerford in the 1980s. You probably don't remember that, you'd've been just a kid, but he shot himself in the end. Like the bloke at Dunblane. It always ends where they shoot themselves.'

Merrily couldn't move. Louis was panting with rage and frustration and probably fear. On a hot night, it was the most unstable combination imaginable. And all Syd had was . . .

'The other ending is death by Armed Response Unit. Like I've already told your father, lots of police marksmen all over the hills. Automatic rifles. Night sights. Make that thing look like a spud gun and you like the crass amateur you undoubtedly are.'

'You make one more . . . remark like that and then—'

'And for a while you get to learn what it was like for all the foxes you used to hunt. Only with not even the faintest possibility of an earth to escape to. No escape at all from those boys. Terrorism-trained, now, and they don't take any chances. At some stage one of them gets you in the cross-hairs and takes you out. You don't even see him taking aim. Like a wasp doesn't see the rolled-up newspaper.'

Syd standing there with his arms by his sides, an unmoving target. Merrily's heart going, *Please God, please God, please God.*

'We can get away,' Louis said. 'Any time we want. Just a question of whether—'

'Nah. It doesn't happen, son, not at this level.'

'—Whether we leave you fucking dead when we go.'

'You don't understand. You graduated to a new level of achievement tonight, mate,' Syd said. 'In the big school now. Where they spend millions hunting you down.'

Preston Devereaux stood up.

'Can I talk to my son?'

'Don't ask *me*, Preston – he's got the weapon.'

'What do I do?' Louis's whole body bending backwards like a water-skier, tensed around the swivelling pistol. '*What do I do?*'

'You probably give the gun to me,' Preston said.

'We can still get out of this. He's got to be lying about armed police. We could—'

Louis turned, the pistol pointing directly at Merrily. She felt a spasm below her heart like a long needle going in.

'—Take Mrs Watkins with us?'

'And then what, Louis?' Syd said. 'Demand a helicopter? Grow up, son.'

'Stay fuck—' Louis spun but not at Syd. 'Stay fucking *there!*'

Merrily, heart jumping, heard a cry from Lol.

'... *Tim!*'

Tim Loste was lumbering out from the tree. In his stained singlet, he looked like an old-fashioned butcher, arms sleeved in sweat, finger out, pointing at Louis.

'You were wearing a . . . a balaclava.'

'Don't come any closer,' Louis said, 'you wanker.'

'Recognize your voice. Wearing a balaclava with eyeholes.'

'Louis,' Preston Devereaux said, 'it's not necessary.'

'Big knife. You had this big— She was screaming at you to stop, screaming and screaming and . . . and crying and you just . . . you bloody bastard—'

Tim tumbled, sobbing, into Louis and Louis shot him twice.

# 62

# Seventeen

'I WENT TO SLEEP,' Tim said. 'Now I'm refreshed.'

He tried to laugh. A dry, skittering noise came out.

Merrily vaguely recognized the first words sung by the soul, after death, in *The Dream of Gerontius*.

'Feel so much lighter,' he said. 'That's good, isn't it?'

'Yes,' Merrily said. 'That's very good.'

Time seemed to have slowed. The white clouds had diminished and so had the humidity. A small night breeze rattled among the boughs.

Tim said, 'You're jolly pretty. I didn't . . . didn't realize you'd be so young. Way Winnie talked, it was as if you were some old . . .' He stopped for a breath. It was a terrifying noise, like a small breeze in a mound of dead leaves. 'Doesn't matter what Winnie said, does it?'

'I suppose not.'

She'd rung for an ambulance, said she'd found a man badly injured, didn't know how. Syd's advice. What they didn't need was an Armed Response Unit. She'd given them directions from the hamlet of Whiteleafed Oak, her name and her mobile number, telling them they could probably get an ambulance across the common without any difficulty if they took it slowly.

Lol had brought half a bale of straw up from the barn, and they put some of it under Tim, raising his legs. Syd's advice.

He walked over.

'Both gone?' Merrily said.

'Nothing I could do. Not without more of this. Maybe they'll get to a vehicle in time. Maybe they have arrangements in hand. Maybe they'll be on a boat out of Fishguard by morning. Can't see that he wouldn't't've made provision: bolt-holes, foreign bank accounts.'

Syd had phoned West Mercia Police on the general number, someone from Worcester coming back to him. Merrily didn't know what had been said, but Spicer'd had the impression that they already knew some of what he was telling them and they'd confirmed this by asking if he was the man who'd left a message on Malcolm France's mobile.

Some explaining, then, for Syd. Later.

She whispered to him, 'There's hardly any blood.'

'Internal, then. Keep him warm. Don't move him.'

Merrily's head was filled with a prayer that she couldn't articulate. She felt as if she was hovering over the entire scene, the wooded arena with its hints of neolithic mounds, its ghost of a processional way and the sacred, magisterial oak stuffed with twinkling symbols of vain hopes and dreams and, at its splayed feet, a man whose plea to be taken away had been answered in a blinding flash.

Tim Loste looked up at her from his bed of straw, his face creamed in sweat.

'Hannah's pretty.'

'Yes, she is.'

'Used to watch out for her when she came past. On her bike. Wished I had a bike. Follow her down. Two of us, whizzing down the hill. Super.'

'Mmm.'

'All I ever wanted, really. Thought I might buy a bike, but . . . Winnie said it would be the wrong kind.'

'Not like Mr Phoebus.'

'No.'

'But you rode Mr Phoebus sometimes. In your . . . daydreams?' With Hannah.

Tim's eyes filled up with tiny pools of moonlight.

'Know what I don't want?'

Merrily bent close to him now. His sweat smelled sour.

'You know what I . . . *really* don't want? Where's Dan?'

'I'm here.'

Lol was kneeling on the other side.

'Dan knows.'

'Remind me?' Lol said.

It was possible to speak with normal voices now, but they were whispering because Tim Loste was whispering. Tim smiled under his Edward Elgar yardbrush moustache, through his sweat.

'Don't want the Angel of the blasted Agony.'

'Would anybody?' Lol said.

Tim looked at Merrily and started to say something. But he was suddenly fighting for breath. She beckoned Syd, urgently, and he pushed more straw under Tim's legs.

'Lessens strain on the heart. Don't move him, and don't let him get too hot.'

Syd being the soldier again – as if too many priests would spoil the prayer. From quite a distance away, Merrily heard a single gunshot. Not uncommon, except this wasn't, she was sure, a shotgun. She exchanged a glance with Syd. He went still.

Tim was mumbling something to Lol, who was shaking his head.

'No, no . . . you haven't failed. Winnie failed, that's all. It couldn't work for someone like Winnie. You must've known that.'

Of course it couldn't. Winnie and her academic magic, her hit-and-miss, mix 'n' match spirituality. *Try this, try that.* Merrily suddenly saw the callousness of it. Whatever happened to Tim, Winnie would have had a book out of it. She could almost see the hovering spirit, outlined in the acid colours of the moon's halo, making notes. An even better book if Tim was dead.

'You just need to change the end,' Lol said. 'It's easy.'

'Seven,' Tim said.

'Seven?'

Lol turned to Merrily as Tim said something else. She shook her head.

'Was that . . . seventeen?'

Lol thought for a moment and then he smiled.

419

Tim's eyes lit up, a quiet glow appearing on the edges of the pupils. Faraway, unknowing eyes, like the light through clouds.

Merrily took in a rapid breath just before the second shot came out of the forestry.

She heard the night-shredding squawks of emergency vehicles and took Tim Loste's hand and began to pray.

# A List

'MERRILY,' BLISS SAID QUIETLY on the mobile. 'Before you say anything, I'm afraid there's nothing I can do. Not tonight, anyway.'

'Frannie,' she said wearily, 'where the *hell* have you been?'

They were in Syd Spicer's kitchen, her and Lol. It was nearly two a.m.

'I just called to leave a message. Never imagined you'd still be up.' He sounded knackered, his accent thickening. 'Just gorrin from Shrewsbury. Went up to talk to a guy my victim Malcolm France was working for. Bloke with serious form, and it looked promising, but it wasn't what we thought and I'm pig-sick, and I know it's your daughter and I know that Parry's a family friend, but this time—'

'*What?*'

'You know I've always liked Gomer, *pairsonally*, but some things . . .'

'What are you on about?'

Bliss paused. 'Where are you?'

'I'm— Tell me what you were talking about, first.'

'The charges against Gomer Parry? I did pick up your messages, but I was on a major investigation. I might be able to pull the odd string, but not tonight. CID were consulted but it's a uniform thing now. Out of my hands.'

'Gomer. Gomer and Jane? What have they *done*?'

'Do you know a place called Coleman's Meadow?'

'Heard of it. Vaguely.'

'They've trashed it with a JCB. Taken a fence out and destroyed an expensive vehicle.'

'Are they all right?'

'Oh *they're* all right. For the present. That old man's a complete maniac, of course, which you know, and Jane . . . Listen, I can suggest someone you might possibly talk to tomorrow, but I can't get involved, Merrily, I can't pull any—'

'That's why you didn't return my calls? You thought I was going to ask you to pull strings on behalf of Jane and Gomer?'

'I've had a bloody long night, Merrily. I've gorra *mairder* inquiry.'

'Not any more, Frannie,' Merrily said.

Hadn't really been his week, had it? Or anyone's she knew.

She needed to go home, but . . .

The police had found both bodies in the forestry. No back-road network, farm to farm to Fishguard and the ferry to Ireland.

Louis had been shot in the back of the head, evidently while relieving himself, his dad presumably having offered to hold the gun for him. Preston had been found some distance away. He'd fumbled it, blown a piece of his head away but was not dead. He'd died, like Lincoln Cookman, in the ambulance.

It was numbing.

'I can't question it,' Syd Spicer said. 'You know what the suicide rate is among ex-SAS? You come out into a shrunken world and it's like your coffin's being assembled around you. Every day another little screw going in. The sudden smallness of everything, the petty regulations, the way your hands are tied by the kind of people you just want to smack.'

He talked about that feeling of *confinement.* How you had to find a way out of that. Preston Devereaux's answer was to slide out of the system by shedding his humanity like excess weight.

Merrily lit a cigarette.

'Ironically, dumping your humanity now seems like the best way to survive in farming. A cow's no longer Daisy, it's a product with a government bar code.'

'The State penetrating your life at every level,' Syd said. 'Nobody's more aware of that than the farmer, whose only rulers used to be the elements. State doesn't like the idea of guys out there being independent. Officials come swarming over your land like maggots, and you're clawing away to get them off before they start eating into your brain. Maybe Preston felt he was finally reclaiming his Norman heritage as a robber baron. The Normans controlled the hunting in the Malverns. The Devereaux dynasty controls the drugs.'

'But knowing that at any time it could all go to pieces? That he could lose everything his family had built up over the centuries? Did that add to the necessary sense of danger?'

'Maybe,' Lol said, 'he thought he'd already lost everything. That it was just useless packaging. And the only part of it worth preserving was the ... whatever was still alight inside him.'

Merrily thought about this. About Devereaux telling her how he'd put all his valuable furniture into the holiday units. Stripping his own life back. She saw him in the Beacon Room in his anonymous, muted green overalls, surrounded by mementoes of the past – the fox heads and the picture of him with Eric Clapton. She looked at Syd.

'You knew that if you could get them to walk away ... ?'

Syd had changed into his cassock, as if in some vain attempt to convince himself that what had happened in the last several hours had happened to someone else.

'Didn't see him having any taste for life as a fugitive. Still less as a prisoner who – even if he hadn't actually personally killed anybody—'

'He had killed, though, hadn't he?' Merrily said. 'What about Lincoln Cookman and his girlfriend?'

'I meant murder.'

'Yes, well ...' Merrily bent her head into her hands. 'This is probably nonsense, but when I went to talk to Raji Khan at the Royal Oak, Roman Wicklow's family were there, collecting his stuff. Including his small sports car. Quite a deep colour of orange, which might look red at night, I don't know. It was just a feeling I had, and I don't get them often.'

Syd sat back. 'A Mazda?'

'I think it was a Nissan, but about the same size and shape, and late at night, coming towards Preston Devereaux at speed, with a black guy inside . . . He told me he was very tired at the time. He said if he hadn't been so tired it wouldn't have happened.'

'An impulse thing?'

'If Wicklow was preying on his mind . . .'

'You said Wicklow killed that man in Pershore?'

'He was tortured before he was shot,' Merrily said. 'Maybe he gave Wicklow information leading Wicklow back to Devereaux.'

'Then Wicklow turns up at Old Wychehill to ask for a job. Blackmail in a thin disguise. What if Wicklow tells Khan? Assuming Khan doesn't already know.'

Suspecting that Khan had a charmed-life arrangement with Annie Howe, Merrily didn't think he did know.

'I could be totally wrong about the Wychehill crash, anyway. How could he know they'd both be killed?'

'He couldn't,' Syd said. 'But he was a massively angry man in a business that brutalizes. I remember he was in a very . . . excited state that night. In fact, I don't rule out that Preston, like Louis, partook of the produce. In his careful way.'

'It could even be that Cookman had been involved with Wicklow. The police did find a bag of crack under his spare wheel.'

'Anything's possible and most of it won't come out. The cops have too many angles to follow up. Could take weeks with several forces involved. Could be dozens of people charged. But it's not our problem. Is it?'

'Meanwhile,' Lol said, 'Do we ring A and E at Worcester Hospital?'

'They'll ring us,' Merrily said. 'Tim has no known relations in the country. Not that anybody knows of.'

She pushed her cup away. One of the parameds had mentioned the possibility of damage to the pulmonary artery. The kitchen seemed dim. The garden, where it was lifted towards the bald hill, was pallid with tired moonlight and what remained of the so-called noctilucence.

'I may've screwed up badly.' Syd plucked at his cassock. 'Probably gonna get out of this now.'

'The cassock?'

'You know what I mean.'

'Quitting's not in your nature, Syd. Or your training.'

He smiled faintly.

'Increasingly, I admire you, Merrily. You've watched it fall to pieces from your point of view. Every deliverance angle going, one after another, down the toilet.'

'That's what you think?' Merrily sank her head into her arms, looking up at him from table-top level. 'You really don't see anything bordering on the paranormal?'

'You mean you do?'

'Syd,' she said. 'When I've slept, I'll make you a list.'

'You think there should still be some form of requiem?'

'I don't know. You think that would make everything all right in Wychehill? Sweetness and light and harmony and Mr Holliday inviting Mr Khan to afternoon tea?'

'What do you think?'

'I suppose I think truth sometimes heals on its own. Winnie said there was a festering wound in the hills. Maybe she added to the infection. Maybe she – let's be fanciful – annoyed Elgar, bringing him to judgement when all he wanted was to pedal up and down, whistling his sad little up-and-down cello tune.'

'Bringing him to judgement?'

'What right did she have? It was essentially a magical ritual, you know, what they were—' She stood up. 'What they're *still* doing, presumably, in your church.'

Merrily had never been a hymn kind of person, but she knew them. Most of the words, if not the tune in this case.

> '*Oh wisest love that flesh and blood*
> *Which did in Adam fail . . .*'

'*Praise to the Holiest in the Height.* That's . . . ?'

'What the heavenly choir sings before the appearance of the Angel of the Agony,' Lol said. 'Tim's expanded it, I think. Dan said it goes into a speaking-in-tongues kind of chant. He said that's when you start to get high.'

They were in the parking bay outside Wychehill Church. The singing was much louder now than when Merrily had last heard it, standing on an upturned bucket below a window. As if the choristers had been pacing themselves like athletes.

'You think we should stop them?' Syd Spicer stood under the cracked lantern, his eyes uncertain. 'How long's it got to go?'

'What time is it now, Syd?'

'Two-twenty.'

'It ends at three,' Lol said.

'Let them finish then.' Syd brought out his keys. 'You want to go in?'

Lol nodded. Merrily had caught a movement in the churchyard. 'Join you in a few minutes. OK?'

Sliding among the bushes and the graves not a moment too soon because within a few seconds there were voices behind her, talking to Syd, and one of them was Annie Howe's. 'No, I'm not sure,' she heard Syd say. 'She was here not long ago. Do you want to talk to me first?'

She was standing under the statue of the Angel of the Agony, pink cardigan over a summer dress with cartwheels and roses on it. Male and female voices cascaded down through the warm air, fluid and ethereal, coloured rain.

> *'God's presence and his very Self*
> *and Essence—'*

'I thought,' Merrily said, 'that on Friday and Saturday night you stayed in behind locked and barred doors.'

'Sometimes I sit at the window,' Mrs Aird said. 'From the front dormer I can just see the church gates. I had the window open tonight, to hear the choir. Then I saw you come in with the Rector and the other gentleman.'

Merrily sat on the edge of the tomb, looked up into her face, meagrely lit by the candles inside the church.

'What don't I know about you, Mrs Aird?'

'Oh dear, is it that obvious?'

'I did think of ringing Ingrid Sollars, but there hasn't been much time.'

'Oh well,' Mrs Aird said. 'Ingrid doesn't know, anything really. I don't make a point of telling people my family history. Not round here, especially. There's still quite a bit of strong feeling in certain quarters.'

She glanced up at the Angel of the Agony, whose face, even by diffused candlelight, reflected none of the compassion that you might expect.

'Oh,' Merrily said. 'I see ... I think.'

'He was my grandfather.'

'Joseph Longworth.'

'I don't remember him. He died when I was very young. I didn't even know where he was buried for a long time. It was quite a shock when I first came here.'

'I can imagine.'

'He left some money, in trust for Wychehill Church. The interest to be handed over as a lump sum every ten years, as directed by the principal trustee. Which at present is me, as the eldest in the family. He wanted the money to perpetuate the church's connection with Elgar.'

'Ah ...'

'What I was told was that Elgar's music was not very popular by the time my grandfather discovered it in the 1920s. He became, you know, besotted with it. He thought it was the greatest music ever made in England. He wanted to help. And to make up, in a small way, for all the damage done by the quarrying. And I suppose he's been proved right, hasn't he, about the music?'

'Somebody said he created Wychehill Church as ... almost an altar to Elgar?'

'Well, I came to tend it,' Mrs Aird said. 'I'm the first of our family – including my grandfather – ever to live in Wychehill, and it's all been very strange. Very strange indeed. I used to be afraid to stand here, especially after dark.'

'You came – twenty-five years ago?'

'Twenty-four. When my husband retired. He was some years older than me. You didn't have to wait long for a house to come on the market here. It's always been like that. It was a very unhappy place when we came. I made it my business to try to cheer people up. It was a . . . a vocation, you might say. It made me feel content here. I felt my grandfather – this will sound silly . . .'

'Probably not to me.'

'I felt he was helping me. So when Mr Loste came and established his choir . . .'

'Good way to . . . perpetuate Elgar's music?'

'I made a donation, from the fund. Towards the choir and hiring musicians sometimes.'

'You gave Tim money?'

'Anonymously. Through my solicitor. I didn't want them to know. I didn't want that woman . . . I heard she . . . is it true?'

'I'm afraid it is.'

'Dear God.' Mrs Aird sank down on to the tomb. 'What's *happening* here, Mrs Watkins?'

Merrily told her, without mentioning names, that the people responsible were no longer a threat. That there was nobody out there any more to be afraid of.

She wondered if that was true and if the divide which had opened up all those years ago, like a fissure in the rocks, between Longworth and the Devereaux family, Old Wychehill and Upper Wychehill, might in some way be closed. What would happen to Old Wychehill now? In theory, it was Hugo's. But what would happen to Hugo?

'As soon as I handed over the money,' Mrs Aird said, 'I knew it was wrong, somehow, and I didn't know why. I had terrible dreams. One night . . .' She hugged her arms. 'I saw him.' She looked up. '*Him.*'

'The angel?'

'I was watching the sunset and just after the sun had gone down, he was there in my garden. Don't think I'm mad—'

'No.'

'And the next day the lorry crashed into the church wall. It was probably a coincidence, but that's not what you think, is it, at the time?'

'Did you ... see him again?'

'No.'

'And the light the lorry driver said he saw ... ?'

'He thought it was the sun, but it was too early. Perhaps it was like the policeman said, he was overtired. But I thought of the ball of light that my grandfather's supposed to have seen. And then Mr Loste ... and then Hannah. I didn't know what to believe. It was getting too much for me. And then I talked to Ingrid and ...' Mrs Aird let her arms drop and turned to Merrily. 'How much of it was lies? Do you know?'

'No,' Merrily said. 'I don't. Sometimes you never do. Sometimes you just have to push on regardless and hope you get ... some ...'

Help? She looked up. Something had happened.

She saw, through the steep, plain-glass window, a *very* small glow, as if only one candle was left alight. And the choir had faltered, voices trailing like ribbon. She stood up.

The last candle didn't go out, but the choir stayed silent. Merrily heard the church door opening, and Lol came out, and she walked over to him. He looked anxious.

'He ... the conductor was this guy, Dan. He'd stepped in at the last minute because the usual guy couldn't make it. And he just ... he stopped it. He said he had to sit down. Suddenly felt cold ... and weak. And then he got up again and went round blowing out the candles. It was ... weird. Who's that?'

Merrily turned and saw Mrs Aird walking back along the drive towards the road. There was darkness there. The cracked lantern at the entrance had gone out.

Cold inside with dread, she took out her mobile and opened it up, its screen flaring orange and white, and called the hospital in Worcester where Tim Loste had been taken.

# 64

# Helium

IT WAS UNEARTHLY SEEING Elgar like this. Disorientating.

In his striped casual jacket and his hat with the brim raffishly upturned at the sides. And was that a cigarette, for heaven's sake, between his fingers?

He wasn't exactly smiling, but you felt that, under that Wild West marshal's moustache, he was on the edge of one, standing on the track with his arms spread as if emphasizing its width. Yes, it had to be a cigarette – that was smoke in the air

You spent all week searching for him in the Malverns, and here he was in Ledwardine.

Something mischievous and yet rueful about that near-smile. The main difference between Watkins and Elgar, at this stage of their lives, was that Elgar was more or less played out in his sixties, while Watkins was only just beginning his greatest work, crackling with vision.

Maybe Elgar, in Ledwardine, was returning a favour – for getting Longworth off his back? No, don't get fanciful.

'Whenever I think I'm getting somewhere.' Jane lowered her face into her hands. 'Just when I think I'm breaking through, I screw up. It's like there's something inside me, something demonic—'

'Stop right there, flower.'

Jane looked up. Annoyance turning to something between hopelessness and an unhealthy kind of repentance.

Anyway, it was almost pitiful.

'I was going to say, "*Don't call me 'flower' like I'm seven years old.*" But yeah, call me flower. Call me flower till I grow up. Maybe getting thrown out of school . . . maybe that's what I need. Maybe I should go away, where I can't harm anybody.'

Merrily thought of telling her that the one person this didn't seem to have harmed was Gomer Parry who, when she'd seen him in the Eight till Late, had looked ten years younger, despite facing charges which could include taking a mechanical digger without the owner's consent and criminal damage to a fence and a silver BMW.

He said he'd deny that this last offence had been *criminal* as he'd had no way of knowing that Pierce had brought his car round in order to drive Gerry Murray home so Murray could leave his JCB on site overnight, which was plain daft, anyway.

'More likely to've banged Pierce,' Gomer said. 'Bloody little crook.'

Merrily had advised resisting making that point to the police. Bliss had suggested that Gomer might get a caution . . . but only if he admitted an offence of, say, Aggravated Taking Without Consent. Which, Gomer being Gomer . . .

She wondered if she should ring Robert Morrell at home and make a crawling apology, telling him how stressed-out she'd been and what a difficult year it had been for Jane. Wondered whether this might actually work, or whether Jane would just despise her.

Probable answers: no and yes.

Just before twelve, Syd Spicer had rung to say that he'd spoken to Tim Loste's parents in France. He'd asked Merrily how she'd feel about conducting the funeral. The full Requiem, as High Church as she was prepared to go.

Incense, even.

She'd said OK.


The young guy at the door was in jeans and a Mappa Mundi T-shirt.

'Neil Cooper. Herefordshire Council.'

'I think I've seen you somewhere before,' Merrily said.

'It's possible, yes. I wondered if Jane was in.'

'Well, she—'

Jane appeared in the hall.

'Oh—'

'This is Mr Cooper, Jane. From the Council.'

'Look,' Jane said. 'I overreacted. I behaved like a kid. But on the other hand I'm not going to apologize.'

'I don't expect you to.' Neil Cooper looked grim. 'But I think you ought at least to come and see the extent of what you've done, you and your ... volatile friend.'

'For what it's worth, I'm accepting full responsibility. Gomer thought I was in danger, and that's why he did it. In fact it was an act of protest.'

Merrily said, 'Jane—'

'Also, he was insulted by Lyndon Pierce. Made to look small. And old and knackered. Gomer's a proud sort of guy in his way, and he's a good guy, and he could drive a JCB in his sleep, and Pierce was stupid to leave his car there with no lights.'

'I really don't want to argue,' Cooper said. 'If you're prepared to face up to—'

'All right, I'll come. OK? But if you're going to offer me any kind of a deal, like the police did, to drop Gomer in it . . .'

Merrily watched them go, wondering what all this was going to cost, in terms of money and their future in the village. Then she went over to Lol's.

Lol was sitting on his sofa with the Boswell guitar. Merrily sat down next to him and listened while he played a couple of strange, drifting chords, singing in a low mumble.

> *'Don't need ... The Angel of the Agony.*
> *Don't want ... the pomp and circumstance.'*

He put the guitar down.

'Lay down here when we got in. Slept for a couple of hours and I woke up and that was in my head. Crap?'

'It's haunting,' Merrily said.

'Develop it, do you think?'

'And when you record it, have Simon St John on cello.'

'Elgar would hate it.'

'Tell me – would that have bothered you before?

'Um . . .'

'Seventeen,' Merrily said. 'You remember?'

'It wasn't.'

'Wasn't seventeen?'

'It was *Severn* . . . *Teme*. Elgar said he wanted to be cremated and have his ashes scattered at the confluence of the River Severn and the River Teme.'

'So Tim meant . . .'

'There wasn't much cremation back then. They talked him out of it, and now he's with Alice in Little Malvern.'

'Where does the Severn meet the Teme?'

'No idea.'

'I wonder if there's a country church near there. And an amenable vicar with a fondness for Elgar. Take some arranging and negotiations with relatives, of course, but . . .'

'You're thinking Tim?'

'Thinking both of them. Tim . . . and Elgar, in essence. But . . .'

Faraway eyes and a lonely bicycle lamp in the dusk. A floating sadness.

'. . . I just don't know,' Merrily said.


It was a mess, no arguing with that. A spreading wound in the belly of the village. OK, some of it had been done by Gerry Murray before they arrived, but a lot of it was clearly down to Gomer. The way the fence had been smashed down and spread across the field. The way the council sign describing the plans for luxury executive homes had been snapped off halfway up its post and crunched and splintered into the mud that used to be Coleman's Meadow.

And Pierce's car, of course. The car was still there. Pierce's BMW with its windscreen smashed and its bonnet turned into a sardine can. Well, it had been dark. How was Gomer supposed to know that Pierce was giving Murray a lift home? And wasn't the fact that Pierce was doing this a clear demonstration that they were in this together? Pierce wouldn't want that coming out. Would he?

He wouldn't give a toss. He had Jane, unhinged, crazy as a binge drinker on New Year's Eve, and dragging an old man into it.

He wouldn't get jail for a first offence – Jane hoped – at his age, but there'd be a heavy fine and, worst of all, the possibility of some kind of ban, and if they stopped Gomer driving his JCB he'd just slink off and die.

All her fault.

If anything happened to Gomer because of what she'd done she just couldn't go on living here.

Didn't want to live here any more, anyway.

The afternoon was dull and sultry. A bleak posse of clouds had gathered around Cole Hill. It was like a sign. Coleman's Meadow was desolate, an old battlefield, but the only blood was hers.

'Why are you doing this to me?' Jane said. 'I've messed up. I admit it.'

Neil Cooper strolled out to the middle of the field. He wasn't bad-looking in an insubstantial kind of way.

'But it *is* a ley,' Jane shouted after him. 'Or it *was.*'

'I'm not sure I believe in leys,' Cooper said.

'Yeah, well, you wouldn't.'

'Look at the state of this.' He bent down. 'Come on. Look at it.'

'Sod you,' Jane said. 'You're determined to rub my nose in it, aren't you?'

'Will you come here?'

Jane sighed. How much more of this? Monday she'd have to face Morrell. Tuesday she'd be looking for a new school. Or a job. Maybe stacking shelves for Jim Prosser.

'It's my day off, actually,' Neil Cooper said. 'I just heard about it on the radio and thought I'd wander over. OK, here—'

She went and looked over Neil Cooper's shoulder to where a great slice of soil and clay had been peeled away like a giant pencil-shaving. Murray's work, but somebody had been at it with a spade and there was a trench there now. Neil Cooper tapped the bottom of it with a trowel. It rang sharply off something.

'Oops, shouldn't've— You know what this is, Jane?'

Jane stood sullenly on the edge of the trench, which was still roughly aligned with the ley.

'No.'

'It's a stone,' Neil Cooper said. 'Approximately four metres long. Like a very big cigar. It was about half a metre under the surface. A large part of it would've been underground, but when it was standing it would've been taller than me.'

Jane said, 'Standing?'

Cooper walked lightly along the bottom of the trench and then stopped.

'It seemed even longer at first and then I realized that . . .' He bent down, tapped again with his trowel. 'That *this* was a separate one.'

'How do you mean?'

'And then I brought in a couple of mates and we found a third.'

'What?'

'Have you ever seen Harold's Stones at Trellech? What's that – forty miles from here?'

'Thereabouts.'

She and Eirion had been. Twice. Harold's stones were magnificent. Jane felt herself growing pale.

'Probably not going to be *quite* that tall,' Neil Cooper said. 'But when we get them up, at least as high as Wern Derys, which is the tallest prehistoric stone in Herefordshire. And, of course, as a stone *row . . .*'

'Who *are* you?'

'I get the feeling we met once before, when I was working on the renovation of the Cantilupe tomb in the Cathedral. I certainly recognized your mum. I'm with the County Archaeologist's Department now.'

Cooper was on his feet.

'Jane, they've been buried for centuries. They're way beyond living memory, and there are no records. There was a time when farmers would do this because the old stones got in the way of ploughing.'

'Bury them?'

'Broke them up, sometimes. Fortunately that didn't happen here, although the one at the far end was quite badly chipped by Mr Murray's JCB. But then, if he hadn't been so determined to destroy your bit of ... ley line, we wouldn't have found out about it – if we ever *did* find out – until the housing estate was well under way, and then it would've been just rescue archaeology because the estate would have planning permission. Whereas now—'

'These are real, actual, prehistoric standing stones?'

Jane felt like her body had filled up with helium and her voice was coming out in this thin squeak.

'I'd stake my future career on it,' Neil Cooper said.

'What ... what does that mean?'

'Means a long and careful excavation, and then, with any luck, the stones will get raised again and carefully repositioned just as they once were.'

'And the ... and the housing estate?'

'What housing estate?' Neil Cooper said.

Jane went down on her knees in the trench, rubbing away the soil, getting dirt all over the big plaster on the back of her hand. She closed her eyes and saw a swirl of faces: Neil Cooper looking down on her with Elgar on one side of him and Alfred Watkins on the other, peering over his glasses, eyes alight, and all of them in the enveloping shadow of the batwing poncho of Lucy Devenish.

'This time, *we*'ll call the media,' Neil Cooper said. 'If that's all right with you?'

'I need to talk to my agent,' Jane said.

# Credits Plus

ALTHOUGH LINKS BETWEEN EDWARD ELGAR and Alfred Watkins have not been mentioned in major biographies of either man, the geographical facts, as discovered by Jane Watkins, speak for themselves. However, confirmation: Jacob O'Callaghan records in *Elgar, A Herefordshire Guide* how the by-then eminent composer joined the famous Woolhope naturalists' club, 'possibly introduced by his neighbour, Alfred Watkins.' And Laurence Meredith notes in *In the News – Herefordshire*, that Elgar, who had a photographic darkroom at Plas Gwyn 'was also a great friend of Herefordian Alfred Watkins, inventor of the modern photographic light-meter, and he and Elgar frequently met to discuss photography.' Thanks to Woolhope member Sue Rice for pointing this out. It seems unlikely that Watkins and Elgar would not also explore their mutual fascination with the landscape.

Whiteleafed Oak, of course, exists as described, right down to the *severely* limited parking. Please treat it with respect. The theory of Whiteleafed Oak and the perpetual choirs was, as explained, first outlined, in comparatively recent times, by John Michell in his inspiring books *City of Revelation* and *New Light on the Ancient Mystery of Glastonbury*, developed by John Merron in an article in *The Ley Hunter* magazine, investigated by members of the Malvern-based British Society of Dowsers and guarded by Val de Heer, of the Aquarius shop, Malvern, who supplied essential background.

Did Elgar know it? None of the biographers mention it, but local people say, Yes ... definitely.

The earliest mention of the Three Choirs Festival seems to have been about 1700. It was established for the performance of sacred music –

originally Handel and Purcell – by the combined choirs of the cathedrals of Gloucester, Worcester and Hereford, with an orchestra behind them. And it was always held in the late summer. A gentrified, fairly formal event ... or so they thought.

Many thanks also to Mike Ashley, author of *Starlight Man*, the excellent biography of Algernon Blackwood, for essential advice and perusal of correspondence; Richard Bartholomew on Elgar and Malvern topography, and Chris Bennett at the Elgar Birthplace Museum; Hereford Cathedral Director of Music Geraint Bowen; the Rev. Peter Brooks for crucial eleventh-hour assistance with the Welsh Triads and other problems; the Rev. Keith Crouch; Paul Devereux, author of *Earthlights, Earthlights Revelation, Haunted Land* and many other essential books on some of the mysteries dealt with here; Ros Ephraim, chorister and proprietor of Burway Books, Church Stretton, for the essential *Gerontius*; David Furlong, author of *Working with Earth Energies*; Nicola Goodwin, author of *Tales from Herefordshire's Graves and Burials*; Paul Gormley for atmosphere; Robert Hale of the *Malvern Gazette*, my agent Andrew Hewson, BBC journalist Dave Howard, Phil Howard, Wendy Howell, Ced Jackson, Helen Lamb, Prof. Bernard Knight, Owen Morgan, John Moss, Mervynne and Ceri Payne and Edith Powell at the Arcade Bookshop in Pershore; Ron Phillips for Elgar-analysis and some inspiring discussions; the playwright David Pownall for Elgar psychology; Alun Rees for Gomer-related offences, Canon John Rowlands, author of *Church, State and Society: the Attitudes of John Keble, Richard Hurrell Froud and John Henry Newman, 1827–1845*; and leading Hay-on-Wye bookseller Tracy Thursfield, who put me on to *The Human Chord* and other Elgar-linked esoterica.

Principal books on Elgar consulted include *Elgar's Sacred Music* by John Allison; *The Life of Elgar* by Michael Kennedy; *Elgar – Child of Dreams* by Jerrold Northrop Moore; *Gerontius, a novel about Sir Edward Elgar* by James Hamilton Paterson – better than any of them at presenting the great man as a complex, mixed-up human being. (No one, however, seems to have *quite* pinned him down. Michael Kennedy, distinguished music critic and former Northern Editor of the *Daily Telegraph*, is quick to squash suggestions that Elgar was a liberal, claiming triumphantly that he went fox-hunting, while Jacob O'Callaghan points out that Elgar allied himself with the campaigns of his vegetarian friend George Bernard Shaw and told a journalist that he had developed 'a horror of the slaughter of wildlife for "sport."')

Also *The Malvern Hills, An Ancient Landscape* by Mark Bowden with contributions by David Field and Helen Winton; *The Malverns* by Pamela Hurle; *The Old Straight Track* by Alfred Watkins; *Alfred Watkins, A Herefordshire Man* by Ron Shoesmith; *The Human Chord* by Algernon Blackwood; the revised *Who Dares Wins* by Tony Geraghty; *Bravo Two Zero* and *Immediate Action* by Andy McNabb; *Freefall* by Tom Read; *The Music of the Spheres* by Jamie James; *Sacred Sounds* by Ted Andrews; Ray Simpson's *Celtic Worship Through the Year*; *The Inner Teachings of the Golden Dawn* by R.G. Torrens and *Not the Least* (that's the title), *The Story of Little Malvern* by Ronald Bryer.

Wychehill, by the way, is not the same place as either the Wyche or Lower Wyche areas of Malvern. However, an interesting ghost-road situation did arise a few years ago not too far away in the Herefordshire village of Stoke Lacy, scene of several unexplained road accidents. In this case, drivers said they felt as if something had taken over the steering. You couldn't make it up; sometimes you don't have to.

Thanks, as ever, to Krys and Geoff Boswell who preserve the website, www.philrickman.co.uk. against all kinds of negative forces and Terry Smith who organises the T-shirts. In America, Rick and Claire Kleffel, Jani Sue Muhlestein, Marla Williams and Andy Ryan, Trudy Williams and Kevin Bowman, Jerry Handspicker and Rob Wilder.

And, on the publishing side: Anthony Cheetham, Nic Cheetham, Rosie de Courcy, Nick Austin and, of course, the lovely and phenomenal Carol who worked double shifts on this extremely taxing novel for about six weeks before we managed to pull it into shape.

Final note. Noctilucent clouds were visible in the northern sky over the Welsh border counties on at least one night towards the end of June, 2006. The aforementioned Paul Devereux (no relation to Preston – different spelling) explained what they were.

I'd seen them around midnight and wished I'd been at Whiteleafed Oak.